S

THE
CELLIST

Daniel Silva is the award-winning, #1 *New York Times* bestselling author of twenty-four novels, including *The Other Woman*, *The New Girl*, and *The Order*. His books are critically acclaimed bestsellers around the world and have been translated into more than thirty languages. He resides in Florida with his wife, television journalist Jamie Gangel, and their twins, Lily and Nicholas.

For more information visit www.danielsilvabooks.com.

DANIEL SILVA
THE CELLIST

HarperCollins*Publishers*

HarperCollins*Publishers*
1 London Bridge Street,
London SE1 9GF

www.harpercollins.co.uk

HarperCollins*Publishers*
Macken House, 39/40 Mayor Street Upper,
Dublin 1, D01 C9W8, Ireland

This paperback edition published by HarperCollins*Publishers* Ltd 2022
1

First published in the UK by HarperCollins*Publishers* 2021
First published in the United States of America by Harper, an imprint of
HarperCollins*Publishers* 2021

A catalogue copy of this book is available from the British Library.

ISBN: 9780008280758 (PB-B)
ISBN: 9780008472153 (PB-A)

This novel is entirely a work of fiction.
The names, characters and incidents portrayed in it are
the work of the author's imagination. Any resemblance to
actual persons, living or dead, events or localities is
entirely coincidental.

Typeset in Meridien by Palimpsest Book Production Limited, Falkirk, Stirlingshire

Printed and Bound in the UK using 100% Renewable Electricity
at CPI Group (UK) Ltd

MIX
Paper from
responsible sources
FSC™ C007454

This book is produced from independently certified FSC™ paper
to ensure responsible forest management.

For more information visit: www.harpercollins.co.uk/green

*For the officers of the United States Capitol Police
and Washington's Metropolitan Police Department
who defended our democracy on
January 6, 2021*

*And, as always, for my wife, Jamie, and my
children, Lily and Nicholas*

Kleptocracy (klep'täkrəsē) *A ruling body or order of thieves.*

—THE OXFORD ENGLISH DICTIONARY

In Russia power is wealth, and wealth is power.

—ANDERS ÅSLUND, RUSSIA'S CRONY CAPITALISM

Strasbourg

GERMANY

FRANCE

Basel

Zurich

Erlenbach

Neuchâtel

Bern

Lucerne

Féchy

Lausanne

SWITZERLAND

Geneva

Chambéry

Courchevel

Massif de
la Vanoise

ITALY

Turin

FRANCE

0   50 Km

50 mi.

Copyright © MMXXI Springer Cartographics LLC

MEDITERRANEAN
SEA

PART ONE

MODERATO

1

JERMYN STREET, ST. JAMES'S

SARAH BANCROFT ENVIED THOSE FORTUNATE souls who believed they controlled their own destinies. For them, life was no more complicated than riding the Underground. Insert your ticket at the fare gate, get off at the correct stop—Charing Cross rather than Leicester Square. Sarah had never subscribed to such drivel. Yes, one could prepare, one could strive, one could make choices, but ultimately life was an elaborate game of providence and probability. Regrettably, in matters of both work and love, she had displayed an uncanny lack of timing. She was either one step too fast or one too slow. She had missed many trains. Several times she had boarded the wrong one, nearly always with disastrous results.

Her latest career move appeared to fit this star-crossed pattern. Having established herself as one of the most prominent museum curators in New York, she had elected to relocate to London to take over day-to-day management of Isherwood Fine Arts, purveyors of quality Italian and Dutch Old Master paintings since 1968. True to form, her arrival was followed in short order by the outbreak of a deadly pandemic. Even the art world, which catered to the whims of the global superrich, was not immune to the contagion's ravages. Almost overnight, the gallery's business slipped into something approximating cardiac arrest. If the phone rang at all, it was usually a buyer or his representative calling to back out of a sale. Not since the West End musical version of *Desperately Seeking Susan*, declared Sarah's acerbic mother, had London witnessed a less auspicious debut.

Isherwood Fine Arts had seen troubled times before—wars, terrorist attacks, oil shocks, market meltdowns, disastrous love affairs—and yet somehow it had always managed to weather the storm. Sarah had worked at the gallery briefly fifteen years earlier while serving as a clandestine asset of the Central Intelligence Agency. The operation had been a joint US-Israeli enterprise, run by the legendary Gabriel Allon. With the help of a lost Van Gogh, he had inserted Sarah into the entourage of a Saudi billionaire named Zizi al-Bakari and ordered her to find the terrorist mastermind lurking within it. Her life had never been the same since.

When the operation was over, she spent several months recuperating at an Agency safe house in the horse country of Northern Virginia. Afterward, she worked at the CIA's Counterterrorism Center at Langley. She also took part in several joint American-Israeli operations, all at Gabriel's behest. British intelligence was well aware of Sarah's past, and of her presence in London—hardly surprising, for she was currently sharing a bed with an MI6 officer named Christopher Keller. Ordinarily, a relationship such as theirs was strictly forbidden, but in Sarah's case an exception had been made. Graham Seymour, the director-general of MI6, was a personal friend, as was Prime Minister Jonathan Lancaster. Indeed, not long after her arrival in London, Sarah and Christopher had dined privately at Number Ten.

With the exception of Julian Isherwood, owner of the enchanted gallery that bore his name, the denizens of London's art world knew none of this. As far as Sarah's colleagues and competitors were concerned, she was the beautiful and brilliant American art historian who had briefly brightened their world one dreary winter long ago, only to throw them over for the likes of Zizi al-Bakari, may he rest in peace. And now, after a tumultuous journey through the secret world, she had returned, thus proving her point about providence and probability. At long last, Sarah had caught the right train.

London had welcomed her with open arms and with few questions asked. She scarcely had time to put her affairs in order before the virus invaded. She contracted the bug in early March at the European Fine Art Fair in Maastricht and had promptly infected both Julian and Christopher. Julian spent a dreadful fortnight at University College Hospital. Sarah was spared the worst of the virus's symptoms but endured a month of fever, fatigue, headache, and shortness of breath that seized her each time she crawled from her bed. Not surprisingly, Christopher escaped unscathed and asymptomatic. Sarah punished him by forcing him to wait on her hand and foot. Somehow their relationship survived.

In June, London awakened from the lockdown. After thrice

testing negative for the virus, Christopher returned to duty at Vauxhall Cross, but Sarah and Julian waited until Midsummer Day before reopening the gallery. It was located in a tranquil quadrangle of paving stones and commerce known as Mason's Yard, between the offices of a minor Greek shipping company and a pub that in the innocent days before the plague had been frequented by pretty office girls who rode motor scooters. On the uppermost floor was a glorious exhibition room modeled on Paul Rosenberg's famous gallery in Paris, where Julian had spent many happy hours as a child. He and Sarah shared a large office on the second floor with Ella, the attractive but useless receptionist. During their first week back in business, the phone rang just three times. Ella allowed all three calls to go to voice mail. Sarah informed her that her services, such as they were, were no longer necessary.

There was no point in hiring a replacement. The experts were warning of a vicious second wave when the weather turned cold, and London's shopkeepers had been advised to expect more government-mandated lockdowns. The last thing Sarah needed was another mouth to feed. She resolved not to let the summer go to waste. She would sell a painting, any painting, even if it killed her.

She found one, quite by accident, while taking inventory of the catastrophically large number of unsold works in Julian's bulging storerooms: *The Lute Player*, oil on canvas, 152 by 134 centimeters, perhaps early Baroque, quite damaged and dirty. The original receipt and shipping records were still lodged in Julian's archives, along with a yellowed copy of the provenance. The earliest known owner was a Count So-and-So from Bologna, who in 1698 sold it to Prince Such-and-Such of Liechtenstein, who in turn sold it to Baron What's-His-Name of Vienna, where it remained until 1962, when it was acquired by a dealer in Rome, who eventually unloaded it onto Julian. The painting had been attributed variously to the Italian School, a follower of Caravaggio, and, more promisingly, to the circle of Orazio Gentileschi. Sarah had a hunch. She showed the work to the learned Niles Dunham of the National Gallery during the three-hour period Julian reserved daily for his luncheon. Niles tentatively accepted Sarah's attribution, pending additional technical examination utilizing X-radiography and infrared reflectography. He then offered to take the painting off Sarah's hands for eight hundred thousand pounds.

"It's worth five million, if not more."

"Not during the Black Death."

"We'll see about that."

Typically, a newly discovered work by a major artist would be brought to market with great fanfare, especially if the artist had seen a recent surge in popularity owing to her tragic personal story. But given the current volatility of the market—not to mention the fact that the newly discovered painting had been *discovered* in his own gallery—Julian decided a private sale was in order. He rang several of his most reliable customers and received not so much as a nibble. At which point Sarah quietly contacted a billionaire collector who was a friend of a friend. He expressed interest, and after several socially distant meetings at his London residence they arrived at a satisfactory price. Sarah requested a down payment of one million pounds, in part to cover the cost of the restoration, which would be extensive. The collector asked her to come to his dwelling at eight that evening to take delivery of the check.

All of which went some way to explaining why Sarah Bancroft, on a wet Wednesday evening in late July, was seated at a corner table in the bar of Wilton's Restaurant in Jermyn Street. The mood in the room was uncertain, the smiles forced, the laughter uproarious but somehow false. Julian was tilted against the end of the bar. With his Savile Row suit and plentiful gray locks, he cut a rather elegant if dubious figure, a look he described as dignified depravity. He was peering into his Sancerre and pretending to listen to something that Jeremy Crabbe, the director of the Old Master department at Bonhams, was murmuring excitedly into his ear. Amelia March of *ARTNews* was eavesdropping on a conversation between Simon Mendenhall, the mannequin-like chief auctioneer from Christie's, and Nicky Lovegrove, art adviser to the criminally rich. Roddy Hutchinson, widely regarded as the most unscrupulous dealer in all of London, was tugging at the sleeve of tubby Oliver Dimbleby. But Oliver seemed not to notice, for he was pawing at the impossibly beautiful former fashion model who now owned a successful modern art gallery in King Street. On her way out the door, she blew Sarah a decorous kiss with those perfect crimson lips of hers. Sarah sipped her three-olive martini and whispered, "Bitch."

"I heard that!" Fortunately, it was only Oliver. Encased in a form-fitting gray suit, he floated toward Sarah's table like a barrage balloon and sat down. "What have you got against the lovely Miss Watson?"

"Her eyes. Her cheekbones. Her hair. Her boobs." Sarah sighed. "Shall I go on?"

Oliver waved his pudgy little hand dismissively. "You're much prettier than she is, Sarah. I'll never forget the first time I saw you walking across Mason's Yard. Nearly stopped my heart. If memory serves, I made quite a fool of myself back then."

"You asked me to marry you. Several times, in fact."

"My offer still stands."

"I'm flattered, Ollie. But I'm afraid it's out of the question."

"Am I too old?"

"Not at all."

"Too fat?"

She pinched his pinkish cheek. "Just right, actually."

"So what's the problem?"

"I'm involved."

"In what?"

"A relationship."

He seemed unfamiliar with the word. Oliver's romantic entanglements rarely lasted more than a night or two. "Are you talking about that bloke who drives the flashy Bentley?"

Sarah sipped her drink.

"What's his name, this boyfriend of yours?"

"Peter Marlowe."

"Sounds made up."

With good reason, thought Sarah.

"What's he do for a living?" blurted Oliver.

"Can you keep a secret?"

"My darling Sarah, I have more dirty secrets stored inside my head than MI5 and MI6 combined."

She leaned across the table. "He's a professional assassin."

"Really? Interesting work, is it?"

Sarah smiled. It wasn't true, of course. It had been several years since Christopher worked as a contract killer.

"Is he the reason you came back to London?" probed Oliver.

"One of the reasons. The truth is, I missed you all terribly. Even you, Oliver." She checked the time on her phone. "Oh, hell! Will you be a love and pay for my drink? I'm late."

"For what?"

"Behave, Ollie."

"Why on earth would I want to do that? It's so bloody boring."

Sarah rose and, winking at Julian, went into Jermyn Street. The rain was suddenly coming down in torrents, but a taxi soon came to her rescue. She waited until she was safely inside before giving the driver the address of her destination.

"Cheyne Walk, please. Number forty-three."

2

CHEYNE WALK, CHELSEA

Like Sarah Bancroft, Viktor Orlov believed that life was a journey best taken without aid of a map. Raised in an unheated Moscow apartment shared by three families, he became a billionaire many times over through a combination of luck, determination, and ruthless tactics that even his apologists described as unscrupulous, if not criminal. Orlov made no secret of the fact that he was a predator and a robber baron. Indeed, he wore those labels proudly. "Had I been born an Englishman, my money might have come to me cleanly," he dismissively told a British interviewer after taking up residence in London. "But I was born a Russian. And I earned a Russian fortune."

In point of fact, Viktor Orlov was born a citizen not of Russia but of the Soviet Union. A brilliant mathematician, he attended the prestigious Leningrad Institute of Precision Mechanics and Optics and then disappeared into the Soviet nuclear weapons program, where he designed multiwarhead intercontinental ballistic missiles. Later, when asked why he had joined the Communist Party, he admitted it was for reasons of career advancement only. "I suppose I could have become a dissident," he added, "but the gulag never seemed like a terribly appealing place to me."

As a member of the pampered elite, Orlov witnessed the decay of the Soviet system from the inside and knew it was only a matter of time before the empire collapsed. When the end finally came, he renounced his membership in the Communist Party and vowed to become rich. Within a few years he had earned a sizable fortune importing computers and other Western goods for the nascent Russian market. He then used that fortune to acquire Russia's largest state-owned steel company and Ruzoil, the Siberian oil giant. Before long, Orlov was the richest man in Russia.

But in post-Soviet Russia, a land with no rule of law, Orlov's fortune made him a marked man. He survived at least three attempts on his life and was rumored to have ordered several men killed in retaliation. But the greatest threat to Orlov would come from the man who succeeded Boris Yeltsin as president. He believed that Viktor Orlov and the other oligarchs had stolen the country's most valuable assets, and it was his intention to steal them back. After settling into the Kremlin, the new president summoned Orlov and demanded two things: his steel company and Ruzoil. "And keep your nose out of politics," he added ominously. "Otherwise, I'll cut it off."

Orlov agreed to relinquish his steel interests, but not Ruzoil. The president was not amused. He immediately ordered prosecutors to open a fraud-and-bribery investigation, and within a week they had issued a warrant for Orlov's arrest. He wisely fled to London, where he became one of the Russian president's most vocal critics. For several years, Ruzoil remained legally icebound, beyond the reach of both Orlov and the new masters of the Kremlin. Orlov finally agreed to surrender the company in exchange for three Israeli intelligence agents held captive in Russia. One of the agents was Gabriel Allon.

For his generosity, Orlov received a British passport and a private meeting with the Queen at Buckingham Palace. He then embarked on an ambitious effort to rebuild his lost fortune, this time under the watchful eye of British regulatory officials, who monitored his every trade and investment. His empire now included such venerable London newspapers as the *Independent*, the *Evening Standard*, and the *Financial Journal*. He had also acquired a controlling interest in the Russian investigative weekly *Moskovskaya Gazeta*. With Orlov's financial support, the magazine was once again Russia's most prominent independent news organization and a thorn in the side of the men in the Kremlin.

As a consequence, Orlov lived each day with the knowledge that the formidable intelligence services of the Russian Federation were plotting to kill him. His new Mercedes-Maybach limousine was equipped with security features normally reserved for the state cars of presidents and prime ministers, and his home in Chelsea's historic Cheyne Walk was one of the most heavily defended in London. A black Range Rover idled curbside, headlamps doused. Inside were four bodyguards, all former commandos from the elite Special Air Service employed by a discreet private security firm based in Mayfair. The one behind the wheel raised a hand in acknowledgment as Sarah alighted from the back of the taxi. Evidently, she was expected.

Number 43 was tall and narrow and covered in wisteria. Like its neighbors, it was set back from the street, behind a wrought-iron fence. Sarah hurried up the garden walk beneath the meager shelter offered by her compact umbrella. The bell push produced a resonant tolling within, but no response. Sarah pressed the button a second time, with the same result.

Typically, a maid would have answered the door. But Viktor, a notorious germophobe even before the pandemic, had slashed the hours of his household staff to reduce his odds of contracting the virus. A lifelong bachelor, he spent most evenings in his study on the third floor, sometimes alone, often with inappropriately young female company. The curtains were aglow with lamplight. Sarah reckoned he was on a call. At least, she hoped he was.

She rang the bell a third time and, receiving no answer, laid her forefinger on the biometric reader next to the door. Viktor had added her fingerprint to the system, no doubt with the hope their relationship might continue after the sale of the painting was complete. An electronic chirp informed Sarah that the scan had been accepted. She entered her personal passcode—it was identical to the one she used at the gallery—and the deadbolts snapped open at once.

She lowered her umbrella, twisted the doorknob, and went inside. The silence was absolute. She called Viktor's name but there was no reply. Crossing the entrance hall, she mounted the grand staircase and climbed to the third floor. The door of Viktor's study was ajar. She knocked. No answer.

Calling Viktor's name, she entered the room. It was an exact replica of the Queen's private study in her apartment at Buckingham Palace—all except for the high-definition video wall that flickered with financial newscasts and market data from around the world. Viktor was seated behind his desk, his face tilted toward the ceiling, as though he were deep in thought.

When Sarah approached the desk, he made no movement. Before him was the receiver from his landline telephone, a half-drunk glass of red wine, and a stack of documents. His mouth and chin were covered in white foam, and there was vomit on the front of his striped dress shirt. Sarah saw no evidence of respiration.

"Oh, Viktor. Dear God."

While at the CIA, Sarah had worked cases involving weapons of mass destruction. She recognized the symptoms. Viktor had been exposed to a nerve agent.

In all likelihood, so had Sarah.

She rushed from the room, her hand to her mouth, and hurried down the staircase. The wrought-iron gate, the bell push, the biometric scanner, the keypad: any one of them could have been contaminated. Nerve agents were extremely fast acting. She would know in a minute or two.

Sarah touched one final surface, the knob on Viktor's leaden front door. Outside, she lifted her face to the falling rain and waited for the first telltale rush of nausea. One of the bodyguards clambered from the Range Rover, but Sarah warned him to approach no closer. Then she dug her phone from her handbag and dialed a number from her preferred contacts. The call went straight to voice mail. As usual, she thought, her lack of timing was impeccable.

"Forgive me, my love," she said calmly. "But I'm afraid I might be dying."

3

LONDON

AMONG THE MANY UNANSWERED QUESTIONS surrounding the events of that evening was the identity of the man who telephoned the emergency line of the Metropolitan Police. An automatic recording of the call revealed that he spoke English with a heavy French accent. Linguistics experts would later determine he was in all likelihood a southerner, though one suggested he was probably from the island of Corsica. When asked to state his name, he abruptly severed the connection. The number of his mobile device, which left no metadata in its wake, could never be established.

The first units arrived at the scene—43 Cheyne Walk in Chelsea, one of London's poshest addresses—just four minutes later. There they were greeted by a most remarkable sight. A woman was standing on the walkway of the elegant brick town house, a few paces from the open front door. In her right hand was a mobile phone. With her left she was furiously scrubbing her face, which was lifted toward the drenching rain. Four sturdily built men in dark suits were observing her from the opposite side of the wrought-iron fence, as though she were a madwoman.

When one of the officers tried to approach her, she shouted at him to stop. She then explained that the owner of the home, the Russian-born financier and publisher Viktor Orlov, had been murdered with a nerve agent, quite probably of Russian origin. The woman was convinced she had been exposed to the toxin as well, hence her appearance and behavior. Her accent was American, her command of the lexicon of chemical weaponry was thorough. The officers surmised she had a background in security matters, an opinion reinforced by her refusal to identify herself or explain why she had come to Mr. Orlov's home that evening.

Seven additional minutes elapsed before the first green-suited CBRN teams entered the home. Upstairs in the study they found the Russian billionaire seated at his desk, pupils contracted, saliva on his chin, vomit on his shirt—all signs of exposure to a nerve agent. Medical personnel made no attempt at resuscitation. It appeared Orlov had been dead for an hour or more, probably as a result of asphyxia or cardiac arrest brought on by a loss of control of the body's respiratory muscles. Preliminary testing of the room found contamination on the desktop, the stem of the wineglass, and the receiver of the phone. There was no evidence of contamination on any other surface, including the front door, the bell push, or the biometric scanner.

Which suggested to investigators that the nerve agent had

been introduced directly into Orlov's study by an intruder or visitor. The billionaire's security team told police that he had received two callers that evening, both women. One was the American who discovered the body. The other was a Russian— at least, that was the assumption of the security detail. The woman did not identify herself, and Orlov did not supply them with a name. Neither of which was unusual, they explained. Orlov was secretive by nature, especially when it came to his private life. He greeted the woman warmly at the front door—all smiles and Russian-style kisses—and escorted her upstairs to the study, where he drew the curtains. She stayed for approximately fifteen minutes and saw herself out, also not unusual where Orlov was concerned.

It was approaching ten p.m. when the senior officer at the scene reported his initial findings to New Scotland Yard. The shift supervisor rang Met commissioner Stella McEwan, and McEwan in turn contacted the home secretary, who alerted Downing Street. The call was unnecessary, for Prime Minister Lancaster was already aware of the unfolding crisis; he had been briefed fifteen minutes earlier by Graham Seymour, the director-general of MI6. The prime minister had reacted to the news with justifiable fury. For the second time in just eighteen months, it appeared the Russians had carried out an assassination in the heart of London using a weapon of mass destruction. The two attacks had at least one element in common: the name of the woman who discovered Orlov's body.

"What in God's name was she doing in Viktor's house?"

"An art transaction," explained Seymour.

"Are we sure that's all?"

"Prime Minister?"

"She's not working for Allon again, is she?"

Seymour assured Lancaster she was not.

"Where is she now?"

"St. Thomas' Hospital."

"Was she exposed?"

"We'll know soon enough. In the meantime, it is imperative we keep her name out of the press."

Because it was a domestic incident, Seymour's rivals at MI5 assumed primary responsibility for the investigation. They focused their inquiry on the first of Orlov's two female callers. With the help of London's CCTV cameras, the Metropolitan Police had already determined that she presented herself at Orlov's home by taxi at 6:19 p.m. Additional review of CCTV video established that she had boarded the same taxi forty minutes earlier at Heathrow's Terminal 5, having arrived on a British Airways flight from Zurich. Border Force identified her as Nina Antonova, forty-two years old, a citizen of the Russian Federation residing in Switzerland.

Because the United Kingdom no longer required arriving passengers to fill out paper landing cards, her occupation was not readily apparent. A simple Internet search, however, revealed that a Nina Antonova worked as an investigative reporter for *Moskovskaya Gazeta*, the anti-Kremlin weekly owned by none other than Viktor Orlov. She had fled Russia in 2014 after surviving an attempt on her life. From her outpost in Zurich, she had exposed numerous examples of corruption involving members of the Russian president's inner circle. A self-described dissident, she appeared regularly on Swiss television as a commentator on Russian affairs.

It was not the curriculum vitae of a typical Moscow Center

assassin. Still, given the Kremlin's track record, it was hardly out of the question. Certainly, an interview with police was warranted, the sooner the better. According to the CCTV cameras, she left Orlov's residence at 6:35 p.m. and made her way on foot to the Cadogan Hotel in Sloane Street. Yes, confirmed the desk clerk, a Nina Antonova had checked in earlier that evening. No, she was not presently in her room. She left the hotel at seven fifteen, apparently for a dinner engagement, and had not yet returned.

Hotel security cameras had recorded her departure. Her expression grave, she had ducked into the back of a taxi, which had been summoned by a raincoated valet. The car delivered her not to a restaurant but to Heathrow Airport, where at 9:45 p.m. she boarded a British Airways flight to Amsterdam. A call to her mobile phone—the Met obtained a number from the hotel registration form—went unanswered. At which point, Nina Antonova became the primary suspect in the murder of the Russian-born financier and newspaper publisher Viktor Orlov.

In one final humiliation, it was Samantha Cooke of the rival *Telegraph* who broke the story of Orlov's assassination, though her account contained few specifics. Prime Minister Lancaster, during an appearance before reporters outside Number Ten the following morning, confirmed that the billionaire had been killed with an as yet unidentified chemical toxin, almost certainly of Russian manufacture. He made no mention of the documents discovered on Orlov's desk, or of the two women who had called on him the night of his murder. One appeared to have vanished without a trace. The other was resting comfortably in St. Thomas' Hospital. For that, if nothing else, the prime minister was profoundly grateful.

SHE WAS SOAKED TO THE skin when she arrived, and shivering with cold. The critical care staff were not told her name or occupation, only her nationality and her approximate age. They removed her sodden clothing, placed it in a crimson biohazard bag, and gave her a gown and mask to wear. Her pupils were responsive, her nasal passages were clear. Her heart rate and respiration were both elevated. Was she nauseated? She wasn't. Headache? A touch, she admitted, but it was probably the martini she'd drunk earlier that evening. She didn't say where.

Her condition suggested she had survived exposure to the nerve agent unharmed. Nevertheless, in order to safeguard against the possibility of a delayed onset of symptoms, she was prescribed atropine and pralidoxime chloride, both of which were administered intravenously. The atropine dried her mouth and blurred her vision, but otherwise she had no serious side effects.

After four additional hours of observation, she was wheeled to a room on an upper floor with a view of the Thames. It was nearly four a.m. before she drifted off to sleep. Her thrashing gave the night nurses a scare—muscle twitches were a symptom of nerve agent poisoning—but it was only a nightmare, the poor lamb. Two uniformed Metropolitan Police officers kept watch outside her door, along with a man in a dark suit and a radio earpiece. Later, hospital administration would deny a contagion-like staff rumor that the officer was from the branch of the Met responsible for protecting the royal family and the prime minister.

It was nearly ten a.m. when the woman awoke. After taking a light breakfast of coffee and toast, she was subjected to yet another examination. Pupils responsive, nasal passages clear.

Heart rate, respiration, and blood pressure all normal. It appeared, said the doctor, she was out of the proverbial woods.

"Does that mean I can leave?"

"Not yet."

"When?"

"Late afternoon at the earliest."

She was clearly disappointed, but she accepted her fate without so much as a word of protest. The nurses did their best to make her comfortable, though all attempts to engage her in conversation beyond the topic of her condition were deftly rebuffed. Oh, she was polite to a fault, but guarded and distant. She spent much of the day watching the television news coverage of the Russian billionaire's assassination. Apparently, she was involved somehow, but it seemed that Downing Street was determined to keep her role a secret. The staff had been warned not to breathe a word about her to the press.

Shortly after five p.m. she received a call on her room phone. It was Number Ten on the line—the prime minister himself, according to one of the operators, who swore she heard his voice. A few minutes after the conversation ended, a boyish-looking man with the demeanor of a country parson appeared with a change of clothing and a bag of toiletries. He wrote something illegible in the visitors' logbook and waited with the police officers in the corridor while the woman showered and dressed. After a final examination, which she passed with flying colors, the doctors consented to her release. The boyish-looking man promptly took possession of the form and instructed the senior nurse to delete the woman's file from the computer system. A moment later, both file and woman were gone.

4

ST. THOMAS' HOSPITAL, LAMBETH

A SILVER BENTLEY CONTINENTAL WAITED OUTSIDE the hospital's main entrance, the driver leaning indifferently against the hood. He wore a Burberry Camden car coat atop a single-breasted suit by Richard Anderson of Savile Row. His hair was sun-bleached, his eyes were bright blue. Sarah lowered her mask and kissed his mouth, which seemed permanently fixed in an ironic smile.

"Do you really think this is wise?" asked Christopher.

"Very." She dragged the tip of her forefinger across the notch in his sturdy chin. His skin was taut and dark. The years he had spent living in the mountains of Corsica had left him with the complexion of a Mediterranean. "You look good enough to eat."

"They didn't feed you in there?"

"I didn't have much of an appetite. Not after seeing Viktor like that. But let's talk about something a bit more pleasant."

"Like what?"

"All the wicked things I'm going to do to you when we get home."

Sarah bit his bottom lip and slid into the Bentley's passenger seat. Shortly after moving to London, she had suggested that Christopher might want to sell the car and purchase something a bit less ostentatious—a Volvo, for example, preferably an estate model. Now, caressed by quilted leather, she wondered how she could have ever been so foolish. One of her favorite standards flowed from the silken audio system. She accompanied Chet Baker as they crossed Westminster Bridge.

I fell in love just once, and then it had to be with you . . .

The rush-hour traffic was anemic. On the opposite bank of the Thames, construction scaffolding had rendered the Elizabeth Tower invisible, altering London's skyline. Even the famous clockface was veiled. Nothing was right in the world, thought Sarah. Things had fallen apart.

Everything happens to me . . .

"I never knew you had such a beautiful voice," said Christopher.

"I thought spies were supposed to be good liars."

"I'm an intelligence officer. The spies are the people we seduce into betraying their countries."

"That doesn't change the fact that I have the world's worst singing voice."

"Nonsense."

"It's true, actually. When I was in the first grade at Brearley, my teacher wrote a lengthy treatise on my report card about my inability to carry a tune."

"You know what they say about teachers."

"Miss Hopper," said Sarah spitefully. "Fortunately, my father was transferred to London the next year. He enrolled me at the American School in St. John's Wood, and I was able to put the entire episode behind me." She gazed out her window at the deserted pavements of Birdcage Walk. "My mother and I used to take the longest walks when we lived in London. That's when we were still speaking to one another."

Christopher's Marlboros were resting on the center console beneath his gold Dunhill lighter. Sarah hesitated, then plucked one from the packet.

"Perhaps you shouldn't."

"Haven't you heard? They say it kills the coronavirus." Sarah struck the lighter and touched the end of the cigarette to the flame. "You could have visited me, you know."

"The NHS forbids all patient visits with the exception of end-of-life scenarios."

"I was exposed to a Russian nerve agent. End of life was a distinct possibility."

"If you must know, I volunteered to stand guard outside your door, but Graham wouldn't hear of it. He sends his best, by the way."

Christopher switched on Radio Four in time to hear the beginning of the *Six O'Clock News*. Viktor Orlov's assassination had managed to displace the pandemic as the lead story. The Kremlin had denied any role in the affair, accusing British intelligence of a plot to discredit Russia. According to the BBC, British authorities had not yet identified the toxin used to murder Orlov. Nor had they determined how the substance found its way into the billionaire's home in Cheyne Walk.

"Surely you know more than that," said Sarah.

"Much more."

"What kind of nerve agent was it?"

"I'm afraid that's classified, darling."

"So am I."

Christopher smiled. "It's a substance known as Novichok. It's—"

"A binary weapon developed by the Soviet Union in the seventies. The scientists who created it claimed it was five to eight times more lethal than VX, which would make it the deadliest weapon ever produced."

"Are you quite finished?"

"How did the Russians get the Novichok into Viktor's office?"

"The documents you saw on his desk were covered in ultra-fine Novichok powder."

"What were they?"

"They appear to be financial records of some sort."

"How did they get there?"

"Ah, yes," said Christopher. "That's where things get interesting."

"AND YOU'RE ABSOLUTELY SURE," ASKED Sarah at the conclusion of Christopher's briefing, "that the woman who came to Viktor's house was in fact Nina Antonova?"

"We compared a surveillance photo of her taken at Heathrow with a recent television appearance. The facial recognition software determined it was the same woman. And Viktor's bodyguards say he greeted her as though she was an old friend."

"An old friend with a batch of poisoned documents?"

"When the Kremlin wants to kill someone, it's usually an acquaintance or business associate who spikes the champagne. Just ask Crown Prince Abdullah of Saudi Arabia."

"No chance of that." They entered Sloane Square. The darkened facade of the Royal Court Theatre slid past Sarah's window. "So what's your theory? Nina Antonova, a well-known investigative reporter and professed dissident, was recruited by Russian intelligence to murder the man who singlehandedly saved her magazine?"

"Did I say recruited?"

"You choose the word."

Christopher guided the Bentley into the King's Road. "It is the considered opinion of both Vauxhall Cross and our brethren at Thames House that Nina Antonova is a Russian intelligence officer who burrowed her way into the *Moskovskaya Gazeta* years ago and has been biding her time."

"How do you explain the assassination attempt that forced her to leave Russia?"

"Excellent Moscow Center tradecraft."

Sarah did not dismiss the theory out of hand. "There is another possibility, you know."

"What's that?"

"She was duped into giving the poisoned documents to Viktor. In fact, given the peculiar circumstances of her escape from London, I'd say it's the most likely explanation."

"There was nothing peculiar about it. She was gone before we even knew her name."

"Why did she check into a hotel instead of going straight to the airport? And why Amsterdam instead of Moscow?"

"There were no direct flights to Moscow at that hour. We assume she flew there this morning on a clean passport."

"If she did, she's probably dead by now. Frankly, I'm surprised she made it to Heathrow alive."

Christopher turned into Old Church Street and headed north into Kensington. "I thought CIA analysts were trained not to jump to conclusions."

"If anyone's jumping to conclusions, it's you and your colleagues from MI5." Sarah contemplated the ember of her cigarette. "Viktor's phone was off the hook when I entered the study. He must have called someone before he died."

"It was Nina."

"Oh, really?"

"She was in her room at the Cadogan. She left the hotel a few minutes later."

"Was GCHQ monitoring Viktor's phones?"

"The British government does not eavesdrop on the communications of prominent newspaper publishers."

"Viktor Orlov was no ordinary publisher."

"Which is why he's dead," said Christopher.

"What do you suppose they talked about?"

"If I had to guess, he was rather miffed at Nina for poisoning him."

Sarah frowned. "Do you really believe a man like Viktor would waste the final moments of his life berating his killer?"

"Why else would he have called her twenty minutes after she left his house?"

"To warn her she would be next."

Christopher turned into Queen's Gate Terrace. "You're quite good, you know."

"For an art dealer," remarked Sarah.

"An art dealer with an interesting past."

"You're one to talk."

Christopher parked the Bentley outside a Georgian house the color of clotted cream. He and Sarah shared the maisonette on the bottom two floors. The owner of the flat above was a vaguely named shell company registered in the Cayman Islands. Nearly one hundred thousand luxury British properties were held by secret owners, many in tony London districts like Kensington and Knightsbridge. Even MI6 had been unable to determine the true identity of Christopher's absentee neighbor.

He switched off the engine but hesitated before opening the door.

"Something wrong?" asked Sarah.

"There's a light on in the kitchen."

"You must have forgotten to turn it off when you left this morning."

"I didn't." Christopher reached inside his suit jacket and drew a Walther PPK. "Wait here. I won't be but a moment."

5

NAHALAL, ISRAEL

As DIRECTOR-GENERAL OF THE OFFICE, Gabriel Allon was permitted to use safe houses largely as he saw fit. He drew an ethical line, however, at borrowing one for the purpose of getting his wife and children out of their cramped apartment on Narkiss Street in locked-down Jerusalem. At his request, Housekeeping presented him with a market-tested monthly rental rate. He promptly doubled it and ordered the government personnel office to deduct the sum from his salary. Additionally, in the spirit of full transparency, he forwarded copies of all the relevant paperwork to Kaplan Street for approval. The prime minister, who was under indictment on charges of public corruption, wondered what all the fuss was about.

The property in question was by no means luxurious. A

smallish bungalow used mainly for debriefings and storage of blown field operatives, it was located in Nahalal, an old moshav in the Valley of Jezreel, about an hour north of King Saul Boulevard. The furnishings were sparse but comfortable, and the kitchen and bathrooms were recently renovated. There were cows in the paddock, chickens in the coop, several acres of cropland, and a grassy garden shaded by eucalyptus trees. Because the moshav was protected by a crack local police force, security was of no concern.

Chiara and the children settled in the bungalow in late March and remained there after the agreeable weather of spring had given way to the blast-furnace heat of high summer. The afternoons were unbearable, but each evening a cool wind blew from the Upper Galilee. The moshav's communal swimming pool was closed by government edict, and a summer surge of infections made play dates with other young children impossible. It was no matter; Irene and Raphael were content to pass their days organizing elaborate games involving the chickens and the neighbor's flock of goats. By the middle of June, their skin was the color of mocha. Chiara slathered them with sunblock, but somehow they grew darker still.

"The same thing happened to the Jews who founded the moshav in 1921," explained Gabriel. "Raphael and Irene are no longer pampered city dwellers. They're children of the valley."

During the first wave of the pandemic, he had been largely absent. Armed with a new Gulfstream jet and suitcases filled with cash, he had traveled the world in search of ventilators, testing material, and protective medical clothing. He made most of his purchases on the black market and then personally ferried the cargo back to Israel, where it was dispersed to hospitals throughout the country. When word of his efforts reached the press, an influential columnist from *Haaretz* suggested he consider a post-Office career in politics. The reaction was so favorable that many in the chattering classes wondered whether it was a trial balloon. Gabriel, who found all the unwanted attention embarrassing, issued a formal statement forswearing any interest in elected office—which the chattering classes interpreted as proof beyond a reasonable doubt that he intended to run for the Knesset when his term expired. The only unresolved question, they said, was his party affiliation.

But by early June the Office was once again engaged in more traditional pursuits. Alarmed by new intelligence regarding Tehran's determination to build a nuclear weapon, Gabriel slipped a large bomb into a centrifuge factory in Natanz. Six weeks later, in a daring operation carried out at the behest of the Americans, an Office hit team killed a senior al-Qaeda operative in downtown Tehran. Gabriel leaked details of the assassination to a friendly reporter at the *New York Times*, if only to remind the Iranians that he could enter their country whenever he pleased and strike at will.

Despite the summer's brisk operational tempo, he often arrived in Nahalal in time for dinner. Chiara would set a table outside in the cool of the garden, and Irene and Raphael would happily recount the details of their day, which invariably were identical to the particulars of the previous day. Afterward, Gabriel would take them for a walk along the dusty farm roads of the valley and tell them stories of his childhood in the young state of Israel.

He was born in the neighboring kibbutz of Ramat David. There were no computers or mobile phones, of course, and no television, either; it didn't arrive in Israel until 1966. Even then, his mother would not permit one in the house, fearing it would interfere with her work. Gabriel explained to the children how he used to sit at her feet while she painted, imitating her brush-strokes on a canvas of his own. He did not mention the numbers tattooed on her left arm. Or the candles that burned in their home for the family members who had not survived the camps. Or the screams he used to hear from the other bungalows in Ramat David, late at night, when the demons came.

Gradually, he told them more about himself—a thread here, a fragment there, bits of truth mixed with subtle evasion, the occasional outright lie, if only to protect them from the horrors of the life he had led. Yes, he said, he had been a soldier, but not a very good one. When he left the IDF, he entered the Bezalel Academy of Art and Design and began his formal training as a painter. But in the autumn of 1972, after a terrorist attack at the Olympic Games in Munich, Ari Shamron, whom the children referred to as their *saba*, asked him to take part in an undertaking known as Operation Wrath of God. He did not tell the children that he personally killed six members of the PLO faction responsible for the attack, or that whenever possible he shot them eleven times. He implied, however, that his experiences had robbed him of the ability to produce satisfactory original paintings. Rather than allow his talents to go to waste, he learned to speak Italian and then traveled to Venice, where he trained to be an art restorer.

But children, especially the children of intelligence officers, are not easily misled, and Irene and Raphael sensed intuitively that their father's account of his life was far from complete. They probed with care and with guidance from their mother, who thought a familial exhumation of Gabriel's skeletons was overdue. The children already knew, for example, that he had been married once before and that the face of his dead son peered at them nightly from the clouds he had painted on the wall of their bedroom. But how had it happened? Gabriel answered with a heavily redacted version of the truth, knowing full well it would open Pandora's box.

"Is that why you always look under our car before we get in?"

"Yes."

"Do you love Dani more than you love us?"

"Of course not. But we must never forget him."

"Where's Leah?"

"She lives in a special hospital not far from us in Jerusalem."

"Has she ever met us?"

"Only Raphael."

"Why?"

Because God, in his infinite wisdom, had created in Raphael a duplicate of Gabriel's dead son. This, too, he withheld from his children, for their sake and his. That night, as Chiara slept contentedly at his side, he relived the bombing in Vienna in his dreams and awoke to find his half of the bed drenched with sweat. It was perhaps fitting, then, that when he reached for the phone on the bedside table, he learned that an old friend had been murdered in London.

He dressed in darkness and climbed into his SUV for the drive to King Saul Boulevard. After submitting to a temperature check and a rapid Covid test, he rode in his private elevator to his sanitized office on the top floor. Two hours later, after watching the British prime minister's evasive appearance before reporters outside Number Ten, he rang Graham Seymour on the secure hotline. Graham volunteered no additional information about the murder, save for the identity of the woman who had stumbled upon the body. Gabriel responded with the same question the prime minister had posed the previous evening.

"What in God's name was she doing in Viktor Orlov's house?"

IF THERE WAS A BRIGHT spot in Gabriel's post-Covid existence, it was the Gulfstream jet. A G550 of astounding comfort and murky registry, it touched down at London City Airport at half past four that afternoon. The passport Gabriel displayed to the immigration authorities was Israeli, diplomatic, and pseudonymous. It fooled no one.

Nevertheless, after passing yet another rapid Covid test, he was granted provisional admittance to the United Kingdom. A waiting embassy sedan delivered him to 18 Queen's Gate Terrace in Kensington. According to the list of names on the intercom panel, the occupant of the lower maisonette was someone called Peter Marlowe. The bell rang unanswered, so Gabriel descended a flight of wrought-iron steps to the lower entrance and drew the thin metal tool he carried habitually in his jacket pocket. Neither of the two high-quality locks put up much of a fight.

Inside, an alarm chirped in protest. Gabriel entered the correct eight-digit code into the keypad and switched on the overhead lights, illuminating a large designer kitchen. The stonework was Corsican, as was the bottle of rosé he unearthed from the well-provisioned Sub-Zero refrigerator. He removed the cork and switched on the Bose radio resting on the granite countertop.

The Russian government has denied any role in Mr. Orlov's death . . .

The BBC news presenter made an awkward transition from Orlov's assassination to the latest pandemic news. Gabriel switched off the radio and drank some of the Corsican wine. Finally, at twenty minutes past six, a Bentley Continental pulled up in the street, and a well-dressed man emerged. A moment later he was standing in the open door of the kitchen, a Walther PPK in his outstretched hands.

"Hello, Christopher," said Gabriel as he raised the wineglass in greeting. "Do me a favor and put down that damn gun. Otherwise, one of us might get hurt."

6

QUEEN'S GATE TERRACE, KENSINGTON

CHRISTOPHER KELLER WAS A MEMBER of an exceedingly small club—the brotherhood of terrorists, assassins, spies, arms dealers, art thieves, and fallen priests who had undertaken to kill Gabriel Allon and were still walking the face of the earth. Christopher's motives for accepting the challenge had been financial rather than political. He was employed at the time by a certain Don Anton Orsati, leader of a Corsican crime family that specialized in murder for hire. Unlike many of the fools who had gone before him, Christopher was an altogether worthy opponent, a former member of the elite SAS who had served under deep cover in Northern Ireland during one of the nastier periods of the Troubles. Gabriel had survived the contract only because Christopher, out of professional courtesy, declined to pull the trigger when presented with the shot. Some years later

Gabriel repaid the favor by convincing Graham Seymour to give Christopher a job at MI6.

As part of his repatriation agreement, Christopher had been allowed to keep the substantial fortune he had amassed while working for Don Orsati. He had invested a portion of the money—eight million pounds, to be precise—in the maisonette in Queen's Gate Terrace. When Gabriel last dropped in unannounced, the rooms had been largely unfurnished. Now they were tastefully decorated in patterned silk and chintz, and there was a faint but unmistakable whiff of fresh paint in the air. Clearly, Christopher had given Sarah free rein and unlimited resources. Gabriel had reluctantly blessed their relationship, secure in his belief it would be both brief and disastrous. He had even arranged for Sarah to work at Julian's gallery despite concerns about her security. He had to admit, the exposure to a Russian nerve agent notwithstanding, she looked happier than she had in many years. If anyone had earned the right to be happy, thought Gabriel, it was Sarah Bancroft.

Barefoot, she was draped across an overstuffed armchair in the upstairs drawing room, wineglass in hand. Her blue eyes were fixed on Christopher, who occupied a matching chair to her right. Gabriel had settled in a distant corner where he was safe from their microbes and they from his. Sarah had greeted him with pleasant surprise but without so much as a kiss on the cheek or a fleeting embrace. Such were the social customs of the brave new Covid world; everyone was an untouchable. Or perhaps, thought Gabriel, Sarah was merely trying to keep him at arm's length. She had never made any secret of the fact she was desperately in love with him, even when asking for his approval of her decision to leave New York and move to London.

It seemed that Christopher had finally broken the spell. Gabriel suspected he had intruded on an intimate moment. He had one or two things he wanted to clear up before taking his leave.

"And you're certain about the attribution?" he asked.

"I wouldn't have offered it to Viktor if I wasn't. It wouldn't have been ethical."

"Since when do ethics have anything to do with being an art dealer?"

"Or an intelligence officer," replied Sarah.

"But Italian Old Masters aren't exactly your area of expertise, are they? In fact, if I recall correctly, you wrote your dissertation at Harvard on the German Expressionists."

"At the tender age of twenty-eight." She moved a stray lock of blond hair from her face using only her middle finger. "And before that, as you well know, I earned my MA in art history from the Courtauld Institute here in London."

"Did you seek a second opinion?"

"Niles Dunham. He offered me eight hundred thousand on the spot."

"For an Artemisia? Outrageous."

"I told him so."

"Still, all things considered, you would have been wise to take it."

"Trust me, I intend to call him first thing in the morning."

"Please don't."

"Why not?"

"Because one never knows when one might need a newly discovered painting by Artemisia Gentileschi."

"It needs work," said Sarah.

"Who did you have in mind for the job?"

"Since you weren't available, I was hoping I could convince David Bull to take it on."

"I thought he was in New York these days."

"He is. I had lunch with him before I left. Such a lovely man."

"Have you discussed it with him?"

Sarah shook her head.

"Who else knew about the sale to Viktor other than Julian?"

"No one."

"And you didn't let it slip at Wilton's?"

"I'm a former intelligence officer and undercover operative. I don't let things *slip*."

"And what about Viktor?" Gabriel persisted. "Did he tell anyone that you were coming to Cheyne Walk last night?"

"With Viktor, I suppose anything's possible. But why do you ask?"

Christopher answered on Gabriel's behalf. "He's wondering whether the Russians were trying to kill two birds with one stone."

"Viktor and me?"

"You do have a rather long track record when it comes to Russians," Gabriel pointed out. "It stretches all the way back to our old friend Ivan Kharkov."

"If Moscow Center had wanted to kill me, they would have made an appointment to see a painting at Isherwood Fine Arts."

Gabriel directed his gaze toward Christopher. "And you're sure the contaminated documents were in fact delivered by Nina Antonova?"

"We didn't see her place the bloody things on Viktor's desk, if that's what you're asking. But someone gave them to Viktor, and Nina is the most likely candidate."

"Why didn't Jonathan mention her name this morning outside Number Ten?"

"National pride, for a start. As you can imagine, there were red faces all round when we realized that she'd slipped out of the country even before we started looking for her. The home secretary is planning to make the announcement tomorrow morning."

"But what if Sarah is right? What if Nina was deceived into delivering those documents? And what if Viktor managed to warn her before he died?"

"She should have called the police instead of fleeing the country."

"She doesn't trust the police. You wouldn't either if you were a Russian journalist."

Gabriel's phone pulsed with an incoming message. He had been forced, at long last, to part company with his beloved BlackBerry Key2. His new device was an Israeli-made Solaris, reputedly the world's most secure mobile phone. Gabriel's had been customized to his unique specifications. Larger and heavier than a typical smartphone, it was capable of fending off remote attacks from the world's most sophisticated hackers, including the American NSA and Russia's Special Communications Service, or Spetssviaz.

Christopher eyed Gabriel's device enviously. "Is it as secure as they say?"

"I could send an email from the middle of the Doughnut with complete confidence that HMG would never be able to read it." The Doughnut was how employees of Britain's GCHQ referred to their circular headquarters in Cheltenham.

"May I at least hold it?" asked Christopher.

"In the age of Covid? Don't even think about it." Gabriel entered his fourteen-character hard password, and the text message appeared on the screen. He frowned as he read it.

"Something wrong?"

"Graham has asked me to come to dinner. Apparently, Helen is making couscous."

"My condolences. I'm only sorry I won't be joining you."

"You are, actually."

"Tell Graham I'll take a raincheck."

"He's the director-general of your service."

"I realize that," said Christopher, staring at the beautiful woman draped across the overstuffed chair. "But I'm afraid I have a much better offer."

7

EATON SQUARE, BELGRAVIA

WHEN HELEN LIDDELL-BROWN met Graham Seymour at a drinks party at Cambridge, he told her that his father worked for a very dull department of the Foreign Office. She did not believe him, for her uncle served in a senior position in the same department, which was known to insiders as the Firm and the rest of the world as MI6. She accepted Graham's proposal of marriage on the condition he take a respectable job in the City. But a year after they wed, he surprised her by joining MI5, a betrayal for which Helen—and Graham's father, for that matter—never quite forgave him.

She punished Graham by adopting stridently left-wing politics. She opposed the Falklands War, campaigned for a nuclear freeze, and was twice arrested outside the South African Embassy in Trafalgar Square. Graham never knew what horrors awaited him in the post each night when he returned home from the office. He once remarked to a colleague that if Helen were not his wife, he would have opened a file on her and tapped her phone.

If it was her secret strategy to derail his career, she failed miserably. After serving for several years in Northern Ireland, he took control of MI5's counterterrorism division and was then promoted to the rank of deputy director for operations. It was his intention, at the conclusion of his term, to retire to his villa in Portugal. His plans changed, however, when Prime Minister Lancaster offered him the keys to his father's old service—a move that surprised everyone in the intelligence trade except Gabriel, who had brought about the set of circumstances that led to Graham's appointment. With the Americans turning inward and torn by political divisions, ties between the Office and MI6 had grown exceedingly close. The two services operated together routinely, and critical intelligence flowed freely between Vauxhall Cross and King Saul Boulevard. Gabriel and Graham saw themselves as defenders of the postwar international order. Given the current state of global affairs, it was an increasingly thankless task.

Helen Seymour's acceptance of her husband's ascent to the pinnacle of British intelligence had been grudging at best. At Graham's request, she had toned down her politics and placed some distance between herself and some of her more heretical friends. She practiced yoga each morning and passed her afternoons in the kitchen, where she indulged her passion for exotic cooking. During Gabriel's last visit to the Seymour residence, he had heroically consumed a plate of paella in violation of Jewish dietary laws. The chicken couscous was a rare triumph.

Even Graham, who was skilled at moving food around his plate to create the illusion of consumption, helped himself to a second portion.

At the conclusion of the meal, he dabbed the corners of his mouth deliberately with his linen napkin and invited Gabriel to join him upstairs in his book-lined study. A draft blew through the open window overlooking Eaton Square. Gabriel was dubious as to the efficacy of such precautions, believing they simply facilitated the transfer of the virus from host to unwitting recipient. He glanced at the wall-mounted television, which was tuned to CNN. A panel of political experts was debating the American presidential election, now only three months away.

"Care to make a prediction?" asked Graham.

"I believe Christopher will propose marriage to Sarah sometime in the next year."

"I was talking about the election."

"It will be closer than the polls are predicting, but he cannot win."

"Will he accept the outcome?"

"Not a chance."

"And then what?"

Graham went to the window and effortlessly lowered the sash. He seemed unsuited for so mundane a task. With his even features and plentiful pewter-colored locks, he reminded Gabriel of one of those male models who appear in ads for gold fountain pens and expensive wristwatches, the sort of needless trinkets that went out of fashion with the pandemic. He made lesser beings feel inferior, especially Americans.

"Rumor has it you arrived in London on a fancy new Gulf-stream," he said, reclaiming his seat. "The registry is rather opaque."

"With good reason. My many friends and admirers in the Islamic Republic are rather angry with me at the moment."

"That's what you get for blowing up their centrifuge factory. Frankly, I'm surprised you found time in your busy schedule to come here on such short notice."

"A dear friend of mine was feeling under the weather. I thought I'd pay her a visit."

"Your dear friend is just fine."

"Unfortunately, the same can't be said of Viktor Orlov."

"Viktor is none of your affair."

"He was my asset, Graham. And if it wasn't for his money, I would be dead. So would my wife."

"As I recall," said Graham, "I was the one who talked Viktor into surrendering his oil company in exchange for your freedom. If he'd had any sense, he would have kept a lower profile. Instead, he purchased the *Gazeta* and deliberately placed himself in the Kremlin's crosshairs. It was only a matter of time before they got to him."

"With Nina Antonova?"

Graham made a face. "At some point, we might have to re-establish some boundaries between your service and mine."

"You don't really believe she's a Moscow Center assassin, do you?"

"Sometimes two plus two does in fact equal four."

"But sometimes it's five."

"Only in Room 101 of the Ministry of Love, Winston."

"Sarah has an interesting theory," replied Gabriel. "She believes Nina was deceived into delivering the contaminated documents."

"And when did Sarah reach this conclusion? During the thirty seconds she was inside Viktor's study?"

"She has excellent instincts."

"That's hardly surprising. After all, you were the one who trained her. But Moscow Center would never have entrusted such a dangerous weapon to someone who wasn't fully under its control."

"Why ever not?"

"What if she had opened the parcel on the British Airways flight from Zurich?"

"But she didn't. She delivered the package to Viktor. And Viktor, who was justifiably paranoid about his security, waited until she had left before opening it. What does that tell you?"

"It tells me that Nina Antonova and her controllers at Moscow Center devised a rather cunning method of slipping a contaminated package past Viktor's formidable defenses. They're probably celebrating their latest success as we speak."

"There's no way she's in Moscow, Graham."

"Well, she isn't in Zurich, and her phone is off the air."

"What about her credit card?"

"No recent activity."

"That's because she knows the Russians are looking for her. Obviously, we need to find her first."

"By midday tomorrow, she will be the world's most wanted woman."

"Unless you delay releasing her name and photograph long enough for me to find her."

Graham was silent.

"Give me seventy-two hours," said Gabriel.

"Not possible." Graham paused, then added, "But you can have forty-eight."

"That's not much time."

"It's all you're going to get."

"In that case," said Gabriel, "I'm sure you won't mind if I borrow Sarah."

"Not at all. Where do you intend to start?"

"I was hoping to have a word with someone who used to work with Nina at the *Gazeta*. Someone who might have an opinion as to whether she was a real journalist or a Moscow Center assassin." Gabriel smiled. "You wouldn't know where I could find someone like that, would you, Graham?"

"Yes," he said. "I think I might."

8

LONDON–NORWICH

Transport left a Vauxhall sedan in Pembridge Square, a key taped beneath the rear bumper, a Beretta 9mm concealed in the glove box. Gabriel collected it at half past nine the following morning and drove to Knightsbridge. Sarah was drinking a cappuccino at Caffè Concerto in the Brompton Road, a mask dangling from one ear. Laughing, she slid into the passenger seat.

"A Vauxhall? What happened? They couldn't find you a Passat?"

"Evidently, there were none available in the whole of the United Kingdom."

"We should have taken Christopher's Bentley."

"Intelligence officers don't drive cars like that unless they're moonlighting for the Russians."

"Says the man who has his own airplane."

"It belongs to the state of Israel."

"Whatever you say, darling." Sarah glanced at the facade of Harrods. Quietly, she said, "The bricks are in the wall."

Gabriel gave an involuntary start.

Sarah placed a hand on his arm. "Forgive me, I shouldn't have done that."

"Obviously, you and Christopher have been engaging in a little pillow talk about past operations."

"We were locked in the maisonette together for three months with nothing to do but watch the pandemic on television and share our deepest, darkest secrets. Christopher told me all about the Eamon Quinn affair and the real story behind the bombing of Harrods. He also mentioned something about a woman he fell in love with while he was working undercover in Belfast."

"I assume you reciprocated with a tragic tale of your own."

"Quite a few, actually."

"Did my name come up?"

"I might have mentioned that I was once desperately in love with you."

"Why on earth would you tell him that?"

"Because it's true."

"But you're not in love with me anymore?"

"Not even a little." She gave him a sidelong glance. "You *are* still a handsome devil, though."

"For a man of advancing years."

"You don't look a day over—"

"Careful, Sarah."

"I was going to say fifty."

"How generous of you."

"What's your secret?"

"I'm young at heart."

She gave a dismissive laugh. "You're the oldest soul I've ever met, Gabriel Allon. It's one of the reasons I fell in love with you."

He followed the Strand to the Kingsway, then headed through the northeastern boroughs of London to the M11. The traffic was pandemic sparse, mainly lorries and essential workers. They reached Cambridge before noon and an hour later were approaching Norwich, the unofficial capital of East Anglia.

Gabriel left the Vauxhall in a car park near the twelfth-century cathedral and led Sarah on an hour-long walking tour of the city's ancient center. After performing a series of time-tested countersurveillance maneuvers, they made their way to Bishopsgate. A terrace of redbrick cottages overlooked the deserted sporting grounds of the Norwich Middle School. Gabriel thumbed the bell push of Number 34 and then turned his back to the camera mounted above the door.

A female voice addressed him in English over the intercom. The accent was vaguely Russian, the tone unwelcoming. "Whatever it is you're selling, I'm not interested."

"I'm not selling anything, Professor Crenshaw."

"Who are you?"

"An old friend."

"I don't have any friends. They're all dead."

"Not all of them."

"How are we acquainted, please?"

"We met in Moscow a long time ago. You took me to Novodevichy Cemetery. You said that to understand modern Russia, you had to know her past. And that to know her past, you had to walk among her bones."

A long moment passed. "Turn around so I can have a look at you."

Gabriel rotated slowly and lifted his eyes to the lens of the security camera. A buzzer groaned, the deadbolt thumped. He placed his hand on the latch. Sarah followed him inside.

"I WAS BEGINNING TO THINK you'd forgotten about me."
"Not for a minute."
"How long has it been?"
"A hundred years."
"Is that all?"
They were seated at a wrought-iron table outside in the un-kempt garden. Olga Sukhova was clutching an earthenware mug of tea to her breasts. Her hair, once long and flaxen, was short and dark and flecked with gray, and there were lines around her blue eyes. A plastic surgeon had softened her features. Even so, her face was still remarkably beautiful. Heroic, vulnerable, virtuous: the face of a Russian icon come to life. The face of Russia itself.

Gabriel had glimpsed it for the first time at a diplomatic re-ception at the Israeli Embassy in Moscow. He had been posing as Natan Golani, a midlevel functionary from the Ministry of Culture who specialized in building artistic bridges between Israel and the rest of the world. Olga was a prominent Russian investigative reporter who had recently come into possession of a most dangerous secret—a secret she shared with Gabriel over dinner the following evening at a Georgian restaurant near the Arbat. Afterward, in the darkened stairwell of her Mos-cow apartment building, they were targeted for assassination. The Russians mounted a second attempt on their lives a few months later in Oxford, where Olga was working as a Russian-language tutor named Marina Chesnikova. She was now known as Dr. Sonia Crenshaw, a Ukrainian-born professor of contemporary Russian studies at East Anglia University.

"What happened to Mr. Crenshaw?" asked Gabriel. "Did he run off with another woman?"

"Deceased, I'm afraid."

"There's a lot of that going around."

"Yes," Olga agreed. "I settled here in Norwich a few months after the funeral. It isn't Oxford, mind you, but East Anglia is one of the better plateglass universities. Ishiguro studied creative writing here."

"*The Remains of the Day* is one of my favorite novels."

"I've read it ten times at least. Poor Stevens. Such a tragic figure."

Gabriel wondered whether Olga, perhaps unconsciously, was referring to herself. She had paid a terrible price for her journalistic opposition to the kleptomaniacal cabal of former KGB officers who had seized control of Russia. Like thousands of other dissidents before her, she had chosen exile. Hers was harsher than most. She had no lover because a lover could not be trusted. She had no children because children could be targeted by her enemies. She was alone in the world.

She eyed Gabriel over the rim of her mug. "I read about your recent promotion in the newspapers. You've become quite the celebrity."

"Fame has its drawbacks."

"Especially for a spy." Her gaze shifted to Sarah. "Wouldn't you agree, Miss Bancroft?"

Sarah smiled but said nothing.

"Are you still working for the CIA?" asked Olga. "Or have you found honest work?"

"I'm managing an art gallery in St. James's."

"I suppose that answers my question." Olga turned to Gabriel. "And your wife? She's well, I hope."

"Never better."

"Children?"

"Two."

Her expression brightened. "How old?"

"They'll soon be five."

"Twins no less! How lucky you are, Gabriel Allon."

"Luck had very little to do with it. Chiara and I would never have made it out of Russia alive were it not for Viktor."

"And now Viktor is dead." She lowered her voice. "Which is why you came to see me again after all these years."

Gabriel made no reply.

"The Metropolitan Police have been rather circumspect about the details of Viktor's murder."

"With good reason."

"Have they identified the toxin?"

"Novichok. It was concealed in a parcel of documents."

"And who gave these documents to Viktor?"

"A reporter from the *Gazeta*."

"Was it Nina, by any chance?"

"How did you know?"

Olga smiled sadly. "Perhaps we should start from the beginning, Mr. Golani."

"Yes, Professor Crenshaw. Perhaps we should."

9

BISHOPSGATE, NORWICH

O N APRIL 25, 2005, RUSSIA'S president declared the collapse of the Soviet Union to be "the greatest geopolitical
catastrophe" of the twentieth century. Olga worked late into
the evening on the *Gazeta*'s editorial response, which accurately
predicted the onset of a new cold war and the end of Russian
democracy. Afterward, she and a few colleagues gathered at Bar
NKVD, a neighborhood watering hole located around the corner from the *Gazeta*'s offices in the Sokol district of Moscow. As
was often the case, they were watched over by a pair of leather-
jacketed thugs from the FSB, who made little effort to conceal
their presence.

The mood that night was funereal. One of Olga's colleagues,
a man named Aleksandr Lubin, became roaring drunk and un-
wisely picked a fight with the FSB officers. He was saved from a

beating only by the intervention of a young freelance journalist who occasionally frequented Bar NKVD. The *Gazeta*'s editor in chief was so impressed by her bravery he offered her a job as a staff reporter.

"Perhaps you remember him," said Olga. "His name was Boris Ostrovsky."

Like many Russian journalists, Ostrovsky's career had ended violently. Injected with a Russian poison while crossing St. Peter's Square, he had collapsed in the basilica a few minutes later, at the foot of the Monument to Pope Pius XII. Gabriel's face was the last he ever saw.

"And you're sure it was Aleksandr who picked the fight with the FSB officers and not the other way around?"

"Why do you ask?"

"Because if I wanted to penetrate a meddlesome news organization, I might have done it exactly the same way."

"Nina? An FSB officer?"

"Actually, the British are under the impression she works for the SVR. They think she's back at Moscow Center waiting for the Tsar to hang a medal round her neck."

"Is that what you think?"

"I'm more interested in your opinion."

"Nina Antonova is no one's spy. She's an excellent reporter and a superb writer. I should know. Boris told me to take her under my wing."

"She looked up to you?"

"She worshipped me."

Olga reminded Gabriel that in the months following Boris Ostrovsky's assassination, she had served as the *Gazeta*'s editor in chief, a title she relinquished after fleeing Russia and settling in Britain. The Kremlin engineered the sale of the *Gazeta* to an associate of the Russian president, and the once authoritative political weekly became a scandal sheet filled with stories about Russian pop stars, men from outer space, and werewolves inhabiting the forests outside Moscow. Nina was summarily fired by the new owner, along with several other members of the staff, but she returned to the *Gazeta* after it was acquired by Viktor Orlov. Her first story exposed a large construction project on the shore of the Black Sea, a billion-dollar presidential retreat financed with funds illegally diverted from Russia's Federal Treasury.

"The minute that story appeared, Nina's life was in danger. It was only a matter of time before the Tsar ordered the FSB to kill her."

"Eighteen shots at close range outside the Ritz-Carlton on Tverskaya Street," said Gabriel. "And yet she walked away without so much as a scratch."

"You're wondering whether the attack was staged?"

"The thought crossed my mind."

"What about the three innocent bystanders who were killed?"

"Since when does Russian intelligence worry about innocent bystanders?" Receiving no answer, Gabriel asked, "Were you in contact with Nina after you came to Britain?"

"Yes."

"And when she settled in Zurich?"

Olga nodded.

"Did you ever meet with her?"

"Only once. It was during Viktor's seventieth birthday party at his estate in Somerset. All the beautiful people were there. Fifteen hundred of Viktor's closest friends. I suspect half of them were Russian intelligence officers. It was a miracle he survived the night."

"How often did you see him?"

"Not often. It was too dangerous. We communicated mainly by encrypted text messages and emails. Occasionally, we spoke on the telephone."

"When was the last time?"

"I believe it was late April or perhaps early May. Viktor had come into possession of some interesting documents concerning a Swiss-based company known as Omega Holdings. Omega owns companies and other assets valued at several billion dollars, all carefully hidden beneath layer upon layer of shell corporations, many of them registered in countries such as Liechtenstein, Dubai, Panama, and the Cayman Islands. Viktor was convinced that Omega was being used by a prominent Russian for the purposes of laundering looted state assets and concealing them in the West."

"And Viktor would know a thing or two about looting state assets."

Olga gave a fleeting smile. "He was far from perfect, our Viktor. But he was committed to a free and democratic Russia, a decent Russia that was aligned with the West rather than at war with it."

"Did he know the identity of the prominent Russian?"

"He said he didn't."

"Did you believe him?"

"Not quite."

"Who could it be?"

"I could recite the names of a hundred possible candidates off the top of my head. They would run the gamut from senior government officials to Kremlin-connected businessmen and mobsters."

"Did Viktor tell you where he got the documents?"

"They were given to him by Nina."

"Was he at all concerned about their authenticity?"

"If he was, he never raised it. Therefore, I assume he believed the documents to be genuine."

"So why did Nina fly to London Wednesday night and give Viktor a package of documents contaminated with Novichok? And why was he foolish enough to open it?"

"Obviously, he trusted her. But I'm certain she had nothing to do with Viktor's death. Nina is a pawn in a much larger game, which means her life is in danger."

"All the more reason why we need to find her as quickly as possible." Gabriel paused, then asked, "You wouldn't happen to know where she is, would you, Olga?"

"No," she answered. "But I know someone who might."

"Who?"

"George-dot-Wickham at Outlook-dot-Com."

SHE ROSE WITHOUT ANOTHER WORD and entered the cottage. When she returned, she was clutching a MacBook Pro, which she placed on the table before Gabriel. On the screen was a Gmail account for someone named Elizabeth Bennet.

"I learned to speak English by reading Jane Austen," she explained. "*Pride and Prejudice* is my favorite novel."

"You're not fooling anyone, you know. Not GCHQ and certainly not the Spetssviaz."

"What's the alternative? Total digital isolation?"

"How many people have the address?"

"Seven or eight, including Nina. But yesterday afternoon I received an email from an Outlook address I didn't recognize." She pointed out the entry in the in-box. "The conniving George Wickham. A wastrel, a scoundrel, a compulsive gambler. Only a close friend would know to use his name."

The email had arrived at 11:37 a.m. on Thursday, approximately twelve hours after Nina's flight arrived in Amsterdam. Gabriel opened it and read the text. It was a single sentence, written in the stilted, dated tone of an early-nineteenth-century novel of manners.

I would be most grateful if you would advise your British friends that I had nothing at all to do with the unpleasantness last evening in Chelsea.

"Did you realize it was from Nina?"

"Not at first. But I was fairly certain the *unpleasantness* to which the author was referring was Viktor's murder."

"What did you do?"

"Check my out-box."

Gabriel clicked SENT. At 11:49 a.m. Olga had replied with a single sentence of her own.

Who is this?

The answer arrived two hours later.

S . . .

Gabriel clicked the REPLY icon and began to type.

Please tell me where you are. A friend of mine will help you.

"What do you think?" he asked.

"It's not exactly Austenian prose, but it will do."

Gabriel fired the email into the ether and stared at the screen. The waiting, he thought. Always the waiting.

———

OLGA FETCHED A BOTTLE OF wine from the fridge and switched on some music on the MacBook. The wine was a sauvignon blanc from New Zealand, crisp and delicious. The music was Rachmaninoff's remarkable collection of preludes in all twenty-four major and minor keys. When lives were at stake, Olga declared, only a Russian soundtrack would do.

When an hour passed with no response, she grew anxious. To distract herself, she spoke of Russia, which only darkened her mood. The Russian president, she lamented, was now truly a tsar in everything but name. A recent sham referendum had given him the constitutional authority to remain in power until 2036. All peaceful means of dissent had been eliminated, and the Kremlin-authorized opposition parties were a farce.

"They are a Potemkin village to create the illusion of democracy. They are useful idiots."

When another half hour had passed without a reply, Olga suggested they order something to eat. Gabriel rang an Indian takeaway on Wensum Street and twenty minutes later collected the food curbside. On the way back to Bishopsgate, he saw no sign of surveillance, British or Russian. Entering the garden, he found Olga seated before the open laptop, with Sarah peering over her shoulder.

"Where is she?" he asked.

"Still in Amsterdam," replied Olga. "She wants to know the identity of the friend who'd like to help her."

"Does she know that I was the one who brought you out of Russia?"

Olga hesitated, then nodded.

"Go ahead."

Olga typed the message and clicked SEND. Three minutes later the MacBook pinged with Nina's reply. "She'll meet you at the Van Gogh Museum tomorrow afternoon at two."

"Perhaps she could be a bit more specific."

Olga posed the question. The reply arrived at once. Gabriel smiled as he read it.

Sunflowers . . .

10

LONDON CITY AIRPORT–AMSTERDAM

THE ADORABLE COUPLE," SAID Christopher Keller. "Imagine meeting the two of you here, of all places."

He was rummaging through a cabinet in the forward galley of Gabriel's Gulfstream G550, which was parked on the floodlit tarmac of London City Airport. Gabriel and Sarah had driven there directly from Norwich. The night manager at the FBO had neglected to mention that a business consultant who went by the name Peter Marlowe had already boarded the aircraft, doubtless because Mr. Marlowe had indicated he worked for the secretive firm based in the large office building at the foot of Vauxhall Bridge.

He opened another cabinet. "I remember when you had to rely on the kindness of strangers when you needed a private plane. Though one wonders how you possibly manage without cabin staff."

"Looking for something?" asked Gabriel.

"A bit of whisky to take the edge off my day. It needn't be anything premium, mind you. Monsieur Walker will do nicely. Black Label, if you have it."

"I don't. But there's wine in the fridge."

"French, I hope."

"Israeli, actually."

Christopher sighed. He was dressed for the office in a dark suit and tie. His Burberry overcoat lay on a seat in the passenger compartment, along with a smart-looking Prada overnight bag.

"Would you mind telling me what you're doing here?" asked Gabriel.

"The Secret Intelligence Service and our brethren from across the river routinely monitor the status of private aircraft used by visiting foreign dignitaries and assorted international troublemakers. Therefore, we were understandably intrigued when your crew filed a flight plan and reserved a departure slot for ten thirty p.m." Christopher opened the refrigerator and withdrew an open bottle of Israeli sauvignon blanc. "Why Amsterdam?"

"I'm fond of cities with canals."

Christopher removed the cork and sniffed. "Try again."

"I'm bringing Nina Antonova in from the cold."

"And what exactly are you planning to do with her?"

"That depends entirely on what she has to say."

"Graham would like to be present for her debriefing."

"Would he?"

"He'd also like it to take place on British soil."

"I was the one who found her."

"With the help of an exiled Russian journalist residing in Britain under our protection. Not to mention my live-in partner and companion." He poured a glass of the wine and handed it to Sarah. "And unless your fancy new aircraft is given clearance to take off, you're not going anywhere."

"I think I liked you better when you were a contract killer."

"I'd be careful if I were you. I have a feeling you're going to need someone like me before this is over."

"I can look after myself."

Christopher glanced around the interior of the luxuriously appointed cabin. "I'll say."

THEY SPENT THE NIGHT IN separate rooms in the De L'Europe Amsterdam and in the morning took coffee and pastries like three socially distant strangers downstairs on the terrace. Afterward, Christopher departed the hotel alone and walked to the Van Gogh Museum, home of the world's largest collection of Vincent's paintings and drawings.

Ordinarily, the museum could accommodate six thousand patrons daily, but coronavirus restrictions had reduced the number to just 750. Christopher purchased two tickets, slipped one into his pocket, and handed the other to the attendant at the door.

In the foyer a uniformed security guard directed him toward an airport-style magnetometer. Having left his weapon at the hotel, he passed through the contraption without objection. The modern glass lobby was eerily quiet. He drank a coffee at the espresso bar, then headed upstairs to an exhibition room devoted to Vincent's work in the French town of Arles, where he lived from February 1888 to May 1889.

The room's most popular attraction was the iconic *Sunflowers*, oil on canvas, 95 by 73 centimeters. The painting's information placard made no mention of the fact that several years earlier it had been stolen by a pair of professional thieves in what Amsterdam's police chief described as the finest example of a smash-and-grab heist he had ever seen. The thieves turned the painting over to an operative of Israeli intelligence, who produced a perfect copy in an apartment overlooking the Seine in Paris—a copy that Christopher, posing as an underworld figure named Reg Bartholomew, sold to a Syrian middleman for twenty-five million euros. The original was discovered in an Amsterdam hotel room four months after its disappearance. Curiously, it was in better condition than when it was pinched.

Christopher stepped to his left and pondered the neighboring canvas, a dour portrait of a seated Madame Roulin. Then he turned and examined the room itself. It was about fifteen meters by ten, with a well-worn wooden floor and a square bench. There were four ways in and out. Two of the passages led to neighboring rooms dedicated to Vincent's work in Saint-Rémy and Paris. The other two led to the museum's central staircase. It was far from perfect, thought Christopher, but it would do.

He spent the next thirty minutes wandering the remarkable collection—*The Langlois Bridge*, *The Bedroom*, *Irises*, *Wheatfield with Crows*—and then headed downstairs to the lobby. It was a walk of approximately a hundred and fifty meters across the

Museumplein to Van Baerlestraat, a busy thoroughfare with bike lanes and a streetcar line. Using the stopwatch function of his MI6 phone, Christopher timed it at ninety-four seconds.

The walk back to the De L'Europe was twenty-three minutes. Gabriel was upstairs in his room.

"How was *Sunflowers*?" he asked.

"To be honest, I always preferred your version to Vincent's."

"Any problems?"

"I'm not crazy about the magnetometers. There's no way you can bring a gun into the museum."

"But you'll be waiting outside. And you'll be carrying this." Gabriel held up Christopher's Walther PPK. "Perhaps you'd like to use my Beretta instead."

"What's wrong with my gun?"

"It's rather small, Mr. Bond."

"But it's easy to conceal, and it packs quite a punch."

"Yes," said Gabriel. "A brick through a plateglass window."

GABRIEL RANG THE VALET AT one fifteen and requested his car. A metallic-gray Mercedes sedan, it was waiting in the street when he and Christopher stepped from the hotel. Sarah was already behind the wheel. She drove to the Museum Quarter and parked near the Concertgebouw, Amsterdam's neo-Renaissance classical music hall.

Christopher handed her the Walther. "Do you remember how to use it?"

"Disengage the safety and pull the trigger."

"It helps if you aim the bloody thing first."

Sarah slipped the weapon into her handbag as Christopher and Gabriel climbed out of the car and started across Van Baerlestraat. Once again, Christopher timed the walk. Ninety-two seconds. At the entrance of the museum, he gave Gabriel the second ticket he had purchased earlier that morning.

"Steal me something nice while you're in there."

"I intend to," said Gabriel, and went inside.

After passing unmolested through the magnetometer, he climbed the stairs to the Arles exhibition room. Eight masked patrons waited in a Covid-safe queue in front of *Sunflowers*. Another half dozen were contemplating the room's other iconic works. Not one appeared to be the fugitive Russian journalist wanted for questioning in connection with the murder of Viktor Orlov.

Gabriel searched the Paris and Saint-Rémy rooms, but saw no sign of her there, either. Returning to the Arles room, he joined the queue for *Sunflowers*. He checked the time on his phone: *1:52* . . . Suddenly, he felt a twinge in his lower back. It was nothing, he assured himself. Only the empty spot where his gun should be.

11

VAN GOGH MUSEUM, AMSTERDAM

DAKOTA MAXWELL, TWENTY-FOUR YEARS OLD, a recent graduate of a small but highly regarded liberal arts college in New England, had come to Amsterdam for love and stayed for the weed. Her parents, who lived grandly on the Upper East Side of Manhattan, had been pleading with her to come home, but Dakota was determined to remain abroad, like the characters in her favorite Fitzgerald novel. An aspiring writer, she hoped to find a suitable lodging where she might begin work on her first manuscript, which had a title but no plot and only the first stirrings of a story. At present, she was a resident of the Tiny Dancer, a hostel located in the Red Light District. Her room had six beds, three to a stack. On any given night they were filled with an interchangeable cast of twentysomethings whose alcohol-and-cannabis-induced musings filled several of Dakota's notebooks.

The woman who arrived late Wednesday evening was different. Older, professionally attired, sober. Over coffee the following morning, she told Dakota that her name was Renata, that she was Polish, and that she lived in London. Her unemployed husband, a plumber, had threatened to kill her in a drunken rage. She was staying at the Tiny Dancer because it accepted cash and he had canceled her credit cards. She asked Dakota to change the color of her blond-brown hair. In the hostel's communal bathroom, with supplies purchased from the pharmacy across the street, Dakota dyed the woman's hair the same color as hers, black with streaks of royal blue. It looked better on the Polish woman. She had cheekbones to die for.

With the exception of a single trip to Vodafone, where she purchased a new burner device, the woman remained locked away at the Tiny Dancer. But at eleven o'clock on Saturday morning, she had awakened Dakota and quite unexpectedly asked whether she would like to visit the Van Gogh Museum. Dakota, who was hungover and still a little stoned, declined. She relented, however, when the woman explained the real reason why she wanted Dakota's company.

Renata wasn't Polish, didn't live in London, and had never been married. Her name was Nina and she was a Russian investigative journalist who was hiding from the Kremlin. A man would be waiting in front of the museum's most famous painting at two p.m. to take her into protective custody. He was a friend of a friend. Nina wanted Dakota to make contact with this man on her behalf.

"Will I be in danger?"

"No, Dakota. I'm the one they want to kill."

"What's his name?"

"It's not important."

"What does he look like?"

Nina showed Dakota a photograph on her Vodafone.

"But how will I recognize him with a mask?"

"His eyes," said Nina.

Which explained why, at 1:58 p.m. on the first day of August, Dakota Maxwell, an aspiring novelist living in self-imposed exile in Amsterdam, was contemplating a self-portrait of Vincent in the Paris room of the Van Gogh Museum. At the stroke of two, she moved into the Arles room, where four patrons waited in an orderly, Covid-safe queue in front of *Sunflowers*. The man standing directly before the canvas was of medium height and build, hardly the superhero type. His hair was short and dark and very gray at the temples. His right hand rested thoughtfully against his chin. His head was tilted slightly to one side.

Dakota sidestepped the queue, eliciting multilingual murmurs of protest from the other patrons, and joined the man in front of the canvas. He glared at her with the greenest eyes she had ever seen. There was no mistaking him for anyone else.

"You have to wait your turn like everyone else," he scolded her in French.

"I didn't come here to see the painting," she replied in the same language.

"Who are you?"

"I'm a friend of—"

"Where is she?" he asked, cutting her off.

"Le Tambourin."

"Has she changed her appearance?"

"A little," answered Dakota.

"What does she look like?"

"Me."

Le Tambourin, the museum's stylish café, was one level down, on the ground floor. A single customer, a woman sitting alone at a table overlooking the Museumplein, had ink-black hair streaked with royal blue. Gabriel sat down uninvited and removed his mask. She regarded him with apprehension, followed by profound relief.

"It must be difficult for you," she remarked.

"What's that?"

"To have so famous a face."

"Fortunately, it's a recent phenomenon." He looked down at her tea. "You're not actually drinking that, are you?"

"I thought it would be safe."

"Viktor obviously thought the same thing." He moved the teacup to the adjacent table. "Using that American girl upstairs was a lovely piece of tradecraft. If the roles were reversed, I would have done it the same way."

"To survive as a Russian journalist, one must operate by a certain set of rules."

"In our business they're known as the Moscow Rules."

"I can recite them from memory," said Nina.

"Which is your favorite?"

"Assume that everyone is under opposition control."

"Are you?" asked Gabriel.

"Is that what you think?"

"I wouldn't be here if I did."

She smiled. "You're not what I expected."

"How so?"

"Given your exploits, I imagined you'd be taller."

"I hope you're not disappointed."

"Quite the opposite. In fact, this is the first time I've felt safe in a very long time."

"I'll feel better when you're on board my plane."

"Where are you taking me?"

"The British would like to clear up a few details of your visit to Viktor's home on the night of his death."

"I'm sure they would. But what happens if they conclude that I was under the control of the opposition?"

"They won't."

"How can you be sure?"

"Because I won't let them."

"You have influence over the British?"

"You'd be surprised." Gabriel looked at her phone. "Disposable?"

She nodded.

"Leave it behind. A colleague of mine is waiting outside. Try to walk at a normal pace. And whatever you do, don't look back."

"Moscow Rules," said Nina.

By 2:05 p.m., Sarah was beginning to grow worried. Having operated against the Russians on numerous occasions, she was well aware of their enormous capabilities and, more important, their utter ruthlessness. Alone in the car, her hand wrapped around the grip of the Walther pistol, she conjured an image of a crowd gathered around a dying man lying at the foot of a Van Gogh masterpiece.

Finally, her phone pulsed.

On our way.

She left the car park and turned into the busy Van Baerle-straat. There was a single lane reserved for cars and absolutely nowhere to park, even for a moment or two. Sarah neverthe-less pulled to the curb and switched on her hazard lamps. She looked to her right and glimpsed Gabriel and a woman who might have been Nina Antonova walking arm in arm across the Museumplein. Christopher was a few paces behind them, his hand in his coat pocket.

Just then, a car horn sounded, followed by another. Sarah glanced into her rearview mirror and saw an annoyed-looking policeman approaching on foot. The officer froze when Gabriel opened the rear passenger-side door and helped the woman into the backseat.

Christopher dropped into the front passenger seat and switched off the hazard lamps. "Drive."

Sarah slipped the car into gear and pressed the accelerator.

"Next left," said Christopher.

"I know."

She made the turn without slowing and sped along a street lined with shops and gabled brick houses. Christopher plucked the Walther from her coat pocket and returned the Beretta to Gabriel. Nina Antonova was staring out her window, her face awash with tears.

"So much for jumping to conclusions," said Sarah.

"Is there anything I can do to redeem myself?"

She smiled wickedly. "I'm sure I'll think of something."

12

WORMWOOD COTTAGE, DARTMOOR

Wormwood Cottage was set upon a swell in the moorland and fashioned of Devon stone that had darkened with age. Behind it, across a broken courtyard, was a converted barn with offices and living quarters for the staff. The caretaker was a former MI6 fieldhand called Parish. As was often the case, he was given only a few hours' warning of the pending arrival. It was Nigel Whitcombe—the chief's boyish acolyte, notetaker, food taster, henchman, and primary runner of off-the-record errands—who made the call. Parish took it on the secure line in his office. His tone was that of a maître d' from a restaurant where tables were impossible to come by.

"And the size of the party?" he wondered.

"Seven, myself included."

"No Covid, I take it."

"Not a speck."

"I assume the chief will be joining us?"

Whitcombe mumbled something in the affirmative.

"Arrival time?"

"Early evening, I should think."

"Shall I ask Miss Coventry to prepare dinner?"

"If she wouldn't mind."

"Traditional English fare?"

"The more traditional the better."

"Dietary restrictions?"

"No pork."

"Might I infer, then, that our friend from Israel will be joining us?"

"You might indeed. Mr. Marlowe, as well."

"In that case, I'll ask Miss Coventry to make her famous cottage pie. Mr. Marlowe adores it."

Owing to the pandemic, it had been many weeks since the cottage had last seen company. There were rooms to open, carpets to vacuum, surfaces to disinfect, and a depleted pantry to restock. Parish helped Miss Coventry with the shopping at the Morrisons in Plymouth Road, and at half past seven he was standing in the twilit forecourt as the chief's sleek Jaguar came nimbly up the long drive. Nigel Whitcombe arrived soon after in an anonymous service van with blacked-out windows. He was accompanied by a beautiful Slavic-featured woman who bore a passing resemblance to a famous Russian journalist who had been resettled in Britain several years earlier. What was her name? *Sukhova* . . . Yes, that was it, thought Parish. *Olga Sukhova* . . .

Whitcombe gave Parish the woman's phone—mobile devices

were forbidden in the cottage, at least where company was concerned—and led her inside. The sun dipped below the horizon, darkness gathered over the moor. Parish noted the appearance of the evening's first stars, followed soon after by a waning gibbous moon. How fitting, he thought. These days everything seemed to be in decline.

He marked the time on his old Loomes wristwatch as another service van came bumping up the drive. Mr. Marlowe emerged first, looking as though he had just returned from a holiday in the sun. Next came two women. Parish reckoned they were in their mid-forties. One was fair-haired and pretty, an American perhaps. The other had hair like a raven's wing, with peculiar blue streaks. Parish pegged her for another Russian.

Finally, the Israeli popped from the van like a cork from a bottle. Parish, who could scarcely rise from his bed without rupturing something, had always envied his agility and limitless stamina. His green eyes seemed to glow in the half-light.

"Is that you, Parish?"

"I'm afraid so, sir."

"Aren't you ever going to retire?"

"And do what?" Parish accepted the Israeli's leaden mobile phone. "I assigned you to your old room. Miss Coventry found some clothing you left behind after your last visit. I believe she placed it in the bottom drawer of the dresser."

"She's too kind."

"Unless you cross her, sir. I have the scars to prove it."

Like Parish, Miss Coventry was old service; she had worked as a listener during the final years of the Cold War. Powdered and churchy and vaguely formidable, she was standing before the stove, an apron tied around her ample waist, when the woman with peculiar black-and-blue hair entered the cottage. The Slavic-looking woman who might or might not have been the famous Olga Sukhova was waiting anxiously in the entrance hall, next to the chief. One of the women let out a joyous shriek—which one, Miss Coventry couldn't say. The man she knew as Peter Marlowe had planted himself in the passageway and was blocking her view.

"Miss Coventry, my love." He gave her a roguish smile. "You're certainly a sight for sore eyes."

"Welcome back, Mr. Marlowe."

In the entrance hall the two women were now conversing in animated Russian. Mr. Marlowe was peering through the oven window. "What are they saying?" he asked quietly.

"One of them is relieved that the other is still alive. It seems they're old friends. Evidently, it's been several years since they've seen one another."

"Are the microphones switched on?"

"That's Mr. Parish's province, not mine." She took down a serving platter from the sideboard. Absently, she asked, "Does your pretty new girlfriend like cottage pie as well?"

"You don't miss much, do you?"

Miss Coventry smiled. "American, is she?"

"Not too."

"She's one of us?"

"A former cousin."

"We won't hold that against her. Though I must admit, I had hopes for you and Miss Watson."

"So did she."

It had been Miss Coventry's intention to serve a socially

distant supper outside in the garden, but when a blustery wind blew suddenly from the northwest, she laid a formal table in the dining room instead. The first course was an onion tart with an endive and Stilton salad, followed by the cottage pie. She and Mr. Parish dined at the small table in the kitchen alcove. Occasionally, she overheard a snatch of conversation in the next room. It couldn't be helped—eavesdropping, like cooking, came naturally to her. They were discussing the Russian billionaire who had been murdered at his home in Chelsea. Apparently, the black-and-blue-haired Russian woman was involved somehow. Mr. Marlowe's American friend, too.

Miss Coventry served a bread-and-butter pudding with custard for dessert. Shortly before nine o'clock, she heard the scrape of chairs on the wooden floor, signaling the meal had concluded. It was a cottage tradition to serve coffee in the drawing room. The chief and the Israeli gentleman took theirs in the adjoining study and invited the black-and-blue-haired Russian woman to join them. The pleasantries were over. The time had come, as they used to say in the old days, to have a look beneath the bonnet.

In another lifetime, before the Wall fell and the West lost its way, Miss Coventry might well have been hunched over a reel-to-reel tape machine in the next room, a pencil in her fist. Now everything was done digitally, even the transcriptions. All it took was a flip of a switch. But that was Mr. Parish's province, she thought as she filled the kitchen basin with water. Not hers.

13

WORMWOOD COTTAGE, DARTMOOR

PARISH HAD FLIPPED THE SWITCH in question at seven that
evening. Nevertheless, owing to a technical glitch brought
about by the nimble fingers of Nigel Whitcombe, no audio
recording or written transcript of the evening's proceedings
would ever find its way into the official record of the affair.
Had such a document existed, it would have revealed that the
debriefing of Nina Antonova, lone suspect in the murder of
Viktor Orlov, began with the email she received in late February. Like many investigative journalists, she publicized her
address on her Twitter feed. It was hosted by ProtonMail, the
encrypted email service founded in Geneva by scientists working at the CERN research facility. ProtonMail utilized client-
side end-to-end encryption, which encoded the message before
it reached the firm's servers. Both were located in Switzerland,

beyond the jurisdictional reach of the United States and the European Union.

"How do you access the account?" asked Graham.

"Only on my computer."

"Never by mobile device?"

"Never."

"Where's the computer?"

"My apartment in Zurich. I live in District Three. Wiedikon, to be precise."

"You work from home, I take it?"

"Don't we all these days?"

She was seated primly before the unlit fire, a cup and saucer balanced on her knee. Graham had settled in the chair opposite, but Gabriel was slowly pacing the perimeter of the room, as though wrestling with a guilty conscience. From beyond the closed door came the murmur of voices. Outside, the wind prowled in the eaves.

"I assume the Russians know your address?" probed Graham.

"I wouldn't be surprised if I was on the embassy mailing list," replied Nina.

"You're careful with your Wi-Fi network?"

"I take all the usual precautions. But I am also well aware of the fact that it is virtually impossible to fully shield one's communications from the various agencies of state surveillance, including Britain's GCHQ. Besides, the Russians aren't terribly discreet. They sometimes post a team outside my apartment, just to let me know they're always watching. They also leave threatening messages on my voice mail."

"Have you ever played them for the Swiss police?"

"And give them an excuse to revoke my coveted residence

permit?" She shook her head. "Zurich is an excellent place from which to monitor the flow of dirty money out of Russia. It's also a rather pleasant place to live."

"And the email?" asked Graham. "Who was it from?"

"Mr. Nobody."

"I beg your pardon?"

"That's how he referred to himself. Mr. Nobody."

"Language?"

English, she answered, with two examples of British spelling. Mr. Nobody said he had left a package of documents for Nina in an athletics field not far from her apartment. Wary of a Kremlin trap, she asked Mr. Nobody to email her the documents instead. But when twenty-four hours passed without a reply, she donned a protective mask and a pair of rubber gloves and ventured into the dystopian void. The athletics field had a red artificial running track, around which four unmasked Zurichers were spewing their droplets. Trees lined the perimeter. At the base of one, she discovered a rectangular parcel wrapped in thick black plastic and sealed with clear packing tape.

She waited until she returned home before cautiously opening it. Inside were about a hundred pages of financial records regarding wire transfers, stock trades, and other investments such as large purchases of commercial and residential property. One corporate entity appeared frequently, a Swiss-registered shell company called Omega Holdings. All of the documents were from the same institution.

"Which one?"

"RhineBank AG. Financial insiders commonly refer to RhineBank as the world's dirtiest bank. Not surprisingly, it has numerous Russian clients."

"What did you do with the documents?"

"I photographed the first ten pages and emailed them to a well-known expert in Kremlin corruption."

"Viktor Orlov?"

She nodded. "He called a few minutes later, practically breathless. 'Where did you get these, Nina Petrovna?' When I explained, he told me to delete the photographs from my phone at once."

"Why?"

"He said the documents were far too dangerous to transmit electronically."

He flew to Zurich the next day on his private jet. Nina met him in the lounge of the FBO at Kloten Airport. His left eye twitched as he leafed through the documents, an affliction that surfaced whenever he was anxious or excited.

"I take it Viktor was excited?"

"He said the documents concerned the personal finances of a very high-profile Russian. Someone close to the president. Someone from his inner circle."

"Did he tell you who it was?"

"He said it was better if I didn't know the man's name. Then he instructed me to deliver the next batch of documents to him without opening the parcel."

Gabriel ceased his slow journey round the perimeter of the room. "How did he know there was going to be a next time?"

"He said the first set of documents were only the tip of the iceberg. He said there had to be more."

"How did you react?"

"I told Viktor that Mr. Nobody was my source. Then I reminded him of the promise he made after acquiring the *Gazeta*."

"What promise was that?"

"That he would never interfere in editorial matters or use the *Gazeta* to settle political scores with the Kremlin."

"And you believed him?"

"Viktor asked me the exact same question."

The next drop, she continued, took place in the second week of March, at a marina on the western shore of the Zürichsee. The third drop was in early April in the town of Winterthur; the fourth, in Zug. There was a lull in May, but June was a busy month, with drops in Basel, Thun, and Lucerne. Nina grudgingly delivered all the parcels to Viktor at Kloten Airport.

"And he always opened the packages in your presence?" asked Graham.

She nodded.

"Did he ever feel ill afterward? A sudden headache? Nausea?"

"Never."

"What about you?"

"Not at all."

"And the package you brought to London on Wednesday evening?" asked Graham. "Where did Mr. Nobody leave it?"

"A little village called Bargen near the German border. He said it would be his last drop. He said the material would be comprehensive and unambiguous."

"Why didn't Viktor collect the documents in Zurich?"

"He said he had a prior commitment."

"What was it?"

"A woman, of course. With Viktor, it was always a woman."

"Did he happen to mention her name?"

"Yes," answered Nina. "Her name was Artemisia."

ORDINARILY, VIKTOR WAS TIGHT-FISTED WHEN it came to travel expenses, but he allowed Nina to fly to London first class. She placed the documents in her carry-on bag, and the bag in the overhead bin. Her seatmate was a prosperous-looking English-speaker whose bespoke protective face mask matched his silken necktie. She engaged him in a few minutes of muffled small talk, if only to establish that he was not an officer of the FSB, the SVR, or any other division of Russian intelligence.

"Who was he?" asked Graham.

"A banker from the City. Lloyds, if I remember correctly." She gave him a false smile. "But then, you already knew that, didn't you, Mr. Seymour?"

She cleared passport control with no delay—which Mr. Seymour surely knew as well—and rode in a taxi to Cheyne Walk. Viktor had just removed the cork from a bottle of Château Pétrus. He didn't offer Nina a glass.

"That's not like Viktor," said Graham. "I've always known him to be an extremely generous host."

"He was expecting another visitor. I suppose it was Artemisia. Whoever she was, she saved my life. Viktor was in such a rush he didn't open the package in my presence."

"You left at six thirty-five p.m."

"If you say so."

"Is there some reason you walked to the hotel instead of taking a taxi?"

"I've always enjoyed walking in London."

"But you had a suitcase."

"It has wheels."

"Did you notice anyone following you?"

"No. Did you?"

Graham ignored the question. "And when you arrived at the hotel?"

"I poured myself a vodka from the minibar. Viktor rang a few minutes later. The instant I heard his voice, I knew something was wrong."

"What did he tell you?"

"Surely you've listened to the recording."

"There isn't one."

She gave Graham a skeptical look before answering. "He said he had just vomited and was having trouble breathing. He was convinced he'd been poisoned."

"Did he accuse you of trying to kill him?"

"Viktor?" She shook her head. "He asked if I was feeling sick, too. When I said that I was fine, he told me to leave Britain as quickly as possible."

"He was afraid the Russians would try to kill you, too?"

"Or that they would try to implicate me in the plot against him," she answered. "As you know, Mr. Seymour, the organs of Russian state security rarely murder someone without a plan to cast the blame on someone else."

"Which is why you should have phoned the police. You implicated yourself when you fled the country."

"Viktor told me not to call the police. He said he would do it himself. It wasn't until my plane landed in Amsterdam that I learned he was dead. Obviously, I blame myself for what happened. If I had never collected that first parcel of documents from Mr. Nobody, Viktor would still be alive. Moscow Center has been plotting to kill him for years. And they used me to place the murder weapon in his hands."

Graham was silent.

"Please, Mr. Seymour. You must believe me. I had nothing to do with Viktor's death."

"He does believe you," said Gabriel from across the room. "But he'd like to see the emails from Mr. Nobody, including the one about the package he left in the Swiss village of Bargen. You *did* save them, didn't you, Nina?"

"Of course. I only hope Moscow Center or the Spetssviaz hasn't hacked into my account and deleted them."

"When was the last time you checked?"

"The morning of Viktor's murder."

"That was three days ago."

"I was afraid they would be able to pinpoint my location if I accessed the account."

"You have nothing to fear here, Nina." Gabriel looked at Graham. "Isn't that right, Mr. Seymour?"

"I'll withhold judgment until I see those emails."

Nina looked around the dated room. "Is there a computer in this place?"

IT WAS LOCATED IN THE converted barn, in Parish's office. Company were strictly forbidden to lay hands upon it, as it was linked securely to Vauxhall Cross. The chief asked Parish to wait outside in the corridor with Nigel Whitcombe while the black-and-blue-haired woman checked her ProtonMail account, an indignity Parish suffered with poorly disguised outrage.

"But she's a bloody Russian!" he said sotto voce.

"One of the good ones," drawled Whitcombe in reply.

"I didn't realize there were any." From the opposite side of the door came a burst of firm, confident typing. "She's a journalist, is she?"

"Not bad, Parish."

When the typing ceased, a silence followed. It was a tense silence, thought Parish—like the silence that hangs ominously in a room after an accusation of infidelity or treachery. Finally, the door was flung open and the chief emerged, along with the black-and-blue-haired Russian woman and the gentleman from Israel. They all three clambered down the stairs, with Nigel Whitcombe in hot pursuit. Mr. Marlowe joined them in the courtyard. A few words were exchanged. Then Mr. Marlowe and the Israeli gentleman plunged headlong into the back of a service van, and the van raced hell-for-leather toward the gate.

Parish returned to his office. The computer was aglow. On the screen was an open email. According to the time code, it had arrived in the woman's in-box earlier that evening, as she was sitting down to Miss Coventry's dinner. Parish quickly closed it, but not before his eyes passed involuntarily over the text. It was addressed to a Ms. Antonova and was three sentences in length. The language was English, the punctuation proper and businesslike. There were no needless exclamation points or ellipses in the place of a full stop. The subject matter was surprisingly mundane given the reaction it provoked, something about a package that had been left in the Old City of Bern. Indeed, the only thing Parish found remotely interesting was the name of the person who had sent it.

Mr. Nobody . . .

14

BERN

THE DROP SITE WAS LOCATED a few paces from the edge of a
leafy footpath stretching along the bank of the river Aare.
The possibility of Russian involvement required Gabriel to assume the worst, that the contents of the parcel, whatever they
might be, were contaminated with the same nerve agent that
had killed Viktor Orlov. If that were the case, it had to be removed immediately by a CBRN team, lest an innocent passerby
or a curious child open it by mistake. Which left Gabriel no
choice but to bring the Swiss into the picture.

Protocol and good manners dictated that he contact his counterpart at the NDB, Switzerland's internal security and foreign
intelligence service. Instead, he telephoned Christoph Bittel,
who ran the domestic side. They had once crossed swords over

an interrogation table. Now they were something like allies. Bittel nevertheless answered his phone warily. A call from Gabriel rarely brought good news, especially when it arrived after midnight.

"What is it now?"

"I need you to pick up a package for me."

"Is there any chance it can wait until morning?"

"None."

"Where is it?"

Gabriel explained.

"Contents?"

"It's possible they might be sensitive financial documents. To be on the safe side, you should assume they're contaminated with ultrafine Novichok powder."

"Novichok?" asked Bittel, alarmed.

"Do I have your attention now?"

"Does this have something to do with Viktor Orlov's assassination?"

"I'll explain when I get there."

"You're not actually thinking about getting on an airplane, are you?"

"A private one."

"Is there anything else you can tell me about the package?"

"I have a feeling the Russians might be watching it. If it's not too much trouble, I'd like you to scare them off before you send in the CBRN team."

"And how might I do that?"

"Make some noise, Bittel. How else?"

NINETY MINUTES LATER, AT 1:47 a.m. local time, units of the Swiss Federal Police established a cordon around the normally tranquil Old City of Bern. They offered no explanation, though subsequent news reports would suggest the Swiss intelligence service had received a credible tip about a bomb hidden along a popular market street. The source of the warning was never reliably identified, and despite a prolonged and robust search of the elegant quarter, no explosive device was ever found. Hardly surprising, for no such device ever existed.

The true target of the early-morning police activity was a benign-looking parcel resting at the base of a poplar tree near the bank of the Aare. Rectangular in shape, it was wrapped in heavy plastic and sealed with clear packing tape. A CBRN team removed the object shortly before four a.m. and transported it to the Federal Institute for NBC-Protection in the nearby town of Spiez. There it underwent a battery of tests for biological, radiological, or chemical contaminants, including the deadly Russian nerve agent known as Novichok. All the tests were negative.

At which point the contents of the package, having been removed from their original plastic wrapper, were placed in an aluminum-sided attaché case for the journey to NDB headquarters in Bern. Gabriel and Christopher arrived there a few minutes after eight a.m., in the back of an Israeli Embassy car. Bittel received them in his top-floor office. Tall and bald, he had the stern countenance of a Calvinist minister and the pallor of a man with little time for outdoor pursuits. Gabriel introduced his traveling companion as an MI6 officer named Peter Marlowe and then delivered the promised briefing on the connection between the package of documents and the murder of Viktor Orlov. Bittel, with some justification, believed about every other word of it.

"And the journalist from the *Gazeta*?" he asked. "Where is she now?"

"Somewhere the Russians will never find her."

The phone on Bittel's desk purred softly. He lifted the receiver and spoke a few words in Swiss German before hanging up. A moment later a young NDB officer appeared in his doorway, attaché case in hand. Gabriel and Christopher reflexively leaned away as Bittel removed the contents, a stack of paper about five centimeters thick. He displayed the first page. It was blank, as were the next twenty-five.

"It looks as though the Russians were having a bit of fun at your expense."

"That would imply they have a sense of humor."

Bittel leafed through another twenty pages, then stopped.

"Well?" asked Gabriel.

Bittel slid the page across the desktop. Six words, sans serif typeface, approximately twenty-point in scale.

I know who killed Viktor Orlov.

"May I make another suggestion?" asked Gabriel after a moment.

"By all means," said Bittel dryly.

"Find out who left this next to that tree."

THE FOOTPATH WAS FRESHLY PAVED and black as a vinyl record. On one side, the land climbed steeply toward the edge of the Old City. On the other flowed the mucus-green waters of the

Aare. The poplar tree clung precariously to the grassy embankment, flanked by a pair of aluminum benches. To reach it, one had to swing a leg over a rustic-looking wooden rail and cross a patch of open ground.

The nearest CCTV camera was about fifty meters downriver. It was mounted atop a lamppost, upon which a graffiti artist had scrawled a slur directed against Muslim immigrants. Bittel obtained a week's worth of surveillance video, commencing at dawn the previous Sunday and concluding with the parcel's removal by the CBRN team. Gabriel and Christopher reviewed it on an NDB laptop, in a glass-enclosed conference room. Bittel used the time to clear the debris from his in-box. Because it was an otherwise quiet Sunday in Switzerland, the office was largely deserted. The only sound was the occasional ring of an unanswered telephone.

The email from Mr. Nobody had arrived in Nina Antonova's ProtonMail in-box at 8:36 p.m. Gabriel synced the CCTV video to the same time and then played it in rewind mode at twice the normal speed.

For several minutes the footpath was deserted. Finally, two figures appeared at the distant end of the image, a man wearing a fedora and a large dog of no discernible breed. Man and beast walked backward toward the camera, pausing briefly next to a rubbish bin, from which the man appeared to extract a small plastic bag. They paused again next to the lamppost, where the canine crouched on the verge of the footpath. What happened next was rendered in reverse order.

"I wish I could unsee that," groaned Christopher.

The evening turned to dusk, and the dusk to a golden

summer afternoon. A fallen leaf rose like a resurrected soul and attached itself to a limb of the poplar tree. Lovers strolled, joggers jogged, the river flowed—all in reverse. Gabriel grew impatient and increased the speed of the playback. Christopher, however, appeared mildly bored. While serving in Northern Ireland, he had once spent two weeks watching a suspected IRA terrorist from a Londonderry attic. The Catholic family living beneath him had never known he was there.

But when the time code reached 14:27, Christopher sat up suddenly in his chair. A figure had slithered over the wooden rail and was walking backward toward the bank of the river. Gabriel clicked PAUSE and zoomed in, but it was no use; the camera was too far away. The figure was little more than a digital smudge.

He clicked REWIND, and the smudge removed the backpack it was wearing. At the base of the poplar tree, it retrieved an object.

A rectangular parcel wrapped in heavy plastic and sealed with clear packing tape . . .

Gabriel clicked PAUSE.

"Hello, Mr. Nobody," said Christopher quietly.

Gabriel clicked REWIND again and watched as Mr. Nobody placed the parcel in the backpack and sat down on one of the aluminum benches. According to the video time code, he remained there for twelve minutes before returning to the footpath.

"Walk this way," whispered Gabriel. "I want to have a look at you."

The distant smudge seemed to hear him, because a moment

later it was walking backward toward the lamppost upon which the CCTV camera was mounted. Gabriel increased the speed of the playback and then clicked PAUSE.

"Well, well," said Christopher. "Imagine that."

Gabriel zoomed in. Shoulder-length blond hair. Stretch jeans. A pair of stylish boots.

Mr. Nobody was a woman.

FLUORESCENT LIGHTS FLICKERED TO LIFE as Gabriel and Christopher followed Bittel along a corridor to the NDB's operations center. A single technician was playing computer chess against an opponent in a distant land. Bittel gave him a camera number and a time code reference, and a moment later the woman who called herself Mr. Nobody appeared on the main video screen at the front of the room. This time they watched the drop in its proper sequence. Mr. Nobody approached from the east, sidled over the wooden rail, and spent twelve long minutes contemplating the river before placing the parcel at the base of the poplar tree and departing to the west.

The technician switched to a new camera, which captured her ascent up a flight of concrete steps to the edge of the Old City. There she made her way to the rail station, where at 3:10 p.m. she boarded a train for Zurich.

It arrived exactly one hour later. In the Bahnhofplatz she boarded a Number 3 tram and rode it to the Römerhofplatz in District 7, a residential quarter on the slopes of the Zürichberg. From there it was a pleasant walk up the incline of the Klosbachstrasse to the small modern apartment block at Hauserstrasse 21.

Two minutes after she entered the building, a light appeared in a third-floor window. A rapid check of a government property database indicated that the unit in question was owned by an Isabel Brenner, a citizen of the Federal Republic of Germany. A further check revealed that she served as a compliance officer in the Zurich office of RhineBank AG, otherwise known as the world's dirtiest bank.

15

NDB HEADQUARTERS, BERN

A S A GENERAL RULE OF thumb, spies from different countries rarely play nicely together. Sharing a juicy piece of regional gossip or a warning about a terrorist cell is commonplace, especially between close allies. But intelligence services avoid joint operations whenever possible, if only because such endeavors inevitably expose personnel and cherished field techniques. Spymasters guard these secrets jealously, like family recipes, and reveal them only under duress. Moreover, national interests rarely align seamlessly, never less so than where matters of high finance are concerned. It was true what they said about money. It definitely changed everything.

Like ultrafine Novichok powder, it was odorless, tasteless, portable, and easy to conceal. And sometimes, of course, it was deadly. Some men killed for money. And when they had enough of it, they killed anyone who tried to take it away from them. Increasingly, much of the money that flowed through the veins and arteries of the global financial system was dirty. It was derived from criminal activity or drained from state coffers by kleptomaniacal autocrats. It poisoned everything it touched. Even the healthy were not immune to its ravages.

Many financial institutions were all too happy to soil their hands with dirty money—for a substantial fee, of course. One such institution was RhineBank AG. At least that was the rumor; money laundering was one of the few financial misdeeds for which the bank had not been punished. Its most recent brush with regulators came in New York, where the state's Department of Financial Services fined RhineBank $50 million over its dealings with a convicted sex trafficker. One red-hot RhineBank derivatives trader remarked that the payment was smaller than his annual bonus. The trader was foolish enough to repeat the claim in an email, which ended up in the pages of the *Wall Street Journal*. During the mini-scandal that followed, RhineBank's spokeswoman sidestepped questions as to whether the trader had in fact earned such an astronomical amount of money. And when the bonus was disclosed in a subsequent corporate filing, it ignited a scandal as well.

The bank was headquartered in a menacing tower in the center of Hamburg that architectural critics had derided as a glass-and-steel phallus. Its busy London office was in Fleet Street, and in New York it occupied a sparkling new skyscraper overlooking the Hudson. Because RhineBank was a truly global bank, it answered to an alphabet soup of regulatory agencies. Any one of them would have been interested to learn that a compliance officer from the Zurich office was leaving packets of sensitive documents at drop sites scattered across Switzerland. Were the nature of those documents ever to become public, RhineBank's share prices would likely tumble, which in turn would adversely impact its infamously overleveraged balance sheet. The damage would quickly spread to RhineBank's business partners, the banks from which it received loans or lent money in return. Dominoes would fall. Given the fragile state of the European economy, another financial crisis was a distinct possibility.

"Obviously," said Christoph Bittel, "such a scenario would not be in the interests of the Swiss Confederation and its all-important financial services industry."

"So what shall we do about her?" asked Gabriel. "Pretend she doesn't exist? Sweep her under the rug?"

"It's a tradition here in Switzerland." Bittel eyed Gabriel across the shimmering rectangular table in the conference room. "But then, you already know that."

"We closed my Swiss accounts a long time ago, Bittel."

"All of them?" Bittel smiled. "I recently had occasion to re-watch the interrogation I conducted with you after the bombing of that antiquities gallery in St. Moritz."

"How was it the second time?"

"I suppose I did the best I could. Still, I wish I'd been able to pin you down on a few more specifics. The Anna Rolfe affair, for example. Your first Swiss adventure. Or was it the Hamidi assassination? It's hard to keep them all straight." Greeted by silence, Bittel sailed on. "I was lucky enough to see Anna perform with Martha Argerich a few weeks before the lockdown. An evening of Brahms and Schumann sonatas. She still plays with the same fire. And Argerich . . ." He held up his hands. "Well, what else can one say?"

"Which Brahms?"

"I believe it was the G Major."

"She always adored it."

"She's living here in Switzerland again, in her father's old villa on the Zürichberg."

"You don't say."

"When was the last time you saw her?"

"Anna?" Gabriel glanced at Christopher, who was watching the Sunday-afternoon traffic flowing along the A6, a half smile on his face. "It's been an age."

Bittel returned to the matter at hand. "We're not the only ones who will suffer if there's a scandal. The British have enormous exposure to RhineBank, as do the Americans."

"If it's handled properly, there won't be a scandal. But if RhineBank has broken the law, it should be punished accordingly."

"What do I say to RhineBank's regulators?"

"Nothing at all."

Bittel was appalled. "That's not the way we do things here in Switzerland. We follow the rules."

"Unless it suits you not to. And then you flout the rules as readily as the rest of us. We're not policemen or regulators, Bittel. We're in the business of stealing other people's secrets."

"Recruit Isabel Brenner as an agent? Is that what you're saying?"

"How else are we going to find out the name of the high-profile Russian who's been looting state assets and stashing them here in the West?"

"I'm not sure I want to know his name."

"In that case, let me handle it."

Bittel exhaled heavily. "Why do I know I'm going to regret this?"

Gabriel didn't bother to offer his Swiss colleague assurances to the contrary. Intelligence operations, like life, were invariably full of regrets. Especially when they involved the Russians.

"What do you need from us?" asked Bittel at last.

"I'd like you to stay out of my way."

"Surely we can provide *some* assistance. Physical surveillance, for example."

Gabriel nodded toward Christopher. "Mr. Marlowe will handle the surveillance, at least for now. But with your approval, I'd like to add another operative to our team."

"Only one?"

Gabriel smiled. "One is all I need."

16

ZURICH

ELI LAVON ARRIVED AT ZURICH's Kloten Airport late the following afternoon. He wore a cardigan sweater beneath his crumpled tweed jacket and an ascot at his throat. His hair was wispy and unkempt; the features of his face were bland and easily forgotten. The immigration authorities who met his aircraft on the tarmac did not bother to inspect his passport. Nor did they check his two large pieces of aluminum-sided luggage, which were crammed with sophisticated surveillance and communications gear.

An attendant at ExecuJet, one of the airport's two fixed-base operators, placed the bags into the back of the BMW X5 waiting outside. Lavon slid into the front passenger seat and frowned. "Shouldn't you have a bodyguard or two?"

"I don't need bodyguards," replied Gabriel. "I have Christopher."

Lavon peered into the empty backseat. "I never knew he was so good."

Smiling, Gabriel turned onto the access road and followed it along the edge of the airfield. "How was the flight?" he asked as an inbound jetliner passed low overhead.

"Lonely."

"Isn't it wonderful?"

"Private air travel? I suppose I could get used to it. But what happens when the pandemic is over?"

"The next director-general of the Office won't be flying El Al."

"Have you given any thought to which unlucky soul will succeed you?"

"That's the prime minister's decision."

"But surely you have a candidate in mind."

Gabriel gave Lavon a sideways glance. "I've been meaning to have a word with you about your future, Eli."

"I'm too old to have a future." Lavon smiled sadly. "Only a very complicated past."

Like Gabriel, Eli Lavon was a veteran of Operation Wrath of God. In the Hebrew-based lexicon of the team, he had been an *ayin*, a tracker and surveillance specialist. When the unit disbanded, he settled in Vienna, where he opened a small investigative bureau called Wartime Claims and Inquiries. Operating on a shoestring budget, he managed to track down millions of dollars' worth of looted Holocaust assets and played a significant role in prying a multibillion-dollar settlement from the banks of Switzerland. Brilliant and unyielding, Lavon quickly earned the contempt of senior Swiss banking officials. The *Neue Züricher Zeitung,* in a scathing editorial, had once referred to him as "that tenacious little troll from Vienna."

He stared gloomily out his window. "Do you mind telling me why I'm back in Switzerland?"

"A problem with a bank."

"Which one is it this time?"

"The dirtiest bank in the world."

"RhineBank?"

"How did you guess?"

"Their claim to the title is undisputed."

"Ever had any dealings with them?"

"No," said Lavon. "But your mother and grandparents did. You see, the distinguished RhineBank AG of Hamburg financed the construction of Auschwitz and the factory that produced the Zyklon B pellets used in the gas chambers. It also trafficked in dental gold removed from the mouths of the dead and earned enormous fees through the Aryanization of Jewish-owned businesses."

"It was a profitable venture, was it?"

"Wildly. Hitler was very good for the bank's bottom line. The relationship went beyond mere expediency. RhineBank was all in."

"And after the war?"

"The bank trimmed its sails and helped to finance the German economic miracle. Not surprisingly, its senior executives were all staunch anti-Communists. There were rumors that several were on the CIA's payroll. The director was a guest at Eisenhower's second inaugural in 1957."

"All was forgiven?"

"It was as if Auschwitz never happened. RhineBank learned that it could get away with anything, and they've tested the proposition time and time again. In 2015, the Americans fined the bank two hundred and fifty million dollars for helping the Iranians to evade international sanctions." Lavon shook his head slowly. "They'll do business with anyone."

"Including a high-profile Russian who's stashing his ill-gotten money here in the West."

"Says who?"

"Isabel Brenner. She's a compliance officer at RhineBank's Zurich office."

"That's a relief."

"Why?"

"Given the firm's track record," said Lavon, "I didn't think it had any."

DURING THE DRIVE INTO CENTRAL Zurich, Gabriel briefed Eli Lavon on the improbable series of events that had heralded their return to Switzerland. His long-overdue reunion with their old friend Olga Sukhova in Norwich. His exfiltration of Olga's former colleague Nina Antonova from Amsterdam. The package that had been left at the base of a poplar tree along the bank of the river Aare. Then he outlined the provisions of the unusual accord he had reached with Christoph Bittel, the deputy director of a reasonably friendly though sometimes adversarial foreign intelligence service.

"Leave it to you to convince the Swiss, the most insular people in the world, to let you run an operation on their soil."

"I didn't give them much of a choice."

"And when they figure out that the one additional operative you brought in for the job is the tenacious little troll from the Holocaust accounts scandal?"

"It was a long time ago, Eli."

"And what about Mr. Marlowe? How many hits did he carry out in Switzerland before joining MI6?"

"He says he can't remember."

"Never a good sign." Lavon ignited a cigarette and then lowered the window to vent the smoke.

"Must you?" pleaded Gabriel.

"It helps me think."

"What are you thinking about?"

"I'm wondering why the Russians haven't taken Isabel Brenner out of circulation. And why they didn't pick up that package of documents she left in Bern."

"What's the answer?"

"The only explanation is that she made each of the drops *before* sending the emails to Nina Antonova. The Russians don't know her identity."

"And the package in Bern?"

"They were probably hoping Nina would be the one to collect it so they could kill her. But you can be sure they didn't fall for that little stunt you and your Swiss friends pulled the other night. They know they have a problem."

"They do, indeed," said Gabriel quietly.

"How long do you intend to watch her before you bring her in?"

"Long enough to make certain she isn't a Russian operative in a clever disguise."

Gabriel turned onto the Talackerstrasse and eased to the

curb along the facade of the Credit Suisse building. On the opposite side of the street, adjacent to the headquarters of UBS, was RhineBank-Zurich.

It was approaching six o'clock; the evening exodus had commenced. At length, Gabriel pointed toward a woman who had just stepped from RhineBank's doorway.

Dark designer pantsuit, white blouse, a pair of expensive-looking pumps. Private banker chic.

"There's our girl. Mr. Nobody."

She was tall and model slender, with long limbs and articulate hands. Her beauty was at once obvious, but partially obscured by the seriousness of her expression. In the half-light of the street, it was impossible to determine the color of her eyes, though one would have been forgiven for assuming they were pale blue. The hair was blond. It swung like the pendulum of a metronome as she walked.

"How old is she?" asked Lavon.

"Her passport says thirty-four."

"Married?"

"Apparently not."

"How could that be?"

"It's different these days, Eli."

Lavon watched her carefully for a moment. "She doesn't look like a Russian to me. She doesn't walk like a Russian, either."

"You can tell a Russian woman by the way she walks?"

"Can't you?"

A moment passed in silence. Then Gabriel asked, "What are you thinking now, Eli?"

"I'm wondering why a beautiful young woman like that would

risk her career to give a Russian journalist confidential financial documents about an important client."

"Perhaps she has a conscience."

"Not possible. RhineBank doesn't hire anyone whose conscience wasn't removed at birth."

She rounded the corner, into the Paradeplatz. Gabriel pulled forward in time to see her board a Number 8 tram. A few seconds later, Christopher entered the same carriage.

"Oaf," said Lavon. "You're supposed to get on *before* the target, not after."

"You'll work with him, Eli."

"I've tried," said Lavon. "He never listens."

17

ERLENBACH, SWITZERLAND

CHRISTOPH BITTEL SUGGESTED THAT GABRIEL run his operation from one of the NDB's existing safe houses. Not surprisingly, Gabriel politely declined. The safe houses, he reckoned, were littered with high-quality microphones and cameras—electronics being one aspect of the trade at which the Swiss excelled. Housekeeping found a lakefront dwelling in the Zurich suburb of Erlenbach last occupied by an executive from Goldman Sachs. Gabriel paid the yearlong lease in full and then quickly dissolved the shell corporation through which the transaction had been carried out, thus depriving his newfound Swiss allies of any means of penetrating his global network of covert finances.

He settled into the villa late Monday afternoon along with the other two members of his nascent operational team. And at

8:15 a.m. on Tuesday, they committed their first criminal offense on Swiss soil. The primary perpetrator was Christopher
Keller, who slipped unobserved into Isabel Brenner's apartment
as she was walking toward the tram stop in the Römerhofplatz.
While inside, he copied the contents of her laptop, compromised
her Wi-Fi network, planted a pair of audio transmitters, and
conducted a swift and minimally invasive search of her possessions. Her medicine cabinet contained no evidence of illness or physical maladies, save for an empty bottle of sleeping
tablets. Her clothing and undergarments were tasteful and re-
strained, nothing suggesting a dark side, and the many serious
works of literature lining her shelves suggested she preferred to
do her reading in English rather than her native German. The
compact discs stacked atop her British-made audio system were
predominantly classical, along with a few jazz masterworks by
Miles Davis, John Coltrane, Bill Evans, and Keith Jarrett. In
the sitting room, next to a music stand, was a fiberglass cello
case.

"Did it contain an actual cello?" asked Gabriel.

"I didn't look," admitted Christopher.

"Why not?"

"Because one rarely keeps a cello case as a decorative piece.
One keeps a cello case to store and transport one's cello."

"Maybe it belongs to her boyfriend."

"There is no boyfriend. At least not one who spends any time
in her apartment."

The laptop yielded the number for Isabel's mobile phone.
And at half past one, while lunching with a colleague at a café
near the office, she succumbed to a malware attack by Unit
8200, Israel's signals intelligence service. Within minutes, the

phone's operating system began uploading eighteen months' worth of emails, text messages, calendar entries, GPS location data, telephone metadata, credit card information, and her Internet browsing history. In addition, the malware seized control of the camera and microphone, turning the device into a full-time video and audio transmitter. Which meant that everywhere Isabel went, Gabriel and his team went with her. In the lexicon of electronic surveillance, they *owned* her.

The tidiness of Isabel's digital life reinforced the impression Christopher Keller had formed during his brief visit to her apartment, that she was a person of enormous intelligence and talent, with no vices or moral shortcomings. The same could not be said, however, of the financial services firm for which she worked. Indeed, the documents taken from Isabel's devices painted a portrait of a bank where the normal rules did not apply, where the prevailing culture was one of profit at any price, and where traders were expected to produce otherworldly returns on investment, even as their risky wagers pushed the bank to the brink of insolvency.

To serve as an ethical and legal watchdog in such an institution was a daily high-wire act, as evidenced by the email Isabel dispatched to Karl Zimmer, chief of RhineBank-Zurich, regarding a series of wire transfers carried out by the wealth management department. In all, more than $500 million had moved from banks in Latvia to RhineBank accounts in the United States. The Latvian banks, she pointed out, were known to be the first financial port of call for much of the dirty money flowing out of Russia. Nevertheless, the Zurich wealth managers had accepted the funds without performing even a modicum of due diligence. To conceal the origin of the money from American regulators, who were well aware of the Russia–Latvia connection, they stripped the country coding from the wire transfers.

"Isabel was concerned it demonstrated a clear consciousness of guilt," explained Lavon. "I have to say, she seemed much less concerned about the legality of the transfers. It was more like a friendly warning from a loyal member of the team."

"And how did Herr Zimmer react?" asked Gabriel.

"He suggested they discuss the matter offline. His word, not mine."

"What was the date?"

"The seventeenth of February. Ten days later, during her lunch hour, she walked to an athletics field in District Three. The one with the red artificial running track," added Lavon. "Her location data matches up with all the other drops as well, with the exception of the package that killed Viktor."

"Any other interesting travel?"

"She went to the United Kingdom in mid-June and again in late July. In fact, she was there two days before Viktor was murdered."

"London is a global financial capital," Gabriel pointed out.

"Which makes it all the more surprising that she never set foot in RhineBank's London office."

"Where did she go?"

"I'm not sure. She switched off her phone for several hours on both visits."

"How long did she stay?"

"A single night."

"Hotel?"

"The Sofitel at Heathrow. She paid the bill with her personal credit card. Her airfare, too. On both trips she caught the first flight back to Zurich and was in the office by nine a.m."

Isabel's telephone, like her apartment, contained no evidence of a fiancé or a long-term romantic partner, male or female. But that evening, after boarding a Number 8 in the Paradeplatz, she arranged to have drinks on Friday with someone called Tobias. When her streetcar reached the Römerhofplatz, she picked up a few things at the Coop market and, followed by Christopher Keller, headed up the slope of the Zürichberg to her apartment. Shortly after her arrival, the two concealed microphones captured the sound of Bach's Cello Suite in D Minor. Several minutes elapsed before Gabriel and Lavon realized they were not listening to a recording.

"Her tone is . . ."

"Intoxicating," said Gabriel.

"And she doesn't seem to be using sheet music."

"Obviously, she doesn't need it."

"In that case," said Lavon, "I have another question for her."

"What's that?"

"Why would a woman who plays the cello like that work for the world's dirtiest bank?"

"I'll be sure to ask her."

"When?"

"As soon as I'm certain she's not a Russian in a clever disguise."

"She might not walk like a Russian," said Lavon as Isabel began the suite's second movement. "But she certainly plays the cello like one."

IN ALL, ISABEL BRENNER'S HOME computer surrendered some
thirty thousand internal RhineBank documents and more than
a hundred thousand emails from her corporate account. It was
far too much material for Lavon to review on his own. He
needed the help of an experienced financial investigator who
was well versed in the wicked ways of the Kremlin's klepto-
crats. Fortunately, Gabriel knew just such a person. She was
an investigative reporter from a crusading Moscow weekly that
regularly exposed the misdeeds of Russia's rich and powerful.
Perhaps more important, she had been in regular if anonymous
contact with Isabel Brenner for several months.

The reporter in question arrived at the safe house on Wednesday afternoon and joined Eli Lavon's excavation of the Rhine-
Bank documents, leaving Christopher to shoulder the burden of
Isabel's surveillance alone. He followed her to work each morning and home again each evening. Most nights she practiced the
cello for at least an hour before making herself something to eat
and phoning her mother in Germany. She never raised the topic
of her work at RhineBank. Nor did she discuss it with the small
circle of friends with whom she was in regular contact. There
was nothing in her communications to suggest she was an asset
or officer of Russian or German intelligence. Christopher saw
no evidence that anyone else was watching her.

On Thursday she had a post-work drink with a female colleague at Bar au Lac on the Talstrasse. Returning home, she
practiced the cello without pause for three hours. Afterward,
she watched a report on Swiss television regarding a missing
Russian journalist named Nina Antonova. It seemed her colleagues at the *Moskovskaya Gazeta* had not heard from her since

the previous Wednesday, when she flew from Zurich to London for a meeting with the magazine's murdered owner. The *Gazeta*'s editor in chief had asked the British government for help in locating her. Perhaps not surprisingly, he had not made a similar request of the Kremlin.

Isabel passed a restless night and the following morning left her apartment twenty minutes later than usual. After dropping her bag in her office, she headed upstairs to the top-floor conference room for a mandatory company-wide call with the Council of Ten, the firm's executive steering committee. She lunched alone and upon returning to the office had a testy exchange with Lothar Brandt, the head of the wealth management department. Evidently, Brandt was burning up the wires with suspect transfers. Isabel advised him to reconsider several of the larger transactions. Otherwise, he risked setting off automatic tripwires in New York and Washington. Brandt in turn advised Isabel to perform a sexual act upon herself before expelling her from his office.

The bitterness of the exchange was still evident on her face when she emerged from RhineBank at six fifteen. Christopher followed her aboard a Number 8 in the Paradeplatz, as did Nina Antonova, who claimed the seat next to her. As the streetcar lurched forward, Nina handed her a single sheet of paper. Six words, sans serif typeface, approximately twenty-point in scale.

I know who killed Viktor Orlov.

Isabel addressed Nina in German, with her eyes downcast. "I hope you sued the person who did that to your hair."

Nina reclaimed the sheet of paper.

"I risked my life giving you those documents. Why didn't you publish a story?"

"Viktor said it was too dangerous."

"Am I responsible for his death?"

"No, Isabel. I am."

"Why?"

"I'll let my friend explain. He'd like to have a word with you tonight. Which means you're going to have to break your date with Tobias."

"How do you know I was meeting him?"

Nina glanced at Isabel's phone. "Tell him you had a work emergency. Trust me, you won't regret it."

Isabel sent the text message, then switched off the phone without waiting for a reply. "It wasn't a date. It was only drinks."

"I can't remember how many times I told myself the same thing."

Isabel squeezed Nina's hand. "I thought you were dead."

"So did I," said Nina.

18

RÖMERHOFPLATZ, ZURICH

A BLOND-HAIRED MAN WITH BRIGHT BLUE eyes and a permanent suntan followed them from the tram at Isabel's usual
stop in the Römerhofplatz. As they were crossing the street, he
nudged her toward a waiting BMW X5. Nina joined them in
the backseat. The man behind the wheel looked like a dealer of
rare books. He eased into the sparse evening traffic as though
he feared there were small children about and headed south on
the Asylstrasse.

The man next to Isabel was now typing something on his
mobile phone. "Who do you work for?" she asked.

"A very dull department of the British Foreign Office."

"MI6?"

"If you say so."

"What's your name?"

"The Swiss seem to think it's Peter Marlowe."

"Is it?"

"Not even close."

Isabel looked at the man behind the wheel. "What about him?"

"If we put our heads together, I'm sure we'll think of something." He gave her a reassuring smile. "You're in good hands, Isabel. You have absolutely nothing to fear."

"Unless you're both from Russian intelligence."

"We hate the bloody Russians." He smiled at Nina. "Present company excluded, of course."

"How did you find me?"

"We got a nice picture of you when you left that package in Bern the other night. Several, in fact."

"You had no right to hack my phone."

"I couldn't agree more. But I'm afraid we had no choice."

"Discover anything interesting?"

"The passwords to your favorite online retailers, every website you've ever visited, and every person you've ever stalked on social media. You've checked Nina's Twitter feed more than four hundred times in the past six months."

"Is that all?"

"We also found more than a dozen email accounts. You have six addresses at ProtonMail alone. You send most of your text messages using the one encrypted service we haven't been able to penetrate."

"That's why we use it."

"We?"

"Employees of RhineBank. Senior management encourages us to conduct sensitive communication using our personal encrypted accounts rather than corporate email addresses."

"Why?"

"To keep our deliberations hidden from regulators. Why else?"

"Do you like Haydn?" he asked suddenly.

"I'm sorry?"

"The composer."

"I know who he is."

"You searched his name several times the week of Viktor Orlov's murder. I was wondering if you had a particular affinity for Haydn's music."

"Who doesn't?"

"I've always preferred Mozart."

"Mozart adored Haydn."

"You also searched for something called the Haydn Group," he informed her. "For some reason, you capitalized the letter G."

"You have good software."

"Are they a string quartet? A trio?"

She shook her head.

"I didn't think so." They passed the Zurich offices of the Russian Commercial Bank and, a few seconds later, Gazprombank. "Enemy territory," remarked the Englishman.

"Not as far as RhineBank is concerned. We do a brisk business with both institutions."

"What about MosBank?"

"Most reputable banks avoid it. But as you know from reading my emails, MosBank is our most important Russian partner." Isabel paused, then asked, "Was that a test?"

He looked down at his phone without answering. They had entered the suburb of Zollikon. The Seestrasse bore them along the lakeshore to the town of Küsnacht and then Erlenbach. There the smallish man behind the wheel turned ponderously through the gates of a walled villa. It was turreted and unwelcoming. Several dark sedans lined the drive. Security men patrolled the lawn.

The smallish man eased to a stop and switched off the engine, as though relieved to have arrived at his destination without incident. At once, a second car drew up behind them. Evidently, they had been followed.

"Come inside, Isabel," said the Englishman amiably. "Meet the others."

The door of the villa was open to receive them. They followed a half-lit central gallery to a large drawing room with soaring windows that gazed westward across the lake. The furniture was brocade-covered, the rugs were oriental and faded. Several oil paintings adorned the walls, landscapes and still lifes, nothing too adventurous. From somewhere came the sound of Haydn's Piano Trio in E Major. Isabel looked at the Englishman, who was once again smiling.

"We chose it specially for you."

Two men were seated in armchairs near one of the windows. One wore the inscrutable expression of a Swiss banker, though the cut and quality of his suit suggested he worked for the government rather than the private sector. The second man looked like a character in an English country-house mystery—villain or protagonist, Isabel could not decide.

Neither appeared to have noticed her arrival. The same was true of the man standing before a still life of fruit and freshly cut flowers, a hand pressed to his chin, his head tilted slightly to one side. His eyes were an unnatural shade of green. Like jade, thought Isabel. She tried to guess his age, but could not settle on a number. When at last he spoke, it was in German, with the distinct accent of someone who had been raised in Berlin.

"Do you like paintings, Isabel?"

"Good paintings. But not second-rate junk like that."

"It's not so bad. It's just very dirty." He paused. "Like the bank for which you work. Fortunately, the painting can be restored. I'm not sure the same can be said for your employer."

"Who do you work for?" she asked. "BaFin or one of the German intelligence services?"

"None of the above. In fact, I'm not even German."

"You certainly speak like one."

"I was taught to speak German by my mother. She was born in the Mitte district of Berlin. I, however, was born in Israel. Once upon a time, I would have given you a pseudonym rather than my real name, which is Gabriel Allon. A simple Internet search would reveal that I am the director-general of Israel's secret intelligence service, but please resist the temptation to type my name in the little white box. There is no such thing as private browsing."

The two men seated near the window were each staring into a private space, like extras in a stage production. "What about them?" asked Isabel. "Are they Israeli, too?"

"Unfortunately, no. The handsome gray-haired gentleman is Graham Seymour, my counterpart at MI6."

"And the other one?"

"A senior Swiss intelligence officer. He would prefer to remain anonymous for now. Think of him as a numbered account."

"They're rather passé."

"What's that?"

"Numbered accounts. Especially for people with real money to hide."

He approached her slowly. "I must admit, we enjoyed listening to your performance a few nights ago. Bach's Cello Suite in D Minor. All six movements. And not a single mistake."

"I made several, actually. I just covered them up well."

"You're good at hiding your missteps?"

"Most of the time."

"We didn't hear the rustle of sheet music."

"I don't need any."

"You have a good memory?"

"Most musicians do. I'm also rather good at math, which is how I ended up at RhineBank."

"But why did you stay?"

"For the same reason ninety thousand other people do."

He returned to the painting and placed his hand to his chin. "And if you had a chance to do it over again?"

"I'm afraid life doesn't work that way."

He licked the tip of his forefinger and rubbed it against the dirty canvas. "Wherever did you get an idea like that?"

19

ERLENBACH, SWITZERLAND

H E SETTLED ISABEL IN A place of honor and took up residence before the dormant fireplace. There he recited the basic details of her impressive curriculum vitae, which he and his friends had unearthed from her mobile phone and personal computer. For the benefit of the non-German-speaking members of his audience, he addressed Isabel in English. His accent was faint and entirely unplaceable. His tone was that of an auctioneer presiding over the sale of a painting. The evening's final lot.

"Isabel Brenner, thirty-four years of age, born in the ancient German city of Trier into a solidly upper-middle-class family. Your father is a prominent lawyer, a man of distinction. Your mother, a devotee of Bach, gave you your first piano lesson at the age of three. But on the occasion of your eighth birthday, she acceded to your wishes and presented you with a cello. Under private instruction, your talent blossomed. At the age of seventeen you were awarded a third prize at the prestigious ARD International Music Competition for your performance of Brahms's Cello Sonata in E Minor."

"That's not true."

"Where did I go wrong?"

"It was the F-major sonata. And I could play both parts."

He frowned at the diminutive man who reminded Isabel of a rare-book dealer. The MI6 chief and Swiss intelligence officer were observing the proceedings from their outpost near the windows. The blue-eyed Englishman was scrolling through the contacts in Isabel's phone. He had not bothered to ask her for the passcode.

"One of Germany's most sought-after instructors offered to take you on as a pupil," Gabriel continued. "Instead, you enrolled at Berlin's Humboldt University, where you studied applied mathematics. You earned your master's degree at the London School of Economics. While completing your dissertation, you met with a recruiter from RhineBank and were offered a job on the spot. Your starting salary was one hundred thousand pounds a year."

"Before bonuses," she pointed out.

"That's a great deal of money."

"It was a pittance by RhineBank's standards, especially in London. But it was three or four times what I would have earned if I was playing the cello in a European orchestra."

"I thought you wanted to be a soloist."

"I did."

"Then why did you study mathematics?"

"I was afraid I wasn't good enough."

"You played it safe?"

"I earned degrees from two prestigious institutions of higher learning and secured a high-paying position with one of the world's largest banks. I don't think of myself as a failure."

"Nor should you. I'm only sorry you allowed your extraordinary talent to go to waste."

"Obviously, it hasn't." Her face flushed with anger. "But what about you? Was it always your dream to be a spy?"

"I did not choose this life, Isabel. It was chosen for me."

"And if you had a chance to do it over again?" she asked provocatively.

"I'm afraid that's a topic for another discussion. You're the reason we're gathered here tonight. You summoned us when you left that message in Bern. You're the star of the show."

She surveyed the room. "It's not exactly the Berliner Philharmonie or Lincoln Center."

"Neither is RhineBank."

"But at least there's never a dull moment."

"You arrived there in 2010."

She nodded. "Two years after RhineBank and its competitors brought the global financial system to the brink of collapse."

"And your first position?"

"Junior analyst in the risk management department of the London office. Rather appropriate, don't you think?" She smiled sadly. "Risk management. The story of my life."

BUT FIRST, ISABEL HAD TO go back to school—the Risk Academy, RhineBank's monthlong training seminar, held at a rented conference center on Germany's Baltic coast. It was presided over by the appropriately named Friedrich Krueger, Rhine-Bank's chief risk officer, a former German paratrooper with a penchant for online pornography and far-right neo-fascist politics. Pupils were lodged in dormitories and subjected to merciless hazing rituals inflicted by Herr Krueger's band of sadistic instructors. One made explicit sexual advances toward Isabel. A week into her stay, she packed her bags and threatened to leave if the conduct did not cease. Herr Krueger convinced her to stay, though later he inserted a report into her file that suggested she was not a team player. It would be the first of her many black marks.

The goal of the course was to simulate *Informationsflut*, or information overload. On the final day, trainees were given one hour to rework the bank's balance sheet to account for a once-in-a-lifetime combination of financial and political calamities. Isabel completed the assignment in just thirty minutes and then used the remaining time to perform Beethoven's Cello Sonata in A Major.

"Where?" asked Gabriel.

She laid the long fingers of her left hand across the upper portion of her right arm. "In my head."

She achieved the highest score possible on the final examination and returned to London in the autumn to take up her new position at RhineBank's offices in Fleet Street, the headquarters of the bank's global markets division. As a German citizen, Isabel was an oddity; most of the traders were American imports. Where once RhineBank made the bulk of its profits the old-fashioned way—by lending to creditworthy businesses—it was now a major player in volatile derivatives. Indeed, the *Economist* had declared that RhineBank was nothing more than a $2 trillion hedge fund engaged in high-risk, high-yield proprietary trading, much of it with borrowed money. The Council of Ten had set a goal of a twenty-five-percent return on every dollar, pound, or euro invested, an exorbitant sum. The London traders accepted the challenge. They viewed the markets as casinos and were encouraged to push the envelope on every deal.

"How did they feel about risk managers?"

"We were the enemy. If we raised an objection to a trade, we were told to keep quiet. Freddy Krueger wasn't much interested in our concerns, either. The money was rolling in—hundreds of millions of dollars a year in fees alone. He wasn't about to pull the plug. Besides, if the London trading floor lost money on one deal, they would make it up on the next. Or so Hamburg assumed."

Occasionally, however, the traders went too far. One was betting hundreds of millions of dollars each day on tiny movements of the Libor index, the interbank lending rate. Isabel took her concerns to the head of the London office and was told in no uncertain terms to mind her own business; the Libor trades were incredibly lucrative. She persisted in her inquiry nevertheless and discovered that the trader in question was conspiring with counterparts at other banks to manipulate the rate itself, thus creating a no-lose investment. The trader was eventually shown the door, and RhineBank was forced to pay a hundred-million-pound fine to British regulators, a small fraction of what it had earned through the dirty dealing.

"One would have thought that I would have been rewarded for my efforts. Instead, Freddy Krueger reprimanded me for putting my concerns in a chain of emails that was later obtained by the British Financial Conduct Authority. Black mark number two."

Even so, Isabel received regular promotions and salary increases. After four years at the bank, she was earning two hundred thousand pounds a year, twice her starting pay. She was also quite miserable. The long hours, pressure-cooker atmosphere, and regular battles with the ethically challenged traders had taken a toll. She took refuge in London's vital classical music scene. She found three women like herself—musicians who worked in the financial services industry—and they formed a string quartet. Two evenings a week she took advanced lessons from an instructor at the London Cello Institute. Before long, she was playing better than ever before.

Isabel's colleagues knew nothing of her double life. Nor would they have cared. For the most part, they were an uncultured lot. She avoided extracurricular office gatherings whenever possible—especially the alcohol-soaked weekend getaways to luxurious European destinations—but her attendance at a risk management retreat in Barcelona in the autumn of 2016 was mandatory. Freddy Krueger was in rare form. RhineBank's share price, which reached a zenith of ninety-seven euros in 2007, was bumping along in the low twenties. The Council of Ten was in a panic; the CEO's head was on the block. Freddy's, too. He told his risk managers that they needed to stand aside and let the traders make money. Otherwise, RhineBank faced the prospect of a painful downsizing.

"The message was unmistakably clear. The bank was in trouble. Investors were heading for the exits. So were some of our biggest clients. Freddy blamed it all on the regulators. He ordered us to mislead them about the amount of risk on

RhineBank's balance sheet. He never once used the word *regulators* alone. It was always the *fucking* regulators."

Isabel returned to London, secure in the knowledge that the bank for which she worked was in serious trouble and that it was hiding something. The reckless traders on the global markets desk had all but stopped returning her calls and emails. Having little else to do, she embarked on a private review of the firm's balance sheet—at least the portion of the balance sheet she was allowed to see. What she discovered shocked even her. The bank's leverage ratio was more than fifty to one, leaving it dangerously dependent on borrowed money. Worse still, the traders had used that money to purchase derivatives, which were notoriously hard to value. Isabel constructed a computer model to predict their performance during a crisis. The model concluded that many of the derivatives on the bank's books were worthless, a fact it was concealing from regulators in Europe and America.

"The bank was a house of cards, a two-trillion-dollar Ponzi scheme that was dependent on its ability to borrow money at extremely low rates. If market conditions changed . . ."

"The bank would fail?"

"In all likelihood."

"What did you do?"

She wrote a detailed report—twenty thousand words in length, with accompanying charts and graphs—and forwarded it to Freddy Krueger. Freddy summoned her to Hamburg the next day and subjected her to an hourlong dressing down. He then suggested that Isabel might want to find employment elsewhere.

"Why didn't he simply fire you?"

"I was far too dangerous to fire. If I had made my findings public, it might well have led to a run on the bank. I had to be handled with the utmost care."

A return to her old job was out of the question; the head of the London office didn't want her in the building. Freddy didn't want her, either. The beleaguered head of compliance, however, was in desperate need of warm bodies, as RhineBank's many ethical lapses had led regulators to demand stronger internal safeguards. Isabel returned to Hamburg for six months of training, which bore no resemblance to the madness of Freddy's Risk Academy. Once again, she received the highest possible marks on her final exam. As a result, she was allowed to select her assignment. After careful deliberation, she chose Zurich, the dirtiest outpost of the world's dirtiest bank.

H ERR KARL ZIMMER, THE HEAD of RhineBank-Zurich, welcomed Isabel to his fiefdom as though she were an unwanted
houseguest. During a tense introductory meeting, he made it
clear he had objected to her transfer but had been overruled
by headquarters. Nevertheless, he claimed he was ready and
willing to give Isabel a chance to salvage her career, provided
she keep her nose clean and do nothing to interfere with the
essential business of the Zurich office, which was making ob-
scene amounts of money by any means necessary. He gave her
a windowless cell of an office two levels beneath the trading
floor. It was just down the hall from a cipher-and-biometric-
protected door, behind which toiled the gnomes of a secret unit
of the wealth management department known as the Russian
Laundromat.

RhineBank's ties to Russia, she explained, dated to the late nineteenth century, leaving the bank uniquely positioned to take advantage of the corrupt and oftentimes violent return to capitalism that followed the collapse of the Soviet Union. RhineBank-Moscow opened during the final years of the Yeltsin era, and in 2004 the Council of Ten approved the purchase of Metropolitan Financial, a small bank that catered to newly rich Russian oligarchs and criminals. RhineBank also extended a billion-dollar line of credit to MosBank, a Kremlin-owned lender directly controlled by the Russian president. MosBank used a portion of the money to fund the overseas activities of the SVR, Russia's foreign intelligence service. It also allowed SVR agents to operate undercover from MosBank branches throughout the world.

"Which meant that RhineBank AG of Hamburg was indirectly facilitating Russian intelligence operations targeting the West. And it was making millions of dollars a year in profits in the process."

That paled in comparison, however, to the profits the bank earned by operating the Russian Laundromat—a smooth-running conveyor belt that funneled dirty money out of Russia and deposited clean money throughout the world, all beneath impenetrable layers of shell companies that shielded the client's identity from regulators, law enforcement, and, of course, investigative journalists. Much of the money began its journey at either MosBank or Metropolitan Financial. From there, it would make its way to dubious financial havens such as Latvia or Cyprus before arriving in Zurich, where the gnomes of the Laundromat worked their magic. They offered their clients a broad range of services, including legal and corporate advice subcontracted through a network of unscrupulous lawyers in Switzerland, Liechtenstein, and London. A unit of the Laundromat searched out investment opportunities. Luxury real estate, especially in the United States and the United Kingdom, was prized. But in many cases, the money was simply repackaged by other divisions of the bank and lent to other customers.

"As you can imagine, the arrangement is highly lucrative. Not only does the bank collect fees for the initial cleaning service, it then collects massive fees from the borrowers as well."

"What kind of cleaning fees are we talking about?"

"That depends on how much soap is required. If the laundry is only lightly soiled, RhineBank pockets about ten percent. If the laundry is bloodstained, RhineBank might demand as much as half of it. Not surprisingly, the gnomes of the Laundromat like dirty customers. The dirtier the better."

"Dealing with Russian mobsters can be a dangerous business."

"Herr Zimmer is well protected. So is Lothar Brandt."

"The chief of the wealth management department."

She nodded. "Head washer boy."

"You were aware of the Russian Laundromat before you arrived in Zurich?"

"Why do you think I asked to come here?"

"You penetrated your own bank? Is that what you're saying?"

"I suppose I did."

"What motivated you to take such a drastic step?"

"Mirror trades."

"In English, please."

"Let's say a dirty Russian has a mountain of dirty rubles he needs to convert into dollars. The dirty Russian can't take the dirty rubles to the local Thomas Cook, so he gives them to a brokerage firm that uses them to purchase a large quantity of blue-chip stocks at RhineBank-Moscow. A few minutes later, the brokerage firm's representative in, say, Cyprus *sells* the exact same number of blue-chip stocks to RhineBank-London, which pays the Cypriot in dollars. The trades *mirror* each other, thus the name."

Isabel learned of the mirror trades while she was in London, and from her new position in Zurich she was able to observe what happened when the money reached the Laundromat. Her view, however, was highly obstructed; the Laundromat was quarantined from the rest of the office. Even so, their activities required a veneer of internal compliance, especially transfers involving large sums of money—in some cases, hundreds of millions of dollars. Each day, Lothar Brandt brought stacks of documents to Isabel's office and loomed over her while she blindly signed where indicated. But occasionally, if he was busy with another client, the documents arrived by inner-office pouch, presenting Isabel an opportunity to review them at her leisure. One corporate entity appeared frequently, almost always in connection with massive wire transfers, stock and real estate purchases, and other investments.

"Omega Holdings," said Gabriel.

Isabel nodded.

"Why did Omega stand out?"

"Its sheer size. Most clients of the Laundromat utilize dozens of corporate shells, but Omega had hundreds. Whenever possible, I photographed the documents on my personal phone. I also ran Omega through our databases."

"How much money did you find?"

"Twelve billion. But I was certain I'd only scratched the surface. It was obvious the man behind Omega Holdings was very high on the Russian food chain." She paused. "An apex predator."

"What did you do?"

She briefly considered filing an anonymous complaint with FINMA, the Swiss regulatory agency, but decided instead to give the material to a woman she had seen on Swiss television. She was an investigative reporter from a crusading Russian newsmagazine who had a knack for ferreting out financial wrongdoing by the men of the Kremlin. On the seventeenth of February, during her lunch hour, Isabel left a parcel of documents in an athletic field in Zurich's District 3. That evening, using the personal computer in her apartment, she sent an anonymous message to the Russian journalist's ProtonMail address. Afterward, she played Bach's Cello Suite in E-flat Major. All six movements. No sheet music. Not a single mistake.

In March, Isabel left a package at a marina on the western shore of the Zürichsee, and in April she made drops in Winterthur and Zug. Several times each day she checked Nina Antonova's Twitter feed and the website of the *Moskovskaya Gazeta*, but there were no stories about an important oligarch or senior Kremlin official utilizing the services of RhineBank's Russian Laundromat. She made three more drops in June—Basel, Thun, Lucerne. Nevertheless, the *Gazeta* remained editorially silent, leaving her no choice but to pursue the investigation herself.

She had met Mark Preston when they were students at the London School of Economics. After completing his degree, he embarked on a career as a business journalist, only to discover he detested London's financial elite. An avid gamer and amateur hacker, he pioneered a new form of investigative journalism, one that relied on keystrokes and clicks rather than phone calls and shoe leather. His sources were never human, for humans often lied and nearly always had a vested interest. Instead, Preston searched for information captured by the cameras of smartphones—on Twitter, Facebook, Instagram, and Google Street View. He also discovered that in Russia there was a thriving black market for CDs crammed with telephone directories, police reports, and even the national passport database. Yearbooks from elite military units and academies were also available.

His first major story came during the Syrian civil war, when he documented that the regime was dropping chemical barrel bombs on innocent civilians. A year later he identified the Russian officers responsible for shooting down Malaysian Airlines Flight MH17 over Ukraine. The story cemented Preston's reputation and earned him the enmity of the Kremlin. Fearful of Russian retaliation, he left London and went into hiding. He also joined the International Consortium of Investigative Journalists, a nonprofit global network of reporters and news organizations headquartered in Washington.

"As you might recall, the ICIJ broke the Panama Papers story. Much of their work focuses on corruption. Mark helps the financial investigators by identifying and tracking the movements of individuals, especially individuals who are connected to Russia's intelligence services."

"How did you communicate with him?"

"The same way I communicated with Nina. ProtonMail."

"I assume you didn't refer to yourself as Mr. Nobody."

"No. But I didn't put my real name in any of the emails, either. It wasn't necessary."

"Because you and Mark Preston are more than friends."

"We dated for a semester."

"Who ended it?"

"He did, if you must know."

"Silly boy."

"I always thought so."

They met at the end of Brighton Place Pier, as if by chance. At Preston's insistence, Isabel had switched off her phone and removed the SIM card before leaving London. She gave him copies of the documents and asked him to undertake a private investigation on her behalf, for which she would pay any amount he asked. He agreed, though he refused Isabel's offer of money.

"It seems he always regretted the way he treated me."

"Perhaps there's hope for him after all."

"Not in that regard."

A month passed before Isabel heard from him. This time they met in a little seaside town called Hastings. Preston gave her a flash drive containing a dossier of his findings. He warned her to be careful. He said Russian journalists had been murdered for less. Swiss bankers, too.

Isabel read the dossier that evening in her hotel room. Two days later she learned that Viktor Orlov had been murdered, apparently with a Russian nerve agent. She waited until Saturday evening before sending an encrypted email to Nina Antonova. She had left a new package along the bank of the river Aare, in the Old City of Bern. All the pages were blank, with one exception. *I know who killed Viktor Orlov* . . . Afterward, she performed Bach's Cello Suite in D Major.

"Any mistakes?"

"Not a one."

"Where's the dossier?"

She dug it from her bag. "The flash drive and the Word document are both locked. The password is the same."

"What is it?"

"The Haydn Group." She looked at the Englishman and smiled. "The letter G is capitalized."

PART TWO

MENUETTO & TRIO

21

ZURICH–VALLEY OF JEZREEL

A GULFSTREAM G550 OF ASTOUNDING COMFORT and murky registry departed Zurich's Kloten Airport shortly before midnight. Eli Lavon reclined his seat and slept, but Gabriel plugged the flash drive into his laptop and with the cabin lights dimmed reread the dossier.

It was an impressive piece of digital detective work, all the more remarkable for the fact it was produced largely with open sources. An Instagram photo here, a name from a Swiss business registry there, real estate transactions, a few nuggets of gold unearthed from the Panama Papers, Moscow vehicle registrations, Russian passport records. When laid out in proper sequence—and viewed in proper context—the data had produced a name. Someone close to the Russian president. Someone from his inner circle. The secret guardian of his unfathomable wealth. The intelligence services of the West had been searching for this man for a very long time. Mark Preston, with documents provided by a gifted young cellist who worked for the world's dirtiest bank, had found him.

The skies above Tel Aviv were blue-black with the approaching dawn when the G550 touched down at Ben Gurion Airport. Two SUVs waited on the tarmac. Lavon headed to his apartment in the Talpiot neighborhood of Jerusalem; Gabriel, to the safe house in the Valley of Jezreel. After placing his clothing in a plastic rubbish bag, he padded soundlessly upstairs and slipped into bed next to Chiara.

"Well?" she asked quietly.

"Well what?"

"What in God's name was Sarah Bancroft doing in Viktor Orlov's house?"

"She found a lost Artemisia in Julian's storeroom. Viktor agreed to buy it."

"Is it really an Artemisia?"

"Apparently so."

"Any good?"

"She says it needs work."

"That makes two of us," whispered Chiara.

Gabriel removed her silken nightgown. At times like these, he thought, there was comfort in familiar routines.

AFTERWARD, HE PLUNGED INTO A dreamless sleep and woke to find his half of the bed ablaze with the sunlight pouring through the unshaded window. The air in the room was still and heavy and perfumed with the scent of earth and bovine excrement. It was the smell of the valley. As a child, Gabriel had always hated it. He much preferred the pine-scented air of Jerusalem. Or the smell of Rome, he thought suddenly, on a chill autumn evening. Bitter coffee and garlic frying in olive oil, woodsmoke and dead leaves.

He reached for his phone and was surprised to see it was nearly one in the afternoon. Chiara had left a caffe latte on the bedside table. He drank it quickly and went into the bathroom to commence his morning labors before the looking glass. Then he dressed in his usual attire, a trim-fitting charcoal gray suit and a white shirt, and headed downstairs.

Chiara, in leggings and a sleeveless pullover, was seated before her laptop at the kitchen table. Her riotous hair was wound into a bun, and a few stray tendrils lay along the damp skin of her neck. Her caramel-colored eyes were narrowed with irritation.

"I thought you were banned from Twitter," said Gabriel.

"I'm helping my father with an article he's writing for *Il Gazzettino*."

Chiara's father was the chief rabbi of Venice and a historian of the Holocaust in Italy. On the rare occasions he wrote for the popular press, it was usually to issue a warning.

"What's the topic?" asked Gabriel cautiously.

"QAnon."

"The conspiracy theory?"

"QAnon isn't a conspiracy theory. It's a toxic, extremist ideology that borrows heavily from anti-Semitic tropes such as the blood libel and the *Protocols of the Elders of Zion*. And thanks to the pandemic, it has arrived in Western Europe."

"You forgot to mention that the FBI considers QAnon a domestic terrorism threat."

She removed a document from the printer. It was a copy of an internal FBI memo from the bureau's Phoenix field office warning of QAnon's rise. "People are going to die because of this lunacy."

"I agree. But don't spend too much time down the rabbit hole, Chiara. You might not find your way out again."

"Who do you suppose he is?"

"Q?"

She nodded.

"I'm Q."

"Are you really?" She regarded Gabriel for a moment through her reading glasses. "I'm suddenly feeling quite cheap."

"Why?"

"I allowed you to have your way with me, and now you're fleeing the scene of the crime."

"If I recall, you were the one who initiated the activity." He took down a mug from the cupboard and poured coffee from the thermos flask. "Where are the children?"

"I haven't a clue, but I'm sure I'll hear about it later." She smiled. "Don't worry, Gabriel. These past few months have been wonderful for them. A part of me is sorry we can't stay longer."

"Why are we leaving?"

"Because the children start school next month. Remember?"

"I have a feeling they won't be in school long."

"Don't say that."

"A rise in infection rates is inevitable, Chiara. The prime minister will have no choice but to shut down the country again."

"For how long?"

"Until next spring, I'd say. But once we get a sufficient percentage of the population vaccinated, life will return almost to normal. I'm confident we'll get there much faster than the rest of the developed world."

"How can you be so sure?"

"I'm the director-general of the Office. I know things."

"Do you know who killed Viktor Orlov?"

"I tried to tell you last night, but I was too busy having my way with you." Gabriel fished the flash drive from his pocket.

"What is that?"

"A portable storage device with a terabyte of memory."

Chiara rolled her eyes. "Where did you get it?"

"A woman who works for the Zurich office of RhineBank. It contains a dossier written by an open-source investigative journalist named Mark Preston."

"And the subject of the dossier?"

"A Russian billionaire living on the shores of Lake Geneva."

"How nice. Does the billionaire have a name?"

"Arkady Akimov."

"Never heard of him."

"That's probably not an accident."

"How does he make his money?"

"He owns an oil trading firm called NevaNeft, among other things. NevaNeft purchases Russian oil at a steep discount and delivers it to clients in Western Europe at a windfall profit."

"What's wrong with that?"

"Preston is convinced that Arkady is the one who's holding the bulk of the Russian president's personal fortune."

"Oh, dear."

"I'm afraid it gets better."

"How is that possible?"

"Many of Arkady's employees are former Russian intelligence officers. Interestingly enough, they all seem to work for the same small subsidiary of his company."

"Doing what?"

"Preston wasn't able to determine that, but I know someone who might be able to help." He paused, then added, "And so can you."

"How?"

"By printing the dossier." Gabriel inserted the flash drive into Chiara's computer. "The password is the Haydn Group. The letter G is capitalized."

22

UPPER GALILEE, ISRAEL

THERE ARE INTERROGATION CENTERS SCATTERED throughout Israel. Some are in restricted areas of the Negev Desert, others are tucked away, unnoticed, in the middle of cities. And one lies just off a road with no name that runs between Rosh Pina, one of the oldest Jewish settlements in Israel, and the mountain hamlet of Amuka. The track that leads to it is dusty and rocky and fit only for Jeeps and SUVs. There is a fence topped with concertina wire and a guard shack staffed by tough-looking youths in khaki vests. Behind the fence is a small colony of bungalows and a single building of corrugated metal where the prisoners are kept. The guards are forbidden to disclose their place of work, even to their wives and parents. The site is as black as black can be. It is the absence of color and light.

At present, the facility housed a single prisoner, a former SVR officer named Sergei Morosov. His colleagues at Moscow Center had been led to believe he was dead, the victim of a mysterious auto accident on a stretch of empty road in Alsace-Lorraine. They had even taken delivery of a set of human remains, courtesy of the French internal security service. In truth, Gabriel had abducted Morosov from an SVR safe flat in Strasbourg, stuffed him into a duffel bag, and loaded him onto a private plane. Under coerced interrogation, he had revealed the existence of a Russian mole at the pinnacle of MI6. Gabriel had taken the mole into custody outside Washington, on the banks of the Potomac River. He had been fortunate to survive the encounter. Three SVR officers had not.

The mole now occupied a senior position at Moscow Center, and Sergei Morosov, loyal servant of the Russian state, was the lone prisoner of a secret interrogation facility hidden in the bony hills outside Rosh Pina. He had spent the first eighteen months of his stay in a cell. But after a prolonged period of agreeable behavior, Gabriel had allowed him to settle into one of the staff bungalows. It was not unlike the Allon family home in Ramat David, a little breeze-block structure with whitewashed walls and linoleum floors. The refrigerator and pantry were stocked weekly with an assortment of traditional Russian fare, including black bread and vodka. Morosov happily saw to his own cooking and cleaning. The mundane chores of daily life were a welcome diversion from the grinding monotony of his confinement.

The furnishings in the sitting room were institutional but comfortable. Many Israelis, thought Gabriel, made do with less. Everywhere there were books and piles of yellowed newspapers and magazines, including *Die Welt* and *Der Spiegel*. Morosov was a fluent speaker of KGB-accented German. He had run the final lap of his career in Frankfurt, where he had posed as a banking specialist from something called Globaltek Consulting, a Russian firm that purportedly provided assistance to companies wishing to gain access to the lucrative Russian market. In reality, Globaltek was an undeclared *rezidentura* of the SVR. Its main task was to identify potential assets and acquire valuable industrial technology. To that end, it had ensnared dozens of prominent German businessmen—including several senior executives from RhineBank AG—in operations involving *kompromat*, the Russian shorthand for compromising material.

The bungalow had no telephone or Internet service, but Gabriel had recently approved the installation of a television with a satellite connection. Morosov was watching a talk show on NTV, the once-independent Russian television network now controlled by the Kremlin-owned energy company Gazprom. The topic was the recent assassination of the dissident Russian businessman Viktor Orlov. None of the panelists appeared troubled by Viktor's passing or the appalling manner of his death. In fact, they all seemed to think he had received the punishment he deserved.

"Another one bites the dust," said Morosov. "Isn't that how the song goes?"

"Careful, Sergei. Otherwise, I might be tempted to lock you in a cage again. You remember what it was like in there, don't you? Paper plates and plastic spoons. Blue-and-white tracksuits. And no vodka or cigarettes, either."

"The tracksuits were the worst."

Absently, Morosov ran a hand over the front of his burgundy

crewneck sweater. It paired nicely with his French-blue dress shirt, gabardine trousers, and suede loafers. His graying hair was neatly trimmed, his aging face recently shaved. One might have assumed that he had been expecting a visitor, but that wasn't the case. As usual, Gabriel had dropped in unannounced.

He pointed the remote at the television and pressed the power button.

Sergei Morosov grimaced. "That remote is now covered with your germs. And if you must know, I'd feel better if you were wearing a mask." He sprayed the remote with disinfectant. "How bad is it out there?"

"Consider yourself lucky that you live here in your little Covid-free bubble."

"I'd be much happier in a place of my own."

"I'm sure you would. But the minute our back was turned, you would head straight for the Russian Embassy, where you would spin a sad tale about how I kidnapped you and brought you here against your will."

"It happens to be the truth."

"But your old service is unlikely to believe a word of it. In fact, if by some miracle they were able to get you back to Russia, they would probably take you to a room in Lefortovo Prison and execute you."

"You know the Russian people very well, Allon."

"Unfortunately, I speak from experience."

"How long do you intend to keep me here?"

"Until you've told me every last secret rattling around that head of yours."

"I already have."

Gabriel removed the printout of the dossier from his attaché case and handed it to Morosov. The Russian slipped on a pair of half-moon reading glasses and scanned the opening pages. His face betrayed no emotion other than grudging admiration.

"You don't seem terribly surprised, Sergei."

"Why would I be?"

"Is it accurate?"

"Not entirely. Arkady was never assigned to the Soviet Foreign Ministry."

"Where did he work?"

"The Komitet Gosudarstvennoy Bezopasnosti."

"The KGB?"

Morosov nodded slowly.

"And the Haydn Group?" asked Gabriel.

"It's a subsidiary of Arkady's oil trading company."

"Yes, I know. But what is it?"

"The Komitet Gosudarstvennoy Bezopasnosti."

Gabriel reclaimed the dossier. "You should have told me about Arkady a long time ago."

Morosov shrugged. "You never asked."

23

UPPER GALILEE, ISRAEL

THE GUARDS PLACED TWO CHAIRS in the camp's main court, with a folding table between them. Sergei Morosov, pleased by the prospect of human interaction, even with his former tormentor, brought along a meal of pickled herring, black bread, and Russian vodka. He feigned mild offense when Gabriel declined his offer of a drink.

"You don't care for vodka?"

"I'd rather drink a glass of diesel."

"I have a lovely Shiraz if you'd like that instead. It's from a winemaker called Dalton."

Gabriel smiled.

"What's so funny?"

"The accent is on the second syllable." Gabriel pointed toward the north. "And the vineyards are right over that hill."

"You have many fine wines here in Israel."

"We do our best, Sergei."

"Perhaps someday you would be kind enough to show me your country."

"On second thought, I think I'll have that vodka after all."

Morosov drained his glass with the snap of his wrist and returned it to the tabletop. "You don't much care for Russians, do you, Allon?"

"Actually, I'm very fond of them."

"Name one Russian you like."

"Nabokov."

Morosov smiled in spite of himself. "I suppose you have a right to hate us. Your confrontation with Ivan Kharkov at that dacha outside Moscow was the stuff of legend. You and your wife would have died that morning if it wasn't for Grigori Bulganov's courage and Viktor Orlov's money. Now Grigori and Viktor are both dead, and you are the last man standing. It is an unenviable position. I should know, Allon. I speak from experience, too."

Morosov then reminded Gabriel of his impeccable lineage. He was, to borrow the term coined by the Russian philosopher and writer Zinoviev, a true *Homo Sovieticus*—a Soviet Man. His mother had served as a personal secretary to KGB chairman Yuri Andropov. His father, a brilliant Marxist theoretician, had worked for Gosplan, the agency that oversaw the Soviet Union's command economy. As party members, they lived a life far beyond the reach of ordinary Russians. A comfortable apartment in Moscow. A dacha in the country. Access to special stores stocked with food and clothing. They even owned an automobile, a cherry-red Lada that on occasion actually performed the function for which it was designed and assembled.

"We weren't elites, mind you. But we had it quite good. That wasn't the case for Vladimir Vladimirovich," he added, using the Russian president's given name and patronymic. "Vladimir Vladimirovich was a member of the proletariat. The son of a factory worker. A true man of the people."

He was raised, Morosov continued, in a tumbledown apartment building at 12 Baskov Lane in Leningrad. Two other families, one devoutly Russian Orthodox, the other observantly Jewish, shared the same cramped flat. There was no hot water, no bathtub, no heat other than a wood-burning stove, and no kitchen save for a single gas ring and a sink in a windowless hallway. Young Vladimir Vladimirovich spent most of his time downstairs in the rubbish-strewn courtyard. Short in stature, slight of build, he was often bullied. He took boxing lessons and later studied judo and sambo, the Soviet martial arts discipline. Incorrigible and quick tempered, he sought out opportunities on the mean streets of Leningrad to put his fighting skills to the test. Whenever words or sinister looks were exchanged, it was invariably Vladimir Vladimirovich who threw the first punch.

Occasionally, he looked after neighborhood boys who could not fend for themselves—including a boy named Arkady Akimov, who lived at 14 Baskov Lane. One day Vladimir Vladimirovich saw two older boys menacing Arkady in the fetid passageway that connected the courtyards of their buildings. Arkady was a frail child who suffered from chronic respiratory illnesses. Worse still, at least in the eyes of Baskov Lane's thugs, he was a promising pianist who was protective of his hands. Vladimir Vladimirovich fought the fight for him, beating both boys to a pulp. And thus was born a friendship that would change the course of Russian history.

The boys attended School No. 193, where Vladimir Vladimirovich got into trouble and Arkady excelled. It was his dream to study music at the Leningrad Conservatory, but at seventeen he was informed he had been denied admission. Heartbroken, he followed his childhood friend to Leningrad State University, and upon graduation they were recruited by the KGB. After intensive language instruction and a stay at the Red Banner Institute spy school, they were sent off to East Germany as newly minted Soviet intelligence officers. Sergei Morosov was working there at the time.

"Vladimir Vladimirovich was assigned to the backwater of Dresden, but Arkady joined me at the main *rezidentura* in East Berlin. I was a traditional PR Line officer. I recruited and ran agents. Arkady was in a different line of work entirely."

"Active measures?"

"The KGB's stock-in-trade," said Morosov with a nod.

"What sort of active measures?"

The usual, answered Morosov. Propaganda, political warfare, disinformation, subversion, influence operations, support for anti-establishment forces on both the far left and far right—all of it designed to tear at the fabric of Western society. Arkady and his counterparts in the Stasi also armed and funded Arab terrorist groups, including the Palestine Liberation Organization and the Popular Front for the Liberation of Palestine.

"Do you remember the La Belle discotheque bombing in West Berlin in April 1986? Sure, Gaddafi and the Libyans were involved. But where do you think the bombers got the plastic explosive and the detonator in the first place? Arkady's finger-prints were all over that attack. He was damn lucky his role wasn't exposed when the Stasi files were made public after the Wall came down."

Even the officers of the Berlin *rezidentura* were caught off guard by the speed of East Germany's collapse. They put in place stay-behind networks, burned their files, and headed home to an uncertain future—Sergei Morosov to Moscow, Arkady and Vladimir Vladimirovich to their hometown of Leningrad. The country had deteriorated during their absence. The lines were longer, the shelves emptier. And in December 1991, four months after an abortive coup led by KGB hard-liners, the Soviet Union was no more. The once-mighty KGB soon passed into history as well, leaving two services in its wake. The FSB, headquartered at Lubyanka Square, handled internal security and counterintelligence, while the SVR, from its wooded compound in Yasenevo, conducted traditional espionage abroad.

Sergei Morosov decided to stay on with the SVR, though for six months he received no salary. By then, Arkady Akimov and Vladimir Vladimirovich had already begun the second acts of their career. Arkady went into the oil business. And Vladimir Vladimirovich, after declaring himself to be a committed democrat, went to work for the mayor of Leningrad, which had reverted to its historic name, St. Petersburg. As head of the Committee for External Relations, it was his job to attract foreign investment to a city where crime was rampant. During the long winter of 1991, with Russia facing the threat of widespread hunger, he supervised a series of international barter deals, trading plentiful Russian commodities such as timber, petroleum, and minerals for badly needed staples such as fresh meat, sugar, and cooking oil. Few of the promised goods ever arrived, and the immense profits derived from the sale of the Russian commodities abroad were never properly accounted for. An investigation would later determine that much of the money ended up in the pocket of Arkady Akimov.

Suddenly wealthy, Arkady hired a small army of former KGB officers and *spetsnaz* special operatives and waged a bloody turf war with the Tambov crime family for control of St. Petersburg's port. Before long, he was Russia's dominant oil trader. With a portion of his rapidly growing fortune, he purchased a plot of lakefront land and constructed a colony of dachas. He gave one to Vladimir Vladimirovich and the others to men such as himself, former KGB officers turned successful businessmen. They gathered at the retreat each weekend with their wives and children and plotted the future. They were going to seize control of Russia and return it to superpower status. And in the process, they were going to make themselves rich. Rich as tsars. Rich beyond imagination. Rich enough to punish the Americans and Western Europeans for destroying the Soviet Union. Rich enough to exact revenge.

"You don't believe that nonsense about Volodya being an accidental president, do you, Allon? It was a straight KGB operation from beginning to end. Nothing was left to chance."

Their chosen candidate arrived at the Kremlin in June 1996 and took up a post in an obscure directorate that managed government-owned properties abroad. With the help of Arkady Akimov and his cadre of former KGB men, a series of rapid promotions ensued. Deputy chief of the presidential staff. Director of the FSB. And, in August 1999, prime minister of the Russian Federation. His path to the presidency seemed all but certain.

"But remember, Allon—nothing was left to chance."

The first bomb, said Morosov, exploded on September 5 in the republic of Dagestan. The target was an apartment building that housed mainly Russian soldiers and their families. Four days later, it was another apartment building, this one on Guryanova Street in Moscow. The combined death toll was 158, with hundreds more wounded. Chechen separatists were blamed.

When two more bombs exploded the following week—one in Moscow, the other in the southern city of Volgodonsk—hysteria swept the country. The new prime minister, on an official visit to Kazakhstan, assured his traumatized people that his response would be swift and merciless.

"That was when he issued his infamous threat about wasting Chechen terrorists in the outhouse. Only a thug from Baskov Lane would say such a thing. It was also a lie. The Chechen separatists had nothing to do with those bombings. They were planned by Arkady Akimov and carried out by the FSB. They were active measures aimed not at a foreign adversary but the Russian people."

"Can you prove it?"

"One does not *prove* such things in Russia, Allon. One simply knows them to be true."

The manufactured crisis, Sergei Morosov continued, had its intended effect. After escalating the war in Chechnya, Vladimir Vladimirovich saw his approval ratings soar. In December, an ailing and alcohol-addled President Boris Yeltsin announced his resignation and appointed a little-known functionary as his successor. Four months later, he faced Russia's voters for the first time. The result was never in doubt. Nothing was left to chance.

The first phase of the operation was complete. Arkady Akimov and his cadre of KGB officers had succeeded in placing one of their own in the Grand Kremlin Palace. The second phase was about to commence. They were going to make themselves rich. Rich as tsars. Rich beyond imagination. Rich enough to exact revenge.

24

UPPER GALILEE, ISRAEL

BUT FIRST, SAID SERGEI MOROSOV, the oligarchs had to be brought to heel. Khodorkovsky, owner of the energy behemoth Yukos, was the richest. But Gusinsky, by dint of his Media-Most broadcast empire, was perhaps the most influential. Police raided his offices in downtown Moscow just four days after the inauguration. Khodorkovsky survived three years before tasting the Kremlin's wrath. Dragged off his private jet during a refueling stop in Siberia, he would spend the next decade in prison, much of it in a labor camp near the Chinese border, where he passed his days making mittens and his nights in solitary confinement.

"Viktor got off easy by comparison. A luxury townhouse in Cheyne Walk, an estate in Somerset, a villa by the sea in Antibes. One wonders why he would risk it all by getting involved with a traitor like Grigori Bulganov." Sergei Morosov paused. "Or with you, Allon."

"Viktor believed Russia could be a democracy."

"Do you subscribe to this fantasy as well?"

"I was cautiously pessimistic."

"Russia will never be a democracy again, Allon. We cannot live as normal people."

"A very wise woman once told me the same thing."

"Really? Who?"

"Go on, Sergei."

Once the original oligarchs had been put in their place, he said, the looting began—a wild orgy of self-dealing, kickback schemes, siphoning, embezzlement, protection rackets, tax fraud, and outright theft that enriched the men around the new president. They saw themselves as a new Russian nobility. They erected palaces, commissioned coats of arms, and traveled the country by a network of private roads. Most became billionaires many times over, but none was richer than Arkady Akimov. His oil trading firm, NevaNeft, was Russia's largest. So was his commercial construction company, which was awarded endless government projects, always with bloated contracts.

"Such as?"

"The presidential palace on the Black Sea. It started out as a modest villa, about a thousand square meters. But by the time Volodya and Arkady were finished, the price tag was more than a billion dollars."

That was pocket change, Morosov continued, when compared to the money Arkady earned from the Olympic Games in Sochi. The cost to the Russian taxpayer for the extravaganza on the shores of the Black Sea was more than $50 billion, nearly five times the original estimate. Arkady's construction firm was awarded the largest slice of the pie, a forty-eight-kilometer highway and rail line running from the Olympic Park to the ski venues in the mountains. The contract was worth $9.4 billion.

"It was one of the greatest grifts in history. The Americans sent a probe to Mars for a fraction of that. Arkady could have paved the road in gold for less."

"How much do you suppose Vladimir Vladimirovich let him keep for himself?"

"You know the old Russian proverb, Allon. What's mine is mine, and what's yours is mine."

"Translation?"

"Volodya effectively controls the entire Russian economy. It's *all* his. He's the one who chooses the winners and losers. And the winners remain winners only if he allows it."

"He takes a cut of everything?"

Morosov nodded. "Everything."

"Is he the richest man in the world?"

"Second, I'd say."

"How much is there?"

"North of a hundred billion, but south of two."

"How far south?"

"Not much."

"Is any of it in his name?"

"He might have a billion or two stashed away in MosBank under his real name, but the rest of the money is held by trusted members of his inner circle like Arkady. He's doing quite well for himself, is Arkady. NevaNeft is now the third-largest oil trading firm in the world. He owns a fleet of oil tankers, and he's invested billions in pipelines, refineries, storage facilities, and terminals in Western Europe. About five years ago he moved his business to Geneva and established a Swiss-registered company called NevaNeft Trading SA. There's also NevaNeft Holdings SA, which includes the rest of his empire."

"Why Geneva?"

"It recently replaced London as the oil trading capital of the world. All the big Russian firms have offices there. It's also located conveniently close to Zurich."

"Home of the Russian Laundromat."

Morosov nodded. "Arkady is a valued customer. RhineBank earns hundreds of millions of dollars a year in fees from laundering his money. As you might expect, they don't ask many questions."

"And if they did?"

"They would discover they are helping Arkady and his childhood friend from Baskov Lane achieve their most important goal."

"What's that?"

"Revenge."

IT WAS ARKADY WHO CHOSE the name of the unit hiding in plain sight within NevaNeft Holdings. He wanted something punchy and memorable, something that paid homage to the musical career denied to him by the rector of the Leningrad Conservatory. Like all young Russian pianists, he had studied the masterworks of Tchaikovsky and Rachmaninoff, whom he revered. But he had also memorized several sonatas written by the Austrian composer regarded as the father of both the string quartet and the modern symphony. He ran it by Vladimir

Vladimirovich, who granted his approval. Two weeks later, after Arkady's lawyers filed the necessary paperwork with the Swiss Commercial Registry, the Haydn Group SA was born.

"What sort of work does it do?"

"On paper? Market research and management consulting."

"And in reality?"

"Propaganda, political warfare, disinformation, subversion, influence operations, the occasional assassination of pro-democracy advocates and exiled Russian billionaires."

"Active measures."

Sergei Morosov nodded in agreement. "All designed to undermine the West from within."

"I thought the SVR and GRU were already doing a fine job of that."

"They are," said Morosov. "But the Haydn Group provides an additional layer of plausible deniability because it's a private business operating outside Russia. It's quite small, about twenty employees. They're all former intelligence officers, the best of the best, and very well paid."

"How much operational latitude does Arkady have?"

"For all intents and purposes, he's the director of an elite intelligence service. But he gets Volodya's approval for the big stuff."

"Like killing Viktor Orlov?"

"Sure."

"And the run-of-the-mill stuff?"

Much of it, said Morosov, involved covertly funneling money to political and social movements that were either pro-Kremlin or anti-establishment, especially those movements on the far right that were opposed to immigration and the economic integration of Europe. The Haydn Group had also created a chain of phantom think tanks and online public policy journals that presented the Kremlin's point of view in a favorable light and questioned the effectiveness of Western democracy and liberalism.

But the unit's most effective financial tool, said Morosov, was the promise of Russian riches. Politicians, lawyers, bankers, businessmen, even senior intelligence officers: all were targeted for corruption with Russian money. Most accepted it without reservation. And once they had taken the initial bait—the contribution, the bribe, the no-lose business opportunity—there was no wriggling off the hook. They were wholly owned assets of Kremlin Inc.

"Have you ever wondered why so many members of the British and French aristocracy are suddenly pro-Russian? It's because Arkady is buying them off one lord, duke, earl, viscount, and marquis at a time. Money is Russia's greatest weapon, Allon. A nuclear bomb can only be dropped once. But money can be wielded every day with no fallout and no threat of mutually assured destruction. Russian money is rotting the institutional integrity of the West from within. And Arkady Akimov is the one writing the checks."

"You seem to have a rather firm grasp of the Haydn Group's activities, Sergei."

"Arkady and I were comrades from the bad old days in Berlin. He's also quite rich, not to mention a close friend of the boss of bosses. I made a point of staying on his good side."

"When was the last time you saw him?"

"A couple of months before you abducted me. We met at

NevaNeft headquarters in Geneva. Arkady owns the building on the western side of the Place du Port. His office is on the top floor."

"And the Haydn Group?"

"They're one floor down, the sixth. Everything is state of the art. Biometric locks, soundproof glass, secure phones. And computers," said Morosov. "Lots and lots of computers."

"What are they using them for?"

"What do you think?"

"I think the Haydn Group is running a troll factory in the middle of Geneva."

"A very good one," said Morosov.

"Do you think Arkady is trying to influence the outcome of the American election?"

"I've been out of circulation for some time, Allon."

"And if you were to hazard a guess?"

"Needless to say, the Kremlin would like the incumbent to remain in office. Therefore, it stands to reason that Arkady and the Haydn Group are putting their thumb on the scale. But they're far more interested in helping the Americans destroy themselves. They spend most of their time sowing discord and rancor on social media and other Internet forums, including message boards used by racists and other extremists. Arkady told me that one of his operatives had managed to inspire several acts of political violence."

"How?"

"By anonymously whispering into the ear of someone who's on the edge. Have you been watching the news from America lately? They're not so hard to find."

Morosov drained another glass of vodka with a snap of his wrist.

"If you keep drinking that stuff, your liver is going to turn to concrete."

"It's not as if I have much else to do."

Gabriel took up the dossier and rose. "Is there anything else you forgot to tell me, Sergei?"

"Just one thing."

"I'm listening."

"If Arkady can get to Viktor Orlov, he can get to you, too."

25

TIBERIAS, ISRAEL

TWENTY-FIVE KILOMETERS SOUTH OF Rosh Pina, rising from the depths of the Jordan Rift Valley, stands Mount Arbel. The ancient Jews who inhabited the mountain during the brutal Roman occupation of Palestine dwelled in fortified caves carved into its sheer cliffs. Now they resided in three tidy agricultural settlements on the tabletop summit. One of the settlements, Kfar Hittim, stood on the scalding plain where Saladin, on a blazing summer afternoon in 1187, defeated the thirst-crazed armies of the Crusaders in a climactic battle that would leave Jerusalem once again in Muslim hands. Ari Shamron claimed that, when the winds were right, he could still hear the clashing of swords and the screams of the dying.

His honey-colored villa stood on the outskirts of Kfar Hittim, atop a rocky escarpment overlooking the Sea of Galilee and the ancient holy city of Tiberias. Gilah, his long-suffering wife, greeted Gabriel in the entrance hall. With her melancholy eyes and wild gray hair, she bore an uncanny resemblance to Golda Meir. She spread her arms wide and demanded to be embraced.

Masked, Gabriel kept his distance. "It's not safe, Gilah. I've been traveling."

She threw her arms around him nonetheless. "We were beginning to think we would never see you again. My God, how long has it been?"

"Don't make me say it aloud. It's too depressing."

"Why didn't you tell us you were coming?"

"I happened to be in the neighborhood. I wanted to surprise you."

She squeezed him tightly. "You're too thin."

"You always say that, Gilah."

"I'll bring you some dinner. Ari is working on a new radio. The isolation has been very hard on him." She laid her hand on Gabriel's cheek. "So has your absence."

She drew away without another word and disappeared into the kitchen. Steeling himself for the worst, Gabriel headed downstairs to the room that doubled as Shamron's study and workshop. The shelves were lined with the memorabilia of a secret life, including a small glass case containing eleven .22-caliber shell casings. Eli Lavon had collected them from the lobby of an apartment building in Rome's Piazza Annibaliano a few minutes after Gabriel killed a Palestinian named Wadal Abdel Zwaiter.

"You really have to get rid of these things, Ari."

"I'm saving them for you."

"I told you, I don't want them."

"One of the American networks is preparing a major new documentary. The producers would like to interview me while I am still among the living. I suggested that they might want to speak to you as well."

"Why on earth would I want to talk about it now, after all these years? It will only reopen old wounds."

"It's not exactly a secret that you were the primary gunman for Operation Wrath of God. In fact, I have it on good authority that you have finally told your children about the things you did to defend your country and your people."

"Is there anything you *don't* know about my life?"

Shamron smiled. "I don't believe so."

He was perched atop a tall stool at his worktable, dressed in neatly pressed khaki trousers and an oxford-cloth shirt. Before him was a Philco rosewood radio. There was no sign of his old olive-wood cane, only an aluminum walker that shone coldly in the glare of his work lamp. With a tremulous right hand—the same hand he had clamped over the mouth of Adolf Eichmann on a darkened street in Argentina—he reached for his packet of Maltepe cigarettes.

"Don't even think about it, Ari."

"Why shouldn't I?"

"Because you don't want to spend your final days on earth attached to a ventilator."

"I resigned myself to such a fate a long time ago, my son." Shamron extracted a cigarette from the packet and ignited it with his old Zippo lighter. "Will you at least take off that mask? You look like one of my doctors."

"It's for your own good."

"My doctors tell me the same thing every time they impale

me with something sharp." He squinted at the radio's exposed innards through a cloud of smoke. "What brings you all the way to Tiberias?"

"You, Abba."

"I might be old, but I'm not senile."

"I needed to have a word with Sergei Morosov."

"About our old friend Viktor Orlov?"

Gabriel nodded.

"I assume Viktor's death had something to do with money."

"Wherever did you get an idea like that?"

"The luxury villa you acquired on the shore of Lake Zurich." Shamron frowned. "A steal at a mere forty thousand Swiss francs a month. Last evening, when you should have been celebrating Shabbat with your wife and children, you were given a dossier by a young woman who works at the Zurich office of RhineBank, home of the so-called Russian Laundromat. The dossier in question was prepared by a British investigator with an impressive track record when it comes to revealing Russian secrets. It suggests that a businessman named Arkady Akimov is the primary keeper of the Russian president's immense wealth."

"Have you placed a transmitter in the Nahalal safe house?"

"A mole," replied Shamron. "Apparently, several of Arkady's employees are former SVR and GRU officers. They work for a subsidiary of his oil trading firm known as the Haydn Group. The British investigator was unable to determine the nature of the unit's work."

"Active measures directed against the West."

"A page from the old Soviet playbook," said Shamron.

"They're nothing if not consistent."

"Is it your intention to put Arkady Akimov out of business?"

"With extreme prejudice. RhineBank, too."

"Given the firm's deplorable history, nothing would make me happier. But an operation of that scale will consume the final precious months of your term." Shamron paused. "Unless, of course, you're planning to stay for a second."

"I learned how to walk and chew gum a long time ago. As for a second term, it hasn't been offered."

"And if it were?"

"I have other plans."

"*Haaretz* seems to think you'd make a fine prime minister."

"Can you imagine?"

"I can, actually. But there's a rumor going around that you plan to take your retirement in a palazzo overlooking the Grand Canal in Venice." Shamron glared at Gabriel with reproach. "I know it was Chiara's idea, but you could have put your foot down."

"My authority ends at the threshold of my home."

"Your country needs you." Shamron lowered his voice. "And so do I."

"I have a year and a half left in my term."

"With any luck, I'll be dead by then." Shamron sighed in resignation. "Have you given any thought to your successor?"

"I was hoping I could talk *you* into taking the job."

"I'm too young," said Shamron. "Too inexperienced."

"That leaves Yaakov Rossman or Yossi Gavish. The fact that Yaakov is the chief of Special Operations gives him the edge. But Yossi has plenty of operational experience and would make a fine chief."

"Neither of them is your caliber."

"In that case," said Gabriel, "perhaps we should make history."

"How?"

"By appointing the first female director-general of the Office."

Shamron was intrigued by the idea. "Do you have any candidates in mind?"

"Only one."

"Rimona?"

Gabriel smiled. "She's the head of Collections, which means she's responsible for recruiting and running a worldwide network of agents. She also happens to be your niece."

"Perhaps I am eternal after all." Shamron's gaze was suddenly clouded by a memory. "Do you remember the day she fell off her scooter outside in the drive and tore the skin from her hip? The poor child was screaming with pain, but I was so distraught by the sight of all that blood I couldn't comfort her. You were the one who applied the field dressing to her wound."

"She still has the scar."

"You were always good at fixing people, Gabriel." Shamron indicated the circuits and vacuum tubes scattered across his worktable. "I can only make old radios sound like new again."

"You built a country, Ari."

"And an intelligence service," he pointed out. "You would be wise to accept my advice every now and again."

"What advice would you give me about Arkady Akimov?"

"Let someone else handle him."

"Like who?"

"The Swiss or the British."

"They've agreed to let me run the operation."

"How generous of them."

"I thought so."

"And if things get messy?"

"The Swiss gave me a get-out-of-jail-free card."

"What are you going to do about the Russian journalist who delivered the contaminated documents to Viktor?"

"By way of deception," said Gabriel, reciting the first four words of the Office's motto.

Shamron crushed out his cigarette. "That leaves Arkady."

"I'm thinking about going into business with him."

"What kind of business?"

"Money laundering, Ari. What else?"

"I thought Arkady did his laundry at RhineBank."

"He does."

"So why would he need you?"

"I'm still working on that."

"There *is* a rather simple solution, you know."

"What's that?"

Shamron lit a fresh cigarette. "Close the Russian Laundromat."

26

KING SAUL BOULEVARD, TEL AVIV

THREE LEVELS BENEATH THE LOBBY of King Saul Boulevard was a doorway marked 456C. The room on the other side had once been a dumping ground for obsolete computers and worn-out furniture, often used by the night staff as a clandestine meeting place for romantic trysts. The keyless cipher lock was set to the numeric version of Gabriel's date of birth, reputedly the Office's most closely guarded secret. At ten the following morning, he punched the code into the keypad and went inside.

Rimona Stern, chief of the Office division known as Collections, niece of Ari Shamron, quickly put on her mask. "I hear you paid a visit to Tiberias last night."

"Is that all you heard?"

"My aunt says you're too thin."

"Your aunt always says that before stuffing me with food."

"How is she holding up?"

"She's been locked in a house with your uncle for nearly six months. How do you think she's holding up?"

Just then, the door opened and Yossi Gavish entered the room. Born in London, educated at Oxford, he still spoke Hebrew with a pronounced British accent. Yossi was the head of Research, the Office's analytical division, but his training as a Shakespearean actor had made him a valuable field asset as well. There was a beachside café in Saint Barthélemy where the waitresses thought him a dream and a hotel in Geneva where the concierge had taken a private vow to shoot him on sight.

He was followed a moment later by Yaakov Rossman and a pair of all-purpose field operatives named Mordecai and Oded. Eli Lavon arrived next, trailed by Dina Sarid, the Office's top terrorism analyst and a first-class researcher who often spotted connections others missed. Petite and dark-haired, Dina walked with a slight limp, the result of a serious wound she had suffered when a Hamas suicide bomber detonated himself aboard a Number 5 bus in Tel Aviv in October 1994. Her mother and two of her sisters were among the twenty-one people killed in the attack.

Mikhail Abramov loped through the door a moment later. Tall and lanky, with pale, bloodless skin and eyes like glacial ice, he had long ago replaced Gabriel as the Office's primary practitioner of targeted killings, though his enormous talents were not limited to the gun. Born in Moscow to a pair of dissident scientists, he had immigrated to Israel as a teenager. He was accompanied by his wife, Natalie Mizrahi. A French-born Algerian Jew who spoke fluent Arabic, she was the only Western intelligence officer to have ever penetrated the insular ranks of the Islamic State.

Within the corridors and conference rooms of King Saul Boulevard, the nine men and women gathered in the subterranean room were known by the code name Barak, the Hebrew word for lightning, for their uncanny ability to gather and strike quickly. They were a service within a service, a team of operatives without equal or fear who had fought together, and bled together, on a chain of secret battlefields stretching from Moscow to the Atlas Mountains of Morocco. Four were now powerful division chiefs. And if Gabriel had his way, one would soon make history as the first female director-general of the Office.

Rimona watched him intently as he approached the chalkboard—the last chalkboard in all of King Saul Boulevard— and with a few deft swipes of his left hand wrote a name: Arkady Akimov, childhood friend of the Russian president, former officer of the KGB specializing in active measures, owner of a private intelligence company known as the Haydn Group that was attempting to undermine the West from within.

The Office, Gabriel told his team, was going to undermine Arkady Akimov instead. They were going to dislodge him from his prominent perch in the West, destroy the Haydn Group, and seize as much of his dirty money as possible, including money he happened to be holding for the president of the Russian Federation. RhineBank AG would be granted no quarter. Nor, for that matter, would any other financial services firm—Swiss, German, British, or American—that might be caught up in the affair.

An attack of that magnitude, he cautioned, could not be mounted from the outside, only from within. Isabel Brenner, a compliance officer at RhineBank's Zurich office, had opened a doorway into Arkady's well-defended citadel. Now the Office was going to walk through it. They were going to forge a business relationship with Arkady, become a partner in the kleptocracy known as Kremlin Inc. Extraordinary care would be taken at every step of their merger. Nothing, said Gabriel, would be left to chance.

BUT HOW TO PENETRATE THE court of a man who assumed that every phone he used was tapped, every room he entered was bugged, and every stranger who crossed his path was out to destroy him? A man who never spoke to the press, who rarely left his protective Russian bubble, and was always surrounded by bodyguards drawn from elite *spetsnaz* units? Even the location of his office in Geneva's Place du Port was a carefully guarded secret. Housekeeping acquired office space in the building opposite, and two of Eli Lavon's surveillance artists set up shop the next day. They snapped photographs of all those who came and went from Arkady's opaque front door and forwarded the images to King Saul Boulevard, where the team attempted to put names to faces. One photo depicted a trim, silver-haired man stepping from the back of a Mercedes-Maybach saloon car. Yossi Gavish's caption was a masterpiece of bureaucratic brevity: Akimov, Arkady. Chairman of NevaNeft Holdings, NevaNeft Trading, and the Haydn Group.

Arkady was even more circumspect when it came to the location of his residence. For several years he had lived quietly in the moneyed enclave of Cologny. But in the summer of 2016, he pulled up stakes and settled into a custom-built palace in Véchy valued at more than one hundred million Swiss francs.

The massive construction project enraged his new neighbors, including an English pop star who went to the press with his complaints. The identity of the new villa's owner was never made public, only that he was thought to be a Russian business-man, perhaps with connections to the Kremlin.

The same anonymous Russian businessman was thought to be the owner of the largest private dwelling in the French ski village of Courchevel, a lavish villa on the Côte d'Azur near Saint-Tropez, a mansion in the walled Moscow suburb of Rublyovka, and an apartment on Manhattan's Billionaire's Row purchased for the astonishing price of $225 million. He owned the obligatory yacht but rarely used it, as he was prone to seasickness. His private jet was a Gulfstream, his private helicopter was an Airbus H175 VIP. He flashed about Geneva in a motorcade fit for a head of state.

His official biography contained no reference to a KGB past, only an unremarkable stint at the Soviet Foreign Ministry, a job that had taken him briefly to East Berlin. Much specula-tion surrounded the nature of his relationship with the Russian president. Through his lawyers he acknowledged that they had known each other when they were young boys in Leningrad, but he rejected any suggestion that he was part of the president's inner circle. Reports regarding his sometimes-messy personal life had been harder for the lawyers to tamp down. There were two known divorces, both quiet, and a string of rumored affairs and mistresses. His newest wife was the former Oksana Miro-nova, a beautiful ballet dancer more than thirty years his junior.

Not surprisingly, the *Moskovskaya Gazeta* was among Arkady's harshest critics. The magazine had exposed his links to the pres-idential palace on the Black Sea and the billions he had made from the bloated construction contracts awarded for the Sochi

Olympic Games. Several of the articles had been written by the missing investigative reporter Nina Antonova. Having returned to Wormwood Cottage to await permanent resettlement, she composed an illuminative twenty-thousand-word dossier of her own that contained every unproven allegation ever made against Arkady. It made for entertaining reading, as did Olga Sukhova's retelling of a heated encounter she had had with Arkady in Moscow in 2007, after reports surfaced that his childhood friend from Leningrad was somehow worth an astonishing $40 billion.

By all accounts, the Russian president's personal fortune had grown substantially since then. So, too, had Arkady Akimov's, skyrocketing from a paltry $400 million in 2012 to $33.8 billion, according to the most recent estimate by *Forbes* magazine, making him the forty-fourth richest man in the world. Directly above him was an American hedge fund manager, and beneath him was a Chinese manufacturer of home appliances. Arkady, not without some justification, was said to have been disappointed by his ranking.

But then, *Forbes* had only part of the picture. Missing from its estimate of Arkady's net worth was the money that the gnomes of the Russian Laundromat had buried anonymously in the West. Fortunately, Gabriel had gnomes of his own—the nine men and women burrowing away in a subterranean room three levels beneath the lobby of King Saul Boulevard.

In nearly every respect, they were the polar opposite of the man whose life they were pulling to pieces. They earned a government salary and lived modestly. They did not steal unless ordered to do so. They did not kill unless innocent lives were at stake. They were kind to their spouses and lovers, and cared for their children to the best of their ability while at the same time working impossible hours. They had no vices, for those with vices were never admitted to their ranks.

They managed to conduct their work with a minimum of rancor, as raised voices tended to facilitate the spread of the coronavirus. Even Rimona Stern, who possessed her famous uncle's quick temper, managed to modulate her normally stentorian tone. Proper social distancing was not possible—not in the cramped quarters of their subterranean lair—so they disinfected their worktables frequently and were subjected to regular testing. Somehow there were no positive results.

Gabriel poked his head through the doorway of Room 456C once or twice each day to check on the team's progress and crack the operational whip. He was anxious to return to the field as quickly as possible, lest the Swiss have a change of heart and declare Arkady off limits. It was obvious to Rimona and the others that he was tempted to give the Russian oligarch the bullet he so richly deserved and be done with it. But Arkady Akimov—trusted member of the Russian president's inner circle, owner of a private intelligence company waging war against the West from within—was far too valuable to kill. He was the one for whom Gabriel had been searching for a very long time. He would leave nothing to chance.

But how to penetrate his court?

Usually, it was a flaw or vanity that left a man vulnerable, but Gabriel instructed the team to find Arkady Akimov's one redeeming quality. Surely, he beseeched them, there had to be at least *one* reason why the Russian oligarch was taking up space on the planet. It was Dina Sarid, while reviewing NevaNeft's otherwise pointless website, who discovered it. Through the company's charitable arm, Arkady Akimov had donated hundreds of millions of dollars to orchestras, conservatories, and art museums in Russia and across Western Europe, oftentimes with little or no publicity.

As it turned out, Arkady was also a frequent underwriter of concerts and festivals, which allowed him to rub shoulders with some of the most prominent figures in the classical music world. A reverse-image search of social media turned up a photograph of the notoriously camera-shy Russian standing at the side of the French violinist Renaud Capuçon, a broad smile on his face. Arkady had worn the identical expression while posed next to the German violinist Julia Fischer. And with her countryman Christian Tetzlaff. And with the pianists Hélène Grimaud and Paul Lewis. And the conductors Gustavo Dudamel and Sir Simon Rattle.

Dina was dubious as to the operational value of her discovery. Nevertheless, she printed the photographs on high-quality paper and placed them on Gabriel's desk. One hour later, during his evening visit to Room 456C, he wrote two more names on the chalkboard. One was an old enemy; the other, an old lover. Then he described for his team the opening act of the planned merger between the Office and the kleptocracy known as Kremlin Inc. It would be a seemingly chance encounter at a grand occasion, an event that Arkady Akimov would move heaven and earth to attend. Cocktails and canapés would not suffice. Gabriel required a star attraction, an international celebrity whose presence would make attendance mandatory for the moneyed elite of Swiss society. He also needed a financier to play the role of the evening's benefactor, a paragon of corporate virtue known for his commitment to causes ranging from climate change to Third World debt relief. Just the sort of man Arkady Akimov would love to corrupt with dirty Russian money.

27

GENEVA

R HINEBANK AG OF HAMBURG WAS not the only financial
institution to do a brisk business with Nazi Germany. Switzerland's National Bank accepted several tons of gold from
the Reichsbank throughout the six years of World War II and
earned a tidy profit of twenty million Swiss francs in the process. The major Swiss banks also took on high-ranking Nazis as
clients—including none other than Adolf Hitler, who deposited
the royalties from his anti-Semitic manifesto *Mein Kampf* in a
UBS account in Bern.

But more often than not, party leaders and senior officers
of the murderous SS enlisted the services of discreet private
bankers such as Walter Landesmann. A minor figure in Zurich banking before the war, Landesmann was by the spring of

1945 the secret guardian of a vast ill-gotten fortune, much of which remained unclaimed after his clients were arrested as war criminals or forced to seek sanctuary in distant South America. Never one to miss an opportunity, Landesmann used the money to transform his bank into one of Switzerland's most prominent financial services firms. And upon his death, he bequeathed it to his only child, a charismatic young financier who was called Martin.

Martin Landesmann knew full well the source of the bank's rapid postwar growth and wasted no time washing his hands of it. With the proceeds of the sale, he created Global Vision Investments, a private equity firm that financed forward-looking start-up enterprises, especially in the field of alternative energy and sustainable agriculture. His abiding passion, however, was his One World charitable foundation. Martin delivered medicine to the sick, food to the hungry, and water to the thirsty, oftentimes with his own hands. Consequently, he was much beloved by the smart set in Aspen and Davos. His circle of influential friends included prominent politicians and the luminaries of Silicon Valley and Hollywood, where his production company bankrolled documentaries on topics such as climate change and the rights of immigrants. His most recent film was the flattering self-portrait *One World*. Its legion of critics, mainly on the political right, wondered why he hadn't called it *Saint Martin* instead.

The first documented use of the sobriquet was an unfavorable profile in the *Spectator*. It was now wielded regularly by his defenders and detractors alike. Martin secretly loathed it, perhaps because it bore no resemblance to the truth. For all his corporate piety, he was remorseless in his pursuit of profit, even if it required ravaging the rain forests or pouring carbon into the atmosphere. Among his more lucrative ventures was Keppler Werk GmbH, a metallurgy firm that manufactured some of the world's finest industrial-grade valves. Keppler Werk was part of a global network of companies that supplied nuclear technology to the Islamic Republic of Iran in violation of United Nations sanctions—a network that Gabriel had penetrated and then used to sabotage four previously undisclosed Iranian uranium-enrichment facilities. Martin's participation in the affair had not been voluntary.

His public pronouncements to the contrary, he did not play exclusively with his own money. GVI was the clandestine owner of Meissner PrivatBank of Liechtenstein, and Meissner PrivatBank was the portal of a sophisticated money-laundering operation utilized primarily by organized crime figures and wealthy individuals averse to taxation. For a substantial fee, and few questions asked, Martin turned dirty money into assets that could be held indefinitely or converted into clean cash. Gabriel and Graham Seymour were aware of Martin's extracurricular activities. Swiss financial regulators were not. As far as they were concerned, Saint Martin Landesmann was the one Swiss financier who had never put a foot wrong.

He had fled cold, gray Zurich after the rapid sale of his father's tainted bank and settled in genteel Geneva. GVI was headquartered on the Quai de Mont-Blanc, but the true nerve center of Martin's empire was Villa Alma, his grand lakeside estate on the rue de Lausanne. Martin's longtime chief of security greeted Gabriel in the forecourt. Their last conversation had been conducted over the barrel of a SIG Sauer P226. Gabriel had been the one holding it.

"Are you armed?" asked the bodyguard in his atrocious Swiss German.

"What do you think?" answered Gabriel in proper *Hochdeutsch*.

The bodyguard held out his hand, palm up. Gabriel brushed past him and went into the gleaming entrance hall, where Saint Martin Landesmann, bathed in a corona of golden light, waited in all his glory. He was dressed, as was his custom, like the lower half of a gray scale: slate-gray cashmere pullover, charcoal-gray trousers, black loafers. When combined with his glossy silver hair and silver spectacles, the clothing lent him an air of Jesuitical seriousness. The hand he raised in greeting was white as marble. He addressed Gabriel in English, with a vaguely French accent. Martin no longer spoke the language of his native Zurich. Unless, of course, he was threatening to have someone killed. If that were the case, only Swiss German would do.

"I hope you and Jonas had a chance to get reacquainted," he said amiably.

"We're having drinks later."

"Do you know your Covid status?"

"Somehow I'm still negative. You?"

"Monique and I are tested every day." Monique was Martin's Parisian-born wife and an international celebrity in her own right. "I hope you'll forgive her for not saying hello. She's not anxious to relive the Zoe Reed affair."

"That makes two of us."

"I bumped into Zoe at Davos last year," Martin volunteered. "She was anchoring CNBC's afternoon coverage. As you might imagine, it was all rather awkward. We both pretended that none of the unpleasantness of that night happened."

"It was a long time ago."

"And your associate who broke into my computer?"

"He sends his best."

"No hard feelings, I hope."

"A few," said Gabriel. "But let's not dwell on the past. I'm here to talk about the future."

Martin frowned. "I didn't realize we had one."

"A bright one, actually."

"What are we going to do?"

"Restore the global order and Western liberal democracy before it's too late."

"And how are we going to do that?"

"By going into business with Arkady Akimov." Gabriel smiled. "How else?"

THE WALLS OF VILLA ALMA were hung with a world-class collection of Impressionist and postwar paintings. Martin showed off a few of his newer acquisitions, including a voluptuous nude by Lucian Freud, as they repaired to the sweeping terrace. The Savoy-blue waters of the lake sparkled in the dazzling sunlight. Martin pointed out the Mont Blanc massif, where the Planpincieux glacier was in danger of imminent collapse after several days of above-normal temperatures. The planet, he feared, was hurtling toward the point of no return. The American withdrawal from the Paris Agreement had been a disaster; four irrecoverable years had been lost. He was confident the Democratic candidate for president, were he to win the election, would create a cabinet-level post devoted solely to combating climate change. He had been told by a campaign source that the leading contender for the job was the former senator and secretary of state who had negotiated the Iran nuclear accords. Martin knew him well. Indeed, he had been a frequent guest at the secretary's homes in Georgetown, Nantucket, and Sun Valley. It was true what they said about the rich, thought Gabriel, listening. They really were different.

"And did you tell your good friend the secretary that you were the one who helped the Iranians construct their centrifuge cascades? That *you* were the one who brought the world to the brink of yet another war in the Middle East?"

"Actually, it never came up. You and your friends at MI6 and the CIA managed to keep my identity secret, even from the man who was sitting across the negotiating table from the Iranians."

"We assured you we would."

"Forgive me for doubting your word. After all, you know what they say about promises, Allon."

"I do my best to keep mine."

"Have you always?"

"No, Martin. But let's not get into a game of moral relativism. The scale of your duplicity is almost as breathtaking as the view from your terrace."

"Let he who is without sin cast the first stone. Isn't that what the good book says?"

"Not our book. In fact, we were the ones who pioneered the technique."

"It's not all a lie," said Martin. "I really do want to make the world a better place."

"We have that in common, you and I. As the inhabitant of a small country with limited water and arable land, I share your concerns about the changing climate. I also appreciate the work you've done in Africa, as uncontrolled migratory flows are inherently destabilizing. For proof, one needs to look no further than Western Europe, where the anti-immigrant extreme right is ascendant."

"They're racist cretins. Not to mention authoritarians. I fear for the future of democracy."

"Which is why you're going to announce a new One World initiative to promote freedom and human rights, especially in Hungary, Poland, the former republics of the Soviet Union, and Russia itself."

"George Soros cornered that market long ago. By the way, he's a friend, too."

"In that case, I'm sure he won't mind if you join his crusade."

"It's a fool's errand, Allon. Russia will never be a democracy."

"Not anytime soon. But your initiative will nevertheless infuriate Arkady Akimov and his good friend the Russian president." Gabriel paused, then added, "Which is why Arkady will want to go into business with you."

"Explain," said Martin.

"Arkady doesn't form business relationships with prominent Westerners out of the goodness of his heart. He uses Russian money as a stealth weapon to rot the West from within. You are an ideal target, a saintly liberal activist who harbors a dark secret. Arkady will use you and compromise you at the same time. And once you've taken the bait, you will be a wholly owned subsidiary of Kremlin Incorporated. At least in their eyes."

"Which is why I never do business with Russians. They're too corrupt, even for me. And far too violent. Mind you, I do business with plenty of gangsters, including the Italians.

They're quite reasonable, actually. They take their cut, I take mine, and everybody lives. But chaps like Boris and Igor are quick to resort to violence if they think they've been cheated. Besides," added Martin, "I was under the impression Arkady took his dirty laundry to RhineBank."

"He does. But he will soon find himself in need of a new cleaning service."

"And if he approaches me?"

"You will play very hard to get. But once you agree to take his money, you will violate as many laws as possible, including in Great Britain and the United States."

"What happens then?"

"Arkady goes down. You, however, will emerge with your glittering reputation intact, just like after the Iran operation."

"And when Boris and Igor come calling?"

"You'll have a roof over your head."

"You?"

"And the Swiss," said Gabriel.

Martin made a show of thought. "I suppose I have no choice but to say yes."

Gabriel was silent.

"And who's going to pay for this democracy project of yours?" asked Martin.

"You are. You're also going to purchase a painting."

"How much will it cost me?"

"A fraction of what you paid for that Lucian Freud of yours. What was it? Fifty million?"

"Fifty-six." Martin hesitated, then asked, "Is that all?"

"No," said Gabriel. "There's one more thing."

28

TALACKERSTRASSE, ZURICH

AT THREE FIFTEEN THAT AFTERNOON, Isabel heard a knock on the door of her windowless office. The tenor and tone suggested it was Lothar Brandt, head washer boy at the Russian Laundromat. Therefore, she allowed an interval of twenty seconds to elapse before inviting him to enter. Lothar closed the door behind him, never a good sign, and placed a stack of documents on Isabel's desk.

"What have you got for me today?" she asked.

He opened the first document to the final page and pointed to the signature line for the compliance officer, which was flagged with a red tab. As was his custom, he volunteered no information as to the nature of the trade or transaction or the parties involved. Isabel nonetheless signed her name.

They fell into an easy rhythm: place, point, sign. *Isabel*

Brenner . . . To alleviate the tedium, and perhaps to distract Isabel from the fact that she was committing serious infractions of numerous banking regulations, Lothar recounted the details of his weekend. He and a friend—male or female, he did not specify—had spent it hiking in the Bernese Oberland. Isabel murmured something encouraging. Privately, she could think of no worse fate than to be trapped in the Alps alone with Lothar. Like Isabel, Lothar was German. He was not unintelligent, only unimaginative. Isabel had once been forced to sit next to him at a company dinner. It was all she could do not to slash her wrists with the butter knife.

"What about you?" he asked suddenly.

"I'm sorry?"

"Your weekend. Anything special?"

She described a dull two days spent sheltering from the coronavirus. Lothar was apoplectic. He believed the virus to be a hoax fabricated by social democrats and environmentalists to slow global economic growth. Exactly where he had stumbled on this theory was unclear.

When Isabel had finished signing the first batch of documents, Lothar returned with a second, then a third. European markets were closing as she rendered her name for the final time. RhineBank had suffered yet another drubbing, falling by more than two percent. It was no matter, thought Isabel. The bad boys on the derivatives desk in London had probably made a killing betting against the firm's stock.

Upstairs, the mood on the trading floor was funereal. Herr Zimmer was sealed in his fishbowl of an office, nearly invisible in a fog of cigar smoke—disabled smoke detectors being one of the most sought-after perquisites of RhineBank senior executives. Seated at his desk, he was engaged in an animated conversation with his speakerphone. Based on his defensive posture, the person at the other end of the line was sitting on the top floor of RhineBank's headquarters in Hamburg.

Isabel saw to a few routine matters of compliance, and at half past six, after bidding farewell to the girls at reception and the security guards in the lobby, she went into the Talackerstrasse. The ruggedly handsome Englishman who called himself Peter Marlowe joined her aboard a Number 8. In the Römerhofplatz they slid into the backseat of a BMW X5. The crumpled little Israeli eased slowly away from the curb and headed south toward Erlenbach.

"I was beginning to think I'd never see you again," she said.

"That's the point, luv." He smiled. "How was your day?"

"A thrill a minute."

"It's about to get a good deal more interesting."

"Thank goodness." Isabel looked at the little Israeli behind the wheel. "Is there any way he can drive a bit faster?"

"I've tried," said the Englishman despairingly. "He never listens."

ISABEL LAID THE FINGERS OF her left hand upon her right arm and played the cello portion of Beethoven's *Triple Concerto* as they made their way along the lakeshore. She was nearing the end of the second movement when they arrived at the villa. Gabriel was waiting inside, along with several people who had not been present during her last visit. She counted at least eight new arrivals. One was a beautiful woman who might or might not have been an Arab. The man seated next to her had skin like porcelain and colorless eyes. A fleshy woman with brownish-blond hair was eyeing Isabel with what appeared to be mild contempt. Or perhaps, she thought, it was merely her natural expression.

Isabel turned to Gabriel. "Friends of yours?"

"You might say that."

"Are they all Israeli?"

"Would that be a problem?"

"Why do you ask?"

"Because many Europeans do not believe the state of Israel has a right to exist."

"I'm not one of them."

"Does that mean you would be willing to work with us?"

"I suppose that depends on what you want me to do."

"I would like you to finish the job you started when you gave those documents to Nina Antonova."

"How?"

"By helping me to destroy Arkady Akimov and the Haydn Group. It's a private intelligence service," Gabriel explained. "And it's waging war on Western democracy from the sixth floor of Arkady's office in Geneva."

"That would explain all the former SVR and GRU officers on the payroll."

"It would indeed." Smiling, Gabriel set out on a slow tour of the sitting room. "You're not the only one here tonight with hidden talent, Isabel." He stopped next to a tall, balding man who looked like one of her professors from the London School of Economics. "Yossi was a gifted Shakespearean actor when he was at Oxford. He also plays a bit of cello. Not like you, of course." He pointed toward the Arab-looking woman. "And

Natalie was one of Israel's top physicians before I sent her to Raqqa to become a terrorist for the Islamic State."

"Do you want me to become a terrorist, too?"

"No," replied Gabriel. "A money launderer."

"I already am."

"Which is why Global Vision Investments of Geneva would like to hire you."

"Isn't that Martin Landesmann's shop?"

"You've heard of him?"

"Saint Martin? Who hasn't?"

"You'll soon discover that Martin isn't the saint he makes himself out to be."

"Are you forgetting I already have a job?"

"Not for long. In fact, I'm confident that in a few short days your position at RhineBank will be quite untenable. In the meantime, I would like you to copy as many incriminating documents from the Russian Laundromat as you can safely lay your hands on. I would also like you to continue to practice the cello."

"Anything in particular?"

"Is Rachmaninoff's 'Vocalise' part of your repertoire?"

"It's one of my favorite pieces."

"You have that in common with one of RhineBank's biggest clients."

"Really? Who?"

He smiled. "Arkady Akimov."

29

KENSINGTON, LONDON

SUCH WAS THE UNRELENTING PACE of the news cycle that the death of Viktor Orlov had all but receded from the collective memory of the British press. Therefore, it came as something of a surprise when the Crown Prosecution Service accused the well-known Russian journalist Nina Antonova of complicity in Orlov's assassination and issued domestic and European warrants for her arrest. The murder weapon, the authorities alleged, was a parcel of Novichok-contaminated documents delivered to Orlov's Cheyne Walk mansion on the night of his death. CCTV images documented the reporter's arrival and departure from the residence, her brief stay at the Cadogan Hotel, and her passage through Heathrow Airport, where she boarded a late-night flight to Amsterdam. According to Dutch authorities, she spent the night in a popular youth hostel in the city's notorious Red Light District and likely left the Netherlands the next day on a false passport supplied by her handlers in Russian intelligence.

Absent from the charging statement was any mention of Sarah Bancroft, the beautiful former CIA officer turned London art dealer who had stumbled upon Viktor Orlov's body. She, too, was caught off guard by the announcement, for no one, not even the MI6 officer whose Kensington maisonette she shared, had bothered to warn her it was coming. She had not seen Christopher since the night of Nina's interrogation at Wormwood Cottage. Nor had she had any meaningful communication with him, only the odd text message rendered in the manner of Peter Marlowe, his cover identity. It seemed his stay in Switzerland would be longer than anticipated. A visit by Sarah was not possible—not in the short term, at least. He would try to get back to London soon, perhaps at the next weekend.

To make matters worse, Sarah's friend the prime minister had imposed new coronavirus restrictions. There was no point in trying to sneak across the West End to the gallery; business had once again slipped into a coma. Instead, Sarah sheltered in place in Kensington and promptly put on five additional pounds of unwanted weight.

Fortunately, the new rules contained an exception for exercise. In black leggings and a new pair of trainers, Sarah bounded along the deserted pavements of Queen's Gate to the entrance of Hyde Park. After pausing briefly to stretch her calves, she set out along a footpath into Kensington Gardens, then headed up Broad Walk to the park's northern boundary. Her stride was smooth and relaxed as she flowed toward Marble Arch, but by the time she arrived at Speakers' Corner, her breath was ragged and her mouth tasted of rust.

It had been her ambition to circle the park twice, but it was out of the question; the pandemic had taken a terrible toll on her fitness. She managed one final burst of good form along Rotten Row and then walk-jogged back to Queen's Gate Terrace. There she found the lower door of the maisonette slightly ajar. In the kitchen, Gabriel was pouring bottled water into the Russell Hobbs electric kettle.

"How was your run?" he asked.

"Depressing."

"Maybe you should stop smoking Christopher's cigarettes."

"Is there any chance I can have him back?"

"Not anytime soon."

"You sound pleased by the prospect."

"I told you not to get involved with him."

"I'm afraid I didn't have much say in the matter." She settled atop a stool at the granite island. "I assume Nina won't be taken into custody anytime soon."

"Unlikely."

"Was there really no other way?"

"It's for her own good," answered Gabriel. "And the good of my operation."

"Do you have any need of a washed-up field agent with a pretty face?"

"You have a gallery to run."

"Perhaps you haven't heard, but business isn't exactly booming."

"You wouldn't have an Artemisia lying around, would you?"

"A nice one, actually."

"How much do you want for it?"

"Who's paying?"

"Martin Landesmann."

"Viktor was going to give me five," said Sarah. "But if Saint Martin is picking up the tab, I think fifteen sounds about right."

"Fifteen it is. But I'd feel better if we put some distance between my client and your gallery."

"How?"

"By running the sale through an intermediary. It would have to be someone discreet. Someone utterly without morals or scruples. Do you happen to know anyone who matches that description?"

Smiling, Sarah reached for her phone and dialed Oliver Dimbleby.

He answered on the first ring, as though he were waiting next to the phone in anticipation of Sarah's call. She asked whether he had a few minutes to spare to discuss a matter of some delicacy. Oliver replied that, where Sarah was concerned, he had all the time in the world.

"How about six o'clock?" she wondered.

Six was fine. But where? The bar at Wilton's was a no-go zone. Bloody virus.

"Why don't you pop over to Mason's Yard? I'll put a bottle of shampoo on ice."

"Be still, my beating heart."

"Steady on, Ollie."

"Will Julian be joining us?"

"He's sealed himself in a germ-free chamber. I don't expect to see him again until next summer."

"What about that boyfriend of yours? The one with the flashy Bentley and the made-up name?"

"Out of the country, I'm afraid."

Which was music to Oliver's ears. He arrived at Isherwood Fine Arts a few minutes after six and laid a sausage-like forefinger on the call button of the intercom.

"You're late," came the metallic reply. "Hurry, Ollie. The champagne's getting warm."

The buzzer howled, the deadbolts thumped. Oliver climbed the newly carpeted stairs to the office Sarah shared with Julian and, finding it deserted, rode the lift up to the gallery's glorious glass-roofed exhibition room. Sarah, in a black suit and pumps, her blond hair falling across half her face, was removing the cork from a bottle of Bollinger Special Cuvée. Oliver was so entranced by the sight of her that it took him a moment to notice the frameless canvas propped upon Julian's old baize-covered pedestal—*The Lute Player*, oil on canvas, approximately 152 by 134 centimeters, perhaps early Baroque, quite damaged and dirty.

Crestfallen, Oliver asked, "Is this the matter of some delicacy to which you were referring?"

Sarah handed him a flute of champagne and raised her own in salutation. "Cheers, Ollie."

He returned the toast and then appraised the painting. "Where did you find her?"

"Where do you think?"

"Buried in Julian's storeroom?"

She nodded.

"Current attribution?"

"Circle of Orazio Gentileschi."

"Pish posh."

"I couldn't agree more."

"Have you got a second opinion?"

"Niles Dunham."

"Good enough for me. But how's the provenance?"

"Airtight." Sarah raised her glass to her crimson lips. "Interested?"

Oliver allowed his eyes to wander over her form. "Definitely."

"In the painting, Oliver."

"That depends on the price."

"Fourteen."

"The record for an Artemisia is four-point-eight."

"Records are made to be broken."

"I'm afraid I don't have fourteen lying around at the moment," said Oliver. "But I might have five. Six in a pinch."

"Five or six won't do. You see, I'm quite confident you'll unload it in short order." Sarah lowered her voice. "Next day, I imagine."

"How much will I get for it?"

"Fifteen."

He frowned. "You're not up to something illegal, are you?"

"Naughty," said Sarah. "But not illegal."

"There's nothing I love more than naughty. But I'm afraid we'll need to adjust the terms of the deal."

"Name your price, Oliver. You have me over a barrel."

"If only." He lifted his gaze toward the skylight and with the tip of his forefinger tapped his damp lips. At length, he said, "Ten for you, five for me."

"For a day's work? I should think a cut of three million is more than sufficient."

"Ten and five. Hurry, Sarah. The gavel's about to fall."

"All right, Oliver. You win." She touched her champagne flute to his. "I'll send over the contract in the morning."

"What about the restoration?"

"The buyer has someone in mind. Apparently, he's quite good."

"I certainly hope so. Because our lute player needs a great deal of work."

"Don't we all," sighed Sarah. "I nearly had a heart attack in Hyde Park today."

"What were you doing?"

"Jogging."

"How positively American of you." Oliver refilled his glass. "Is that boyfriend of yours really out of the country?"

"Behave, Oliver."

"Why on earth would I want to do that? It's so bloody boring."

30

MARTIN LANDESMANN, FINANCIER, philanthropist, philan-
derer, money launderer, evader of international nuclear
sanctions, scion of a proud if dubious Zurich banking dynasty,
threw himself into his newest endeavor with an energy and a
sense of purpose that astonished even his wife, Monique, who
had seen through his saintly public persona long ago and was
among his harshest critics, as wives often were.

A master of branding and image-making, he focused first
on a name for his undertaking. He thought Freedom House
had a nice ring to it and was bereaved to learn it was the name
of a respected think tank based in Washington. Gabriel suggested the Global Alliance for Democracy instead. Admittedly,
it was dull, and its English-language acronym was atrocious.
But it left nothing to the imagination, especially the Russian

imagination, which was the entire point of the exercise. Martin commissioned a suitably grandiose logo, and the One World Global Alliance for Democracy, dedicated to the promotion of freedom and human rights, was born.

It took time, of course. But Gabriel, if he felt the pressure of a ticking clock, gave no sign of it. He had a story to tell, and he was going to pay it out slowly, with each plot element revealed in its proper sequence and with appropriate detail given to each character and setting. It was not necessarily a story with mass appeal. But then, Gabriel's audience was small—a wealthy former KGB officer who had at his disposal an elite unit of cyber operatives. Nothing would be left to chance.

Such was the case with the unveiling of the One World Global Alliance for Democracy. The group's interactive, multilingual website went live at nine a.m. Geneva time, on the one-month anniversary of Viktor Orlov's murder in London. With content written and edited largely by Gabriel and his team, it depicted a planet drifting inexorably toward authoritarianism. Martin issued the same dire warning in a whirlwind series of television interviews. The BBC granted him thirty minutes of precious airtime, as did Russia's NTV, where he engaged in a spirited debate with a popular pro-Kremlin host. Not surprisingly, Martin got the better of him.

The reviews broke along ideological and partisan lines, but that was to be expected. The progressive press found much to admire in Martin's initiative, the populist fringe less so. One far-right American cable news host dismissed the Global Alliance for Democracy as "warmed-over George Soros." If there was a threat to democracy, he added, it was from know-it-all, nanny-state lefties like Martin Landesmann. Gabriel was pleased to see that the website of Russia Today, the Kremlin's English-language propaganda arm, wholeheartedly agreed.

No news outlet or purveyor of opinion, regardless of its ideological tilt, questioned Martin's sincerity. Neither, it seemed, did the Russians, who mounted their first spearfishing probe of the Global Alliance for Democracy the following afternoon. Unit 8200 traced the attack to a computer in an office building in the Place du Port in Geneva—the same building that housed the offices of NevaNeft Holdings SA and its subsidiary, the Haydn Group.

Clearly, Gabriel's opening gambit had caught the eye of his target. He did not permit himself the luxury of a celebration, however, for he was already crafting the next chapter of his story. The setting was the Zurich office of RhineBank AG, otherwise known as the dirtiest outpost of the world's dirtiest bank.

THE FIRST TO RECEIVE AN email was a *New York Times* correspondent who had written authoritatively on RhineBank in the past. It purported to be from an employee of the firm's headquarters. It was not. Gabriel had composed it himself, with Yossi Gavish and Eli Lavon standing over his shoulder.

Attached were several hundred documents. A small portion were drawn from the archives of Isabel Brenner. The rest had been acquired clandestinely by Unit 8200, which conducted its hack so skillfully that RhineBank never knew its system had been breached. Taken together, the documents provided indisputable proof that the firm's Zurich office was operating a secret unit known as the Russian Laundromat, a smooth-running conveyor belt that funneled dirty money out of Russia and deposited clean money throughout the world. No other office or division of RhineBank was implicated, and none of the documents pertained to the activities of Arkady Akimov or his anonymous shell corporation, Omega Holdings.

The reporter's story appeared on the *Times* website a week later. It was followed in short order by similar stories in the *Wall Street Journal*, *Bloomberg News*, the *Washington Post*, the *Guardian*, *Die Welt*, and the *Neue Züricher Zeitung*—all of which had received document-laden emails as well. At Rhine-Bank headquarters, its glossy spokeswoman dodged and denied while upstairs on the top floor the Council of Ten considered its options. All were in agreement that only a complete massacre would satisfy the bloodlust of the press and the regulators.

The order went out at midnight on a Thursday, and the executions commenced at nine the following morning. Twenty-eight employees of the Zurich office were terminated, including Isabel Brenner, a compliance officer who had signed much of the Russian Laundromat's paperwork. Somehow, Herr Zimmer managed to survive. In his fishbowl office, in full view of the trading floor, he presented Isabel with a termination agreement. She signed the document where indicated and accepted a severance check for one million euros.

She walked out of RhineBank for the final time at four fifteen that afternoon, clutching a cardboard box of her possessions, and the following evening moved into a fully furnished apartment in the Old Town of Geneva owned by her new employer, Global Vision Investments. The bulk of Gabriel's team went to Geneva with her. Their new safe house was located in the upscale diplomatic neighborhood of Champel, a steal at sixty thousand a month.

Gabriel, however, remained behind in Zurich, with only Eli Lavon and Christopher Keller for company. All in all, he thought, his operation was off to a promising start. He had his painting. He had his financier. He had his girl. All he needed now was his star attraction. It was for that reason, after carefully weighing the risks, both professional and personal, he reached for his phone and dialed Anna Rolfe.

31

ROSENBÜHLWEG, ZURICH

THE VILLAS LINING THE ROSENBÜHLWEG were big and old and huddled closely together. One, however, stood atop its own promontory and was surrounded by a formidable iron fence. Gabriel arrived at the appointed hour, half past seven p.m., to find the security gate locked. Pelted by fat balls of rain, a flat cap pulled low over his brow, he laid his thumb on the call button of the intercom and endured a wait of nearly a minute for a response. He supposed he had it coming. The dissolution of their brief and tumultuous relationship had hardly ranked among his finest hours.

"May I help you?" a female voice asked at last.

"I certainly hope so."

"Poor you. Let me see if I can figure out how to let you in. Otherwise, you'll catch your death."

Another long moment passed before the automatic lock finally snapped open. Drenched, Gabriel scaled a flight of steps to the soaring portico. The front door yielded to his touch. The entrance hall had not changed since his last visit; the same large glass bowl stood atop the same carved wooden table. He peered into the formal drawing room and in his memory glimpsed a well-dressed man of advancing years and obvious wealth lying in a pool of his own blood. His socks, Gabriel remembered suddenly, had been mismatched. One of the suede loafers, the right, had a thickened sole and heel.

"Hello?" he called out, but there was no reply other than a silken G-minor arpeggio. He climbed the stairs to the second floor of the villa and followed the sound to the music room, where Anna had spent much of her unhappy childhood. She appeared unaware of his arrival. She was lost to the simple arpeggio.

Tonic, third, fifth . . .

Gabriel removed his sodden cap and, wandering the perimeter of the room, scrutinized the outsize framed photographs adorning the walls. Anna with Claudio Abbado. Anna with Daniel Barenboim. Anna with Herbert von Karajan. Anna with Martha Argerich. In only one of the photographs was she alone. The setting was the Scuola Grande di San Rocco in Venice, where she had just completed an electrifying performance of her signature piece—Giuseppe Tartini's *Devil's Trill Sonata*. Gabriel had been standing not ten feet away, beneath Tintoretto's *Temptation of Christ*. At the conclusion of the recital, he had accompanied the soloist to her dressing room, where she had found a Corsican talisman hidden in her violin case, along with a brief note written by the man who had been contracted to kill her that night.

Tell Gabriel he owes me one . . .

The violin fell silent. At length, Anna said, "I never played the *Devil's Trill* better than I did that night."

"Why do you suppose that was?"

"Fear, I imagine. Or perhaps it had something to do with the fact that I was falling in love." She played the sonata's languid opening passage, then stopped abruptly. "Were you ever able to find him?"

"Who?"

"The Englishman, of course."

Gabriel hesitated, then said, "No."

Anna eyed him down the barrel of the violin's neck. "Why are you lying to me?"

"Because if I told you the truth, you wouldn't believe me." He looked at the violin. "What happened? Did you get tired of the Stradivarius and the Guarneri?"

"This one isn't mine. It's an early-eighteenth-century Klotz on loan from the estate of its original owner."

"Who was that?"

"Mozart." She displayed the violin vertically. "He abandoned it in Salzburg when he came to Vienna. I'm going to use it to record his five violin concertos the minute it's safe to go back into the studio. Unlike most older violins, it was never upgraded in the nineteenth century. Its sound is very smooth and veiled." She offered it to Gabriel. "Would you like to hold it?"

He declined.

"What's wrong? Are you afraid you're going to drop it?"

"Yes."

"But you touch priceless objects all the time."

"A Titian, I can repair. But not that."

She placed the violin beneath her chin and played an arresting, dissonant double-stop from Tartini's sonata. "You're dripping on my floor."

"That's because you intentionally made me stand in the rain."

"You should have brought an umbrella."

"I never carry umbrellas."

"Yes," she said distantly. "It's one of the things I remember most about you, along with the fact that you always slept with a gun on the bedside table." She placed the violin carefully in its case and folded her arms beneath her breasts. "What does one do in a situation like this? Shake hands or exchange a passionless kiss?"

"One uses the excuse of the pandemic to keep one's distance."

"What a shame. I was hoping for a passionless kiss." She laid her hand atop the Bechstein Sterling grand piano. "I have been involved with many men in my life—"

"Many," agreed Gabriel.

"But never has one vanished so thoroughly as you."

"I was trained by the best."

"Do you remember how long you stayed at my villa in Portugal?"

"Six months."

"Six months and fourteen days, actually. And yet I've received not a single phone call or email in all these years."

"I'm not a normal person, Anna."

"Neither am I."

Gabriel surveyed the photographs lining the walls. "No," he said after a moment. "You most certainly are not."

She was, by any objective standard, the finest violinist of her generation—technically brilliant, passionate and fiery, with a matchless liquid tone that she pulled from her instrument by the sheer force of her indomitable will. She was also prone to immense swings of mood and episodes of personal recklessness, including a hiking accident that had left her with a career-threatening injury to her famous left hand. In Gabriel she had seen a stabilizing force. For a brief time, they were one of those endlessly fascinating couples one reads about in novels, the violinist and the art restorer sharing a villa on the Costa de Prata. Never mind that Gabriel was living under a false identity, or that he had the blood of a dozen men on his hands, or that she was never, under any circumstances, allowed to point a camera in his direction. Were it not for a few Swiss surveillance photos, there would be no proof that Gabriel Allon had ever made the acquaintance of the world's most famous violinist.

To the best of his knowledge, she had kept him a secret as well. Indeed, a part of Gabriel was surprised she remembered him at all; her love life since their parting had been as tempestuous as her playing. She had been linked romantically to an assortment of moguls, musicians, conductors, artists, actors, and filmmakers. Twice she had married, and twice she had been spectacularly divorced. For better or worse, neither union had produced offspring. She had told a recent interviewer that she was through with love, that she planned to spend the final years of her career in search of perfection. The pandemic had played havoc with her plans. She had not set foot in a studio or on a stage since her appearance at Zurich's Tonhalle with Martha Argerich. Not surprisingly, she was desperate to perform in public again. The adulation of a crowd was for Anna like oxygen. Without it, she would slowly die.

She looked at the ring on his finger. "Still married?"

"Remarried, actually."

"Did your first wife—"

"No."

"Kids?"

"Two."

"She's Jewish, your wife?"

"A rabbi's daughter."

"Is that why you left me?"

"Actually, I found your constant practicing unbearable." Gabriel smiled. "I couldn't concentrate on my work."

"The smell of your solvents was atrocious."

"Obviously," said Gabriel archly, "we were doomed from the start."

"I suppose we're lucky it ended before someone got hurt." Anna smiled sadly. "Well, that about covers it. Except, of course, why you showed up at my door after all these years."

"I'd like to hire you for a recital."

"You can't afford me."

"I'm not paying."

"Who is?"

"Martin Landesmann."

"His Holiness? I saw Saint Martin on the television just the other day warning about the end of democracy."

"He does have a point."

"But he's an imperfect messenger, to say the least." Anna moved to the window, which overlooked the villa's rear garden.

"When I was a child, Walter Landesmann was a frequent visitor to this house. I know exactly where Martin got the money to form that private equity firm of his."

"You don't know the half of it. But he's agreed to help me with a matter of some urgency."

"Will I be in any danger?"

"None whatsoever."

"How disappointing." She turned to face him. "And where will this performance be?"

"The Kunsthaus."

"An art museum? What's the occasion?"

Gabriel explained.

"The date?"

"Mid-October."

"Which will give me more than enough time to shake off the coronavirus cobwebs." She retrieved Mozart's violin from the case. "Any requests?"

"Beethoven and Brahms, if you don't mind."

"Never. Which Beethoven?"

"The F Major sonata."

"A delight. And the Brahms?"

"The D Minor."

She raised an eyebrow. "The key of repressed passion."

"Anna . . ."

"I performed the D Minor that night in Venice. I believe it goes something like this." She closed her eyes and played the haunting opening theme from the sonata's second movement. "It sounds better on the Guarneri, don't you think?"

"If you say so."

Anna lowered the violin. "Is that all you need from me? Two little sonatas?"

"You seem disappointed."

"To be honest, I was hoping for something a bit more . . ."

"What?"

"Adventurous."

"Good," said Gabriel. "Because there's one more thing."

32

LONDON–ZURICH

I T WAS AMELIA MARCH OF *ARTnews* who got wind of it first. Her source was the fashion model turned art dealer Olivia Watson, who for reasons never made clear had been granted a private viewing. But where on earth had he found it? Even Olivia, with all her obvious physical endowments, hadn't been able to coax it out of him. Nor had she been able to ascertain the name of the art historian who had supplied the updated attribution. Evidently, it was unassailable. Stone tablets on Mount Sinai. Word of God.

Amelia knew better than to ring him directly; like most London art dealers, he was an unusually skilled spinner of half-truths and outright lies. Instead, she made quiet inquiries among his equally disreputable circle of cohorts, collaborators, and occasional competitors. Roddy Hutchinson, his closest friend, swore total ignorance, as did Jeremy Crabbe, Simon Mendenhall, and Nicky Lovegrove. Julian Isherwood suggested Amelia speak to his new partner, Sarah Bancroft, who was herself the source of endless rumors. Amelia left a message on her voice mail and dropped her a line on email as well. Neither received a reply.

Which left Amelia no choice but to approach the dealer directly, always a risky endeavor when one was a female. Like the enigmatic Sarah Bancroft, he ignored her phone calls, and refused to answer his bell when she popped round to his gallery in Bury Street. In the window was a small sign that read NO COMMENT.

It was, thought Amelia, the perfect vignette with which to lead her story, which she commenced writing later that afternoon. She was still laboring over the first draft when her editor forwarded her a link to an article that had just appeared in the *Neue Züricher Zeitung*. It seemed the London art dealer Oliver Dimbleby had sold a previously misattributed painting by Artemisia Gentileschi—*The Lute Player*, oil on canvas, 152 by 134 centimeters—to the Swiss financier and political activist Martin Landesmann. The saintly Landesmann had generously agreed to donate the painting to the Kunsthaus in Zurich, where it would go on display after an extensive restoration. The museum planned to unveil it at a gala reception, at which the internationally renowned Swiss violinist Anna Rolfe would perform for the first time since the start of the pandemic. The sponsor of the event was Landesmann's newly formed One World Global Alliance for Democracy. Regrettably, the general public was not invited.

Having been thoroughly beaten to the punch, Amelia penned

a flaccid but thoughtful piece that cast Artemisia—a gifted Baroque painter whose work had long been overshadowed by the rape she suffered at the hands of Agostino Tassi—as a feminist icon. Elsewhere in the British art press, there was disappointment that a major London art dealer had facilitated the transfer of one of Artemisia's paintings to Switzerland, of all places. The one bright spot, grumbled the *Guardian*, was that *The Lute Player* would hang in a museum for all to see rather than on yet another rich man's wall.

For its part, the Kunsthaus reveled in its good fortune. Owing to the lingering threat of the pandemic, only two hundred and fifty guests would be invited to the gala. Not surprisingly, the competition for tickets was fierce. Anyone who was anyone— the celebrated and the scorned, the offensively rich and the merely wealthy, the world and its mistress—fought tooth and nail to attend. Martin was besieged with calls from friends, associates, and even a few blood enemies. Each was instructed to dial a number that rang in the Erlenbach safe house, where Gabriel and Eli Lavon delighted in deciding their fate. It was Christopher, posing as an event coordinator from the Global Alliance for Democracy, who delivered the verdicts. Among those who were denied an invitation were Karl Zimmer, head of RhineBank's Zurich office, and two senior members of the firm's ruling Council of Ten.

After three days, only twenty tickets remained. Gabriel held two in reserve for Arkady Akimov and his wife, Oksana. Unfortunately, they showed no interest in attending.

"Maybe he has a scheduling conflict," suggested Eli Lavon.

"Like what?"

"Perhaps he's planning to subvert a democracy that night.

Or maybe Vladimir Vladimirovich has asked him to come to Moscow to review his investment portfolio."

"Or maybe he's somehow unaware of the fact that the social event of the season will be taking place at the Kunsthaus in Zurich and he hasn't received an invitation."

"And he's not going to receive one," said Lavon gravely. "Not unless he sits up on his hind legs and begs for one."

"What if he doesn't?"

"Then we will have nothing to show for our efforts other than a painting by Artemisia Gentileschi and a new pro-democracy NGO. But under no circumstances are you to invite Arkady Akimov to attend that reception. It goes against all our operational orthodoxy." Lavon glanced at Christopher. "We get on the streetcar *before* the target, not after. And we always, *always*, wait for the target to make the first move."

Gabriel conceded the point. But when another three days passed with no contact, he was beside himself with worry. It was Yuval Gershon, director of Unit 8200, who finally put his mind to rest. The Unit had just intercepted a phone call from a Ludmilla Sorova of NevaNeft to the Global Alliance for Democracy. She rang the number in the safe house five minutes later. After listening to her request, Christopher placed the call on hold and addressed Gabriel.

"Oksana Akimova and her husband would be honored to attend the reception at the Kunsthaus."

"If you had an ounce of self-respect," said Lavon, "you'd tell her it's too late."

Gabriel hesitated, then nodded slowly.

Christopher brought the receiver to his ear and took the call off hold. "I'm so sorry, Ms. Sorova, but I'm afraid there are no more tickets available. I only wish you'd reached out to us sooner." After a silence, he said, "Yes, a donation to the Global Alliance for Democracy would certainly influence our thinking. What sort of contribution did Mr. Akimov have in mind?"

THE SUM, ARRIVED AT AFTER several offers and counteroffers, was an astonishing twenty million Swiss francs, slightly more than Martin had paid for *The Lute Player*. He had pledged to deliver the painting to the Kunsthaus, restored to its original glory, in time for the gala. The museum's chief conservator, the esteemed Ludwig Schenker, was skeptical. Having reviewed high-resolution photographs of the canvas, he reckoned a proper restoration would take six months, if not longer. A specialist in Italian Baroque art, he had offered to serve as a consultant. Martin had politely demurred. The restorer he had in mind for the project didn't play nicely with others.

"He's good, your man?" inquired Dr. Schenker.

"I'm told he's one of the very best."

"Do I know his work?"

"Undoubtedly."

"Might I at least share with him some of my observations?"

"No," said Martin. "You might not."

The high-resolution photographs had revealed only a portion of the damage. They did not accurately represent, for example, the shocking degree to which the four-hundred-year-old canvas had sagged with age. Gabriel concluded he had no choice but to reline the painting, a delicate undertaking that involved adhering a swath of new linen to the back of the original canvas and then reattaching it to a stretcher. When the procedure was complete, he commenced the most tedious portion of the restoration, the removal of the old varnish and surface grime using cotton wool swabs soaked with a carefully calibrated mixture of acetone, methyl proxitol, and mineral spirits. Each swab could clean about a square inch of the painting before it became too soiled to use. At night, when he was not dreaming of blood and fire, he was removing yellowed varnish from a canvas the size of the Piazza San Marco.

He worked in the garden room of the safe house, with the windows open to vent the dangerous fumes of his solvent. For the most part, he was spared unwanted observation of his efforts; Christopher and Eli Lavon both knew better than to watch him while he worked. An Office courier brought his brushes and pigments from Narkiss Street, along with his old paint-smudged portable CD player and a collection of his favorite opera and classical music recordings. The rest of his supplies, including his chemicals and a pair of powerful halogen lamps, he acquired locally.

Twice each week, Isabel traveled to the safe house from Geneva for a crash course in the basics of tradecraft. Having successfully penetrated the defenses of the Russian Laundromat, she was a natural deceiver. All she required was a bit of polish. Christopher and Eli Lavon served as her instructors, and the techniques they instilled in her were borrowed from both the British and Israeli traditions. Her education did not suffer as a result. Among the international brotherhood of intelligence officers, MI6 and the Office were universally regarded as the finest handlers of human assets in the business.

Gabriel remained a distant observer of Isabel's training, for he had a restoration to finish and a service to run. He shuttled regularly between Zurich and Tel Aviv, and twice popped in to London to confer with Graham Seymour. With just ten days remaining until the gala, *The Lute Player* was nowhere near ready for her reemergence into public view. Several large swaths required retouching, including the young musician's amber-colored garment and her face, which Artemisia had depicted exquisitely in semi-profile, with an expression both serene and concentrated. There was also a trace of foreboding, thought Gabriel, perhaps an allusion to the danger that awaited the young girl just beyond the safety of her music room.

Having never restored a painting by Artemisia, Gabriel would have preferred to work with painstaking slowness. His looming deadline, however, would not allow it. It was no matter; trained in the Italian method of restoration, he was when necessary the swiftest of painters. The operas of Puccini, especially *La Bohème*, were his usual background music. The restoration of *The Lute Player*, however, was set mainly to a pair of violin sonatas—one by Beethoven, the other by Brahms—and a haunting piece by Sergei Rachmaninoff, the favorite composer of the oil trader and oligarch Arkady Akimov.

On the second Wednesday evening of October, Isabel came to the safe house for a final session with Christopher and Eli Lavon. This time she was joined by a woman she idolized, the renowned Swiss violinist Anna Rolfe. Their rehearsal involved no music, only choreography—the seemingly serendipitous and effortless conveyance of Arkady Akimov into the hands of Martin Landesmann. Afterward, Anna stole into the garden room to watch Gabriel work, knowing full well it drove him to distraction.

He loaded his brush and placed it against the cheek of the lute player. "What do you suppose she's thinking?"

"The girl in the painting?"

"The girl in the next room."

"She's probably wondering how it is we know one another." Anna frowned. "Did my practicing really annoy you?"

"Never."

"Good. Because I never tired of watching you work."

"Trust me, it gets old."

"Like me." She probed at the skin along her jawline. "I don't suppose you could do a little work on me before the recital on Saturday night."

"I'm afraid I don't have a minute to spare."

"Will you finish it in time?"

"That depends on how many more questions you intend to ask me."

"Actually, I have only one more."

"You want to know what happened to the Englishman who was hired to kill us that night in Venice."

"Yes."

"He's talking to the girl in the next room," said Gabriel.

"The dishy one with the lovely suntan?" Anna sighed. "Must you make a joke about everything?"

33

KUNSTHAUS, ZURICH

To reach the entrance of the Kunsthaus museum, repository of Switzerland's largest and most important collection of paintings and other objets d'art dating to the thirteenth century, one did not traverse a historic square or scale monumental steps of stone. One merely crossed a small esplanade off the Heimplatz, which at eight o'clock on Saturday evening was ablaze with television lights and the logo of the One World Global Alliance for Democracy. The museum's director had implored attendees of the gala to utilize public transportation so as to reduce the event's carbon footprint. With the exception of four young women who alighted from a Number 5 streetcar, none complied. Most hovered for a moment outside the museum's portico to allow their photographs to be taken by the press. And a few, including the CEO of Credit Suisse, consented to brief interviews. Martin held forth for nearly ten minutes while Monique dazzled in a gown by Dior Haute Couture. Not surprisingly, it was the dress, with its dramatic neckline, that was soon trending on social media.

Christopher Keller, in a dark suit and tie, clipboard in hand, observed the parade of money and temporary beauty from his post in the lobby. The laminated badge affixed to his lapel identified him as Nicolas Carnot and his place of employment as Global Vision Investments. It was Monsieur Carnot, at half past four that afternoon, much later than the museum's director would have preferred, who had delivered *The Lute Player* to its new home. At present, the painting was under armed guard in a room near the event hall. In an adjacent room, also under armed guard, was Anna Rolfe. Monsieur Carnot had left strict instructions with the museum's staff that under no circumstances—save *perhaps* the outbreak of nuclear war—was she to be disturbed before the performance.

Christopher's phone pulsed with an incoming message. It concerned the whereabouts of the evening's secret guest of honor, the oil trader and oligarch Arkady Akimov. Having traveled to Zurich from his home on Lake Geneva by executive helicopter, Mr. Akimov was now approaching the Kunsthaus in a fleet of hired limousines. Through his representative, a certain Ludmilla Sorova, he had requested two additional tickets to the gala for his security detail. His request had been denied, and it had been made clear to Mr. Akimov that bodyguards were not considered appropriate to the occasion.

Another prosperous-looking couple entered the lobby—the Basel-based pharmaceutical magnate Gerhard Müller and his underfed wife, Ursula. Christopher placed a proper schoolboy tick mark next to their names on his list and, looking up again, spotted a procession of three matching Mercedes S-Class sedans drawing up outside in the Heimplatz. From the first and third cars emerged a sextet of bodyguards. All veterans of elite *spetsnaz* units, all with blood on their hands. And all armed, thought Christopher, who was not. He had only his clipboard and his pen and a laminated badge that identified him as Nicolas Carnot, a name he had dredged up from his complicated past.

He had his ironic half smile, too, which he donned like body armor as Arkady Akimov and his wife, Oksana, alighted from the second Mercedes. The phalanx of bodyguards escorted them across the esplanade to the entrance of the museum. Much to Christopher's relief, they made no attempt to follow them into the lobby.

There he was able to regard them at his leisure. Arkady Akimov, the sickly boy from Baskov Lane, was now a trim, linear figure of upright bearing and imperious demeanor, with thinning silver hair combed carefully over his broad Russian pate, and smooth skin stretched tightly over his square Russian cheekbones. The mouth was small and unsmiling, the eyes were hooded and observant. They were the eyes, thought Christopher, of a Moscow Center–trained hood. They swept over him without pause before settling approvingly on Oksana. In Christopher's professional estimation, Arkady regarded his beautiful young wife as little more than a possession. Heaven help her if she ever crossed him. He would kill her and find another.

The Arkady Akimovs followed the Gerhard Müllers toward the event hall along a designated path that took them past some of the museum's most popular attractions, including works by

Bonnard, Gauguin, Monet, and Van Gogh. Christopher, armed with his clipboard and badge, headed to the venue by a direct route. White-jacketed waiters were serving champagne and hors d'oeuvres to the early arrivals in the foyer. Inside the hall, neat ranks of auditorium chairs were arrayed before a rectangular raised platform, upon which stood a concert grand piano and a baize-covered display pedestal. Technicians from the museum's production department were making a final adjustment to the microphones and the lighting.

Christopher slipped through a doorway at the left side of the stage and instantly heard the muted sound of Anna Rolfe's violin, a simple D-minor scale played over two octaves. The security guard posted outside her door was making small talk with the unflappable Nadine Rosenberg, Anna's longtime accompanist. Isabel was in a room across the hall. Gowned, her hair professionally styled, she was contemplating her reflection in the lighted mirror over her dressing table. Her 1790 William Forster II cello was propped on a stand in the corner.

"How do I look?" she asked.

"Remarkably calm for someone who's about to share a billing with Anna Rolfe."

"Trust me, it's all an act."

"Any last questions?"

"What happens if he doesn't approach me after the performance?"

"I suppose you'll have to improvise."

She lifted the cello from its stand and played the melody of "Someday My Prince Will Come." Christopher hummed the tune as he headed through the event hall to the foyer. The crowd of invited dignitaries had broken into opposing camps, one surrounding Martin Landesmann, the other Arkady Aki-mov. Tray-bearing waiters shuttled between the two blocs, but otherwise a cold peace prevailed. It was, thought Christopher, an altogether perfect start to the evening.

IN THE ERLENBACH SAFE HOUSE, Gabriel and Eli Lavon were observing the same scene on an open laptop computer. The video feed arrived to them courtesy of Unit 8200, which had seized control of the museum's security system and internal audiovisual network—all with the knowledge and tacit approval of the Swiss intelligence service.

Shortly before eight p.m., the doors of the event hall were opened from within, and a ceremonial bell was rung. Because the invited guests were all terribly rich and unused to follow-ing instructions, they ignored it. Indeed, by the time they were all settled in their assigned seats, Gabriel's carefully planned program was already running twenty minutes behind schedule. Martin and Monique, the event's sponsors and hosts, occupied two chairs in the center of the first row. Arkady and Oksana Akimov, having donated twenty million Swiss francs to the One World Global Alliance for Democracy, had also been granted preferential seating. Martin, as instructed, acted as though the Russian and his wife were invisible.

At last, the museum's director stepped onto the stage and spoke at length regarding the importance of art and culture in an age of conflict and uncertainty. His remarks were only slightly less sedative than those delivered by the chief conser-vator Ludwig Schenker on the subject of Artemisia Gentileschi and the unlikely rediscovery of *The Lute Player*, little of which bore any resemblance to the truth. Martin was for once merci-fully taciturn. At his command, two curators placed the paint-ing atop the pedestal, and Monique and the director removed the white veil with a flourish. In the event hall of the Kunst-haus, the applause was rapturous. In the Erlenbach safe house, it was brief but genuine nonetheless.

Gabriel and Eli Lavon watched as *The Lute Player* was con-veyed from the stage and Martin introduced the evening's fea-tured entertainment. The mere mention of her name brought the audience to its feet, including the oil trader and oligarch Arkady Akimov. Her acknowledgment of the adulation was perfunctory, automatic. Like Gabriel, she possessed the ability to block out all distraction, to enclose herself in an impene-trable cocoon of silence, to transport herself to another time and place. For the moment, at least, the two hundred and fifty invited guests did not exist.

There was only her accompanist and her beloved Guarneri. Her fiddle, as she liked to call it. Her graceful lady. She placed the instrument against her neck and laid the bow upon the A string. The silence seemed to last an eternity. Too anxious to watch, Gabriel closed his eyes. A villa by the sea. The sienna light of sunset. The liquid music of a violin.

THE SONATAS WERE BOTH FOUR movements in structure and nearly identical in duration—twenty minutes for the Brahms, twenty-two for the Beethoven. Isabel watched the final mo-ments of Anna's performance from the open doorway next to the stage. Anna was ablaze, the audience spellbound. And to think Isabel would soon take her place. Surely, she thought suddenly, it was not possible. She was experiencing one of her frequent anxiety dreams, that was all. Or perhaps there had been an oversight of some sort, a scheduling error. It was Alisa Weilerstein who would perform next. Not Isabel Brenner, a former compliance officer from the world's dirtiest bank who had once earned a third prize at the ARD International Music Competition.

Lost in thought, she gave an involuntary start when the event hall erupted with thunderous applause. Martin Landesmann was the first to rise, followed instantly by a silver-haired man a few meters to his right. Isabel, try as she might, could not seem to recall his name. He was no one, a nothing man.

Microphone in hand, Anna requested silence, and the two hundred and fifty luminaries arrayed before her obeyed. She thanked the audience for their support of the museum and the cause of democracy, and for giving her an opportunity to play in public again after so long an absence. Wealthy and privileged, she had managed to hide from the lethal virus. But nearly two million people worldwide—the aged, the sick, the indigent, those who were crammed into substandard housing or who toiled for hourly wages in essential industries—had not been so fortunate. She asked the audience to keep the dead in their hearts and to remember those who lacked the basic resources most of them took for granted.

"The pandemic," she continued, "is taking a terrible toll on the performing arts, especially classical music. My career will resume when the concert halls finally reopen. At least I hope so," she added modestly. "But unfortunately, many talented young musicians will have no choice but to start over. With that in mind, I would like to introduce you to a dear friend of mine who will perform a final piece for us this evening, a lovely composition by Sergei Rachmaninoff called 'Vocalise.'"

Isabel heard her name reverberate through the hall, and somehow her legs managed to carry her to the stage. The audience disappeared the instant she began to play. Even so, she could feel the weight of his steady gaze upon her. Try as she might, she could not seem to recall his name. He was no one. He was a nothing man.

34

KUNSTHAUS, ZURICH

IT HAD BEEN ANNA ROLFE's intention to make only a brief final appearance on the stage, but the audience would not permit her to leave. Admittedly, much of the adulation was directed toward Isabel. Her performance of Rachmaninoff's haunting six-minute composition had been incendiary.

At last, Anna took Isabel's hand, and together they departed the event hall. It seemed a sudden onset of headache—it was common knowledge Anna suffered from crippling migraines—would not allow her to mingle with the invited guests at the post-recital reception as planned. Dazzling young Isabel had consented to take her place. For reasons having to do with operational security, Gabriel had not told Anna all the reasons he had concocted tonight's elaborate charade. She knew only that it had something to do with the Slavic-looking man who had been feeding on Isabel with his eyes from his place in the front row.

Anna bade farewell to Isabel with stilted formality in the corridor, and they retreated to their separate green rooms. A museum security guard stood watch outside Anna's. Her violin case lay on the dressing table, next to her packet of Gitanes. She lit one in violation of the museum's strict no-smoking regulations and instantly thought of Gabriel, brush in hand, shaking his head at her with reproach.

I suppose we're lucky it ended before someone got hurt . . .

The sound of feminine footfalls in the corridor intruded on Anna's thoughts. It was Isabel leaving her dressing room for her star turn at the reception. Anna was relieved that her attendance was not required, as she found nothing quite so terrifying as a room filled with strangers. She much preferred the company of her Guarneri.

She pressed her lips gently to the scroll. "Time for bed, graceful lady."

She dropped the Gitane into a half-drunk bottle of Eptinger and opened the violin case. Nestled among her things—a spare bow, extra strings, rosin, mutes, peg compound, cleaning cloths, nail clippers, emery boards, a lock of her mother's hair—was an envelope with her name written in longhand across the front. It had not been there when she went onstage, and she had left strict instructions with the security guard not to allow anyone to enter her room in her absence. So, too, had the dishy Englishman with the lovely suntan. He had done so in quite possibly the least convincing French accent Anna had ever heard.

She hesitated a moment, then reached for the envelope. It was of high quality, as was the bordered correspondence card inside.

Anna recognized the handwriting.

Rising, she wrenched open the door and rushed into the corridor. The security guard looked at her as though she were a madwoman. Obviously, her reputation preceded her.

"I thought I told you not to let anyone in my room while I was onstage."

"I didn't, Frau Rolfe."

She waved the envelope in his face. "Then how on earth did this get in my violin case?"

"It must have been Monsieur Carnot."

"Who?"

"The Frenchman who delivered the painting to the museum this afternoon."

"Where is he now?"

"He's right here," came a distant reply.

Anna wheeled round. He was standing next to the half-lit stage, an ironic half-smile on his face.

"You?"

He raised a forefinger to his lips, then disappeared from Anna's view.

"Bastard," she whispered.

THE LUTE PLAYER, OIL ON canvas, 152 by 134 centimeters, formerly assigned to the circle of Orazio Gentileschi, now firmly attributed to Orazio's daughter Artemisia and restored to its original glory by Gabriel Allon, stood atop a pedestal in the center of the foyer, flanked by a pair of docile-looking museum guards. The invited dignitaries orbited the painting reverently, like pilgrims around the Kaaba at Mecca. The bare floors and walls echoed with the sound of their incantations.

Isabel, as yet unnoticed, reflected upon the set of circumstances, the chain of misadventure and providence, that had brought her to the gala. The story she told herself contained several glaring omissions but otherwise adhered to a few confirmable facts. A child prodigy, she had won an important prize at the age of seventeen but had decided to attend a proper university rather than conservatory. After completing her graduate degree at the prestigious London School of Economics, she had worked for RhineBank, first in London, then Zurich. Having left the firm under circumstances she was not at liberty to discuss—hardly uncommon where employees of RhineBank were concerned—she now worked for Martin Landesmann at Global Vision Investments of Geneva.

And why is that man looking at me like that?

The unsmiling gray-haired man with the raven-haired Slavic centerfold on his arm. Avoid at all costs, Isabel told herself.

She plucked a glass of champagne from a passing tray. The effervescence carried the alcohol from her lips to her bloodstream with startling speed. She heard someone call her name and, turning, was confronted by a woman of late middle age whose most recent appointment with her plastic surgeon had left her with an expression of sheer terror.

"The piece you performed was by Tchaikovsky?" she asked.

"Rachmaninoff."

"It's quite beautiful."

"I've always thought so."

"Will Anna be joining us? I'm so looking forward to meeting her."

Isabel explained that Anna had taken ill.

"It's always something, isn't it?"

"I beg your pardon?"

"She's cursed, the poor thing. You know about her mother, of course. Awful."

The woman was carried away, as if by a gust of wind, and another took her place. It was Ursula Müller, the emaciated wife of Gerhard Müller, a client of RhineBank.

"You play like an angel! You look like one, too."

Herr Müller clearly agreed. So did the gray-haired man with the centerfold on his arm. They were advancing on Isabel through the crowd. She allowed herself to be pulled in the opposite direction and was passed like a serving dish from one shimmering, bejeweled couple to the next.

"Breathtaking!" exclaimed one.

"I'm so glad you liked it."

"A triumph!" declared another.

"You're too kind."

"Tell us your name again."

"Isabel."

"Isabel what?"

"Brenner."

"Where's Anna?"

"Unwell, I'm afraid. You'll have to make do with me."

"When is your next performance?"

Soon, she thought.

She had run out of places to hide. She surrendered her glass to a waitress—the champagne was doing her no good—and started toward the painting, but the gray-haired man and his child bride blocked her path. He wore on his broad Slavic face an approximation of a smile. He addressed Isabel in perfect German, with the accent of an Ostländer.

"With the possible exception of Rostropovich, I have never heard 'Vocalise' performed any better."

"Come now," replied Isabel.

"It's the truth. But why Rachmaninoff?"

"Why *not* Rachmaninoff?"

"Is his cello sonata part of your repertoire?"

"God, yes."

"Mine as well."

"You're a cellist?"

"A pianist." He smiled. "You're not Swiss."

"German. But I live here in Switzerland."

"In Zurich?" he probed.

"I used to. But I moved to Geneva not long ago."

"My office is in the Place du Port."

"Mine is across the bridge on the Quai de Mont-Blanc."

He frowned, confused. "You're not a professional musician?"

"I'm a project analyst for a Swiss private equity firm. A number cruncher."

He was incredulous. "How can that be?"

"Number crunchers make much more money than musicians."

"Which firm do you work for?"

She pointed toward Martin Landesmann. "The one owned by the man standing right over there."

"Saint Martin?"

"He hates when people call him that."

"So I've heard."

"Do you know him?"

"Only by reputation. For some reason, he seems to be ignoring me tonight. Which is odd, considering the fact I donated twenty million Swiss francs to his pro-democracy organization to attend tonight's performance."

Isabel made a show of thought. "Are you—"

"Arkady Akimov." He glanced at the girl. "And this is my wife, Oksana."

"I'm sure Martin would be honored to meet you."

"Would you mind?"

Isabel smiled. "Not at all."

Two MUSEUM SECURITY CAMERAS PEERED into the corner of the foyer where Martin had established his court—one from his right, the other directly overhead. With the first camera, Gabriel and Eli Lavon watched as Isabel Brenner, formerly of RhineBank-Zurich, lately of Global Vision Investments in Geneva, threaded her way through the dense crowd. Several times she was obliged to pause to accept another compliment. None of her well-wishers paid any heed to the silver-haired Russian following in her wake—the oil trader and oligarch Arkady Akimov, childhood friend of Russia's kleptocratic authoritarian leader, estimated net worth $33.8 billion, according to the most recent estimate by *Forbes* magazine. For now, at least, he was no one. A nothing man.

When at last Isabel arrived at her destination, Gabriel switched to the second camera, which offered a satellite view of the stage upon which the evening's final performance would take place. Once again there was a delay, as the acolytes and admirers gathered around Martin welcomed Isabel elatedly to their midst. Eventually she placed a hand on Martin's arm, a deliberately intimate gesture the oil trader and oligarch was sure to notice. The phone in the breast pocket of Martin's tuxedo, handmade by Senszio of Geneva, provided audio coverage.

"I'm so sorry to interrupt, Martin. But I'd like to introduce you to someone I just met . . ."

There were no handshakes, only guarded nods of greeting, one billionaire to another. Their conversation was cordial in tone but confrontational in content. At the midway point, the oil trader and oligarch offered Martin a business card, which prompted a final tense exchange. Then the oil trader and oligarch murmured something directly into Martin's ear and, taking his wife by the hand, withdrew.

The party resumed as though nothing untoward had occurred. But ten kilometers to the south, in a safe house on the shores of Lake Zurich, Eli Lavon's applause was spontaneous and sustained. Gabriel reset the time code on the recording of the conversation and clicked the PLAY icon.

"Thank you for the generous contribution to the Global Alliance, Arkady. I'm planning to use it to finance our efforts in Russia."

"Save your money, Martin. As for the twenty million, it was a small price to pay for the privilege of attending your little soiree tonight."

"Since when is twenty million a small price?"

"There's much more where that came from, if you're interested."

"What did you have in mind?"

"Are you free next week?"

"Next week is bad, but I might have a minute or two to spare the week after."

"I'm a busy man, Martin."

"That makes two of us."

"Making the world safe for democracy?"

"Someone has to do it."

"You should stick to climate change. How do I reach you?"

"You call the main number at GVI like everyone else."

"I have a better idea. Why don't you call me instead?"

"What's that in your hand, Arkady?"

"A business card. They're all the rage."

"If you'd done your homework, you would know I never accept them. Call Isabel. She'll set something up."

"She was quite extraordinary tonight."

"You should see her with a spreadsheet."

"Where did you find her?"

"Don't even think about it, Arkady. She's mine."

It was at that instant the oil trader and oligarch leaned forward and spoke directly into Martin's ear. The din of the reception drowned out the remark, but Martin's expression suggested it was an insult. Gabriel reset the recording, activated a filter that reduced much of the background noise, and clicked PLAY. This time the final words of the oil trader and oligarch were clearly audible.

"Lucky you."

35

QUAI DU MONT-BLANC, GENEVA

L UDMILLA SOROVA RANG ISABEL AT ten o'clock on Monday
morning. Isabel waited until Thursday before returning the
call. Her tone was businesslike and brisk, a woman whose plate
was overflowing. Ludmilla's was petulant—clearly, she had
been expecting to hear from Isabel sooner. Nevertheless, she
attempted to engage her in preliminary small talk regarding
her performance at the Kunsthaus. Evidently, Mr. Akimov had
enjoyed it immensely.

Isabel quickly diverted the flow of the conversation back to
the original reason for her call, which was Mr. Akimov's request for a meeting with Martin Landesmann. He had two
small windows in his schedule the following week—Tuesday
at three and Wednesday at five fifteen—but otherwise he was
booked solid with meetings and video conference calls for his

newest initiative, the Global Alliance for Democracy. Ludmilla said she would consult with Mr. Akimov and get back to Isabel by the end of the day. Isabel advised her not to dawdle, as Mr. Landesmann's time was limited.

She terminated the call and then memorialized the date, time, and topic in her leather-bound GVI logbook. Looking up again, she noticed a text message waiting on her mobile phone.

Well played.

She deleted the message and, rising, followed her new colleagues into GVI's luminous conference room. It was a surprisingly small workforce—twelve overeducated analysts of requisite gender and ethnic diversity, all young and attractive and committed, and all convinced that Martin was indeed the patron saint of corporate responsibility and environmental justice he claimed to be.

They gathered twice each day. The morning meeting was devoted to proposed or pending investments and acquisitions; afternoons, to over-the-horizon projects. Or, as Martin put it grandly, "the future as we would like it to be." The discussions were deliberately undisciplined in nature and unfailingly courteous in tone. There were none of the blood feuds and office pissing matches that were typical of meetings at RhineBank, especially in the London office. Martin, in his open-necked dress shirt and bespoke sport jacket, shimmered with intelligence and vision. Rarely did he utter a sentence that did not contain the word *sustainable* or *alternative*. It was his intention to unleash the post-pandemic economy of tomorrow—a green, carbon-neutral economy that met the needs of workers and consumers alike and spared the planet further damage. Even Isabel could not help but be moved by his performance.

He asked her to remain behind as the others filed out of the room. "How was your phone call?" he asked.

"If I had to guess, you'll be meeting with Arkady on Tuesday afternoon at three."

Smiling, Isabel returned to her office to find the red message light on her phone flashing like a channel marker. It was a breathless Ludmilla Sorova calling to say that Mr. Akimov was free to meet with Mr. Landesmann on both Tuesday and Wednesday, with Tuesday being his preference. She was hoping to hear from Isabel before the day was out, as Mr. Akimov's time was limited as well.

"I wonder why." Isabel deleted the message. Then, to no one in particular, she asked, "What do you think?"

A few seconds later her mobile phone shivered with an incoming message.

Nothing that can't wait until morning.

"My thought exactly."

Isabel placed a few papers in her shoulder bag, pulled on a lightweight quilted coat, and headed downstairs. Outside, the highest peaks of the Mont Blanc massif blushed in the last tawny light of sunset, but the neon Rolex and Hermes signs burned atop the elegant buildings lining the South Bank of the Rhône. In the Place du Port, she passed the ugly modern office building where, on the uppermost floor, Ludmilla Sorova eagerly awaited her call. The next square was the trapezoidal Place de Longemalle. The Englishman, disreputably attired in denim and leather, was drinking a Kronenbourg at a table outside the Hôtel de la Cigogne. The label of the bottle was pointed directly toward Isabel, which meant she was not being followed.

To reach the Old Town she first had to cross the rue du Purgatoire. Her apartment building overlooked the shops and cafés of the Place du Bourg-de-Four. The little Israeli who reminded Isabel of a rare book dealer was seated cross-legged on the cobbles next to the ancient wellhead. Dressed in the soiled clothing of a vagrant, he was clutching a tattered sign requesting food and money from passersby. At present, the sign was right side up, meaning he shared the opinion of the Englishman that Isabel was not being followed.

Upstairs in her apartment, she opened the windows and shutters to the chill autumn air and poured herself a glass of wine from an open bottle of Chasselas. Her cello beckoned. She removed it from its case, placed a mute upon its bridge, and laid her bow upon the strings. Bach's Cello Suite in G Major. All six movements. No sheet music. Not a single mistake. Afterward, the habitués of the square beneath her window demanded an encore, none with more enthusiasm than the little vagrant sitting on the cobbles at the base of the wellhead.

ISABEL RANG LUDMILLA SOROVA THE following morning and greenlit Tuesday at three. She then laid down a number of conditions for the encounter, none of which were negotiable, as she was pressed for time. The duration of the meeting, she explained, would be forty-five minutes, not a minute more. Mr. Akimov was to come alone, with no associates, attorneys, or assorted hangers-on.

"And no security detail, please. Global Vision Investments isn't that sort of place."

For the next four days, Isabel was entirely unreachable, at least where Ludmilla Sorova was concerned. Emails went unreturned, phone calls unanswered—including the urgent call Ludmilla placed at 2:50 p.m. on Tuesday regarding Mr. Akimov's imminent arrival at GVI headquarters. It was unnecessary, for Isabel, from her office window, could see his appalling motorcade barreling toward her over the Pont du Mont-Blanc.

By the time she reached the lobby, he was bounding from the back of his limousine. Chased by a band of bodyguards, he marched across the pavement and came whirling through the revolving door. The pose he struck was that of a victorious general come to dictate terms of surrender. His expression softened when he spotted Isabel standing next to the security desk.

"Isabel," he called out. "So wonderful to see you again."

Hands clasped behind her back, she nodded formally. "Good afternoon, Mr. Akimov."

"I insist you call me Arkady."

"I'll do my best." She checked the time on her phone, then gestured toward the elevators. "This way, Mr. Akimov. And if you wouldn't mind, please instruct your security detail to remain here in the lobby or in their vehicles."

"Surely you have a waiting room upstairs."

"As I explained to your assistant, Martin finds them disruptive."

Arkady muttered a few words to the bodyguards in Russian and followed Isabel into a waiting elevator carriage. She pushed the call button for the ninth floor and stared straight ahead as the doors closed, a leather folio case clutched defensively to her breasts. Arkady tugged at his French cuff. His expensive cologne hung between them like tear gas.

"You mentioned the other night that you used to live in Zurich."

"Yes," replied Isabel vaguely.

"What sort of work did you do there?"

"Banking. Like everyone else."

"Why did you leave this bank of yours and come to Geneva?"

I left because of you, she thought. Then she said, "I was given the sack, if you must know."

Arkady regarded her reflection in the elevator doors. "What was your crime?"

"They caught me with my hand in the till."

"How much did you steal?"

She met his reflected gaze and smiled. "Millions."

"Were you able to keep any of it?"

"Not a centime. In fact, I was living on the streets until Martin came along. He cleaned me up and gave me a job."

"Perhaps he is a saint, after all."

When the doors opened, Arkady insisted Isabel depart the carriage first. The hallway along which she led him was hung with photographs of Martin engaged in philanthropic pursuits in the developing world. Arkady offered no commentary on the shrine to Martin's good works. In fact, Isabel had a nagging suspicion he was at that moment assessing the quality of her ass.

She paused at the conference room door and held out a hand. "This way, Mr. Akimov."

He brushed past her without a word. Martin appeared distracted by something he was reading on his mobile phone. A single chair stood on each side of the long wooden table, upon which was arrayed an assortment of mineral water. The carefully staged setting seemed more suited to high-stakes East-West summitry than a criminal conspiracy. All that was missing, thought Isabel, was the obligatory handshake for the press photographers.

Instead, the two men exchanged a cheerless, unspoken greeting across the divide of the table. Martin scored the first goal of the contest owing to the fact he was tieless and his opponent was hopelessly overdressed. In an attempt to even the score, Arkady dropped into his chair without first receiving an invitation to sit. Martin, in a shrewd display of boardroom jujitsu, remained on his feet, thus retaining control of the high ground.

He looked at Isabel and smiled. "That will be all for now, Isabel. Thank you."

"Of course, Martin."

Isabel went out, closing the door behind her, and returned to her office. The digital clock on her desk read 3:04 p.m. Forty-one minutes, she thought. And not a minute more.

36

QUAI DU MONT-BLANC, GENEVA

NOT SURPRISINGLY, MARTIN HAD RESISTED the installation of hidden cameras and microphones in the conference room of Global Vision Investments. He acquiesced only after receiving a solemn pledge from Gabriel that the devices—*all* of them—would be removed at the conclusion of the operation. There were four cameras in all, and six high-resolution microphones. The encrypted feed bounced from a receiver in the telecom closet to the team's new safe house in diplomatic Champel. They hadn't bothered with much of a cover story to explain their presence. The local security service was a silent partner in their endeavor.

They received their first update at half past two, when Eli Lavon's watchers in the Place du Port reported the arrival of a motorcade—a Mercedes-Maybach sedan and two Range Rovers—at the NevaNeft headquarters. Arkady Akimov stepped from the building's opaque doorway fifteen minutes later, and at 2:55 p.m. he was listening to Isabel explaining that his security detail was not welcome in the carbon-neutral confines of Global Vision Investments. The transmission from her phone died when she entered the lift, and when the audio feed resumed, she was standing in the door of the conference room. Martin and Arkady were glaring at one another over the table like prizefighters in the center of a ring.

"That will be all for now, Isabel. Thank you."

"Of course, Martin."

Isabel withdrew, leaving the two billionaires alone in the conference room. At length, Martin opened one of the bottles of mineral water and slowly poured two glasses.

"Do you think he'll drink any of it?" asked Eli Lavon.

"Arkady Akimov?" Gabriel shook his head. "Not if it was the last drop of water on earth."

"If you would prefer," said Martin, "I have some without gas."

"I'm not thirsty, thank you."

"You don't drink water?"

"Not unless it's my water."

"What are you so afraid of?"

"Capitalism in Russia is a contact sport."

"This is Geneva, Arkady. Not Moscow." Martin finally sat down. "For the record—"

"I don't see anyone keeping a record, do you?"

"For the record," Martin repeated, "I agreed to take this meeting as a courtesy to you, and because we live and work in close proximity to one another. But I have no intention of going into business with you."

"You haven't heard my offer."

"I already know what it is."

"Do you?"

"It's the same offer you've made to countless other Western businessmen."

"I can assure you, they've all done remarkably well."

"I'm not like them."

"I'll say." Arkady surveyed the photographs hanging on the wall of Martin's conference room. "Who do you think you're fooling with this bullshit?"

"My charitable foundation has changed millions of lives around the world."

"Your charitable foundation is a fraud. And so are you." Arkady smiled. "I'll have some of that water, please. No gas, if you don't mind."

Martin poured a glass of the sparkling water and nudged it across the table. "Where did you learn your negotiating tactics? The KGB?"

"I was never a KGB officer. That, as they say, is an old wives' tale."

"That's not what I read in *The Atlantic*."

"I sued them."

"And you lost."

Arkady moved the glass aside without drinking from it. "You clearly have a better publicity department than I do. How else to explain the fact that the press has never written about your relationship with a certain Sandro Pugliese of the Italian 'Ndrangheta? Or your ties to Meissner PrivatBank of Liechtenstein? And then there were those centrifuge components you were selling to the Iranians through that German company of yours. Keppler Werk GmbH, I believe it was."

"I'm afraid you have me confused with someone else."

"I suppose it's possible. After all, successful men like us are always being accused of wrongdoing. They accuse me of being a KGB officer, that I owe all my wealth to my relationship with Russia's president. It is nothing more than anti-Russian bigotry. Russophobia!" He thumped the tabletop for emphasis. "Consequently, I sometimes find it necessary to conduct my affairs in a way that shields my identity. As do you, I imagine."

"Global Vision Investments is one of the most respected private equity firms in the world."

"Which is precisely why I would like to be in business with you. I have an enormous amount of excess capital sitting on the sidelines. I would like you to invest that capital on my behalf, using the unimpeachable imprimatur of GVI."

"I don't need your money, Arkady. I have plenty of my own."

"Your net worth is a paltry three billion, if the most recent *Forbes* list is to be believed. I'm offering you the chance to be rich enough to truly change the world." He paused. "Would that be of interest to you, Saint Martin?"

"I don't like to be called that."

"Ah, yes. I believe I read that in the same article that mentioned your disdain for business cards."

"And just where is this excess capital of yours now?"

"A portion of it is already here in the West."

"How much?"

"Let's call it six billion dollars."

"And the rest?"

"MosBank."

"Which means it's in rubles."

Arkady nodded.

"How many rubles are we talking about?"

"Four hundred billion."

"Five and a half billion dollars?"

"Five-point-four-seven, at today's exchange rate. But who's counting?"

"Where did it come from?"

"My construction company was recently awarded a contract for a large public works project in Siberia."

"Do you intend to actually *construct* any of it?"

"As little as possible."

"So the money has been siphoned from the Federal Treasury."

"In a manner of speaking."

"I don't deal in looted state assets. Or in rubles, for that matter."

"Then I suppose you'll have to convert my looted rubles into a reserve currency before investing the money on my behalf."

"In what?"

"The usual. Privately held companies and industrial concerns, large real estate assets, perhaps a port or two. These assets will be held by Global Vision Investments, but the true ownership will reside with several corporate shell companies that you will create for me. You will keep these assets on your books until such time as I see fit to dispose of them."

"I just founded a nongovernmental organization dedicated to promoting the spread of democracy around the world, including to the Russian Federation."

"You would have a better chance of slowing the rise of the seas than bringing democracy to Russia."

"But you see my point."

"The fact that you are now a self-declared opponent of the Russian government plays to our advantage. No one would ever dream that you are doing business with someone like me." Arkady admired his wristwatch—Patek Philippe of Geneva, one million Swiss francs—and then rose to his feet. "I was told your time was limited, as is mine. If you are interested in my offer, send word to my office by no later than five p.m. on Thursday. If I don't hear from you, I'll take my business elsewhere. No hard feelings."

"And if I'm interested?"

"You will draw up a detailed prospectus and deliver it to my villa in Féchy on Saturday. Oksana and I are having a few friends for lunch. I'm sure you and your lovely wife will find the other guests interesting."

"I have plans this weekend."

"Cancel them."

"I'm addressing a gathering of civil society leaders in Warsaw on Saturday."

"Another lost cause."

"I'll have my lawyer deliver the prospectus."

Arkady smiled. "I don't deal with lawyers."

ISABEL RETURNED TO THE CONFERENCE room at the stroke of 3:45 p.m. It appeared as though nothing had changed since she left. Now, as then, one man was seated and another was standing, though it was Arkady, not Martin, who was on his feet. The air between them was charged with the electricity of their final exchange.

Isabel escorted Arkady to the lifts and bade him a pleasant evening. Returning to the conference room, she found Martin standing contemplatively at the window, as though posing for a One World Foundation promotional video.

"How did it go?"

"Arkady Akimov would like us to launder and conceal eleven and a half billion dollars."

"Is that all?"

"No," Martin answered. "I'm afraid there's one more thing."

AT SEVEN FIFTEEN THAT EVENING, while tidying up her already spotless desk, Isabel received a text message from a number she didn't recognize, instructing her to purchase some wine on her way home. The sender was good enough to suggest a shop on the boulevard Georges-Favon. The proprietor recommended a Bordeaux of moderate price but exceptional vintage and placed it in a plastic bag, which Isabel carried through the quiet streets of the Old Town to the Place du Bourg-de-Four. The vagrant was in his usual spot near the wellhead. He appeared oblivious to the fact he was holding his sign upside down.

Isabel dropped a few coins in his cup and crossed the square to the entrance of her building. Upstairs, she opened the wine and poured a glass. Once again, her cello beckoned, but this time she ignored it, for her thoughts were elsewhere. The oil trader and oligarch Arkady Akimov had invited her to attend a luncheon on Saturday at his villa in Féchy. And she was now under surveillance by the private Russian intelligence service known as the Haydn Group.

37

GENEVA-PARIS

MARTIN RANG ISABEL AT HALF past seven the following morning while she was attempting to revive herself with a pulverizing shower after a largely sleepless night.

"I'm sorry to call so early, but I wanted to catch you before you left for the office. I hope it's not a bad time."

"Not at all." It was the day's first lie. Isabel was certain there would be more to come. "Is there a problem?"

"An opportunity, actually. But I'm afraid it will require you to travel to Paris this afternoon."

"What a shame."

"Not to worry. I promise to make your stay as pleasant as possible."

"How long will I be away?"

"Probably one night, but you should pack for two, just to be on the safe side. I'll tell you the rest when you arrive."

With that, the call went dead. Isabel finished showering, then checked the weather forecast for Paris. It was nearly identical to Geneva's, chilly and gray but no chance of rain. She packed accordingly and slipped her passport into her handbag. Her clothing for the day, a tailored pantsuit, hung from the back of her bedroom door. Dressed, she ordered an Uber and headed downstairs to the Place du Bourg-de-Four.

There was no sign of the vagrant, but two male employees of the Haydn Group were breakfasting at one of the cafés. One of the men, the darker-haired of the two, followed Isabel to the rue de l'Hôtel-de-Ville, where her car was waiting. When she arrived at GVI headquarters, Martin was gaveling the morning meeting to order. Nearly one hour in duration, it included no discussion of a lucrative offer by the oil trader and oligarch Arkady Akimov to launder and conceal eleven and a half billion dollars' worth of looted Russian state assets in the West.

At the conclusion of the meeting, Martin summoned Isabel to his office to explain why she would soon be leaving for Paris. A breakfast meeting at the Hôtel Crillon with an innovative French entrepreneur—or so Martin claimed. He gave Isabel some materials to review on the train and a key to an apartment. The address was handwritten on a notecard bearing his initials, as was the eight-digit passcode for the street-level entrance. Isabel memorized the information and then fed the notecard into Martin's shredder.

Her train departed the Gare de Cornavin at half past two. The dark-haired operative from the Haydn Group, having followed her on foot to the station, accompanied her on the three-hour journey to the Gare de Lyon. A waiting car delivered her to 21 Quai de Bourbon, an elegant residential street on the northern flank of the Île Saint-Louis.

The apartment was on the uppermost floor, the fifth. With Martin's key in hand, she stepped from the lift, only to find the door ajar. Gabriel waited in the entrance hall, a forefinger pressed to his lips.

He relieved Isabel of her bag and drew her inside. "Forgive me for deceiving you," he said, closing the door without a sound. "But I'm afraid there was no other way."

THE SITTING ROOM WAS IN darkness. He threw a wall switch, and a constellation of overhead recessed lighting extinguished the gloom. The decor surprised Isabel. She had expected grandeur, a miniature Versailles. Instead, she found herself in a showplace of affected casual elegance. It was no one's primary residence—or even secondary, she thought. It was a comfortable crash pad for those occasions when its very rich owner found himself in Paris for a few days.

"Yours?" she asked.

"Martin's, actually."

"Does he let all of his employees use it?"

"Only those with whom he's romantically involved."

Her scandalized expression was contrived. "Martin and me?"

"These things happen."

"Poor Monique."

"Fortunately, she'll never know." He dimmed the lights. "I would like you to make a brief appearance in the window."

"Why?"

"Because that is what a young woman does when she arrives at her lover's grand apartment on the Seine."

Isabel started toward the windows.

"Remove your coat, please."

She did as he asked and tossed it carelessly over the back of an armchair. Then she slipped between a pair of ivory-colored curtains and opened the room's center casement window. The evening wind took her hair. And five floors beneath her, an employee of the private intelligence company known as the Haydn Group took her photograph.

She closed the window and emerged from behind the curtains to find Gabriel rearranging her coat. "You don't like things out of place, do you?"

"You've noticed?"

"It's rather hard to miss. Everything is always just so. Paintings, violinists, Swiss financiers, disgruntled employees of the world's dirtiest bank. And you seem to have a cover story for every occasion."

"It is an essential part of our operating doctrine. We call it the small lie to cover the big lie."

"What's the small lie?"

"That you are having an affair with Martin Landesmann."

"And the big lie?"

"That you are here with me."

"Why?"

"Because it wasn't safe for us to meet in Geneva." He paused. "And because I have a difficult decision to make."

"Lunch at Arkady's on Saturday?"

He nodded.

"Is there any chance he didn't know that Martin was going to be in Warsaw this weekend?"

"None whatsoever. It was a clever ploy on his part. He wanted to invite you all along to test our bona fides. If you don't attend, he will suspect there's a problem."

"And if I agree?"

"You will be observed closely by several current and former Russian intelligence officers for any signs of discomfort or deception. You will also face seemingly benign questions about your past, especially your time at RhineBank. If you somehow manage to pass this examination, Arkady will in all likelihood go forward with the deal."

"And if I fail?"

"If we're lucky, Arkady will send you on your way, and we'll never hear from him again. If we are unlucky, he will subject you to a far different kind of questioning. And you will tell him everything, because that is what one does when a loaded Russian gun is pointed at one's head." He lowered his voice. "Which is why I'm inclined to cash out my chips and call it a night."

"Do I get a say in the matter?"

"No, Isabel. You do not. I asked you to lend your professional expertise to Martin Landesmann and to make an introduction at a crowded reception where you were in absolutely no danger. But I never prepared you to enter Arkady's world alone."

"It's only lunch."

"It's *never* only lunch. Arkady will begin testing you the second you walk through his door. He will assume that you are not who you claim to be. Once he has guided you through your usual repertoire, he will take away your sheet music and force you to improvise. The recital will not end until he is satisfied that you are not a threat."

"I'm capable of improvisation."

He regarded her doubtfully. "I must say, I've never heard 'Someday My Prince Will Come' played on the cello before. Your tone was quite lovely, but otherwise the performance was less than convincing."

"Then I suppose we'll have to do another take."

"There are no second takes, Isabel. Not where Russians are concerned."

"But in a few hours' time, Arkady will be under the impression I'm Martin's lover—isn't that correct?"

"That is my hope."

"So why on earth would Martin Landesmann allow his beautiful young girlfriend to attend a luncheon at Arkady's villa if he didn't think it was safe?"

Gabriel smiled. "Was that an improvisation on your part?"

She nodded. "What do you think?"

Before he could answer, his phone pulsed with an incoming message. "Your lover's plane just landed at Le Bourget."

"What are our plans?"

"A quiet dinner at a bistro around the corner."

"And then?"

"The small lie to cover the big lie."

"What's the small lie?"

"That you are spending the night making love to Martin."

"And the big one?"

"You'll be spending it with me."

38

ÎLE SAINT-LOUIS, PARIS

MARTIN AND ISABEL WALKED HAND in hand along the lamplit Quai de Bourbon to a brasserie at the foot of the Pont Saint-Louis. On the opposite side of the narrow channel loomed Notre-Dame, its flying buttresses concealed by scaffolding, its spire missing. The Russian who had followed Isabel from Geneva dined at an adjacent restaurant; Yossi Gavish and Eli Lavon, at an establishment across the street. Halfway through his meal, Yossi suddenly declared his coq au vin inedible, provoking a heated confrontation with the outraged chef that soon spilled on to the pavement. Lavon managed to defuse the situation, and the two combatants made their apologies and pledged eternal friendship, much to the delight of the spectators in the surrounding eateries. Gabriel, who monitored the incident via Isabel's phone, was only sorry he had not witnessed the performance, for it was one of the better pieces of operational street theater he had heard in some time.

He had instructed Martin to ply Isabel with a glass or two of wine over dinner. They drank Sancerre with their appetizers and with their main course a rather good Burgundy. As they walked back to the apartment, Isabel's step was languorous, her laughter brighter in the night. The Russian saw them to their door, then made his way across the Pont Marie to a floating café bar on the opposite embankment. His table offered an unobstructed view of Martin's bedroom window, where Isabel appeared shortly before midnight, wearing only a men's dress shirt. The Russian snapped several photos with his smartphone—hardly ideal but, when combined with his firsthand visual observations, more than sufficient.

Martin appeared in the window briefly, shirtless, and drew Isabel inside. The Russian at the floating café would have been forgiven for assuming the couple returned to bed. In truth, they made their way to Martin's splendid dining room, where Gabriel waited in the half-light, his hands resting on the tabletop. He instructed Isabel to sit down in the chair opposite and refused her request to put on additional clothing. Her seminudity made her uncomfortable. It had the same effect on Gabriel. He averted his eyes slightly as he posed his first question.

"What is your name?"

"Isabel Brenner."

"Your real name."

"That is my real name."

"Where were you born?"

"In Trier."

"When did you receive your first cello?"

"When I was eight."

"Your father gave it to you?"

"My mother."

"You competed in the ARD International Music Competition when you were nineteen?"

"Seventeen."

"You won a second prize for your performance of Brahms's Cello Sonata in E Minor?"

"Third prize. And it was the F Major."

"How long have you been working for Israeli intelligence?"

"I don't work for Israeli intelligence. I work for Martin Landesmann."

"Is Martin working for Israeli intelligence?"

"No."

"Are you involved in a sexual relationship with Landesmann?"

"Yes."

"Are you in love with Landesmann?"

"Yes."

"Is he in love with you?"

"You would have to ask him."

Gabriel's questions ceased.

"How did I do?"

"If your wish is to die on Saturday afternoon, you did just fine. If, however, you wish to survive your lunch at Arkady's villa, we have a great deal of work to do. Now tell me your name."

"It's Isabel."

"Why did you give those documents to Nina Antonova?"

"I didn't."

"How long have you been working for Gabriel Allon?"

"I don't know anyone by that name."

"You're lying, Isabel. And now you're dead."

THE NEXT MOCK INTERROGATION WAS worse than the first, and the one after that was the equivalent of a signed confession. But by four that morning—with a few valuable insights from a criminal who had managed to convince the world he was a saint—Isabel lied with the ease and confidence of a highly trained intelligence officer. Even Gabriel, who was looking for any excuse to press the kill switch, had to admit she was more than capable of answering a few questions at a luncheon party. He was under no illusions, however, about her ability to stand up under sustained KGB-style pressure. If Arkady and his thugs strapped her to a chair, she was to immediately revert to her first fallback, that she had been coerced into working for British intelligence while she was working for RhineBank in London. And if that didn't work, she was to offer them Gabriel's name.

By then, it was approaching five a.m. Isabel managed to sleep for a few hours and at nine fifteen crawled into the back of a taxi for the drive to the Gare de Lyon. Martin departed for Le Bourget a short time later, but Gabriel remained in the apartment until late afternoon, when Eli Lavon determined it was no longer under surveillance by the Haydn Group. Together they made their way to the Israeli Embassy in the first arrondissement and headed downstairs to the secure communications vault. In the lexicon of the Office, it was known as the Holy of Holies.

On the video screen was a feed from GVI headquarters.

Martin, looking none the worse for wear after a sleepless night, was presiding over the afternoon staff meeting. At its conclusion, Isabel gathered up her papers and returned to her office, where she rang Ludmilla Sorova at NevaNeft. Ludmilla placed Isabel on hold, and a moment later Arkady came on the line.

"*I was beginning to think I'd never hear from you.*"

"Hello, Mr. Akimov."

"*Please, Isabel. You must call me Arkady.*"

"*I'm still working on that.*"

"*You sound tired.*"

"*Do I? It's been a busy day.*"

"*I hope it was on my account.*"

"*It was, actually.*"

"*I take it Martin is interested in my offer?*"

"*We're working on the prospectus as we speak. He asked me to deliver it to Féchy on Saturday afternoon.*"

"*You're staying for lunch, I hope.*"

"*I wouldn't miss it. What time should I arrive?*"

"*Around one. But don't worry about arranging a car. I'll send one.*"

"*That's not necessary, Mr. Akimov.*"

"*I insist. Where should he meet you?*"

Isabel recited the name of a prominent Geneva landmark rather than the address of her apartment building. Then, after a final exchange of pleasantries, the connection went dead. In the Holy of Holies, the silence was absolute.

At length, Eli Lavon said, "Maybe classical musicians can't improvise, after all."

"And what should she have said differently?"

"She should have told Arkady that she was more than capable of finding her way to Féchy on her own."

"I'm quite sure she did. In fact, we can listen to the recording if you like."

"She didn't push hard enough."

"And when Arkady threatened to take his business elsewhere?" Receiving no reply, Gabriel reset the time code and clicked the PLAY icon. "Does she sound tired to you?"

"Not a bit."

"So why did Arkady say that?"

"Because he knows where she spent last night. And he wants Isabel and Martin to know that he knows."

"Why?"

"*Kompromat.*"

"And what will Arkady do with this juicy piece of *kompromat* we've so generously placed before him?"

"He'll use it to keep Martin in line. Who knows? He might even use it to sweeten the deal if he thinks Martin's taking too big a cut."

"So we've got him? Is that what you're saying, Eli?"

Lavon hesitated, then nodded.

Gabriel raised the volume on the feed from Isabel's compromised mobile phone. "What's she humming?"

"Elgar, you rube."

"Why Elgar?"

"Perhaps she's trying to tell you that she'd rather not have lunch with a Moscow Center–trained hood."

"There's no way he'll kill her in Switzerland—right, Eli?"

"Absolutely not. He'll drive her across the border to France," said Lavon. "Then he'll kill her."

39

FÉCHY, CANTON VAUD

SATURDAY DAWNED OVERCAST AND GRAY, but by late morning the sun shone brightly upon the pavements of the rue du Purgatoire. Isabel waited on the steps of the dun-colored Temple de la Madeleine, one of the oldest churches in Geneva. Her clothing, all newly purchased, was appropriate for a lakeside luncheon with a crowd of grotesquely rich Russians—Max Mara trousers, Ferragamo pumps, cashmere sweater and jacket by Givenchy, a Louis Vuitton tote bag. Inside was a detailed proposal to launder and conceal eleven and a half billion dollars in looted Russian state assets. She and Martin had put the finishing touches on the document late the previous evening during a marathon session at GVI headquarters.

She checked the time on her wristwatch—a Jaeger-LeCoultre

Rendez-Vous, diamond accent, a gift from Martin—and saw that it was noon precisely. Looking up, she spotted a sleek Mercedes S-Class sedan approaching along the narrow street. The driver stopped at the base of the steps and lowered the passenger-side window.

"Madame Brenner?"

She settled in the backseat for the thirty-minute drive to Féchy, a wealthy wine-producing village in Canton Vaud, on the northern shore of Lake Geneva. Not surprisingly, Arkady's villa was the largest in the municipality. The garish entrance hall was a replica of the Andreyevsky Hall of the Grand Kremlin Palace, smaller in scale, but no less ornate.

"What do you think?" he asked.

"Words fail me," said Isabel truthfully.

"Wait until you see the rest of the place."

They passed through a pair of golden doors and entered a reproduction of the Alexandrovskiy Hall. Next came a series of formal drawing rooms, each with a distinct motif. Here a country house, here a palace by the sea, here the book-lined study of a great Russian intellectual. Only one of the rooms was inhabited, a luminous parlor where three long-limbed young girls were posed as if for a fashion shoot. They eyed Isabel with obvious envy.

Eventually they emerged onto a large terrace where a hundred Russians sipped champagne in the chill autumn sunlight. Isabel had to raise her voice to be heard over the music.

"I was expecting a small luncheon."

"I don't do small."

"Who are all these people?"

Arkady directed his gaze toward a well-fed man with his arm

around the waist of an impossibly pretty young woman. "I assume you recognize him."

"Of course."

The man was Oleg Zhirinovsky, chairman of the Russian state energy giant Gazprom. The young woman he was pawing was wife number four. Getting rid of number three had cost him several hundred million pounds in a London courtroom.

Arkady pointed out another guest. "What about him?"

"Good heavens." It was Mad Maxim Simonov, the nickel king of Russia.

"Or him?"

"Is that—"

"Oleg Lebedev, otherwise known as Mr. Aluminum."

"Is it true he's the richest man in Russia?"

"Second richest." Arkady plucked two glasses of champagne from the tray of a passing waiter and gave one to Isabel. "I trust the drive from Geneva was comfortable?"

"Very."

"And you brought the proposal?"

Isabel patted the Vuitton bag.

"Perhaps we should review it now. That way we can relax and enjoy the rest of the afternoon."

Inside, they scaled a grand stairway and entered Arkady's private office suite. It lacked the gold-plated tsarist vulgarity of the rest of the villa. Holding her champagne glass aloft, Isabel laid her right hand on the keys of a Bösendorfer piano and played the opening passage of Beethoven's *Moonlight Sonata*.

"Is there anything you can't do?" asked Arkady.

"I can't play the rest of this sonata. Not anymore, at least."

"I rather doubt that." He led her to a seating area near the windows and opened a decorative box on the lacquered coffee table. "Place your mobile phone inside, please."

Isabel did as she was told. Then she removed the prospectus from her bag and handed it to Arkady.

"Is this the only copy?"

"Except for the original file. It's on an air-gapped computer in my office."

He slipped on a pair of reading glasses and turned slowly through the pages. "There's a great deal of British and American commercial real estate."

"That's because the pandemic has created a glut of available properties. We believe these assets can be acquired at favorable prices and that they will appreciate in value once the American economy regains its pre-pandemic footing."

"How long will I have to retain possession to see a profit?"

"Three to five years, to be on the safe side."

He looked down again. "Fifty million dollars for an organic food company in Portland?"

"We believe it's undervalued and primed for future growth."

"One hundred million for a maker of solar panels?" He turned another page. "Two hundred million for a company that manufactures wind-driven turbines?" He peered at Isabel over his reading glasses. "Have you forgotten that I'm in the oil business?"

"Owning these companies will allow you to atone for your carbon sins."

Smiling, he looked down again. "Three hundred million for an aftermarket aircraft parts distributor in Salina, Kansas?"

"If you purchase the firm's main competitor, you'll be the dominant player in the American market."

"Is it for sale?"

"We're hearing rumors."

He returned to the real estate section of the document. "The tallest office building in London's Canary Wharf?"

"A not-to-be-missed opportunity."

"A commercial-and-residential tower on Brickell Avenue in downtown Miami?"

"It's a steal at six hundred million. What's more, you'll be able to process tens of millions of dollars through the resale of the luxury condominiums on the upper floors."

"Process?"

Isabel smiled. "Launder is such an ugly word."

"Which brings us to your fee." Arkady flipped to the back of the document. "One and a half billion dollars in consulting and other fees, payable to a limited-liability shell corporation registered in the Channel Islands." He looked up. "Rather steep, don't you think?"

"You're paying for Martin's good name. It doesn't come cheap."

"Neither, it seems, does currency conversion."

Isabel made no reply.

"I assume you have someone in mind for the job?"

"The London office of RhineBank. They're the best in the business."

"And you would know. After all, that's where you began your career. You were recruited by RhineBank after you finished your graduate degree at the London School of Economics."

"You've obviously looked into my background."

"Did you expect otherwise?"

Isabel ignored the question. "Find anything interesting?"

"You weren't fired from RhineBank-Zurich because you got caught with your hand in the till. You were fired because you worked for the so-called Russian Laundromat. Most of your colleagues are still looking for work, but you managed to land on your feet at Global Vision Investments of Geneva." Arkady lowered his voice. "And now you are sitting in my private study, offering to *process* more than eleven and a half billion dollars of my money."

"I'm here, Mr. Akimov, because for some reason you insisted that I come."

"I assure you, my intentions were honorable."

"Were they?"

"I was merely hoping to get to know you better."

"In that case, where would you like me to begin?"

"By playing the rest of the *Moonlight Sonata*."

"I told you, I can't remember it."

"I heard you the first time, Isabel. But I don't believe you."

40

FÉCHY, CANTON VAUD

MECHANICAL AND PASSIONLESS," ARKADY DECLARED at the conclusion of the first movement. "But it's obvious you could play it quite well if you chose to."

"How about this?" Isabel played the opening passage of "When I Fall in Love."

"Have you ever?" asked Arkady.

"Fallen in love? Once or twice."

"And are you in love now?"

Isabel rose from the piano without answering and reclaimed her seat. "Where were we?"

"RhineBank," answered Arkady.

"Founded in 1892 in the Free and Hanseatic City of Hamburg, which, as you know, is located on the river Elbe rather than the Rhine. Currently the world's fourth-largest bank, with approximately twenty-seven billion in revenue and one-point-six trillion in assets."

Arkady regarded her without expression. "Tell me about your work there."

"I signed a nondisclosure agreement as part of my settlement package. I'm not at liberty to discuss anything I did for Rhine-Bank."

"Did you ever handle transactions related to a company called Omega Holdings?"

"Arkady, please."

"Finally!" His smile appeared almost genuine.

"I didn't know the identity of *any* of the clients," explained Isabel. "I just signed off on the transactions."

"Then why on earth were you fired?"

"I was part of the Laundromat. We all had to go."

"Were you the person who leaked the documents to the newspapers?"

"Yes, Arkady. I was the one who did it."

"I'm glad we cleared that up." Another smile. "Now tell me how you ended up working for Martin Landesmann."

"The usual way. He offered me a job."

"Why you?"

"I suppose he wanted my expertise."

"Expertise?"

"I know how to process funds without getting caught."

"And when did you begin sleeping with him?"

Isabel deliberately allowed a false note to creep into her denial. "Martin is a happily married man."

"As am I," replied Arkady. "And it is quite obvious that the two of you are involved in a passionate affair. I only hope that for Martin's sake it never becomes public. His sterling reputation would suffer."

"That sounds like a threat."

"Does it?"

"What are you so worried about?" asked Isabel. "Martin and I are the ones who are required to abide by the rules of the Anti–Money Laundering Act. And we're the ones who will be fined or even prosecuted for our actions if we're caught. You, as the customer, face no such risk."

"My concerns are geopolitical, not legal. But please continue."

"You were the one who came to us, Arkady. Remember?"

"I remember that you performed one of my favorite compositions by my favorite composer at a reception that cost me twenty million Swiss francs to attend. And I remember that when I expressed interest in doing business with Martin, you both played hard to get."

"We played hard to get because we didn't think it was a good idea to go into business with Russians." She slipped the prospectus into her bag and rose. "For reasons that are now all too obvious."

"Where do you think you're going?"

"Back to Geneva."

"Why?"

"Sorry, Arkady. The deal's off."

"Don't you think you should consult with Martin before walking away from a billion-dollar payday?"

"Martin will do whatever I tell him."

"I don't doubt it."

Isabel opened the lid of the decorative signal-blocking box, but Arkady closed it with a sharp *crack* before she could remove her phone. "Please sit down."

"I'm leaving."

"How do you intend to get back to Geneva?"

"I'll call an Uber." She managed a smile. "They're all the rage."

"That won't be easy without your phone, will it?" His hand was still resting on the lid of the box. "Besides, you haven't had lunch."

"I've lost my appetite." Isabel fished the prospectus from her bag and dropped it on the table. "What's it going to be, Arkady?"

"I need a few days to think it over."

Isabel looked at her wristwatch. "You have one minute."

ARKADY'S VOICE WAS THE FIRST Gabriel and his team heard when Isabel's phone, after an absence of twenty-seven minutes, reconnected with the Swisscom cellular network. Curiously, the Russian oligarch was gently chastising her for having rushed through an important passage of Beethoven's *Moonlight Sonata*. The phone's geolocation and altitude data indicated they were still in his office, as did the video images captured by its camera. It focused briefly on Isabel's face as she checked her text messages. There was nothing in her expression to suggest she was under duress, though it was evident from the unstable quality of the shot that her hand was trembling slightly.

She dropped the phone into the darkened void of her Vuitton handbag and followed Arkady downstairs to the villa's terrace, where they circulated through the all-Russian crowd. Arkady introduced Isabel as "an associate," a description that covered all manner of sins. The Gazprom chairman Oleg Zhirinovsky was delighted; Mad Maxim Simonov, the nickel king, clearly smitten. He invited Isabel to join him aboard his yacht, the appropriately named *Mischief*, for his annual summer cruise of the Mediterranean. Isabel wisely declined.

At three fifteen she informed Arkady that she had numbers to crunch—a legitimate investment opportunity in a Norwegian e-commerce firm—and needed to be getting back to Geneva. Reluctantly, he saw her to her car. The driver dropped her at the Temple de la Madeleine and, followed by two operatives of the Haydn Group, she walked to the Place du Bourg-de-Four. Upstairs in her apartment, she performed Bach's Cello Suite in D Minor. All six movements. No sheet music. Not a single mistake.

PART THREE

ADAGIO CANTABILE

THREE DAYS AFTER THE LUNCHEON at Arkady Akimov's palace in Féchy, the inhabitants of the ancient lakeside city of Geneva held their collective breath as America went to the polls. The Republican incumbent seized what appeared to be a commanding early advantage in the key battleground states of Wisconsin, Michigan, and Pennsylvania, only to see his lead evaporate as early votes and mail-in ballots were tabulated. Visibly shaken, he appeared before supporters in the White House East Room early Wednesday morning and, astonishingly, demanded that state election officials cease counting ballots. The counting nevertheless continued, and on Saturday the television networks declared the Democrat the victor. Millions of Americans poured into the streets in a spontaneous eruption of joy and utter relief. To Isabel, it looked as though they were celebrating the fall of a tyrant.

On Monday, life in Geneva resumed largely as normal, though with a new government-imposed mask mandate owing to a sudden spike in coronavirus cases. Isabel worked from her apartment in the Old Town until late morning and then flew to London aboard Martin's Gulfstream, the smaller of his two private jets. Upon arrival at London City Airport, she endured a cursory check of her German passport before settling into the back of a waiting limousine. It bore her westward to the Fleet Street offices of RhineBank-London, her former place of employment.

Directly opposite the building was a café where Isabel had often taken her lunch. Masked, she took a table on the pavement and ordered coffee. At half past four, she checked the FTSE 100 index and saw that London share prices had closed down nearly two percent. Consequently, she waited until 4:45 before ringing Anil Kandar.

"What the fuck do you want?"

"I'm well, Anil. How are you?"

"Have you seen our stock price lately?"

"I believe it's just under ten. Hold on, I'll check."

"What's on your mind, Isabel?"

"Money, Anil. Lots of money."

"You have my attention."

"It's not something I can discuss on the phone."

"My favorite kind of deal. Where are you?"

"Across the street."

"Twenty minutes," said Anil, and rang off.

It was nearly half past five when he finally emerged from RhineBank's entrance. As usual, he was dressed entirely in black, a style he had adopted while still in New York, where he had earned a reputation as one of RhineBank's most reckless traders. For his reward, he was given control of the global markets division, a position that had allowed him to amass a nine-figure personal fortune. He lived in a vast Victorian mansion in a posh London suburb and commuted to work each morning in a chauffeur-driven Bentley. Born in Northern Virginia, educated at Yale and the Wharton School, he now spoke English with a pronounced British accent. Like his coal-black attire, it was something he put on first thing in the morning.

He sat down at Isabel's table and ordered an Earl Grey tea. The smell of cologne, hair tonic, and tobacco was overwhelming. It was the smell, Isabel remembered, of RhineBank-London.

He removed the lid from his drink and popped a fresh piece of Nicorette. "You look good, Isabel."

"Thanks, Anil." She smiled. "You look like shit."

"I suppose I deserved that."

"You did. You were horrible to me when I worked here."

"It wasn't personal. You were a pain in the ass."

"I was only trying to do my job."

"So was I." Anil blew on the surface of his tea. "But I hear you got with the program after you moved to the Zurich office. Lothar Brandt told me that you signed every scrap of paper he placed in front of you."

"And look what that got me," she murmured.

"A job with Saint Martin Landesmann."

"Word travels fast."

"Especially when everyone else who was fired is still seeking gainful employment. Fortunately, we were able to contain the damage to the Zurich office."

Anil was fond of using the word *we* when referring to senior management. It was his ambition to one day become a member of the Council of Ten, perhaps even the firm's chief executive officer. American by birth, Indian by ancestry, he would have to pay for the privilege. Thus his reckless trading habits. Anil was utterly bereft of personal or professional morality. In short, he was the model RhineBank employee.

"How's your trading book these days?" asked Isabel.

"Not as interesting as it once was. The Council of Ten presented us with a cease-and-desist order after the Zurich massacre. No more dicey Russian trades until the dust settles."

"Has it?"

"I've done a few test runs. Small stuff, mainly. Twenty million here, forty million there. Nickel-and-kopek."

"And?"

"Smooth as silk. Not a peep from the British regulators or the Americans."

"Does the Council of Ten know what you're up to?"

"You know the old saying, Isabel. What Hamburg doesn't know . . ." Anil peeled the wrapper from another piece of Nicorette. "I'm about to go into withdrawal, and I'm afraid it won't be pretty. So why don't you tell me what this is all about."

"Global Vision Investments would like to retain the services of RhineBank's global markets division. In return for these services, we are prepared to be very generous."

"What kind of services?"

Isabel smiled. "Mirror, mirror on the wall."

"How much are we talking about?"

"Not nickel-and-kopek, Anil. Not even close."

ANIL INHALED HIS FIRST DUNHILL before they reached Victoria Embankment. By then, Isabel had outlined the basic parameters of the deal. Now, as they walked along the Thames toward the Houses of Parliament, she went into greater detail—mainly for the sake of her listening audience, which was monitoring the conversation via the phone in her handbag. Representatives of her client, she explained, would purchase blocks of blue-chip stocks from RhineBank-Moscow in rubles. Simultaneously, Anil would purchase identical amounts of the same blue-chip stocks from representatives of Isabel's client in Cyprus, the Channel Islands, the Bahamas, or the Cayman Islands. All told, four hundred billion rubles were to be converted and transferred from Russia to the West. Given the extraordinary size of the project, it would necessarily have to be accomplished piecemeal—five billion here, ten billion there, a trade or two a day, more if there was no regulatory reaction. Eventually the money would make its way into accounts at Meissner PrivatBank of Liechtenstein, a fact she did not divulge to Anil. Nor did she tell him the name of her mysterious Russian client, only the amount of money they were prepared to pay RhineBank-London in fees and other service charges.

"Five hundred million?" Anil was predictably appalled. "I won't touch it for less than a billion."

"Of course you will, Anil. You're practically salivating. The only question is whether you're going to call Hamburg tonight to get approval from the Council of Ten."

He flicked the end of his cigarette into the river. "What Hamburg doesn't know . . ."

"How are you going to explain the additional five hundred million on your book?"

"I'll spread it around. They'll never figure out where it came from."

"It's good to know nothing's changed since I left." Isabel handed Anil a flash drive. "This has all the relevant accounts and routing numbers."

"When do you want to start?"

"How about tomorrow?"

"No problem." Anil slipped the flash drive into the pocket of his black overcoat. "I guess those rumors about Martin Landesmann are true after all."

"What rumors are you referring to?"

"That he's no saint. And neither, it seems, are you." He gave her a sidelong leer. "If only I'd known."

"You're salivating again, Anil."

"Have time for a celebratory drink?"

"I've got to get back to Geneva tonight."

"Next time you're in town?"

"Probably not. Don't take this the wrong way, Anil, but you really do look like shit."

BY THE TIME ISABEL ARRIVED at London City Airport, Martin's plane was fueled and cleared for departure. The Englishman looked up from his laptop computer as she entered the cabin.

"How about that drink now?" he asked.

"I'd kill for one."

"I think champagne is in order, don't you?"

"If you insist."

The Englishman entered the galley and emerged a moment later with an open bottle of Louis Roederer Cristal. He poured two glasses and handed one to Isabel.

"What shall we drink to?" she asked.

"Another remarkable performance on your part."

"I have a better idea." Isabel raised her glass. "To the world's dirtiest bank."

The Englishman smiled. "May it rest in peace."

42

QUAI DU MONT-BLANC, GENEVA

AT ELEVEN A.M. THE FOLLOWING morning, a Russian stock-broker named Anatoly Bershov rang his man at RhineBank-Moscow on behalf of an unidentified client and purchased several thousand shares in an American biotech company that developed and produced a widely used coronavirus testing kit. Five minutes later the same Russian stockbroker instructed his representative in Cyprus, a certain Mr. Constantinides, to *sell* an identical number of shares in the company to one Anil Kandar, head of RhineBank's global markets division in London. The first transaction was conducted in rubles, the second in dollars. Mr. Constantinides immediately wired the proceeds to a correspondent Cypriot bank—it was located in the same Nicosia office building, which was owned by anonymous Russian interests—and the correspondent Cypriot bank wired it to the

Caribbean, where it bounced from one shady house of finance to the next before finally making its way to Meissner Privat-Bank of Liechtenstein.

By then, the money had passed through so many flimsy corporate shells its point of origin was all but impossible to determine. For good measure, Meissner cloaked the money beneath a final layer of corporate murk before squirting it to Credit Suisse in Geneva, where it landed in an account controlled by Global Vision Investments. A fonctionnaire at Credit Suisse sent an email confirmation to a GVI executive named Isabel Brenner, who, unbeknownst to the fonctionnaire, was the hidden hand behind the entire appalling deception.

Anatoly Bershov placed a second call to his man at RhineBank-Moscow shortly after three p.m. This time his client wished to purchase several thousand shares in a giant American food-and-beverage conglomerate. The banker from whom Anil Kandar purchased an identical number of shares in dollars was located in the Bahamas. The funds ricocheted among several dubious Bahamian banks, all located on the same Nassau street, before crossing the Atlantic in the opposite direction and finding temporary lodging at Meissner PrivatBank of Liechtenstein. Credit Suisse took possession of the money at four fifteen Geneva time. Email confirmation to Isabel Brenner, Global Vision Investments.

The transactions produced more than a hundred pages of records, including two internal GVI documents requiring both Isabel's signature and the signature of Anatoly Bershov's mysterious client. Fortunately, his office was located directly across the river Rhône, in the Place du Port. Isabel arrived at five p.m. and, after placing her phone in a decorative signal-blocking box, was admitted into Arkady's inner sanctum on the seventh floor—one floor above the offices of the mysterious NevaNeft subsidiary known as the Haydn Group. Much to her surprise, Arkady personally signed the documents where indicated.

Isabel photocopied the papers upon her return to GVI headquarters, along with the other relevant records, and placed the originals in a safe in her office. The copies she gave to a courier, who delivered them to a rented villa in the diplomatic quarter of Champel. Their arrival was cause for a brief celebration. Three months after its unlikely inception, the operation had borne its first fruit. Gabriel and the Office were now minority stakeholders in the kleptocracy known as Kremlin Inc.

ANIL KANDAR SUGGESTED THEY TAP the brakes long enough to determine whether RhineBank's regulators at the Financial Conduct Authority had taken note of the unusual trades. Isabel could have assured her former colleague that FCA was well aware of their activities, as was Her Majesty's Secret Intelligence Service. Instead, she agreed to a pause, so long as it was brief. Her client, she wrote in an obliquely worded email, was not by nature a patient man.

Forty-eight hours proved sufficient to put Anil's concerns to rest, and by Friday morning, Anatoly Bershov was bullish about Microsoft. So, too, was Anil Kandar. Indeed, not five minutes after Bershov placed a multibillion-ruble bet on the conglomerate at RhineBank-Moscow, Anil purchased an identical number of shares from Mr. Constantinides of Cyprus, though Anil paid for his chips with American dollars. The money appeared in a GVI account at Credit Suisse in late morning, and the proceeds of a second mirror trade appeared in midafternoon. Arkady signed the documents that evening at NevaNeft headquarters.

Afterward, he invited Isabel to join him for a glass of champagne. Citing a pressing matter at the office, she tried to beg off, but Arkady was insistent. Ludmilla Sorova brought a bottle of Dom Pérignon and two glasses, and for the better part of the next hour, as the last light drained from the skies above Geneva, they debated the merits of Rachmaninoff's four piano concertos. Isabel declared that the second was clearly his greatest. Arkady agreed, though he had always had a soft spot for the mighty third and was particularly fond of a recent recording by the Russian pianist Daniil Trifonov.

The conversation left him in a reflective mood. "If only I could talk to Oksana like this," he lamented.

"She doesn't like Rachmaninoff?"

"Oksana prefers electronic dance music." He offered Isabel a sheepish smile. "You might find this difficult to believe, but I did not marry her for her intellect."

"She's very beautiful, Arkady."

"But childish. I was quite relieved when she behaved herself during Anna Rolfe's recital. Not long before the pandemic, I took her to a performance of Tchaikovsky's violin concerto. Afterward, I swore, never again."

"Who was the soloist?"

"The young Dutchwoman. Her name escapes me."

"Janine Jansen?"

"Yes, that's the one. Do you know her, too?"

"We've never met," answered Isabel.

"She's no Anna Rolfe, but she's quite talented." Arkady added champagne to Isabel's glass. "I'm sorry, but I can't recall how it is you know Anna."

"We were introduced by Martin."

"Yes, of course. That makes sense," said Arkady. "Martin knows everyone."

While walking home through the darkened streets of the Old Town, Isabel reached the unsettling conclusion that Arkady was interested in expanding the parameters of their relationship to include a romantic or, heaven forbid, a sexual component. She shared her concerns with Gabriel on Monday evening during another carefully choreographed meeting in Martin's apartment on the Île Saint-Louis in Paris. Next morning, over coffee at the café in Fleet Street, she informed Anil Kandar that they needed to quicken the pace of the illicit mirror trades. He responded with four large transactions that produced nearly a hundred million dollars.

Anil engineered four more mirror trades on Wednesday and another four on Thursday. But it was Friday's haul—six large transactions with more than two hundred million in proceeds—that put them over the top. Isabel obtained the required signatures during a late-afternoon appearance at Neva-Neft headquarters and for a second time was invited to linger for a glass of champagne. The intimate nature of the conversation left little doubt that Arkady was hopelessly infatuated with the beautiful German cellist who was laundering his dirty Russian money. She was therefore relieved when, shortly after six p.m., Martin appeared on the screen of the giant wall-mounted television in Arkady's office.

At length, Arkady said, "You never answered my question."

"About my relationship with Martin?"

"Yes."

"Martin and I are colleagues." Isabel paused, then added, "As are we, Arkady."

He aimed a remote at the screen and increased the volume. "He's quite good on television, isn't he? And to think that not a single word of what he's saying is true."

"It's not all a lie. He just neglected to mention one or two pertinent details."

"Such as?"

"The name of the man who's financing his planned spending spree."

"There is no such man." Arkady smiled. "He's Mr. Nobody."

Isabel squeezed the stem of her champagne glass so tightly she was surprised it didn't snap. Arkady appeared not to notice; his gaze was fixed on the television.

"And you're mistaken about one other matter as well," he said after a moment. "Ludmilla Sorova is my colleague. You, Isabel, are something else entirely."

THE HOST OF THE CNBC program upon which Martin appeared was none other than Zoe Reed. The topic concerned rumors swirling about Wall Street that Global Vision Investments was considering several deals in the United States, including in the distressed commercial real estate sector, which the firm had avoided in the past. Martin was as elusive as ever. Yes, he acknowledged, he had several irons in the American fire. Most were in the forward-looking energy and technology sectors where he had traditionally been active, but commercial real estate was not out of the question. GVI expected a sharp post-pandemic rebound in the United States once a sufficient percentage of the population had been vaccinated. The perception that the pandemic would forever change the nature of work was mistaken. Americans, declared Martin, would soon be returning to their offices.

"But that doesn't mean we can go back to our old ways. We have to make our places of work greener, smarter, and much more energy efficient. Remember, Zoe, there's no vaccine for a rising sea level."

"Is it true you're looking at a high-rise in downtown Chicago?"

"We're looking at a number of different projects."

"And what about America's current political turmoil? Are you at all concerned about the stability of the market?"

"America's democratic institutions," said Martin diplomatically, "are strong enough to withstand the current challenge."

The interview left little doubt as to Martin's intentions. It was only a matter of when and where and how much. The wait for an answer was not long—five days, in fact—though the asset in question came as something of a surprise. Isabel obtained the necessary signatures at NevaNeft headquarters and forwarded copies of the documents to the rented villa in Champel. Kremlin Inc. was now the proud owner of a sixty-story office-and-condominium tower on Miami's Brickell Avenue, which meant that Gabriel was now the proud owner of Arkady Akimov. The time had finally come to take on an additional partner—a partner with the financial firepower to turn Arkady's empire to ashes. He had one small piece of unrelated business to attend to at King Saul Boulevard first.

43

TEL AVIV–LANGLEY, VIRGINIA

MOHSEN FAKHRIZADEH CLAIMED TO BE nothing more than a lowly professor of physics at Imam Hussein University in downtown Tehran. In point of fact, he was a senior official in the Iranian Ministry of Defense, a career officer of the Revolutionary Guard Corps, and the leader of Iran's nuclear weapons program. Four of its top scientists had died violently at the hands of Office assassins. But Fakhrizadeh, who lived in a walled compound and was surrounded always by a large detail of bodyguards, had survived several attempts on his life. His run of good fortune ended, however, on the last Friday of November 2020, on a road near the town of Absard. The operation, months in the planning, unfolded with the precision of a Haydn string quartet. By nightfall, the entire twelve-member

Office hit team had slipped out of the country, and the leading light of Iran's nuclear program was lying in his coffin, wrapped in a burial shroud.

Gabriel presided over Fakhrizadeh's assassination from the ops center at King Saul Boulevard. Among the first phone calls he received in the aftermath was from CIA director Morris Payne—hardly surprising, for Gabriel had neglected to inform Langley the hit was imminent. After offering his grudging congratulations, Payne wondered whether Gabriel was free to come to Washington for an operational postmortem. Payne had a hole in his schedule on Monday. The hole, he said, had Gabriel's name on it.

"Tuesday would be better, Morris."

"In that case," replied Payne, "I'll see you Monday morning at ten."

In truth, Gabriel was anxious to make the trip, for it was long overdue. He spent the weekend with Chiara and the children in Jerusalem and, late Sunday evening, boarded his plane for the twelve-hour flight to Washington. An Agency reception committee met him on the tarmac of Dulles Airport and drove him to Langley. Morris Payne, never one to stand on ceremony, received Gabriel in his seventh-floor office rather than the gleaming white lobby. Big and bluff with a face like an Easter Island statue, Payne was West Point, Ivy League law, private enterprise, and a deeply conservative former member of Congress from one of the Dakotas. A devout Christian, he possessed a volcanic temper and a remarkable mastery of profanity, which he displayed for Gabriel while berating him over the Fakhrizadeh assassination. In Payne's version of events, Gabriel had committed a betrayal of biblical proportions by failing to warn him in advance of the operation. Eager to resolve the matter, Gabriel admitted wrongdoing and asked for absolution.

Payne's anger eventually subsided. They were, after all, close allies who had accomplished much together during the president's four years in office. Payne was one of the so-called adults in the room who had attempted to constrain the president's worst impulses. Unlike the other grown-ups—the decorated generals and the experienced foreign policy hands—he had managed to stay in the president's good graces, mainly through constant flattery of his fragile ego. There was talk he intended to take up the president's populist mantle and make a run for the White House in the next election cycle. For now, he was the leader of an agency his boss loathed. Each day, he dutifully signed off on the intelligence to be included in the President's Daily Brief. He admitted to Gabriel that he carefully curated the material to keep America's most sensitive secrets out of the hands of the commander in chief.

"Has he noticed?"

"He hasn't even bothered to read the PDB in months. For all intents and purposes, the national security apparatus of the world's most powerful nation is on autopilot."

"How much longer does he intend to contest the results of the elections?"

"I'm afraid it's a fight to the death. It's the only way he knows how to play the game. Just ask his ex-wives." Payne glanced at his watch. "The chief of the Persia House would like to join us, if you don't mind."

"In a minute, Morris. There's something I need to discuss

with you in private first. It concerns an operation we launched after Viktor Orlov's assassination in London."

"How did you get mixed up in the Orlov business?"

"It's a long story, Morris."

"Where is this operation of yours taking place?"

"Geneva."

With his expression, Payne made it clear that Geneva, a city of culture and international diplomacy, was not to his liking. "The target?" he asked.

"Arkady Akimov. He runs a company called—"

"I know who Arkady Akimov is."

"Did you know that he's smuggling the Tsar's money out of Russia and hiding it in the West? Or that he's running a private intelligence service known as the Haydn Group from his office in the Place du Port?"

"We've heard rumors to that effect."

"Why haven't you done anything about it?"

"Because the president is allergic to operations against Russian financial interests. He turns purple if I even mention the word *Russia*."

"Which is why I didn't invite you to the party, Morris."

"So why are you telling me about this now?"

"Thirteen ninety-five Brickell Avenue. It's a sixty-story tower in Miami's financial district."

"What about it?"

"Arkady and I bought it last week with money looted from Russia's Federal Treasury." Gabriel smiled. "It was a steal at four hundred million."

"WHICH FIRMS ARE HANDLING THE mirror trades?" asked Payne when Gabriel had finished the briefing.

"Actually, only one financial institution is involved."

"American?"

"German."

"RhineBank?"

"How did you guess?"

"You are aware of the fact," said Payne carefully, "that Rhine-Bank is the president's primary lender."

"I'm not interested in the president's finances, Morris. I just want you to quietly ask the Treasury Department and the Fed to turn a blind eye to my activities for the moment."

"You neglected to mention the name of the Geneva-based private equity firm you're using."

"Global Vision Investments."

"Saint Martin Landesmann? That tree-hugging leftist?"

"That's one way of describing him."

"I hear he's in the democracy business now."

"He got into it at my suggestion. I created the Global Alliance for Democracy in order to place Martin on the Haydn Group's radar."

Morris Payne smiled in spite of himself. "Not bad, Gabriel. But what is the goal of this operation?"

"Once Arkady and I complete our shopping spree, I will ask the United States to seize the assets we purchased with looted Russian funds and freeze Arkady's bank accounts worldwide. Given the pro-Russian sympathies of your boss, this reckoning will necessarily have to wait until after the inauguration."

"What makes you think the new crowd will go for it?"

"Come on, Morris. Really."

"And the British?" asked Payne.

"Downing Street will target Arkady's assets in the United Kingdom, and simultaneously the Swiss authorities will shut down his operation in Geneva and expel his workforce, including the employees of the Haydn Group. Arkady will have no choice but to return to Moscow."

"If you're right about the Haydn Group, their computers are the intelligence equivalent of the Holy Grail."

"I've already laid claim to them."

"Who gets the money?"

"Anyone but the Tsar."

"If we seize it, the blowback from Moscow will be intense."

"That money is a weapon of mass destruction, Morris. He's using it to weaken the West from within. The West's internal political divisions are real, but the Russians have been fanning the flames. They're good at this game. They've been playing it for more than a century. But now they have a new weapon at their disposal. The supremacy of the dollar gives the United States the power to disarm them. You must act."

"Not me. I'm out of here on January twentieth at noon." Payne paused, then added, "If I survive that long."

"Are you in trouble?"

"Apparently, I haven't shown sufficient loyalty in the aftermath of the election."

"What did he want you to do?"

"Next subject," said Payne.

"The mirror trades."

"I'll talk to Treasury and the Fed."

"Quietly, Morris."

"The Agency knows how to keep a secret."

"It's not you I'm worried about," said Gabriel. "Do you remember that code-word operation I was running in Syria against the Islamic State? The one your boss described in great detail to the Russian foreign minister in the Oval Office?"

"I turned purple," said Payne.

"That makes two of us, Morris."

44

GENEVA

NEXT MORNING THE OPERATION SHIFTED into high gear.
No longer constrained by the threat of American financial
surveillance, Gabriel instructed Isabel to pressure Anil Kandar into making ever larger mirror trades. The daily hauls of
laundered dollars increased sharply, and by week's end there
was enough cash in the till to finance another purchase. This
time it was the rumored office tower on West Monroe Street
in Chicago, which Martin purchased for $500 million from a
Charlotte-based real estate trust. He turned over management
of the building to the same company that was looking after 1395
Brickell Avenue. No one involved in the deal ever considered
the possibility that the true owner of the property was Arkady
Akimov and his childhood friend from Baskov Lane. No one,
that is, but the director of the Central Intelligence Agency, who

sent Gabriel a secure cable of congratulations over his latest move in the American commercial real estate market.

Gabriel's Russian partner, however, appeared blissfully unaware that his financial empire—not to mention his private intelligence service—was in grave peril. Each afternoon he welcomed the instrument of his demise into his office and signed the documents that would seal his fate. So complete was Arkady's trust of Isabel that by the second week of December she was no longer required to place her phone in the signal-blocking box on Ludmilla Sorova's desk. The recordings lent support to her concerns about the state of Arkady's emotions. In a bid to cool the Russian's ardor, Gabriel dispatched Isabel to Paris for a Wednesday-evening tryst with Martin, but the ruse seemed to have the opposite of its intended effect. A billionaire many times over, Arkady Akimov was used to getting what he wanted. And what he wanted was Isabel Brenner in his bed.

Gabriel had no intention of allowing his agent to be drawn into a love triangle—even a fictitious one. Used judiciously, however, Arkady's affections could be put to good use in helping to run out the operational clock. Gabriel had already engineered more than enough financial misconduct to smash NevaNeft and the Haydn Group to pieces. All he needed now was a change of administration in Washington. On December 14, the Electoral College officially affirmed the president's defeat. The final step in the process, a largely ceremonial congressional certification, would take place in three weeks' time, on Wednesday, January 6. The defeated president called on Republicans in the House and Senate to use the occasion to overturn the results of the election. "Too soon to give up," he wrote on Twitter. "People are really angry." They were also dying of the coronavirus in record numbers. But the president, desperate to remain in power, seemed not to notice or care.

Nor did he seem to notice that the Swiss financier and left-leaning political activist Martin Landesmann had dipped his toe into the American commercial real estate market. Martin's next acquisition, however, was more in keeping with his track record: an Arizona-based manufacturer of wind turbines. The very next day he snapped up SunTech, a maker of solar panels headquartered in Fort Lauderdale. AeroParts of Salina, Kansas, was next, followed soon after by Columbia River Organic Foods of Portland.

His final purchase of the year, an office tower in London's Canary Wharf, came on the Friday of that week, the unofficial start of what promised to be the most depressing winter holiday since the darkest days of the Second World War. Isabel delivered the accompanying documents to NevaNeft headquarters at half past five, and for the first time in many days, Ludmilla Sorova demanded she surrender her phone before entering Arkady's office. One hour later, when she emerged into the Place du Port, her handbag was hanging from her left shoulder rather than the right, a signal there was a problem. While crossing the rue du Purgatoire, she rang Martin and calmly explained what it was.

"You'll never guess who invited me to dinner tomorrow night."

"What did you tell him?"

"I said I would give him an answer in the morning."

"Who else is going to be there?"

"No one."

"What are you talking about?"

"Oksana is leaving for Moscow for a few days. It will just be the two of us. What do you want me to do, Martin?"

HE RANG HER AT NINE the following morning with his answer. His airy tone betrayed the fact he was speaking on behalf of Gabriel.

"It's fine with me. In fact, it might be good for future business."

"And if he tries to seduce me?"

"Improvise." After a pause, Martin added, "If you think you can handle him."

"If I can handle you, I can handle Arkady Akimov."

"I didn't realize I was being *handled*."

"I suppose I'll have to try harder next time."

"Please do."

Isabel planned to telephone Arkady with the news at midday, but he called her five minutes after Martin rang off. He didn't sound at all surprised when she accepted his invitation, though he was quite obviously pleased.

"My driver will pick you up at your apartment at seven," he said, and abruptly rang off.

He didn't bother to ask Isabel for the address.

45

FÉCHY, CANTON VAUD

Arkady's garish villa sparkled like a yuletide tree, but in its cavernous ceremonial rooms the atmosphere was one of sudden abandonment. Isabel imagined the driver had mistakenly delivered her to Gatsby's mansion in West Egg the morning after Myrtle's tragic death in the valley of ashes. Indeed, she half expected to find Arkady as Nick Carraway had found his enigmatic neighbor—leaning against a table in the hall, heavy with dejection or sleep. Instead, Arkady received Isabel cheerfully in his formal drawing room. Like his office upstairs, it was impeccably decorated, though here the piano was a Bechstein Concert B 212 rather than a Bösendorfer.

He lifted an open bottle of Montrachet from a crystal ice bucket and poured two glasses. Handing one to Isabel, he kissed her lightly on each cheek. The shock was like a spark of static electricity.

"You look lovely, Isabel. But then, you always do." Arkady raised his glass. "Thank you so much for accepting my invitation. I was afraid you wouldn't come."

"Why?"

"Because your last visit here was . . ."

"At times unpleasant," said Isabel.

"But lucrative, yes?"

"Incredibly."

"I hope Martin has looked after your interests."

"He's been very generous."

"Does he know you're here?"

"What do you think?"

"I think you called him the minute you left my office last night and asked him what you should do."

"Are you listening to my calls?" asked Isabel playfully.

"Of course." His smile was disarming. "And we're reading your text messages and emails as well."

"Is that how you discovered my address?"

"Absolutely not. We simply followed you home one evening after you left work." Arkady opened a Chinese lacquered box. "Your phone, please."

Isabel placed it inside and closed the lid. "Is this the way you treat all the women you're trying to seduce?"

"Is it that obvious?"

"It has been for some time."

"And yet Martin allowed you to come."

"Because I assured him it was a business dinner and that nothing would happen."

"This *is* a business dinner. As for whether anything will happen . . ." Arkady shrugged. "That is entirely up to you."

Outside, Arkady's terraced gardens were illuminated like the Roman Forum at night. "It's beautiful," remarked Isabel.

"Yes," said Arkady distantly. "But not as beautiful as you."

She accepted his compliment in silence.

"May I ask you a question, Isabel?"

"No."

"Why is a woman like you involved with a married man? And please don't bother to deny it."

"Have you been following me to Paris as well?"

"The apartment is located on the Quai du Bourbon."

"I'll take that as a yes."

Arkady sighed. "Surely you realized that, when working for a man like me, you could expect no zone of privacy."

"I don't work for you. I work for Martin."

"And when he grows bored with you?"

"I'll take solace in the fact that I am now a very wealthy woman."

"How wealthy?"

"Arkady, please."

"Seven figures? Eight perhaps?" He made a dismissive movement of his hand. "This is nothing. I'm prepared to make you seriously rich. Rich enough to own a villa like this. Rich beyond your wildest dreams."

"And what would I have to do in return?"

"Leave Martin Landesmann and come to work for me."

Isabel laughed in spite of herself.

"What's so funny?"

"I thought you wanted me to become your mistress."

"I do," said Arkady. "But I am a very patient man."

———————

THE DINING ROOM WAS HUNG with crystal chandeliers and aglow with candlelight. Two places had been laid at one end of the ludicrously long table. White-jacketed waiters served a first course of green lentils and caviar.

"You must have toiled all day on this," joked Isabel.

"My chef used to work for Alain Ducasse in Paris."

"What a coincidence. So did mine."

"Do you have household help in that little hutch of yours in the Old Town?"

"I have a very nice woman from Senegal who straightens up for me every Friday afternoon."

"You need something larger."

"I'm thinking about a place in Cologny."

"Good idea. Perhaps this will help."

He presented Isabel with a single-page document outlining the terms of his offer. It included a one-time signing bonus of fifty million Swiss francs—the equivalent of $56 million—and a yearly salary of ten million francs. Isabel would earn most of her money, however, through her annual bonuses. The letter promised that they would never be less than eight figures in size.

"I know nothing about the oil business."

"You won't be working in that part of the company. In fact, you won't even have an office in NevaNeft headquarters. Yours will be around the corner on the rue de Rhône."

"What will I do there?"

"Nominally, you will be the owner of a small investment firm."

"What will I *really* be doing?"

Arkady smiled. "Processing."

Isabel laid the offer letter on the table. "It's a mistake, Arkady. I'm more valuable to you at GVI."

"My relationship with Martin has been extremely successful. Those beautiful office towers in America and London are proof of that. But GVI alone can't handle the volume of processing I require. I need a dozen Martins working around the clock. You will be standing atop the podium with a baton in your hand. You will serve as my kapellmeister."

Isabel tapped the document with the tip of her forefinger. "It doesn't mention anything about me sleeping with you."

"My lawyer advised me not to put it in writing."

"Is it a job requirement?"

"Don't be ridiculous."

"And if I'm not interested?"

"I will be heartbroken, but it will have no impact on our working relationship." He pushed the letter across the tabletop. "That is yours to keep. Take all the time you need."

With that, he allowed the matter to drop. Isabel prepared herself to be sexually propositioned but was pleasantly surprised when he asked about her childhood in Trier. He had visited the city in 1985, he claimed, while working as a Soviet diplomat. Isabel listened to Arkady's lies with false attentiveness, a hand pressed to her chin. She only hoped she was half as convincing. Obviously, she had played her part well. How else to explain the fact that Arkady had offered her a senior position at Kremlin Inc.? Regrettably, she would be unable to accept it, as Kremlin Inc. would soon face an unprecedented period of market turbulence.

They returned to the drawing room for coffee. Arkady sat

down at the Bechstein and played the *Moonlight Sonata*. It was a performance worthy of Murray Perahia or Alfred Brendel.

"You missed your calling," said Isabel.

"We have that in common, you and I." He lowered the piano's fallboard. "Women usually melt when I play that piece. But not you, Isabel."

She glanced at her wristwatch. "It's late."

"Was my playing that bad?"

"It was the perfect end to a lovely evening."

"And you'll consider my offer?"

"Of course."

He rose from the piano and lifted the lid of the signal-blocking box. "What are you doing for the holidays?"

"Hiding from the virus. You?"

"Oksana and I are spending Christmas here in Féchy, but we're celebrating New Year's Eve with a few friends in Courchevel."

"A *few* friends?"

"Actually, it will be a rather large gathering."

"I thought the ski resort was closed because of the pandemic."

"It is. But I've purchased every snowmobile in Les Trois Vallées to get my guests to the top of the mountain. Several important figures from Moscow are flying in for the occasion." He handed Isabel her phone. "I insist you join us."

"I wouldn't want to be an imposition."

"You won't be. In fact, one of my guests specifically asked me to invite you."

"Really? Who?"

Arkady took Isabel by the arm. "My driver will take you back to Geneva."

46

GENEVA–COSTA DE PRATA, PORTUGAL

ISABEL WAS AWAKENED BY HER phone shortly after eight the following morning. She tapped the ACCEPT icon and raised the device to her ear.

"Didn't I read somewhere that you never get out of bed before noon?"

"Reporters," said Anna Rolfe disdainfully.

"If I remember correctly, it was a direct quote."

Anna laughed. "I hope I didn't wake you."

"You did, actually. I had a rather late night."

"What was his name?"

"I'd rather not say."

"I've had a few nights like that myself," admitted Anna.

"I've read about those, too."

Anna asked about Isabel's plans for the holidays. Isabel gave her the same answer she had given Arkady the previous evening, that she intended to shelter in place in her apartment in the Old Town.

"I have a better idea," said Anna. "Let's take a trip. Just the two of us."

"Where?"

"It's a surprise."

"How shall I pack?"

"In a suitcase, I suppose."

"Warm or cold?"

"Cold," said Anna. "And wet."

"I was afraid you were going to say that."

"Meet me at Geneva Airport at noon. Martin has agreed to let us borrow his plane."

"Noon *today*?"

"Yes, of course."

"Cello or no cello?"

"Cello," replied Anna before ringing off. "Definitely cello."

Isabel closed her eyes and tried to sleep a little longer, but it was no use; the sun was streaming through her window, and her thoughts were spinning. She doubted Anna's unexpected call had been as spontaneous as it sounded. In fact, Isabel was all but certain it had something to do with the invitation Arkady had extended after his performance of Beethoven's *Moonlight Sonata*. She had been holding her phone at the time, and the signal meter indicated it had reconnected to the cellular grid. Others had been listening.

In the kitchen, Isabel brewed a pot of coffee and watched the latest election news from America. The outgoing president's lawyers were reportedly preparing a last-ditch appeal to the US Supreme Court to overturn the results in the pivotal battleground state of Pennsylvania. It was, said one legal analyst, the last desperate act of a desperate man.

Isabel switched off the television. Showered and dressed, she packed enough clothing for a stay of several days in a cold, wet climate. At 11:45, observed by two employees of the Haydn Group, she maneuvered the suitcase and her cello into the back of an Uber on the rue de l'Hôtel-de-Ville. Because it was a Sunday, the drive to the private terminal at Geneva Airport was only ten minutes. Anna was aboard Martin's Gulfstream, her mobile phone to her ear.

"My agent," she whispered, and continued the conversation until the plane was airborne and the connection was lost. Isabel's phone read NO SERVICE as well. Anna nevertheless placed both their devices in a signal-blocking pouch and sealed the Velcro flap.

"Since when do you travel with a Faraday bag?"

Anna smiled but made no reply.

"Where are we going?" asked Isabel.

"My villa in Portugal."

"Just the two of us?"

"No. Our mutual friend will be there, too."

"May I ask a question?"

"It's a long story, Isabel."

"Does it have a happy ending?"

Anna smiled sadly. "No such luck."

AN AUDI SEDAN WAS WAITING for them at the FBO at Lisbon Airport. Much to Isabel's dismay, Anna insisted on driving. As they hurtled recklessly northward along the A8, she spoke without pause about her career, her failed marriages, her disastrous love affairs, and her lifelong struggle with bipolar disorder—all for the benefit of Isabel's phone, which was resting on the center console, fully charged and connected to Portugal's MEO mobile cellular network.

"And what about you?" asked Anna at last. "Tell me about your work for Martin."

"We're buying everything in sight."

"I read something about a skyscraper in Miami."

"And Chicago and London, too." Isabel glanced at the speedometer. "Don't you think you should slow down a bit?"

"Faster, you say?"

By the time they reached the Costa de Prata, the sun was a fiery orange disk suspended above a copper sea. Anna's villa occupied a wooded hilltop overlooking the fishing village of Torreira. She flashed through the open security gate and a moment later braked to a halt in the gravel forecourt, where an elderly man waited in the fading afternoon light. With his white hair and saddle-leather skin, he reminded Isabel of Pablo Picasso. He seemed relieved that they had arrived from Lisbon in one piece.

"This is Carlos," explained Anna. "When he's not looking after my roof and my vineyard, he looks after me. If it wasn't for him, I wouldn't have a left hand, much less a career. Isn't that right, Carlos?"

Ignoring her question, he directed his gaze toward a Volkswagen Passat estate car. "You have a visitor," he said gravely.

"Really? Who?"

"Senhor Delvecchio. He arrived earlier this afternoon."

"After all these years?"

"He said you were expecting him."

"You were rude to him, I hope."

"Of course, Senhora Rolfe."

Isabel left her phone in the Audi and followed Anna into the villa. In the comfortably furnished sitting room they encountered another worried-looking member of the staff. It was Maria Alvarez, Anna's longtime cook and housekeeper.

"What have you done with him?" asked Anna.

The housekeeper pointed toward the terrace, where a silhouetted figure stood at the balustrade, watching the sun sinking into the Atlantic.

"You'd better set an extra place for dinner."

"If you insist, Senhora Rolfe."

Anna remained in the sitting room while Isabel went onto the terrace. "Who's Senhor Delvecchio?" she called out to the figure standing at the balustrade.

Gabriel delivered his answer over his shoulder. "He was someone I used to be."

"Anna's staff doesn't seem to like him very much."

"With good reason, I'm afraid."

"You hurt her?"

"Evidently."

"Scoundrel," hissed Isabel.

Inside, Anna was filling three glasses with chilled tawny Port wine. She handed one to Gabriel and smiled. "I trust my staff treated you cordially when you arrived?"

"I can only imagine the things you said about me after I left."

He drew his phone from the breast pocket of his jacket. "I need to have a word with Isabel alone."

Anna walked over to the couch and sat down.

"If you do not leave this room, you will remain here under armed guard for the foreseeable future."

"That sounds wonderful to me. In fact, I think I'll quarantine here until the plague subsides."

"Please quarantine yourself in the next room. Or better yet, why don't you go upstairs and practice? You know how much I used to love listening to you play the same arpeggio over and over again."

Anna took up her glass and withdrew. Gabriel sat down in her place and entered a long password into his phone. A moment later it emitted the sound of a man speaking stilted German, in the accent of an Ostländer.

"Several important figures from Moscow are flying in for the occasion. I insist you join us."

"I wouldn't want to be an imposition."

"You won't be. In fact, one of my guests specifically asked me to invite you."

"Really? Who?"

He paused the recording. "It sounds as though the evening went well."

"Not as well as Arkady had hoped."

"He made a pass at you?"

"That's one way to describe it."

"And another?"

"Arkady would like us to enter into a long-term arrangement."

"Sexual?"

"And professional." Isabel handed over Arkady's offer letter.

"The terms are rather generous," said Gabriel after reviewing it. "But what exactly does he want you to do for all this money?"

"He'd like me to be his kapellmeister."

"Meaning?"

"He wants me to serve as the liaison between Kremlin Incorporated and the financial services industry in the West." She paused. "Head washerwoman."

"He's obviously impressed by your work."

"So it would seem."

Gabriel reset the time code on the recording and tapped the PLAY icon.

"In fact, one of my guests specifically asked me to invite you."

"Really? Who?"

He paused the recording a second time. "After you arrived home safely last night, I rang an old friend who works for the DGSI, the French internal security service. And I asked the old friend whether his government knew of any high-profile Russians who were planning to celebrate the New Year in Courchevel. And the old friend, after calling a contact at the Service de la Protection, told me his name."

"What's the Service de la Protection?"

"The SDLP is an elite unit of the Police Nationale that looks after the president and visiting foreign dignitaries."

"He's a government official, this important figure from Moscow?"

"Quite a senior one."

"Who is he?"

"The CEO of Kremlin Incorporated." Gabriel smiled. "Mr. Big."

47

COSTA DE PRATA, PORTUGAL

GABRIEL'S OLD FRIEND FROM FRANCE'S DGSI was a man named Paul Rousseau. Working together, they had destroyed the external terrorism division of the Islamic State, earning Gabriel the admiration and gratitude of France's security establishment. For that reason, Rousseau had revealed closely guarded details of the Russian president's pending private visit to France—details that Gabriel shared with Isabel in the familiar surroundings of Anna Rolfe's villa on the Costa de Prata.

The Russian president, he explained, was scheduled to arrive at two p.m. on New Year's Eve. His aircraft, a modified Ilyushin Il-96, would land at Chambéry Airport. There he would board a French government helicopter for the short flight to Courchevel, where he would attend a party at a luxury chalet owned by the oil trader and oligarch Arkady Akimov. A number of French businessmen and politicians were expected to attend the gathering as well, including several leading figures from the far right, which the Russian president supported clandestinely. A team of twelve officers from the Russian Presidential Security Service—a so-called light footprint, in the lexicon of the protective trade—would look after him inside the chalet. The SDLP would handle the perimeter, with support from uniformed Police Nationale officers. Anticipated departure from the chalet was one minute past midnight. Departure from Chambéry Airport was scheduled for one fifteen.

"Unless, of course, he's running late, which is usually the case."

Like most things about the New Russia, Gabriel continued, the Russian Presidential Security Service was a remnant of the KGB. Formerly known as the Ninth Chief Directorate, it had served as the praetorian guard of the Communist Party elite. Now it protected only the Russian president, his family, and the prime minister. The officers were drawn mainly from elite *spetsnaz* units. They were killers in nice suits, and fanatically devoted to the man they served.

"Nevertheless, the French will have primacy as long as the Russian president is on their soil. Courchevel is very isolated, one road in and out, a mountaintop airstrip that's little more than a helipad. If there's a problem, I can ask my friends in the French government to lock it down."

"So there's no risk?"

"There's always a risk when Russians are involved. But I believe it can be managed. Otherwise, I wouldn't consider allowing you to attend."

"Won't Arkady be suspicious if I refuse?"

"Not if you have a good excuse."

"Like what?"

"A severe case of Covid that requires you to be hospitalized in Geneva."

"The small lie to cover the big lie?"

From upstairs came the sound of a G-minor arpeggio. Rising, Gabriel walked over to the large stone fireplace and arranged a pyre of dried olive wood on the grate, atop a bed of kindling.

"How long did you live here?" asked Isabel.

"Six months and fourteen days. A few months later, while I was working on a painting in Venice, I met the woman I would one day marry."

"One day?"

"My life was rather complicated."

"Not as complicated as mine."

"You have me to thank for that."

"I was the one who gave those documents to Nina."

"And now you've been invited to spend New Year's Eve with the president of Russia."

"Just the way you planned it from the beginning?"

"Hardly." He touched a lighted match to the kindling and returned to the couch. "The Russian president and I have been locked in a blood feud for many years now. I've gotten the better of him lately, but he evened the score when he killed my friend Viktor Orlov. He would love nothing more than to kill me, too. In fact, he's tried on several occasions. Twice he tried to kill me with a bomb. The last was attached to a child."

"My God," Isabel whispered.

"I'm afraid God had nothing to do with what happened that

night. The Russian president is not a statesman, Isabel. He is the godfather of a nuclear-armed gangster regime. They are not ordinary, run-of-the-mill gangsters. They are Russian gangsters, which means they are among the cruelest, most violent people on earth. That is why we've gone to such lengths to protect you. And why I'm reluctant to allow you to go to Courchevel."

"Why do you suppose he wants to meet me?"

"If I had to guess, he'd like to ask you a question or two before he allows Arkady to hire you. After all, it's his money. Arkady is only the bagman."

"And if I pass the test?"

"We would have an asset in the heart of Kremlin Incorporated." He paused. "We would own him."

"Mr. Big?"

He nodded.

"And when it's over?"

"I'm afraid you will have plenty of time to practice the cello."

"How long will I have to remain in hiding?"

"If you walk away now, not long. But if you take a job with Kremlin Incorporated . . ." He left the thought unfinished.

"I appreciate your honesty."

"I've never lied to you. Only to Arkady."

"He believes your lies. Mine, too."

"Are you improvising again?"

Upstairs, Anna was playing Paganini's Caprice no. 10. Smiling, Isabel lifted her gaze toward the ceiling. "Don't you love to listen to her practice?"

"Immensely."

"Are you lying to me now?"

Gabriel closed his eyes. "Never, Isabel."

LATER THAT EVENING, AFTER CONSUMING a traditional Portuguese meal served by a contemptuous Maria Alvarez, Gabriel tried to prepare Isabel for the shock of being in the same room with the most powerful man in the world. A cursory review of press photographs and video revealed the marked change in his appearance in the two decades since his rise to power. Gone were the sunken cheeks and dark circles beneath his eyes. Now he had the waxen face of a corpse on display in a mausoleum. His right arm, broken during a street brawl in Leningrad, hung stiffly at his side when he walked. Intentionally rude and vulgar, he took pleasure in the discomfort of others. Successive American and Western European leaders had emerged from meetings appalled by his conduct. The slouch, the displayed crotch, the dead-eyed stare.

"Like his friend Arkady Akimov, he speaks fluent German, so he will undoubtedly address you in your native language rather than in English, which he speaks poorly. Feel free to wish him a pleasant New Year, but make no other attempt to engage him in conversation. Allow him to ask the questions, and keep your answers brief and to the point. And if you feel nervous, don't hesitate to say so. He's a serial killer. He's used to people being nervous in his presence."

Isabel's preparation continued the following morning after Eli Lavon and Christopher Keller arrived from Geneva. Lavon, who spoke both Russian and German, volunteered to portray Vladimir Vladimirovich in a dry run of the encounter. The exercise ended soon after it began, however, when his attempt to appear menacing provoked nothing in Isabel except an expression of pity. Later, following a break for lunch, she breezed through several mock interrogations. Gabriel conducted the last. When it was over, he laid his Beretta 9mm on the table.

"And what happens if they start waving one of these around? Or if they hit you with it? What do you do then, Isabel?"

"I tell them everything they want to know."

"Everything," Gabriel repeated. "Including my name and phone number. Is that clear?"

She nodded.

"Recite it, please."

She did as she was told.

"Again, please."

She sighed. "I reworked RhineBank's entire balance sheet in less than hour. I can remember a phone number."

"Humor me."

Isabel repeated the number accurately and then slumped in her seat, exhausted. What she needed, thought Gabriel, was not additional training but several days of well-deserved rest.

He left her in the hands of Anna Rolfe and turned his attention to the task of moving his operation from Switzerland to the enchanted ski village of Courchevel. Located 135 kilometers south of Geneva, it was an exclusive playground of the beautiful and the rich, especially rich Russians. Arkady's chalet was on the rue de Nogentil. Housekeeping snared a vacant property on the same street for a mere thirty thousand a night, minimum stay of seven nights, no exceptions during the high season, no refunds in the event of a cancellation. Like the Russian president, Gabriel planned to arrive with a light footprint. With the exception of Christopher Keller, all his personnel would be Israeli, though their passports, drivers' permits, and credit cards would identify them as anything but.

By Christmas morning the preparations were complete. All that remained was Arkady's invitation, which Isabel had yet to accept. Once again, Gabriel waited for the Russian billionaire to take the initiative. He passed the holiday quietly with his young wife in Féchy; Isabel, with her friend Anna Rolfe on the Costa de Prata. They walked the windswept beach in midmorning and that evening shared a festive meal with three old friends, including a handsome Englishman who had once been hired to kill Anna during a recital in Venice. It was, she declared, the most enjoyable dinner party she had thrown in many years.

There was no contact from Arkady on Boxing Day, or the day after that. But on Monday the twenty-eighth, he rang Isabel's mobile and, receiving no answer, left a lengthy message on her voice mail. She waited until late Tuesday morning before calling him back.

"But why not?" asked Arkady, deflated.

"Because I won't know a soul there, and I don't speak a word of Russian."

"The guest list includes plenty of non-Russians. And if you don't attend, my friend from Moscow will be upset."

"Who is he, Arkady?"

"A very important figure in the Kremlin. That's all I'm at liberty to say."

Isabel exhaled slowly.

"That sounded like a yes to me," said Arkady.

"On two conditions."

"Name them."

"I will see to my own transportation."

"It's not such an easy drive up the mountain."

"I'm German. I'll manage."

"And the other?"

"You will behave yourself, especially when I'm around your wife."

"I'll do my best."

Isabel glanced at Gabriel, who nodded once. "All right, Arkady. You win."

"Brilliant. I've already taken the liberty of booking you the largest suite at the Hôtel Grand Courchevel. The head of reservations is named Ricardo. He promised to take excellent care of you."

"You shouldn't have."

"It's the least I could do."

"What time is the party?"

"The first guests should begin to arrive around nine. My chalet is on the rue de Nogentil in the Jardin Alpin. It's the largest in Courchevel," he boasted before ringing off. "You can't possibly miss it."

48

COURCHEVEL, FRANCE

IT WAS JEAN-CLAUDE DUMAS, GENERAL manager of the chic K2 Palace, who famously dismissed the clientele of the Hôtel Grand Courchevel as "the elderly and their parents." Her rooms were thirty in number, modest in size, and discreet in appointment. One did not come to the Grand for gold fixtures and suites the size of football pitches. One came for a taste of Europe as it once was. One came to linger over a Campari in the lounge bar or dawdle over coffee and *Le Monde* in the breakfast room. But never in ski attire, mind you; guests waited until after breakfast before dressing for the slopes. The hotel's wireless Internet service, a recent if reluctant addition to her abbreviated list of amenities, was universally regarded as the worst in Courchevel, if not the entire French Alps. Devotees of the Grand rarely complained.

At half past one p.m. on New Year's Eve, the Grand's tidy lobby was as silent as a crypt. The lounge bar was closed by government edict, as was the breakfast room, the grill room, the gym, the spa, and the indoor swimming pool. The kitchen was operating on a skeleton crew, with "no contact" room service being the only option for on-premises dining. At present, only two of the Grand's rooms were occupied. With the resort's ski lifts shut down and its nightclubs shuttered, Courchevel was a gilded ghost town.

Consequently, most of the resort's hotels were closed for the all-important winter holidays. But not the proud Grand. For the sake of its longtime seasonal employees, management had refused to surrender to the surging pandemic, even if it meant incurring day-to-day operational losses. Quite unexpectedly, the hotel had been rewarded with an onslaught of New Year's Eve bookings. It seemed the oil trader and oligarch Arkady Akimov had decided to throw caution to the wind and host a blowout at his monstrous chalet in the Jardin Alpin. Twenty-four of Arkady's guests had wisely decided to sleep it off at the Grand rather than risk the treacherous drive down the mountain. Regrettably, most were Russians, for whom management did not care. Before the plague, they would have been informed—by polite email or with a phone call from Ricardo the reservations manager—that there was no room at the inn. The harsh economic realities of the day, however, had required the Grand to relax its exacting standards and open its doors to the invaders from the East.

One of Arkady's guests, however, was a certain Isabel Brenner—German citizen, resident of Geneva, one night in a Deluxe Prestige Suite, very VIP. Or so claimed the abrasive personal assistant who had made the reservation on Arkady's behalf. Ricardo had pledged to personally look after Madame Brenner's every need before placing the assistant on eternal hold. For his insolence, he received a call from none other than Arkady himself, who issued a not-so-veiled threat of bodily violence if Madame Brenner's stay fell short of absolute perfection. Ricardo, a Spaniard from the restive Basque region, had no reason to doubt the authenticity of the billionaire's warning. Twelve years earlier, a Russian investigative journalist named Aleksandr Lubin had been stabbed to death in Room 237. It was Ricardo, nearly twenty-four hours after the killing, who found the body.

Owing to the hotel's perilously low current occupancy rate, he had granted Arkady's guests the option of a two p.m. check-in at no additional charge. Therefore, at the stroke of 1:45, he stepped hesitantly from the grotto of Reception and took up a defensive position just inside the Grand's double glass doors. He was joined a moment later by the reassuring presence of Philippe, a neatly built former French paratrooper who wore the crossed keys of the International Concierge Institute on his spotless lapel.

Philippe automatically consulted his wristwatch as a Mercedes sedan braked to a halt at the base of the Grand's front steps. "Maybe this was a mistake," he said quietly.

"Maybe not," replied Ricardo as the limousine's only passenger emerged from the backseat.

Attractive female, mid-thirties, blond hair parted on one side, casually but expensively dressed. The driver was a towering brute, more bodyguard than chauffeur. Ricardo pointed out the slight bulge at the left side of his jacket, suggesting the presence of a concealed firearm.

"Ex-military," declared Philippe.

"Russian?"

"Does he look Russian to you?"

"What about the woman?"

"We'll know in a minute."

Thierry the bellman lifted a single piece of luggage from the boot of the Mercedes.

"Russians," said Ricardo, "never come to Courchevel with only one suitcase."

"Never," agreed Philippe.

The woman bade farewell to her driver and started up the steps. Her gaze was vaguely remote, as though she were listening to distant music. It was beautiful music, thought Ricardo. Proper music. Not the EDM technocrap they blasted at deafness-inducing levels every night at Les Caves.

He retreated to the grotto of Reception and watched Philippe fling open the door with more than his usual flourish. The concierge greeted the woman in syrupy French, and she responded in the same language, though it was readily apparent that French was not her native tongue. Ricardo, who typically spent several hours each day on the phone with foreigners, had a well-honed ear for accents. The graceful young woman who seemed to be listening to music only she could hear was a citizen of Germany.

"Madame Brenner?" he asked when she presented herself at the check-in counter.

"How could you tell?"

"Lucky guess." Ricardo flashed his polished hotelier's smile and handed her the cardkey to her room. "Monsieur Akimov has seen to all your charges. If there's anything at all we can do to be of service, please don't hesitate to ask."

"I could use a coffee."

"I'm afraid the lounge is closed, but there's a Nespresso in your suite."

"How's the gym?"

"Closed."

"The spa, too?"

Ricardo nodded. "All the public spaces in the hotel are closed by order of the government."

"I think I'll take a walk."

"A fine idea. Thierry will place your bag in your room."

"Is there a pharmacy nearby?"

"Follow the rue de l'Église down the hill. The pharmacy will be on your right."

"Merci," said the woman, and went out.

Ricardo and Philippe stood side by side in the doorway, watching her descent down the steps.

"No wonder Arkady wants us to take such good care of her," said Ricardo as she disappeared from view.

"You think she's—"

"His mistress? No way," said Ricardo. "Not that one."

A pair of limousines drew up in the street. Four Russians. A mountain of luggage. Not a mask in sight.

Ricardo shook his head. "Maybe this was a mistake."

"Maybe you're right," agreed Philippe.

49

COURCHEVEL, FRANCE

THE BASE OF COURCHEVEL'S MAIN ski lift stood with the stillness of a monument built by a long-vanished civilization, its empty gondolas swaying gently in the brilliant afternoon sunlight. Isabel strolled past a parade of exclusive shops—Dior, Bulgari, Vuitton, Fendi—all of which were shuttered. Next was a ski rental outlet, also closed, and a small café where two patrons, a man and a woman, were drinking coffee from paper cups at a table on the pavement. The man wore a Salomon cap and wraparound sunglasses. The woman, black-haired and olive-complected, was chastising him in rapid, vehement French.

The small lie to cover the big lie . . .

Smiling, Isabel crossed the street and entered the pharmacy.

As she was describing her symptoms to the white-jacketed woman behind the counter, she heard the ping of the electronic door chime. A moment later a sultry Russian-accented voice said, "Isabel? Is that you?"

It was Oksana Akimova. She was wearing a formfitting Fusalp ski suit. Her skin was aglow with the cold and the sun.

Breathlessly, she asked, "When did you arrive?"

"A few minutes ago."

"Are you unwell?"

"Just a little carsick."

"Why don't you come skiing with us? The snow is perfect, and the slopes are absolutely empty."

"I'm not much of a skier, to be honest. I think I'll just go back to my room and rest before the party."

"At least come have a drink with us. We've taken over the terrace of Le Chalet de Pierres."

The *pharmacienne* placed the medication on the counter. Isabel paid with her credit card and followed Oksana into the street. Watched by the couple at the café, they walked past the same parade of shuttered shops to the base of the lift, where Oksana had left a red-and-black Lynx snowmobile.

"I guess it's true," said Isabel.

"What's that?"

"That Arkady bought every available snowmobile in Les Trois Vallées."

"I don't doubt it." Oksana settled behind the controls and fired the engine.

"I'm not dressed for this," shouted Isabel over the racket.

"It's just a few hundred meters up the hill."

Isabel squeezed on to the back of the saddle and wrapped her arms around Oksana's waist. It was shockingly slender, like the waist of an adolescent girl.

"I really think I need to lie down before the party."

"Don't be ridiculous. You can sleep tomorrow."

Oksana turned up the slope of the hill and opened the throttle. Rather than progress in a straight line, she delighted in showing off her skill at handling the powerful machine. Like Anna Rolfe, she ignored Isabel's pleas to slow down.

Le Chalet de Pierres, a Courchevel institution, stood on the left side of the slope. Four more Lynx snowmobiles were parked outside, and a collection of brightly colored skis and poles leaned drunkenly against the storage rack. Their Russian-speaking owners were gathered in a sunlit corner of the large terrace. The tables were littered with uneaten food and several bottles of Bandol rosé, most of them empty.

A sunburned Russian man thrust a glass of the wine into Isabel's hand as Oksana made the introduction. "Everyone, this is Isabel. Isabel, this is everyone."

"Hello, Isabel!" the Russians replied in unison, and Isabel responded by saying, "Hello, everyone."

Oksana was lighting a cigarette. "Aren't you going to take some?" she asked.

"I'm sorry?"

"The medicine you bought at the pharmacy."

Isabel unscrewed the cap from the container and washed down a tablet with the rosé. "Where's Arkady?"

"At the airport awaiting the arrival of tonight's guest of honor."

"Who is he?"

"Arkady didn't tell you?"

Isabel shook her head. "Only that he was very keen to meet me."

"You should consider yourself lucky," said Oksana. "You have been touched by the magic hand."

"What does that mean?"

"In Russia you cannot succeed or become wealthy unless someone in a position of power or influence places his hand on your shoulder. Arkady has placed his hand on you. Soon you will be as rich as an oligarch."

"But I'm not Russian."

"Look around you, Isabel. Do you see any other non-Russians here? You're one of us now. Welcome to the party that never ends." Oksana gave an ironic smile. "Enjoy it while it lasts."

Suddenly, the valley echoed with the distant *thump-thump-thump* of rotors. A moment passed before the first helicopter came into view. Two more soon followed. As they descended toward Courchevel's mountaintop airfield, the revelers gathered on the terrace broke into a boisterous version of the state anthem of the Russian Federation.

Oksana's eyes shone with emotion. "Why aren't you singing?" she asked.

"I don't know the words."

"How is this possible?"

"I'm German."

"Nonsense!" Oksana threw an arm around Isabel's shoulder. "Look around you, Isabel. You're one of us now."

THE HELICOPTERS WERE AIRBUS H215 Super Pumas operated by the French military. Aboard the first was the president of the

Russian Federation, a small entourage of traveling aides, and four officers of the Russian Presidential Security Service. Eight additional Russian bodyguards were squeezed into the second helicopter along with several crates of secure communications equipment. The third Airbus was reserved for a detail from the French Service de la Protection. Relegated to standing watch at the perimeter, the officers would spend their New Year's Eve outside in inclement Alpine weather rather than with friends and loved ones in Paris. Morale was said to be exceedingly low.

An advance team from the SDLP had arrived in Courchevel that morning for a site survey of the hotel-size chalet on the rue de Nogentil where the Russian president would celebrate the New Year with his childhood friend from Leningrad and three hundred invited guests. Had the officers bothered to knock on the door of the more modest dwelling at Number 172—thirty thousand a night, seven-night minimum, no exceptions, no refunds—they would have discovered a multinational group of holidaymakers who had come to Courchevel, seemingly on a whim, despite the fact the ski area was closed. A further inspection of the premises would have uncovered the presence of a large quantity of sophisticated electronic equipment and several firearms.

It would have also revealed that the holidaymakers were in fact officers of Israel's vaunted secret intelligence service. One was Gabriel Allon, a man who had waged a long and bitter struggle against revanchist Russia and its malign organs of state security. Another was his old friend and accomplice Eli Lavon, chief of the physical-and-electronic-surveillance division known as Neviot. Two other division chiefs, Rimona Stern of Collections and Yossi Gavish of Research, had also slipped into Courchevel unobserved. At present, they were drinking coffee at the café across the street from the pharmacy. The previous occupants of their table were strolling past the darkened storefronts lining the rue de la Croisette. The man wearing a Salomon hat and wraparound sunglasses was Mikhail Abramov. He was accompanied by his French-speaking wife, Natalie Mizrahi.

The final member of the team—he was known variously as Nicolas Carnot, Peter Marlowe, or, more accurately, Christopher Keller—was borrowed from the ranks of Britain's Secret Intelligence Service. Concealed beneath the attire of a cross-country skier, he was drinking hot cider on the terrace of Le Chalet de Pierres, watching a band of inebriated Russians singing a lusty, dissonant rendition of their national anthem. Two attractive women, one Russian, the other German, stood slightly apart from the group. An audio feed from the German woman's phone, which was tucked into her fashionable shearling coat, was audible in the rented chalet on the rue de Nogentil.

"Why aren't you singing?"

"I don't know the words."

"How is this possible?"

"I'm German."

"Nonsense! Look around you, Isabel. You're one of us now."

The singing faded, as did the beating of the helicopter rotors. For that much, at least, Gabriel was grateful. The sound had stirred in him an unpleasant memory.

Enjoy watching your wife die, Allon . . .

He moved to the window of the chalet's vaulted great room and watched a motorcade winding its way down the serpentine rue de l'Altiport. As it passed beneath his feet, he fashioned his hand into the shape of a pistol and aimed it toward the figure in the back of an armored Peugeot 5008. The thug from Baskov Lane in Leningrad. The godfather of a nuclear-armed gangster regime.

The motorcade continued along the rue de Nogentil for another one hundred meters before turning into the forecourt of the hotel-size chalet. Instantly, officers of the SDLP and Police Nationale established a checkpoint at the northern end of the street—a checkpoint through which the beautiful German woman on the terrace of Le Chalet de Pierres would soon be compelled to pass. At four fifteen, after a harrowing snowmobile ride down the mountain, she returned to her hotel, where the Spanish-born head of reservations informed her that Monsieur Akimov had taken the liberty of arranging her car for the evening.

"How thoughtful of him. What time?"

"Nine o'clock, Madame Brenner."

"Tell the driver not to expect me before nine thirty. There's nothing worse than arriving for a party too early. Wouldn't you agree, Ricardo?"

"No, Madame Brenner. Nothing at all."

50

COURCHEVEL, FRANCE

ISABEL AWOKE WITH A FEELING of paralysis, and with no memory of having slept. The bed on which she lay was unfamiliar, as was the darkened room that enclosed her. The alarm on her mobile phone was bleating—curious, for she did not recall setting it. The sound of two men speaking in Russian somewhere nearby only added to her confusion.

At length, she silenced the phone and raised it to her eyes. Evidently, it was 8:15 p.m. on New Year's Eve. But where on earth was she? She entered her eight-digit password and tapped the weather icon, and the forecast for the French ski resort of Courchevel appeared on the screen. And then she remembered. She was to attend a party that evening at the home of a Russian oligarch who wanted her to serve as his chief concealer of looted wealth and, if she were amenable, his extramarital sexual partner. At some point during the evening—the precise timing had never been made clear—she would be invited to meet a very important figure from the Kremlin. A speaker of fluent German, he would address Isabel in her native language. She was authorized to wish him a pleasant New Year but was to make no other attempt to engage him in conversation. If she was anxious during the encounter, she was at liberty to tell him so.

He's a serial killer. He's used to people being nervous in his presence . . .

According to Isabel's phone, a light snow was falling. Pulling away the blackout curtain from the window, she confirmed this to be true. Then she padded into the suite's kitchenette and switched on the Nespresso. A double Diavolitto cleared the last cobwebs of sleep from her head but left her feeling jittery and unsettled.

The sensation abated in the shower. To avoid any last-minute indecision over her clothing, she had packed a single black Max Mara cocktail-length dress, which she accessorized with a diamond bracelet, a double strand of Mikimoto pearls, and her outrageously expensive Jaeger-LeCoultre Rendez-Vous wristwatch. She had brought along a protective face mask—black, to match her dress—but she consigned it to her clutch purse. The party, illegal under France's strict national lockdown, would undoubtedly turn out to be a superspreader event. Isabel reckoned she would be lucky to survive the night.

At nine fifteen the phone on her bedside table fluttered and flashed with an incoming call. It was Ricardo, her car had arrived. She remained in the suite for another fifteen minutes, adding a final touch of decadence to her makeup, before heading down to the lobby. Philippe the concierge practically snapped to attention as she stepped from the lift.

Outside, Thierry the bellman held an umbrella above Isabel's head as she slipped into the back of the waiting Mercedes. Much to her relief, the driver was a handsome Frenchman called Yannick and not another Russian. As the car rolled from the curb, he switched on the sound system. Haydn's Cello Concerto in C Major, the beautiful second movement.

Isabel felt a stab of panic. "Did Monsieur Akimov tell you to play that?" she asked.

"Who, Madame?"

"Never mind."

Isabel contemplated her reflection in the car window. She had been touched by the magic hand, she reassured herself. She was one of them now. She owned them.

ISABEL'S DRIVER WAS YANNICK FOURNIER, thirty-three, a married father of two with no criminal record who supported the Olympique Lyonnais football team. His dispatcher had instructed him to remain in the Jardin Alpin section of Courchevel until such time as the client was ready to return to her hotel. While guiding the car along the rue de Bellecôte, he recited the number for his mobile phone, which the client stored in her own device. Eli Lavon, hunched over a computer in the chalet's makeshift ops center, snapped her photograph with the phone's camera before she returned it to her clutch purse.

"She looks nervous," observed Gabriel.

"He would find it odd if she wasn't."

"Vladimir Vladimirovich?"

"Who else?"

A silence fell between them. There was only the music from the car's sound system.

"Why is the driver playing Haydn?" asked Gabriel. "And why a cello concerto?"

"It's a coincidence."

"I don't believe in them, Eli. And neither do you."

Lavon tapped a few keys on the laptop, and the icon for an audio file appeared on the screen. He opened it, adjusted the time code, and clicked PLAY.

"Arkady has placed his hand on you. Soon you will be as rich as an oligarch."

Lavon clicked PAUSE. "Don't lose your nerve now."

"Maybe he's toying with me."

Lavon clicked PLAY a second time.

"Look around you, Isabel. Do you see any other non-Russians here? You're one of us now. Welcome to the party that never ends."

Lavon paused the recording. "The words of Oksana Akimova would suggest your asset is in no danger."

"Play the rest of it."

Lavon tapped the trackpad.

"Enjoy it while it lasts."

The winking blue light on the computer screen indicated that Isabel's car had arrived at the checkpoint. A moment later came the sound of two men conversing in French. One was Isabel's driver. The other was an officer of the French Service de la Protection.

"Name?"

"Isabel Brenner."

"Open the trunk, please."

The inspection was brief, ten seconds, no more. Then the lid closed with a thud. Gabriel watched as the winking blue light crept forward, into the temporary Russian zone of Courchevel. In a moment his asset would be at the mercy of the Kremlin's praetorian guard. They were fanatically devoted to the man they served, he thought. Killers in nice suits.

51

RUE DE NOGENTIL, COURCHEVEL

TWO OF THE RUSSIAN BODYGUARDS were at that moment standing like pillars at the entrance of Arkady's chalet. One was holding a clipboard, the other a portable magnetometer. Evidently, Isabel had been singled out for additional scrutiny; the pat-down she endured at the hands of the one with the magnetometer bordered on sexual assault. When it was finally over, Comrade Clipboard rummaged through her handbag as though searching for something of value to steal. He found nothing of interest other than her phone, which he demanded she unlock in his presence. She entered the eight digits as swiftly as possible, and the home screen appeared. Satisfied, the Russian returned the device and ordered Isabel to enjoy the party.

Inside, a skinny, mannequin-like girl in stage makeup and a

formfitting sequined gown relieved Isabel of her overcoat and then carelessly directed her toward the chalet's great room. She had expected the decor to match the timbered exterior, but the room was white and modern and hung with large, colorful works of contemporary art. On one side was an open staircase leading to a loft on the second level, where two more expressionless Russian bodyguards stood watch along a balustrade. Beneath them, two hundred or so stylishly attired revelers, drinks in hand, were shouting at one another over the deafening music. Isabel could feel the vibration of the sound waves crawling like insects over her bare arms. Or perhaps, she thought, it was merely particles of coronavirus. She considered pulling on her mask but decided against it. Even the poor French catering staff were absent protection.

A second mannequin girl, her clothing identical to the first, wordlessly pointed out the cocktail table. Several more women moved like dead souls amid the guests, occasionally alighting on the arm of an unaccompanied male. Isabel supposed they were party favors. One was attached to Mad Maxim Simonov, the nickel king, who was engaged in an intense conversation with the Kremlin press secretary. An unusually accomplished liar, the press secretary owned several luxury homes, including an apartment on Fifth Avenue, and vacationed regularly in hot spots such as Dubai and the Maldives. On his left wrist was a limited-edition Richard Mille watch worth $670,000, more than he had earned during his entire career as a humble servant of the Russian people.

He was not the only example of unexplained riches in the room. There was, for example, the former hot-dog salesman who was now the proud owner of record of several highly valuable Russian firms, including the shadowy Internet company that had meddled in the American presidential election of 2016. And the former judo instructor who now built gas pipelines and electric power stations. And the former director of the Mariinsky Theatre who had somehow amassed a personal fortune in excess of $10 billion.

And then, of course, there was the former KGB officer who now owned the Geneva-based oil trading firm known as Neva-Neft. At present, he was standing next to the bodyguards along the balustrade, no doubt searching for Isabel. Adopting the unseeing gaze of the mannequin girls, she walked over to the nearest cocktail table, where she lent her ear to a wholesome-looking man of around forty.

"Can I buy you a drink?" he roared in American-accented English.

"I believe they're complimentary," shouted Isabel in reply. She asked the server for a glass of champagne, and the American ordered vodka.

"You're not Russian," he pointed out.

"You seem disappointed."

"I've always heard Russian girls are easy."

"Especially girls like her." Isabel nodded toward one of the ambulatory mannequins. "If I had to guess, they were flown in for the occasion."

"Like the caviar."

Isabel smiled. "Why are you here?"

"Business," he bellowed.

"What do you do?"

"I work for Goldman Sachs."

"My condolences. Where?"

"London. What about you?"

"I play the cello."

"Nice. How do you know Arkady?"

"It's a long story."

"Is that your phone?"

"What?"

He pointed toward the bag she was clutching in her left hand. "I think you have a call."

Glancing toward the loft, she saw Arkady standing at the balustrade with a phone to his ear. His eyes were searching the crowd, which suggested he had not yet discovered Isabel's whereabouts. She decided to remain in the company of the wholesome-looking stranger a little longer. Though she was allergic to Americans, this one seemed relatively harmless.

"Nice bag," he said when the phone stopped ringing.

"Bottega Veneta," explained Isabel.

"Nice watch, too. How much do cellists make?"

"My father is one of the richest men in Germany."

"Really? Mine is one of the richest in Connecticut. What are you doing for the rest of your life?"

"To be honest, I haven't a clue." The phone started up again. "Will you excuse me?"

"You forgot this." He handed her a glass of champagne. "What's your name?"

"Isabel."

"Isabel what?"

"Brenner."

"I won't forget you, Isabel Brenner."

"Please don't."

She stepped away and engaged in a futile attempt to remove

her phone from the clutch while at the same time holding the champagne. Eventually she lifted her gaze toward the balustrade and saw Arkady observing her struggle with obvious amusement. He beckoned to her with one hand and with the other pointed to the base of the staircase. A moment later he greeted her on the landing with a kiss on each cheek. The display of affection did not go unnoticed by Oksana, who was eyeing them from below.

"I see you met Fletcher Billingsley," Arkady blared.

"Who?"

"The handsome young banker from Goldman Sachs."

"Have you been unfaithful, Arkady?"

"My relationship with Fletcher is entirely legitimate."

"What does that make me?"

He caressed her shoulder. "I assume you now know the name of the man who would like to meet you."

"I believe I do. In fact, one of his bodyguards gave me a thorough groping before letting me through your door."

"I'm afraid you're about to get another."

He led her through a doorway, into a small sitting room—an anteroom, thought Isabel. The walls were adorned with framed photographs of the man who awaited her on the other side of the next door. Most of the photos depicted him meeting with important people and tending to important matters of state, but in one he was walking along a rocky streambed, his hairless chest exposed to the pale Russian sunlight.

"Does he come here often?" asked Isabel, but Arkady made no reply other than to lift the lid of yet another decorative signal-blocking box. Automatically, Isabel placed her phone inside.

Arkady closed the lid and nodded toward the waiting officer

of the Russian Presidential Security Service. His pat-down was even more invasive than the one Isabel had received earlier. When it was over, he demanded her purse.

Arkady placed his hand on the latch of the door. "Ready?"

"Yes, I think so."

"Excited?"

"A bit nervous, actually."

"Don't worry," whispered Arkady as he opened the door. "He's used to it."

52

RUE DE NOGENTIL, COURCHEVEL

IN THE RENTED CHALET ON the opposite side of the rue de Nogentil, Gabriel and the six other members of his team were at that moment gathered around a single laptop computer, monitoring the encrypted feed from Isabel's compromised smartphone. For a period of approximately three minutes, the device had been disconnected from the SFR Mobile cellular network, presumably as a result of being placed in a signal-blocking containment vessel. It was now in the hands of an officer of the Russian Presidential Security Service. Having correctly entered the password on his first attempt, he was scrolling through the directory of recent voice calls.

"Now we know why the boys at the front door ordered her to unlock her phone," said Eli Lavon.

"Is there any way they can find our malware?" asked Gabriel.

"Not unless they attach the phone to a computer. And even then, the technician would have to be damn good to find it."

"They *are* good, Eli. They're Russians."

"But we're better. And you were meticulous when it came to her communications."

"So why did they steal her password?" Gabriel glanced at the computer. "And why is Igor now reading her text messages?"

"Because Igor's boss told him to read them. That's what a Russian gangster does before hiring a non-Russian to launder his money."

"Do you think she can handle him?"

"If she hits her toe marks . . ."

"What, Eli?"

"We'll own him."

THE DECOR OF THE ROOM matched the rest of the chalet, bright and modern, nothing timbered or rustic or suggestive of a ski lodge. For that matter, there seemed to be nothing of Arkady in the room, either. Nothing but the piano, another Bösendorfer. Polished to a high black gloss, it stood forlornly atop a pale gray carpet, unplayed. In one corner of the room sat four men. Two were quite obviously members of the Russian president's security detail. The other two reeked of bureaucracy; doubtless they were Kremlin apparatchiks. Nearby was a stack of lead-gray electronic components, red and green signal lights winking. It was the hardware, thought Isabel, of a head-of-state-level secure phone. The receiver was wedged between the shoulder and ear of the Russian president.

He wore a black rollneck sweater rather than a dress shirt,

and a costly-looking cashmere sport jacket. His fair hair, carefully parted and combed, covered less of his scalp than was suggested by recent photographs. The expression on his medically pampered face was one of irritation, as though he had been placed on hold. It was the same expression, thought Isabel, that he routinely displayed to Western counterparts before embarking on an hourlong airing of grievances, real and imagined.

Arkady escorted Isabel to an arrangement of contemporary furniture adjacent to the room's soaring picture window. The view was to the west, toward the darkened slopes of the ski area. As they sat down, the president began to speak, a burst of rapid Russian followed by a long pause. A minute or two later, he spoke a second time, and once again a lengthy silence ensued. Isabel reckoned there was translation involved.

"It sounds important."

"It usually is."

"Perhaps I should wait outside."

"You told me you don't speak Russian."

"Not a word."

"Then please stay where you are." Arkady was staring out the window, a forefinger resting speculatively along one cheek. "I'm sure he won't be long."

Isabel looked down at her hands and noticed that her knuckles were white. The Russian president was speaking again, though now it was in English; he was wishing the person at the other end of the call a happy New Year. At the conclusion of the conversation, he handed the phone to an aide and in Russian addressed Arkady from across the room.

"A minor crisis at home," Arkady explained to Isabel. "He'd like us to wait outside while he makes another call or two."

They rose in unison and, watched by the Russian president, returned to the anteroom. During their brief absence, three additional officers of the Presidential Security Service had arrived. One was Comrade Clipboard, the sentry from the front door.

Arkady was looking at his phone. "How is your hotel?" he asked.

"Lovely. I'm only sorry I can't stay longer."

"When are you planning to leave?"

"Martin's driver is picking me up at noon."

Arkady looked up from the phone abruptly but said nothing.

"Is something wrong?"

His smile appeared forced. "I was hoping you might join us for brunch tomorrow."

"I really need to be getting back to Geneva."

"Numbers to crunch?"

"Always."

Arkady's phone purred with an incoming call. The conversation was brief and largely one-sided. "It turns out the crisis isn't so minor, after all," he said after killing the connection. "I only hope you can forgive me for dragging you all the way to Courchevel for nothing." He nodded toward Comrade Clipboard. "Gennady will escort you back to the party. Please let me know if there is anything you need."

"All I need," said Isabel, "is my phone."

Arkady removed it from the box and handed it over. The movement did not awaken the device from its slumber. Isabel thumbed the side button, but there was no response. The phone was powered off.

She slipped it into her handbag and followed Comrade

Clipboard down a hallway and into a waiting lift. Two other security men squeezed inside as well. One pressed a call button labeled B.

"Where are you taking me?"

"To the party," answered Comrade Clipboard.

"The party is on the first floor."

When the door slid open, the stench of chlorine was overwhelming. Comrade Clipboard seized Isabel by the arm and pulled her from the carriage. A single figure stood on the deck at the pool's edge, faintly lit by watery blue light. It was Fletcher Billingsley, the rich American from Goldman Sachs whom she had met at the bar upstairs.

He approached her slowly, a benevolent smile on his face, and addressed her in Russian-accented English. "I told you that I wouldn't forget you, Isabel."

He issued no threat or warning, which was inadvertently chivalrous on his part, for it gave Isabel no opportunity to prepare herself for the pain. One moment she was standing ramrod-straight, the next she was doubled over like a folding knife. He eased her with surprising tenderness to the cold tile floor, where she fought in vain to draw a breath. The chalet seemed to be spinning. Welcome to the party that never ends, she thought. Enjoy it while it lasts.

53

RUE DE NOGENTIL, COURCHEVEL

HE HAULED ISABEL TO HER feet and frog-marched her into a luxuriously appointed dressing room. There he hurled her into a ceramic wall before thrusting her head beneath the briny, scalding water of a Jacuzzi. For all she knew, he drowned her, for when she regained consciousness, she was sprawled across the tile floor, covered in her own vomit.

"What is your name?" asked a voice from above.

"Isabel Brenner."

"Your *real* name."

"It is my real name."

"Who are you working for?"

"Global Vision Investments."

He picked her up like a rag doll and forced her head beneath the water a second time. She was scarcely conscious when he finally lifted her face above the surface.

"What is your name?"

"Isabel. My name is Isabel."

"Who are you working for?"

"I used to work for RhineBank. Now I work for Martin Landesmann."

He gave her an openhanded blow that filled her mouth with blood and sent her tumbling to the floor.

"Why are you doing this?" she sobbed.

He shook her violently. "What is your name? Your real name."

"Isabel," she shouted. "My name is Isabel."

He released her and left the dressing room—for how long, she did not know. A few minutes, an hour. When he returned, he was holding an enormous fixed-weight dumbbell. He waved it about effortlessly, as though it were fashioned of papier-mâché.

"Which hand would you like to keep?"

"Please," begged Isabel.

"Right or left? It's up to you."

"I'll tell you everything."

"Yes, I know." He seized her left hand. "This is the most important one, isn't it?"

He pressed her palm to the limestone tile and placed a leaden foot atop her forearm. Isabel could feel her radius bending to the point of fracture. She pummeled his leg with her right hand, but it was no use. It was as if he were made of stone.

He raised the dumbbell above his head and aimed it toward Isabel's splayed left hand.

"Don't drop it," she pleaded.

"Too late." He raised the weight a few centimeters higher. "You might want to close your eyes."

She looked away and saw Arkady standing in the doorway of the dressing room, a look of revulsion on his face. He spoke a few words icily in Russian, and the man Isabel knew as Fletcher Billingsley of Goldman Sachs lowered the weight and removed his foot from her forearm.

Arkady was now frowning at the droplets of Isabel's blood on the tile floor, as though concerned about their adverse effect on the property's resale value. He covered the blood with a plush white towel and poked at it with the toe of his shoe.

"You'll never remove it that way," said Isabel.

"Don't worry, we'll give it a thorough cleaning when you're gone."

She wiped the blood from her face and rubbed it into the cushion of a reclining lounge chair. "What about that?"

Arkady gave her a humorless smile. "He never liked that chair to begin with."

"Who?"

Ignoring her question, he spoke a few additional words in Russian, and Isabel's assailant withdrew.

"I don't suppose his name is really Fletcher Billingsley."

"Felix Belov."

"Where did he learn his English?"

"His father was assigned to the SVR *rezidentura* in New York."

"What does he do when he's not beating up women?"

"He works for a small subsidiary of NevaNeft. Perhaps you've heard of it. It's called the Haydn Group."

Isabel sat upright and looked deliberately at the resplendent wood cabinetry and gold fittings of the dressing room. "No sauna or steam room?"

Arkady nodded toward a passageway.

"How much did you pay for the place?"

"I believe it was twenty-five million."

"Anonymous purchase?"

"Is there any other kind?"

"Omega Holdings?"

"Tradewinds Capital."

"What about the place in Féchy? Is that Tradewinds, too?"

"Harbinger Management."

"And who owns Harbinger?"

Arkady said nothing.

"Does he own NevaNeft, too?"

"Most of it."

"Is any of it actually yours?"

"Oksana, I suppose. At least, she used to be." He scooped up the towel from the floor and used it to wipe Isabel's blood from the edge of the Jacuzzi. Absently, he asked, "When did you begin working for him?"

"Martin?"

"Gabriel Allon."

Isabel didn't bother with a denial. "How long have you known?"

"I'm the one asking the questions. And I would advise you to answer them quickly and truthfully. Otherwise, I'll ask Felix to finish the job he started on that hand of yours."

"I went to work for him not long after you murdered Viktor Orlov."

"Are you a professional intelligence officer?"

"Heavens, no."

"Were you the one who gave those documents to Nina Antonova?"

"Yes, of course."

"Is that why you were fired from the Russian Laundromat?"

"No," she answered. "That was Gabriel's doing."

Arkady folded the bloody towel carefully. "The Global Alliance for Democracy?"

"Gabriel created it in order to put a target on Martin's back."

"The newly discovered Artemisia? The reception at the Kunsthaus? Anna Rolfe? It was all . . ." His voice trailed off. "What about Anil Kandar? Was he in on it, too?"

"Anil's just a greedy bastard. RhineBank is going down, Arkady. And so are you. We had you the minute you signed the paperwork for that office building in Miami."

"Then why did you come here tonight?"

"A once-in-a-lifetime opportunity."

From upstairs came a swell of rapturous applause. A moment later the Russian president began to speak. No doubt from the balustrade, thought Isabel. Thugs the world over loved nothing more than to look down on their vassals from a balcony.

Arkady made a face at something his master said. "He's rather crude, our Volodya. But then again, he always was. He would be nothing if it wasn't for me. I was the one who chose him. I was the one who facilitated his rise through the ranks of the Kremlin bureaucracy. And I was the one who made certain he won that first presidential election. And how does he repay me? By treating me the same way he did when I was a sickly little boy from Baskov Lane who wanted to be a pianist."

"You should have followed your dreams, Arkady."

"I tried." He closed his eyes and squeezed the bridge of his nose between his thumb and forefinger. "You've made a fool out of me."

"I'm sure I wasn't the first."

"I trusted you."

"You shouldn't have."

"Do you know what's going to happen when I get back to Moscow? With a bit of luck, I will fall from a window. Backwards, of course. That's how all Russian businessmen jump from windows these days. It's a tradition in the brave new Russia that I helped to create. We never face forward when we jump. We only fall backwards." Quietly, he added, "At least that way we don't see the cobbles of the courtyard rushing up to greet us."

"Perhaps there's a deal to be made."

"There is," said Arkady. "But it is *you* who will have to come to terms."

"What do you want?"

"I want you to deliver Gabriel Allon into my hands so that my oldest friend in the world doesn't kill me." He drew his phone from the breast pocket of his jacket. "How much do you want? A billion? Two billion? Name your price, Isabel."

"Do you really think I would take your filthy money in order to save myself?"

"It's not my money, it's his. And why should you be any different from all the others who've taken it?" He seized a handful of Isabel's hair, his face so contorted with desperation she scarcely recognized him. "What's it going to be, Isabel? You have one minute."

"Sorry, Arkady. No deal."

"A very unwise decision on your part." He released his grip

on her hair. "Perhaps you're not the shrewd, unprincipled businesswoman I imagined you to be."

"You'll only make it worse for yourself by killing me."

"Who said anything about killing?" He stretched a hand toward her swollen cheek, but she recoiled from his touch. "Tell me something. Whose idea was it for you to play 'Vocalise' at the reception? Yours or Allon's?"

"Mine," she lied.

"You really did give a beautiful performance that night. It's a shame no one will ever hear you play it again." He returned the phone to the breast pocket of his jacket. "Happy New Year, Isabel."

54

RUE DE NOGENTIL, COURCHEVEL

AT 11:30 P.M., APPROXIMATELY NINETY minutes after Arkady Akimov summoned Isabel for her meeting with the Russian president, her phone remained off the air. It was possible the encounter had lasted longer than anticipated. It was also possible Isabel had left the phone in the signal-blocking receptacle after returning to the party. The more likely explanation, however, was that something had gone wrong inside the monstrous chalet on the opposite side of the rue de Nogentil.

A prudent and battle-scarred operational planner, Gabriel had prepared for such an eventuality. Five members of his team had slipped from the safe house in rented vehicles and were now positioned at key points around Courchevel. Yossi was parked across the street from Isabel's hotel; Rimona and Natalie, in a deserted gas station near the entrance of the village. Christopher and Mikhail, the violent tip of Gabriel's spear, were in an Audi Q7 on the rue du Jardin Alpin, near the gondola station. Keller, an accomplished outdoorsman and climber, had protectively brought along snowshoes and hiking poles. Mikhail had nothing other than an altitude-induced headache and a gun, a Barak SP-21 .45-caliber pistol, a man-stopper.

Only Eli Lavon remained with Gabriel in the safe house. At 11:59 p.m. they stepped onto the balcony and listened as Arkady's inebriated guests thunderously counted down the final seconds of a most dreadful year. The motorcade departed at twelve fifteen. Yevgeny Nazarov, the ubiquitous Kremlin spokesman, had joined the president in the armored Peugeot SUV. Directly behind it was a Mercedes-Maybach. Inside were Arkady and Oksana Akimov.

"Late as usual," said Lavon. "But why do you suppose Arkady is going with him to the airport?"

"It's possible he wants to wave goodbye to the helicopter. The presence of his wife, however, would suggest he intends to be *on* the helicopter."

"So would this."

Lavon showed Gabriel a text message from the surveillance team in the Place du Port in Geneva. Several employees of the Haydn Group had just entered Arkady's offices. Lights were burning on the sixth floor.

"If I had to guess," said Lavon, "they're shredding documents and erasing hard drives."

Gabriel quickly dialed Christoph Bittel. "It looks as though Arkady is making a run for Moscow."

"Say the word, and I'll order a raid on his offices."

"The villa in Féchy, too. And do me a favor, Bittel."

"What's that?"

"Make some noise." Gabriel killed the connection and watched the flashing blue lights of the motorcade winding its way up the mountainside. "They wouldn't try to take her to Russia—would they, Eli?"

"Do you really want me to answer that?"

The motorcade had reached the airport. A moment later the first Airbus Super Puma helicopter was airborne and turning toward the northwest.

"You know," said Lavon after a moment, "if Arkady had any sense, he'd stay here in the West."

"He handed me eleven and a half billion dollars of Mr. Big's money on a silver platter. I rather doubt he was given that option."

The second helicopter rose into the black sky, then the third.

"You'd better get it over with," said Lavon.

Gabriel hesitated, then dialed. "This is going to be ugly."

OWING TO A RECENT STRING of deadly lone-wolf attacks by Islamic militants, Paul Rousseau, leader of an elite counterterrorism unit known as the Alpha Group, had decided to spend New Year's Eve in his office on the rue Nélaton in Paris. Consequently, when his phone rang at 12:22 a.m., he assumed the worst. The fact that it was Gabriel Allon at the other end of the connection only added to his sense of impending doom. The Israeli's briefing was rapid-fire and, without doubt, only partially accurate.

"Are you sure they're planning to take her to Russia?"

"No," answered Gabriel. "But at the very least, they know where she is."

"She's Israeli, this agent of yours?"

"German, actually."

"Do the Germans know—"

"Next question."

"Have the Swiss issued a domestic warrant for Monsieur Akimov's arrest?"

"Not yet."

"Filed a Red Notice request with Interpol?"

"Paul, please."

"We can't detain him without legal justification. We need a piece of paper."

"Then I suppose we'll need to think of an extrajudicial way to prevent him from leaving the country."

"Such as?"

"Close the airport, of course."

"That would effectively ground the Russian president's aircraft."

"Exactly."

"There will be diplomatic repercussions."

"We can only hope."

Rousseau sought bureaucratic shelter. "It's not something I can do on my own. I need the approval of higher authority."

"How much higher?"

"For something like this . . . Élysée Palace."

"How does the French president feel about his Russian counterpart these days?"

"He loathes him."

"In that case, will you allow me to make a suggestion?"

"By all means."

"Call the palace, Paul."

Which is precisely what Rousseau did, at 12:27 a.m. The French president was celebrating the New Year with a few close friends. Much to Rousseau's surprise, he was not opposed to the idea of grounding his Russian counterpart's plane. In fact, he rather liked it.

"Call the tower at Chambéry," he said to Rousseau. "Tell them you're acting on my behalf."

"The tower will have to give the Russian pilots a reason for the delay."

"Switch off the airport's radar. The runway lights, too. That way, the pilots won't try something stupid."

"And if they do?"

"I'm sure you and Allon will think of something," said the French president, and the line went dead.

55

RUE DE NOGENTIL, COURCHEVEL

Isabel's Jaeger-LeCoultre wristwatch was frozen at 10:47, its crystal smashed. Therefore, she did not know the precise amount of time that had elapsed since Arkady had taken his leave. She reckoned it had been at least twenty-five minutes, for that was the approximate running time of Brahms's Cello Sonata in E Minor. She thought her imaginary performance of the piece was rather remarkable, given the fact her left forearm, having been crushed beneath the shoe of Felix Belov, had likely suffered at least a hairline fracture.

At the conclusion of the recital, she opened her eyes and saw the Russian leaning in the doorway of the dressing room, watching her intently. "What were you doing just now?" he asked.

"Playing the cello."

"On your arm?"

"Very good, Fletcher."

He entered the dressing room, slowly. "Were you playing Haydn, by any chance?"

"Brahms."

"You can play from memory?"

She nodded.

"Were you playing your imaginary cello when you sent this?"

He handed her his mobile phone. Displayed on the screen was a copy of an email regarding a parcel of documents that had been left in a sporting ground in Zurich's District 3. The sender was someone called Mr. Nobody. The recipient was a well-known Russian investigative reporter named Nina Antonova.

"The Haydn Group had already taken control of Nina's computer when you sent that," Felix explained. "I wish to thank you for finally giving us the opportunity to give the traitor Viktor Orlov the miserable death he deserved."

"What would have happened if Nina had opened that contaminated package on the plane to London?"

"She would have died, along with several people seated around her. But she didn't open it. She took the package straight to Viktor's house in Cheyne Walk and placed it on his desk. It was one of the most perfect assassinations in our long and glorious history. The traitor Orlov was finally eliminated, and the meddlesome Nina Antonova was thoroughly discredited."

"I hope you someday receive the recognition you so richly deserve."

"I was only the delivery boy," replied Felix, failing to notice the irony in Isabel's remark. "Arkady was the one who planned it. He specialized in false-flag operations and active measures when he worked for the KGB."

"I'm glad we cleared that up." She tossed the phone into the Jacuzzi. "But one wonders why you've chosen this moment to confess your involvement in Viktor Orlov's murder."

Upstairs, the music died.

"Party's over," said Felix. "Time to take a ride."

IT OCCURRED TO ISABEL THAT, with the deafening music switched off, someone might hear her call for help. But the first breath of air had scarcely escaped her lungs when Felix clamped a hand over her mouth. Her attempt at physical rebellion likewise failed. All it took was a bit of pressure to the base of her neck, and her body went limp.

He dragged her from the pool pavilion, past the entrance of a faux English pub. Like the drinking establishments of London, it was empty. Next door was the indoor tennis court, which for some reason was ablaze with light, as was the indoor skating rink and the marquee outside the movie theater. The featured attraction was *From Russia with Love.*

Beyond the movie theater was an arcade filled with pinball machines and vintage video games, and adjacent to the arcade was a strip club with a stage and a pole. It was a new low, thought Isabel. Not even Anil Kandar, her ethically challenged former colleague from RhineBank-London, had a home strip club.

Finally, they came to the chalet's enormous six-car garage. Isabel, her dress soaked from the Jacuzzi, shivered in the sudden cold. Only two of the bays were occupied, one with a Mercedes AMG GT coupe, the other with a Range Rover. The door of the last bay was open. Outside in the drive was a Lynx snowmobile with a cargo sled attached.

An arctic suit lay on the spotless concrete floor along with a pair of night-vision goggles, a quilted moving blanket, a roll of heavy-duty packing tape, a tarpaulin, and a length of nylon rope. Isabel folded her arms across her chest as Felix wrapped her inside the quilt and bound it with the packing tape. A moment passed, presumably while he changed into his arctic suit. Then he hoisted Isabel over his shoulder and flung her like war dead onto the cargo sled of the Lynx.

She was lying on her back, with her head at the front of the sled. It sagged a few degrees as Felix climbed aboard the saddle and started the engine. As they drew away from the chalet, Isabel screamed for help until her throat gave out. She doubted even Felix was able to hear her. The high-pitched drone of the engine was like a buzz saw.

Her left hand was lying on the upper portion of her right arm. She closed her eyes and tried to play the opening of the Elgar concerto, but it was no use. For once, she could not hear the music in her head. Instead, she reflected upon the set of circumstances, the chain of misadventure and providence, that had placed her in her current predicament. It was the phone call, she thought—the call the Russian president had taken before their meeting. That was when it happened. That was when everything went wrong.

FIVE MINUTES AFTER THE MUSIC stopped, a line of chauffeur-driven luxury motorcars materialized at Arkady Akimov's door. They set off at regular intervals, one by one, and joined a second queue of vehicles at the southern end of the rue de Nogentil. There, by order of the Élysée Palace, the departing guests were subjected to a second search. In none of the cars did the French police find what they were looking for—a German woman, thirty-four years of age, wearing a black Max Mara cocktail dress and carrying a clutch purse by Bottega Veneta.

Gabriel monitored the proceedings from the balcony of the safe house, a phone to his ear. It was connected to Paul Rousseau in Paris. Rousseau was in turn connected to the control tower at Chambéry Airport, which had just experienced an unexplained and catastrophic loss of power. Or so the control tower had informed the flight crew of the Russian president's Ilyushin Il-96 aircraft.

"Is there any chance they could have smuggled her out of the chalet before the president's departure?" asked Rousseau.

"Not by the front door, and not by car. She's either on one of those helicopters or still inside the house."

"The chief of the SDLP detail says the only additions to the president's traveling party were Monsieur Akimov and his wife."

"That leaves the house."

"Don't even think about it," cautioned Rousseau.

"I was hoping your side might handle it."

"On what grounds?"

"Something innocuous. A complaint from the neighbors, for example."

"In Courchevel on New Year's Eve?"

"There's a first for everything."

"As evidenced by this phone call. Be that as it may," Rousseau continued, "the palace is rather keen to avoid world war three.

Once we confirm your agent isn't aboard any of the helicopters, the power at Chambéry Airport will be miraculously restored."

Gabriel was about to offer up a protest when he heard the sound, like the grinding of a buzz saw, rising over Les Trois Vallées.

"Can you hear that, Paul?"

"I hear it," answered Rousseau.

"What does that sound like to you?"

"It sounds like they just took her out the back door."

FROM THEIR OBSERVATION POST ON the rue du Jardin Alpin, Mikhail Abramov and Christopher Keller heard the same sound. Like Gabriel, Mikhail did not immediately recognize the source, but Christopher knew at once that it was the engine of a snowmobile. Gazing across the ski area, he glimpsed no movement of light. Clearly, the operator of the snowmobile had doused the headlamp to avoid detection, which suggested the machine was being used to transport a German woman, thirty-four years of age, wearing a black Max Mara cocktail dress and carrying a clutch purse by Bottega Veneta.

Christopher climbed atop the Audi's roof to have a better look and remained there, his eyes searching the darkened landscape, as the sound of the engine faded. It was definitely moving on a southwesterly heading, toward the mountain peak known as Dent de Burgin. In the valley beyond it lay the village of Morel and the Méribel ski resort. They were connected to Albertville by the D90, a perfect escape route. Unless, of course, they intended to drop her into a crevasse at the top of the ridge and call it a night.

He eased from the roof of the Audi to find Mikhail gazing calmly at his secure Solaris phone. "Message from headquarters," he explained without looking up.

"What does it say?"

"Headquarters is of the opinion that our girl might very well be aboard that snowmobile. Furthermore, headquarters would like us to remove our girl from the aforementioned snowmobile before any harm comes to her."

"And how are we supposed to do that without a snowmobile of our own?"

"Headquarters suggests we improvise. His word, not mine." Mikhail smiled. "Good thing you packed your snowshoes."

"I'll show you how to put them on."

"It's not really my sort of thing. Besides," Mikhail added, patting the steering wheel, "I'm driving."

Christopher frowned. "Tell *headquarters* to put a police checkpoint on the D90 north of Morel."

Mikhail popped the release for the rear cargo door. "Will do."

Christopher quickly pulled on the snowshoes and clipped a light to the front of his Gore-Tex jacket. Five minutes later, while traversing an ungroomed ski slope about two hundred meters west of Le Chalet de Pierres, he found a set of fresh tracks in the snow. Just as he suspected, they were headed to the southwest. He switched off his light, lowered his head into a knifelike wind, and kept walking.

56

CHAMBÉRY AIRPORT, FRANCE

Arkady Akimov had been relegated to the second helicopter. His seat, the only one available, was at the back of the drafty cabin, next to the crates of secure communications equipment. Oksana was balanced childlike atop his knee, pouting. The thunderous beating of the rotors made conversation all but impossible, which was a blessing. In the car she had pummeled him with questions. Why were they returning to Moscow with Volodya? Were they in trouble? What would happen to the money? Who would look after her? Did it have something to do with Isabel? That was when she had pummeled him with her fists instead of more questions. And he had acquiesced, at least for a moment, for he had earned it. He was confident it would not be the first indignity he would suffer. More would follow once they arrived in Russia. Isabel had stripped away his veneer of wealth and power. She had destroyed him. He was no one, he thought. A nothing man.

The other eight passengers crammed into the second Airbus were all officers of Volodya's security detail. As they were approaching Chambéry, the mood in the cabin grew anxious. Arkady could not make out what they were saying, but it appeared as though there was a problem at the airport. He shifted Oksana to his opposite knee and peered out the rear starboard-side window. The lights of Chambéry sparkled like gemstones, but there was a large black spot where the airport should have been.

Only the gleaming white Ilyushin Il-96, its landing and logo lights burning brightly, was visible in the gloom. The helicopter touched down about a hundred meters behind the tail. Oksana angrily rejected Arkady's attempt to hold her hand as they crossed the darkened tarmac. The bodyguards walking behind them exchanged a few contemptuous remarks at his expense.

A nothing man . . .

Volodya, having left his helicopter, was trudging up the forward airstair, trailed by Yevgeny Nazarov and his other close aides. A second airstair stretched from the Ilyushin's rear door. Arkady looked to one of the bodyguards for direction and was informed, with an insolent nod, that he would make the return trip to Moscow in the back of the plane, with the rest of the hired help.

Inside the cabin, he and Oksana parted company, perhaps for the last time. Oksana collapsed into a seat on the port side of the aircraft, next to one of Volodya's bodyguards—the best-looking one, of course. Arkady sat across the aisle and stared into the night. His thoughts were filled with images of his own

death. Given the available menu of options, a fall from an elevated window would indeed be preferable. Death by nerve
agent, the death he had inflicted on the traitor Viktor Orlov,
would be quick and relatively painless. Death by polonium,
however, would be prolonged and excruciating, a Shostakovich
symphony of suffering.

And then, he thought, there was the sort of death the KGB had
meted out to those who betrayed it. A savage beating, a merciful
bullet to the back of the head, a grave with no marker. *Vysshaya
mera* . . . The highest measure of punishment. For the crime of
giving eleven and a half billion dollars of his money to the likes
of Gabriel Allon, Arkady feared he would leave this world in the
worst way imaginable. He only hoped Volodya looked after Oksana when he was gone. Perhaps he would keep her for himself.
When it came to women, his appetite was insatiable.

Suddenly, Arkady realized that Oksana was calling to him
from across the aisle. He turned sharply, hopeful of clemency,
but she pointed with irritation toward the left side of his suit
jacket. He hadn't noticed his phone was ringing.

The call was from a number he didn't recognize. He declined
it and tossed the phone on to the next seat. Instantly, it began to
ring again. Same number. This time Arkady tapped the ACCEPT
icon and raised the phone hesitantly to his ear.

"Am I catching you at a bad time, Arkady?" asked a voice in
Berlin-accented German.

"Who is this?"

"Who do you think?"

"Your German is quite good, Allon. How can I help you?"

"You can call the driver of that snowmobile before he gets
out of cellular range and tell him to turn around."

"Why would I do that?"

"Because if he doesn't, I'm going to kill him. And then I'm going to kill you, Arkady."

"I'm comfortably seated on Russian soil. Which means I'm quite beyond your reach."

"That plane isn't going anywhere unless you give me Isabel."

"And if I do? What do I get in return?"

"You don't have to go back to Moscow to face the music. Trust me, it won't end well."

Arkady squeezed the phone tightly. "I'm afraid I need something more tangible. An office building on Brickell Avenue in Miami, for example."

"The money is gone, Arkady. It's never coming back."

"But I have to offer him *some*thing."

"In that case, I suggest you improvise. And quickly."

The connection died.

Outside on the tarmac, the flight crew and several members of Volodya's security detail were engaged in a heated argument with two airport officials. Arkady closed his eyes and saw something else, a bloody and battered man on his knees in a small room with walls of concrete and a drain in the center of the floor.

The highest measure of punishment . . .

He opened his eyes with a start and contemplated the number stored in his phone's directory of recent calls. Perhaps it was not inevitable, he thought. Perhaps Gabriel Allon, of all people, had just offered him a way out.

Oksana was now flirting shamelessly with her seatmate. Rising, Arkady headed up the center aisle to the partition separating the luxurious forward compartment from the rest of the cabin. The door was locked. He knocked politely and, receiving no answer, knocked again. At length, the door swung open, revealing the elegant form of Tatiana Nazarova, retired Olympic sprinter and current wife of Yevgeny Nazarov. She sneered at Arkady as though he were late delivering her main course.

"Volodya does not wish to see you at this time. Please return to your seat."

She tried to close the door, but Arkady blocked it with his foot and pushed past her. The lights were dimmed, the mood tense. One aide was trying to awaken the Élysée Palace. Another was shouting in Russian at someone in Moscow—presumably the Russian foreign minister. A lot of good that would do. It was New Year's Eve, and the foreign minister was one of the world's great drunks.

Only Volodya appeared untroubled. He was slouched in a swivel chair, hands dangling from the armrests, an expression of terminal boredom on his face. Arkady stood before him, eyes averted, and awaited permission to speak.

It was Volodya who spoke first. "Is it safe to assume that this so-called power outage is not a coincidence?"

"It was Allon's doing," answered Arkady.

"You've spoken to him?"

"A moment ago."

"Did he switch off the power supply on his own, or are the French involved, too?"

"He didn't say."

"What *did* he say?"

"He wants the woman."

"The one you allowed to steal my money?"

"I didn't know she was working for Allon."

"You should have."

With his penitential silence, Arkady conceded the point.

"Is there a deal to be made?"

"He says not. But I had the impression he might be prepared to be reasonable. Let me speak to him again. Face-to-face, this time."

Volodya adopted a dead-eyed stare. "Thinking about crossing over to the other side? Selling our secrets to Allon and his friends at MI6 in exchange for a nice little cottage in the English countryside?"

"Of course not," lied Arkady.

"Good. Because you're not going anywhere." Outside, the tarmac was suddenly ablaze with light. Volodya smiled. "Perhaps you should return to your seat now."

Arkady started toward the door of the compartment.

"Aren't you forgetting something, Arkady Sergeyevich?"

He stopped and turned around.

Volodya held out his hand. "Give me your phone."

57

MASSIF DE LA VANOISE, FRANCE

THE RUSSIAN PRESIDENT'S ILYUSHIN AIRCRAFT departed Chambéry Airport at 1:47 a.m., some thirty-two minutes later than scheduled. Gabriel asked Paul Rousseau whether anyone on board the plane had unexpectedly disembarked before takeoff. Rousseau put the question to Chambery's tower staff, and the tower staff double-checked with the ground crew. The answer bounced back a few seconds later. There were no members of the Russian president's traveling party on the tarmac, or anywhere else for that matter.

"Where are the helicopters?" asked Gabriel.

"Still at the airport."

"I need one."

"You're not going to find her in the middle of the night. We'll mount a search-and-rescue operation first thing in the morning."

"She'll be dead in the morning, Paul."

Rousseau put the request to the senior Service de la Protection officer, and the SDLP man raised it with the helicopter pilots. All three volunteered.

"One is all I need," said Gabriel.

"He'll be there in about twenty minutes."

Mikhail Abramov ran Gabriel up the winding road to Courchevel's tiny airport. The Airbus Super Puma touched down at 2:14 a.m. Gabriel hurried across the tarmac and climbed aboard.

"Where should we start?" shouted the pilot.

Gabriel pointed to the southwest, toward the peaks of the Massif de la Vanoise.

WHEN THE SNOWMOBILE'S ENGINE FINALLY died, Isabel's ears sang in the sudden silence—a persistent note, sweet and pure, like the sound Anna Rolfe produced when she laid her bow upon the strings of her Guarneri violin.

The next sound she heard was the crunch of Felix dropping into crisp snow. He loosened the nylon rope holding the tarpaulin in place and cut away the packing tape he had wrapped around the padded blanket. Isabel made two counterclockwise rotations and came to rest next to the sled. She tried to free herself, but it was no use. The snow had her in its grip.

Felix stood over her, laughing. Finally, he reached down and jerked her upright. She wrapped her arms around her torso, clutching the last remaining warmth to her body.

He lowered the zipper of his arctic suit and drew a gun. "Chilly?" he asked.

The involuntary vibration of Isabel's jaw temporarily robbed her of the ability to respond. A bright three-quarter moon illuminated their surroundings. They were in a small valley, rimmed by mountain peaks. There were no lights visible, nothing she might use to orient herself.

Clenching her teeth, she managed a single word. "Where . . ."

"Are we?"

She nodded.

"Does it matter?"

"Please . . ."

He pointed to the tallest mountain in sight. "That's the Aiguille de Péclet. Three and a half thousand meters, give or take."

A gust of wind carried away the loose tarpaulin. Isabel looked at the blanket lying on the bed of the cargo sled.

"It won't save you. It's minus ten Celsius, at least. You'll be dead within two hours."

So that was how he intended to do it—death by exposure. Isabel reckoned Felix's estimate was generous. In her sodden Max Mara cocktail dress and Jimmy Choo suede pumps, she would likely begin suffering from the effects of hypothermia within a few minutes. She would experience confusion, her speech would slur, her heart rate and respiration would slow. At some point, she would lose the ability even to shiver. That was the beginning of the end.

She looked again at the blanket. "Please . . ."

Felix placed a hand between Isabel's shoulder blades and shoved her toward the tree line. The snow conditions were reasonably favorable for walking—a few inches of fresh powder atop a rock-solid base—but the Jimmy Choo pumps were definitely a mistake. With each step, the four-inch heels impaled themselves in the snow.

"Faster," demanded Felix.

"I can't," replied Isabel, shivering.

He gave her another shove, and she pitched face-forward into the snow. This time she made no effort to free herself from its frozen embrace, for she was listening to a distant sound and wondering whether it was only a hallucination brought on by the cold.

It was the same sound she had heard while standing on the terrace of Le Chalet de Pierres with Oksana Akimova.

It was a helicopter.

THOUGH ISABEL DID NOT KNOW it, the helicopter in question, an Airbus H215 Super Puma operated by the French military, was one hundred meters above the gap-toothed peak of Dent de Burgin, its searchlight sweeping across the snowpack on the eastern slope. There was no sign of a Lynx snowmobile, but Gabriel glimpsed what appeared to be a small sphere of light in the narrow glacial valley below. The sphere of light, when illuminated by the Airbus, turned out to be a solitary hiker. He signaled the helicopter by crossing his poles overhead and then pointed to the snow to indicate that he was following a set of tracks. The helicopter banked to the south, toward the Aiguille de Péclet. The solitary hiker planted his poles in the snow and trudged on.

FELIX LIFTED ISABEL FROM HER place of rest. "Walk," he commanded.

She wasn't sure she was capable of it. "Where?" she asked, trembling.

A hand appeared over her shoulder and pointed toward a conical tree, spruce or pine, its lower limbs submerged beneath the snow. She labored forward, two awkward steps, then a third. She could only imagine how ridiculous she must have looked. She forced the thought from her mind and focused instead on the sound of the helicopter. It was growing louder.

She took another step, and her legs collapsed beneath her. Or perhaps she allowed them to buckle; even she wasn't quite certain. Felix again heaved her upright and ordered her to keep walking toward the tree. But what was the point of this ritual death march? And why had he selected a tree as her destination?

At once, Isabel understood.

Beneath the canopy of the tree limbs was a cylindrical weak spot in the snow known as a tree well, one of the most dangerous hazards on any mountain. If she tumbled into it, she would be unable to free herself. Indeed, any attempt to claw her way back to the surface would only hasten her demise. The unstable snow surrounding the tree would pour into the well like water down a drain. She would be buried alive.

She held her ground and turned slowly. Felix didn't notice; he was searching the sky for the helicopter. The zipper of the arctic suit was lowered several inches; his neck was exposed. The gun was in his right hand, pointed toward the snow.

Improvise . . .

The cold had done nothing to diminish the pain in Isabel's throbbing left arm. But her bow arm, strengthened by nearly thirty years of practice, felt fine. Reaching down, she removed the pump from her right foot and grasped it firmly around the arch. She formed an image in her mind, a smiling Felix clutching an immense fixed-weight dumbbell, and then swung the stiletto heel of her shoe toward the exposed flesh of the Russian's throat.

In the instant before the blow landed, he lowered his gaze from the blackened sky. The tip of Isabel's stiletto heel cleaved into the soft skin below his left cheekbone and ripped a gash in his face that extended to the corner of his mouth.

Howling in pain, he covered the wound with his left hand. His right was now empty. Isabel released her shoe and seized the gun in both hands. It was heavier than she imagined it would be. She aimed it at the center of Felix's chest and backpedaled slowly away from him.

Blood pumped from the wound to his face and flowed over his left hand. When at last he spoke, it was in the moneyed American accent of Fletcher Billingsley.

"Ever used one before?"

"Please," she said.

"Please what?" He took a step forward. "You might want to chamber the first round and release the safety. Otherwise, nothing is going to happen when you pull the trigger."

She took another step backward.

"Careful, Isabel. It's a long way down."

She stopped. She was no longer shivering. It was the beginning of the end, she thought.

The gun was now steady in her grasp. She made a slight adjustment to her aim and said, "Leave."

"Why would I do that?"

"Because if you don't—"

Felix lowered his hand, exposing the terrible wound to his

face, and blundered toward Isabel through the snow. Pulling the trigger proved more difficult than she had anticipated, and the recoil nearly knocked her from her feet. Nevertheless, the round somehow managed to find its intended target.

He was now lying on his back in the snow, clutching the base of his neck, writhing in agony. Isabel lowered her aim and pulled the trigger a second time. The sharp crack of the gunshot echoed among the surrounding mountain peaks and then died. After that, there was only the beating of the helicopter rotors. It was the most beautiful sound Isabel had ever heard.

PART FOUR

FINALE

58

GENEVA–LONDON–TEL AVIV

I T BEGAN THE USUAL WAY, with an anonymous leak to a respected journalist. In this instance, the leaker was Christoph Bittel of the Swiss NDB, and the recipient of his editorial largesse was a financial reporter from the *Neue Züricher Zeitung*. The information concerned a New Year's Eve raid conducted by Swiss Federal Police on the home and office of the oil trader and oligarch Arkady Akimov. Details of the investigation were scarce, but the words "suspected money laundering" and "theft of Russian state assets" found their way into the reporter's spotless copy. Arkady Akimov could not be reached for comment, as he had taken refuge in Moscow—curious, for his private plane was parked on the tarmac at Geneva Airport, grounded by order of the Swiss government.

Later that morning, with the help of Paul Rousseau in Paris, it emerged that Arkady Akimov had hosted a New Year's Eve party at his chalet in the French ski village of Courchevel. Among those in attendance was the Russian president, who had traveled to France without public fanfare and left sometime after midnight, evidently with Arkady Akimov aboard his plane. The guest list, which somehow became public, included several prominent French businessmen and numerous politicians from the far right. None of those reached for comment remembered anything unusual. Indeed, few could recall much of anything at all.

The next shoe to drop landed on the Zurich office of Rhine-Bank AG, which was the target of an extraordinary Saturday-morning raid. The firm's Fleet Street office in London was likewise raided, and the chief of the bank's global markets division, a certain Anil Kandar, was taken into custody at his Victorian mansion in tony Richmond-on-Thames. Swiss and British financial authorities were unusually taciturn regarding the motivation for the searches, saying only that they were related to the Akimov case. RhineBank's executive steering committee, the Council of Ten, hastily issued a statement denying any wrongdoing, a sure sign the bank had been up to no good.

The sweeping scale of the misconduct was made public later that evening in a lengthy exposé published jointly by the *Moskovskaya Gazeta* and the *Financial Journal* of London, both of which were controlled by the estate of the late Viktor Orlov. The story detailed RhineBank's long-standing ties to members of the Russian president's inner circle and characterized the business empire of Arkady Akimov as a mechanism for the acquisition and concealment of ill-gotten wealth. According to internal RhineBank documents, Akimov was a longtime client of the so-called Russian Laundromat, a secret unit at the firm's Zurich office. But in late 2020, he had been lured into an illicit relationship with the Geneva-based financier and political activist Martin Landesmann, who was working with Swiss and British investigators. At Akimov's behest, Landesmann had purchased several companies and real estate assets, including office buildings in Miami, Chicago, and London's Canary Wharf. The true owner of those assets, however, was none other than the president of Russia.

Among the more shocking aspects of the article were its London dateline and the name of the reporter who had written it: Nina Antonova. As it turned out, the missing Russian journalist had been granted secret refuge in Britain. In a sidebar to her main story, Antonova admitted that she had unwittingly given Viktor Orlov a packet of documents contaminated with ultrafine Novichok powder. The packet had been prepared, she alleged, by an associate of Arkady Akimov named Felix Belov. Interestingly enough, Belov was among those who had attended the New Year's Eve party in Courchevel. His whereabouts, like those of Arkady Akimov, were said to be unknown.

The developments sent shockwaves up and down the length of Whitehall. There were some in the opposition Labour Party, and at rival newspapers as well, who found fault with Downing Street's handling of the matter, especially the formal charges that had been filed against Nina Antonova by the Crown Prosecution Service. Prime Minister Jonathan Lancaster gleefully admitted they were an unorthodox but necessary ruse to protect the reporter from Russia's vengeful intelligence services. He then engaged in a little vengeance of his own, ordering the National Crime Agency to seize a long list of high-value properties, including the Canary Wharf office building. Swiss authorities simultaneously froze the assets of NevaNeft Holdings SA and seized Akimov's airplane and his villa on Lake Geneva. Sources in both countries suggested it was only the beginning.

But why had the Russian businessman been targeted in the first place? And why had he gone into business with Saint Martin Landesmann, of all people? Was it possible that Martin's pro-democracy NGO was some sort of operational front? And what about the splashy gala at the Kunsthaus museum in Zurich? News footage revealed that Akimov and his beautiful young wife had been in attendance that evening. Could it be that the renowned Swiss violinist Anna Rolfe was somehow involved as well?

And then there was *The Lute Player*, oil on canvas, 152 by 134 centimeters, formerly assigned to the circle of Orazio Gentileschi, now firmly attributed to Orazio's daughter, Artemisia. The director of the Kunsthaus curtly rejected questions regarding the painting's authenticity, as did the noted London art dealer Oliver Dimbleby, who had brokered its sale. But where had Dimbleby acquired it? It was Amelia March of *ARTNews* who supplied the answer. Dimbleby, she reported, had purchased the painting from Isherwood Fine Arts, where it had resided since the early 1970s. Sarah Bancroft, the gallery's alluring managing partner, said the circumstances of the sale were private and would remain so.

Amelia March notwithstanding, the reporters who probed for morsels at the edges of the affair found little that was satisfactory. A spokesman for the Global Alliance for Democracy promised that the important work of the NGO would continue well into the future. Through her publicist, Anna Rolfe said she performed at the gala as a favor for an old and treasured friend. Presumably, that friend was Martin Landesmann, but Martin refused all comment. His legion of right-wing critics said his sudden silence was proof that miracles can indeed happen.

Yevgeny Nazarov, the Kremlin's silver-tongued spokesman, was as loquacious as ever. During a combative Moscow press conference, he denied reports that the Russian president was the anonymous owner of the assets in question, or that he possessed secret wealth hidden in the West. A spokeswoman for the incoming American administration dismissed the claim as laughable and suggested the president-elect would not wait long to take appropriate action. The outgoing administration—or at least what remained of it—washed its hands of the mess. The president, who had given up any pretense of governing, was focused on a last-ditch attempt to overturn the results of the November election. The White House press secretary refused to say whether he had even been briefed on the matter.

There was at least one senior American official, CIA director Morris Payne, who followed the demise of Arkady Akimov with more than a passing interest, for he had played a small but not insignificant role in bringing it about. Payne knew what others did not, that the operation against Akimov and his financial enablers at RhineBank had been orchestrated not by the Swiss and British but by the legendary Israeli spymaster Gabriel Allon. Owing to certain technical capabilities of the National Security Agency, Payne was also aware of some unpleasantness that had occurred after Akimov's New Year's Eve party in

Courchevel—something having to do with a German woman named Isabel Brenner and a dead Russian called Felix Belov.

Though Payne was not long for his job, he was anxious to obtain a readout of the evening's events. Truth be told, he believed he was entitled to one. Nevertheless, he waited until eleven a.m. on the morning of Wednesday, January 6, before ringing Allon on the Langley–to–King Saul Boulevard hotline. Much to Morris Payne's dismay, his call received no answer. His profanity-laced tirade was audible the length and breadth of the seventh floor.

59

TZAMAROT AYALON, TEL AVIV

NOT FAR FROM KING SAUL Boulevard, in the Tel Aviv district known as Tzamarot Ayalon, there stands a colony of thirteen new luxury high-rise apartment towers. In one of the buildings, the tallest, was an Office safe flat. The current occupant played the cello day and night, much to the exasperation of her neighbor, a multimillionaire software magnate. The magnate, who was used to getting his way, complained to the building's management, and management complained to Housekeeping. Gabriel retaliated by arranging for the young cellist to take daily lessons from Israel's most sought-after instructor. He was not concerned about a security breach. The instructor's daughter worked as an analyst for Research.

He was leaving as Gabriel arrived. "She played quite beautifully today," he said. "Her tone is truly remarkable."

"How about her mood?"

"Could be better."

She was seated before a westward-facing window, her cello between her knees, the light of the setting sun on her face. It bore no trace of the ordeal she had suffered at the hands of Felix Belov, apart from a bit of trapped blood, the result of a subconjunctival hemorrhage, in one eye. Gabriel was envious of her recuperative powers. It was her youth, he assured himself.

She looked up suddenly, surprised by his presence. "How long have you been listening?"

"Hours."

She lowered her bow and rubbed her neck.

"How are you feeling?"

She moved aside the cello and raised her shirt, revealing a huge magenta-and-garnet-colored bruise.

Gabriel winced. "Does it still hurt?"

"Only when I laugh." She lowered the shirt. "I suppose it could have been worse. Every time I close my eyes, I see his body lying in the snow."

"Do you want to talk to someone?"

"I thought I was."

"You had every right to do what you did, Isabel. It will take time, but one day you will forgive yourself for having the courage to save your own life."

"According to the newspapers, he's missing."

"I believe I read something about that, too."

"Will his body ever turn up?"

"If it does, it won't be in France."

"His English was flawless," said Isabel. "I still find it hard to believe he was actually Russian."

"I'm sure his many American readers would agree with you." She frowned. "What American readers?"

"Felix Belov was the chief of the Haydn Group's U.S.A. desk. My cyber specialists are analyzing the hard drives as we speak. The entire Russian playbook for information operations directed against the West, all at our fingertips." He paused. "And all because of you."

"How have you managed to keep my name out of the press?"

"Quite easily, actually. The only people who know about you are Martin and the Russians."

"What about Anil Kandar?"

"He's been told that if he so much as mentions your name, he'll spend the next two centuries in prison."

"And how long is *my* sentence?" she asked.

"I'm afraid you'll have to remain in hiding until I'm certain the Russian president's desire for vengeance has receded."

"He doesn't strike me as someone who lets bygones be bygones." She placed the cello in its case. "Have you determined who he was talking to when I entered that room?"

"The British signals intelligence service has concluded the call came from a secure phone in Washington, but there's no intercept of the conversation."

"Arkady was a different person after that call. I had them, Gabriel. And then they had me." Rising, she moved to the window. "Where's your office?"

"Its location is officially a secret."

"And unofficially?"

Gabriel pointed to the southwest.

"Very close."

"Everything is close in Israel."

"Do you live here in Tel Aviv?"

"Jerusalem."

"You were born there?"

Gabriel shook his head. "A small agricultural settlement in the Valley of Jezreel. Most of the people who lived there were German-Jewish survivors of the Holocaust. Quite a few were musicians."

"Can you ever forgive us?" she asked.

"I've never subscribed to the notion of collective guilt. But the Holocaust proved once and for all that we could not depend on others to look after our security. We needed a home of our own. And now we have one. You're welcome to stay, if you like."

"Here?"

"Our economy is thriving, our democracy is stable, and we will be vaccinated long before the rest of the world. We also have an extraordinary philharmonic orchestra."

"I'm German."

"So were my parents."

"And I oppose the occupation."

"Many Israelis do. We must find a just solution to the Palestinian question. Permanent occupation is not the answer." Noticing the surprise on her face, he added, "It's a somewhat common affliction among those who have spent their lives killing to defend this country. In the end, we all become liberals."

"It's tempting," said Isabel after a moment. "But I think I would prefer to go back to Europe."

"Our loss."

"Is Germany safe?"

"If that is your wish, I'll arrange it with the head of the BfV.

The Swiss have also agreed to resettle you, as have the British. But if I were you, I'd be inclined to accept Anna Rolfe's offer."

"What's that?"

"Her villa on the Costa de Prata."

"Who will provide the security?"

"Mr. Big."

Isabel stared at him in disbelief.

"There are several billion dollars in uninvested funds sitting in Martin's account at Credit Suisse."

"It does have a certain poetic justice."

"I've always preferred *real* justice. And once the new American administration finds its footing, I'm confident they're going to track down a great deal of his money."

"But will it change anything?"

"In Russia power is wealth, and wealth is power. The Russian president knows that if the money goes away, his power will go away, too. The protests have already started. It is my intention to help them along." Gabriel smiled. "I'm going to meddle in *his* politics, for a change."

IT WAS A FEW MINUTES after seven p.m. when Gabriel's motorcade turned into Narkiss Street. Upstairs, he shared a quiet dinner with Chiara and the children, a rare extravagance. Nevertheless, his gaze wandered often to the television in the next room. In Washington, a joint session of Congress was preparing to certify the results of the presidential election. The outgoing president was addressing an enormous crowd of supporters gathered in frigid weather on the grassy expanse known as the

Ellipse. The audio was muted, but according to the updates crawling across the bottom of the screen, he was repeating his baseless claims that the election had been stolen from him. The crowd, some of whom were clad in military tactical gear, was growing more agitated by the minute. It looked to Gabriel like a combustible situation.

At the conclusion of dinner, he supervised the children's baths, to little discernible effect. Afterward, he sat on the floor between their beds while they drifted off to sleep—first Raphael, then, twenty minutes later, talkative Irene. Out of habit, he marked the time. It was 10:17 p.m. He gave each child a final kiss and, closing their door soundlessly behind him, went to watch the news from Washington.

60

NARKISS STREET, JERUSALEM

THE INSURRECTION BEGAN EVEN BEFORE the president had concluded his remarks. Indeed, not ten minutes after he warned his supporters that they would never take back their country with weakness, that they had to show strength and fight like hell, thousands were streaming eastward along Constitution Avenue. A militant vanguard—white supremacists, neo-Nazis, anti-Semites, QAnon conspiracy theorists—had already gathered at the barricades surrounding the Capitol. The assault commenced at 12:53 p.m., and at 2:11 p.m., the first insurrectionists breached the building. Two minutes later they reached the base of the staircase adjacent to the Senate chamber. Inside, a Republican senator from Oklahoma was objecting to the certification of Arizona's eleven electoral votes. The vice president, who was presiding, adjourned the session and was hurriedly evacuated by his security detail.

For the next three and a half hours, the rioters roamed the marble temple of American democracy, smashing windows, breaking down doors, ransacking offices, defacing works of art, stealing documents and computers, emptying their bowels and bladders, and searching for lawmakers to kidnap or kill— including the speaker of the House and the vice president, whom they intended to hang for treason, apparently from the gallows they had erected on the lawn. Emblems of racism and hate were everywhere. A wildly bearded creature from southern Virginia roamed the halls wearing a hooded sweatshirt that read CAMP AUSCHWITZ. A man from Delaware carried a Confederate battle flag across the floor of the Great Rotunda, an ignoble first in American history.

After assuring his supporters that he intended to join them on their march to the Capitol, the delighted president watched the mayhem on television. Reportedly, his only concern was the scruffy appearance of the violent, hate-filled mob, which he thought reflected badly upon him. Despite numerous pleas from horrified White House staff and congressional allies, he waited until 4:17 p.m. before asking the rioters, whom he described as "very special," to leave the building.

By 5:40 p.m., the siege was finally over. The Senate reconvened at 8:06 p.m.; the House of Representatives, at nine o'clock. At 3:42 a.m. the following morning, while the rest of Washington was under a strict curfew, the vice president formally affirmed the results of the election. The first attempted coup in the history of the United States of America had failed.

AMERICA'S ALLIES, STUNNED BY WHAT they had witnessed, condemned the president's actions in words usually reserved for Third World tyrants and thugs. Even the authoritarian ruler of Turkey called the insurrection a disgrace that shocked humankind. Gabriel thought it was the darkest day in American history since 9/11, though somehow worse. The attack had been launched not by a distant enemy but by the occupant of the Oval Office. Israel's closest ally, he told his astonished senior staff the following morning, was no longer an example to be emulated. It was a flashing red warning light to the rest of the free world that democracy was never to be taken for granted.

Not surprisingly, Russia's pro-Kremlin media outlets reveled in America's misfortune, for it provided a welcome change of subject from the widening scandal surrounding the Russian president and his finances. Gabriel fanned the flames by ordering a hack of MosBank, the Russian bank used by the president's inner circle, and turning over the stolen records to Nina Antonova. They formed the basis of another explosive exposé of rampant theft and unexplained wealth. Kremlin spokesman Yevgeny Nazarov, finding himself at a rare loss for words, dismissed the article as fake news written by an enemy of the people.

Of the oil trader and oligarch Arkady Akimov, there was no sign. His well-paid lawyers waged a halfhearted defense on his behalf, but to no avail; the Swiss government seized or froze every asset it could identify. NevaNeft, leaderless, rudderless, ground to a halt. The pipelines stopped flowing, the refineries stopped refining, the tankers sat in port or wandered the seas, aimlessly. The company's European customers understandably went in search of a more reliable supplier. Energy analysts predicted that Russia's oil exports, down sharply in 2020, would plunge further in the coming year, dealing a severe blow to the Russian economy and, perhaps, the stability of the regime.

RhineBank fared little better. With each new revelation of corporate misconduct, its share price plummeted. On the Friday following the Capitol siege, the once-mighty Hamburg lender closed below four dollars in New York—ventilator territory, according to a wit from CNBC, who was later forced to apologize for the remark. The German government, desperate to keep the country's largest bank afloat, suggested a merger with a domestic rival. But the rival, after reviewing RhineBank's catastrophically overleveraged balance sheet, withdrew from the negotiations, which sent the stock lower still. As the firm approached the point of no return, Karl Zimmer, chief of the Zurich office, hanged himself. Next morning Lothar Brandt, head washer boy from the now-defunct Russian Laundromat, chose death by speeding cargo truck.

Brandt's suicide note, which found its way into print, included the name of a former colleague whom he accused of being the source of the leaked documents. Gabriel was disappointed by the disclosure, but not surprised; like RhineBank's imminent collapse, he supposed it was inevitable. For her part, Isabel was relieved. She was proud of what she had done and eager to tell her story, preferably in a major television interview. Gabriel was not altogether opposed to the idea. In fact, he thought raising Isabel's international profile might serve to reduce the likelihood of Russian retribution.

"Especially if the interview is properly timed for maximum impact."

They were sitting on the windblown terrace of the safe flat. Isabel had just finished her daily lesson. She was wearing a fleece pullover against the cold late-afternoon air and drinking a glass of Galilean sauvignon blanc.

"Did you have a date in mind?" she asked.

"Sometime in early June, I'd say."

"Why June?"

"Because that's when your debut recording is scheduled to be released."

"What recording?"

"The one you're going to make for Deutsche Grammophon. Your friend Anna Rolfe has arranged everything."

Isabel's eyes shone. "When do I go into the studio?"

"As soon as you're ready."

"Why didn't you tell me?"

"I just did."

"What do they want me to record?"

"They say it's your choice."

"You decide."

Gabriel laughed. "Anything but Haydn."

THAT EVENING THE HOUSE OF REPRESENTATIVES voted to impeach the president of the United States for a second time. Ten members of his own party, including the chairwoman of the House Republican Conference, Representative Liz Cheney of Wyoming, joined with Democrats in supporting the article, making it the most bipartisan impeachment in American history. One hundred and ninety-seven Republicans voted against removing the president for inciting the insurrection. Many seemed more concerned about the metal detectors that had been placed outside the House chamber, believing the devices interfered with their right to carry firearms in the halls of Congress.

With just a week remaining in the president's term, a Senate trial appeared unlikely. Of more immediate concern was the upcoming inauguration. The president-elect was determined to take the oath of office in public, on the platform that had been erected on the West Front of the Capitol—the same platform that had been overrun by the insurrectionists on January 6. With Washington on high alert, and extremist Internet sites ablaze with ominous chatter, organizers of the inauguration declared it a National Special Security Event, which placed the Secret Service in command of the preparations.

The threat stream shook experienced professionals to the core. The scenarios included vehicle bombings, snipers, simultaneous active shooters, a direct assault on the inauguration platform, and the occupation of the eighteen-acre White House complex by armed supporters of the outgoing president. Planners were also compelled to contemplate the once unthinkable, that an attacker might wear the uniform of a soldier or a police officer. FBI and Pentagon vetters attempted to root out anyone with extremist ties or sympathies. Twelve members of the National Guard assigned to inauguration security were relieved of duty.

Astonishingly, none of the serious threats emanated from

abroad. All flowed from the violent racist sewer of gunned-up, spun-up America. That changed, however, with the phone call that Gabriel received from Ilan Regev at 3:15 a.m. on Monday, January 18. Ilan was the chief of the cyber-and-technical unit that was scouring the Haydn Group's computers. He had found something that Gabriel needed to see at once. He declined to characterize the discovery over the phone, only that it was time sensitive.

"Extremely time sensitive, boss."

It was approaching six a.m. when Gabriel arrived at King Saul Boulevard. Ilan, ghostly pale and thin as a pauper, was waiting in the underground parking garage. He was the cyber equivalent of Mozart. First computer code at five, first hack at eight, first covert op against the Iranian nuclear program at twenty-one. He had worked with the Americans on a malware virus code-named Olympic Games. The rest of the world knew it as Stuxnet.

He thrust a file into Gabriel's hand as he stepped from the back of his SUV. "We found it on Felix Belov's hard drive yesterday afternoon, but it took some time to break the encryption. The original was in Russian. The machine translation isn't great, but it's good enough."

Gabriel opened the file. It was an internal Haydn Group memorandum dated September 27, 2020. Ilan had flagged the relevant passage. After reading it, Gabriel looked up with alarm.

"It could be rubbish, boss. But given the current environment . . ."

"Have you found any of the text messages?"

"We're working on it."

"Work harder, Ilan. I need a name."

Gabriel hurried upstairs and collected a prepacked suitcase with three days' worth of clothing and kit. Thirty minutes later he carried the bag up the airstair of his Gulfstream jet. It departed Ben Gurion Airport at 7:05 a.m., bound for the flashing red warning light once known as the world's beacon of democracy.

61

WILMINGTON, DELAWARE

GABRIEL WAITED UNTIL HE WAS on the ground at New Castle Airport before ringing Jordan Saunders, the president-elect's designated national security adviser.

"What brings you to town?" he asked.

"I need a word with the boss."

"The boss isn't talking to any foreign leaders or officials before the inauguration. For that matter, neither am I. We'll get together when the prime minister visits the White House."

"I didn't know there was a meeting scheduled."

"There isn't," said Saunders, and rang off.

Gabriel called him back. "Don't hang up, Jordan. I wouldn't be calling if it wasn't serious."

"I'm serious, too, Allon. We're not communicating with foreign officials. Not after the Flynn fiasco."

"I'm not the Russian ambassador, Jordan. I'm the director-general of a friendly intelligence service. And I have something I need to share with you and your boss."

"Why don't you share it with Langley?"

"Because I'm not confident the information will get into the right hands."

"What's the nature of this information? Broadly speaking," Saunders added hastily.

"Broadly speaking, it concerns your boss's security."

Saunders made no reply.

"Did I lose you, Jordan?"

"Where are you?"

Gabriel told him.

"As you might expect, the boss's dance card is rather full today. So is mine."

"As long as I see him before Inauguration Day, it's fine."

"Why Inauguration Day?"

"Not on the phone, Jordan."

"Do you know the address of the house?"

Gabriel recited it.

"I'll be in touch," said Saunders, and the connection went dead a second time.

Gabriel rented a Nissan from the Avis counter and drove to a Dunkin' Donuts on North Market Street in downtown Wilmington. He ordered a large coffee and two jelly sticks and listened to the news on the car radio as the old redbrick buildings darkened around him.

Jordan Saunders called a few minutes after six. "I think I can get you ten minutes at seven fifteen."

"Can I bring you anything from Dunkin'?"

"A Boston Kreme."

"You got it, Jordan."

Google Maps estimated the driving time to the president-elect's house to be sixteen minutes. Gabriel tacked on an additional ten and took his time. He followed North Market Street to West Eleventh, made a left, and picked up Delaware Avenue. It changed names a couple of times before becoming Kennett Pike. Barley Mill Road was two lanes, rolling, and lined with leafless trees.

A Delaware State Police cruiser blocked the entrance of the private lane that led to the president-elect's compound. Gabriel surrendered an Israeli passport to a Secret Service agent and stated his real name. The officer didn't seem to recognize it. Evidently, he was not expected.

The agent stepped away, got on his radio, and after a few minutes determined to his satisfaction that the Israeli with gray temples and unusually green eyes was to be admitted to the grounds without further delay. Gabriel accepted his passport and advanced to the next Secret Service checkpoint, where he was directed into the president-elect's circular drive.

Jordan Saunders, elegantly attired and impeccably groomed, waited outside the entrance of the large colonial-style home. In twenty years, Saunders would look like the archetypal diplomat, the sort who wore waistcoats, drank tea with his breakfast, and lived grandly in Georgetown. For now, at least, he might have been mistaken for one of the interns.

Gabriel handed Saunders the bag from Dunkin' Donuts. "A peace offering."

"Have you been vaccinated?"

"Two weeks ago."

They walked around the side of the house to the rear garden. Through the black boughs of trees, Gabriel glimpsed a small, frozen lake.

"Wait here," said Saunders, and entered the house.

Five minutes elapsed before he reappeared. At his side was the next president of the United States. Unlike the previous Democratic president, he had not emerged from obscurity to dazzle a nation with his oratory and good looks. Indeed, Gabriel could scarcely recall a time when he was not a part of American political life. Twice before he had sought the presidency, and twice he had failed. Now, in the twilight of his life, he had been called upon to heal a sick and divided nation—a difficult task for a leader in his prime, harder still for one who had been slowed by age. Regrettably, he and Gabriel had that affliction in common.

He approached Gabriel warily. He wore slim-fitting wool trousers, a zippered sweater, and a smart-looking car-length coat. Like his young national security aide, he was double-masked.

"This meeting never happened. Are we clear, Director Allon?"

"We are, Mr. President-elect."

He glanced at the file folder in Gabriel's hand. "What is this all about?"

"Your inauguration, sir. I believe you should consider moving it inside, with very few guests."

"Why would I do that?"

"Because if you don't," said Gabriel, "you might have the shortest presidency in American history."

62

WILMINGTON, DELAWARE

GABRIEL BEGAN HIS BRIEFING NOT with the document he had brought from Tel Aviv but with the operation that had produced it—the operation against Arkady Akimov and the private intelligence unit hidden within his Geneva-based company. The president-elect's knowledge of the unfolding scandal involving NevaNeft and the Russian leader's personal finances was limited to what his staff had culled from the media. His daily intelligence briefings, which he had only belatedly begun to receive, had contained no mention of the story.

"Did Langley know about your operation?" he asked.

"Not until late in the game."

"Why not?"

"Because the current administration showed little interest in operating against the Russians."

"How diplomatic of you, Director Allon. Try again."

"I didn't brief the Agency because I was afraid the president would tell his friend in the Kremlin. Unfortunately, I learned early on that he was not to be trusted with sensitive information. My counterpart at MI6 was also extremely careful about the intelligence he let him see. For that matter, so was the director of the CIA."

"Are you suggesting he's a Russian asset?"

"That's a question for your intelligence chiefs."

"I'm not asking them. I'm asking you."

"Assets come in all shapes and sizes. And some assets don't realize they're assets. Oftentimes, they're the best kind."

They were seated at Covid-safe intervals around a wrought-iron table on the patio. Only Gabriel, the briefer, was maskless. A glance at his wristwatch established he had used four of his allotted ten minutes. He opened the file folder and removed the translation of the document found on Felix Belov's computer.

"The Haydn Group's main weapon was dirty Russian money, which it used it to fund anti-establishment parties and to corrupt prominent Western businessmen and politicians. But the Haydn Group also possessed a sophisticated information warfare unit similar to the Internet Research Agency."

"The St. Petersburg company that meddled in the 2016 election."

"Exactly. Our analysis of the Haydn Group's computers revealed that early last summer, their fake Twitter accounts began to amplify the president's false claims the election was going to be stolen from him. But more ominously, the Haydn Group also began planning for the future." Gabriel held up the document. "A future in which their preferred candidate lost the election and you were about to enter the White House."

"What do you have there, Director Allon?"

"A memorandum written by a top operative of the Haydn Group named Felix Belov. It details a plot to deliver a catastrophic blow to American democracy by covertly encouraging an attack on your inauguration. The beauty of the plot, at least from Russia's point of view, is that it will be carried out by an American citizen."

"Who?"

"An asset known as Rebel. Evidently, one of the Haydn Group's cyberwarriors encountered Rebel on an 8kun message board. Rebel is a far-right extremist who supports the imposition of white nationalist, authoritarian rule in the United States, by violence if necessary. Rebel is also an official of the US government who will have access to the inauguration ceremony."

"How?"

"Needless to say, the document doesn't say where Rebel works. The Haydn Group communicated with him anonymously. Rebel has no idea that the texts and direct messages he's been receiving were sent by a private Russian intelligence company."

"Are you sure Rebel is a man?"

"I was using the male pronoun for the sake of brevity. The document doesn't specify Rebel's gender."

"May I see it?" asked Jordan Saunders.

Gabriel handed over the document.

Saunders switched on his phone's flashlight. "Do you know whether the plot is active?"

"No," admitted Gabriel. "In fact, for all we know, Arkady

Akimov dropped that document in his shredder five minutes after it landed on his desk. But if I were in your position, I would assume that he showed it to his friend in the Grand Kremlin Palace, and that his friend gave it the green light."

"There's no way the Russian president would approve something so reckless," said Saunders.

"Viktor Orlov might disagree."

The future national security adviser looked down at the document. "Where's the man who wrote this?"

"He had an unfortunate accident in the French Alps on New Year's Eve."

"What kind of accident?"

"He was shot twice at close range." Gabriel frowned. "And I'd feel better if you threw that phone of yours in the lake."

"The lake is frozen, and the phone is secure."

"Not as secure as you think." Gabriel turned to the president-elect. "Is there any chance you might reconsider—"

"None," the president-elect interjected. "It is essential that I take my oath on the West Front of the Capitol, especially in light of what happened there on January sixth. Besides, the security next Wednesday will be unprecedented. There's no way anything is going to happen."

"Will you at least make sure the Secret Service is told about what we discovered?"

"Jordan will see to it."

Gabriel rose. "In that case, I won't take up any more of your time."

The president-elect pointed toward Gabriel's chair. "Sit down."

He did as he was told.

"Who shot Felix Belov?"

"A young woman who penetrated Arkady Akimov's operation."

"Israeli?"

"German, actually."

"A professional?"

"She plays the cello."

"Any good?"

"Not bad," said Gabriel.

The president-elect smiled. "What are you doing on Wednesday?"

"I was planning to watch your inauguration with my wife and children."

"Would you like to attend the ceremony as my guest?"

"I would be honored, Mr. President-elect."

"Excellent." He nodded toward his national security adviser. "Jordan will make the arrangements."

But Saunders appeared not to hear him; he was still reading Felix Belov's memo. He didn't look like an intern any longer, thought Gabriel. He looked like a very nervous young man.

63

CAPITOL HILL, WASHINGTON

REBEL, THE RUSSIAN ASSET WHO did not know she was a Russian asset, awoke the next day at six fifteen. The bedroom of her tiny basement apartment near Lincoln Park was in its usual morning disarray. She opened the blackout shade, and a bit of gray light seeped through the opaque safety glass of the room's only window. A pair of women's Nikes hurried along the sidewalk of Kentucky Avenue, followed a few seconds later by a well-dressed terrier. This was the view of the nation's capital to which Rebel was entitled for the sum of $1,500 a month, lower extremities and canines, the occasional rat for a change of pace.

Life was different in the small town in southeastern Indiana where Rebel maintained her primary residence. A hundred and fifty thousand bought you a nice house, and for two fifty you could have a couple of acres. The median income was a bit above thirty thousand, with a third of its residents living below the poverty line. There was an old distillery in town, but otherwise there weren't many jobs, only a bit of retail-and-restaurant work along High Street or, for a lucky few, a job as a teller at United Commercial. A lot of the town was wasted most of the time—eighty percent had prescriptions for painkillers—and crime was the one growth industry. At the height of the opioid crisis, Rebel's Indiana county, population fifty thousand, sent more people to prison in a single year than did San Francisco.

It was understandable, then, that folks in Rebel's town were angry. The educated urban elites—the Wall Street bankers, the Connecticut hedge fund managers, the Silicon Valley software engineers, the ones who went to Ivy League schools and made millions pushing buttons—were prospering as never before while the people in Rebel's hometown were falling farther and farther behind. The elites bought their clothes at Rag & Bone, the folks in Rebel's town at Dollar General. On summer weekends they took their kids to the Water World splash park, except at the end of the month, when almost everyone was broke.

Thanks to the enigmatic Internet postings of a former government official known only as Q, Rebel now knew the reason for her town's plight. It was the cabal of Satan-worshipping, blood-drinking, liberal pedophiles who controlled the financial system, Hollywood, and the media. The cabal raped and sodomized children, drank their blood, and ate their flesh in order to extract the life-extending chemical adrenochrome. Q was the prophet, but the president was a divine being sent by God to destroy the cabal and save the children. His battle would culminate in the Storm, when he would declare martial law and begin arresting and executing his enemies. Only then would an age of salvation and enlightenment known as the Great Awakening begin.

Rebel, one of Q's earliest adherents, was now regarded as an expert in the field—a Qologist, as she referred to herself on social media, where she had a half-million followers. Her pages were pseudonymous; no one knew she was a follower of Q. She called herself the Q Bitch. The beautiful blond woman in the profile picture looked nothing like her.

There were many followers of Q who were disappointed that the Storm did not begin after the insurrection at the Capitol—or, as Q Bitch referred to it, the Qsurrection. They were disappointed, too, by Q's long silence. He had made only a single drop during the final two months of 2020, and none in the new year. But Rebel had kept faith with Q, mainly because Q had kept faith with her. For much of the last year, they had been in direct communication using the encrypted message service Telegram. Q had warned Rebel not to publish what he was saying, or to tell anyone that she was in contact with him. She had followed his instructions to the letter, if only because she feared he might vanish. She was Q's dirty little secret.

Some of their conversations were quite lengthy, hours long, late at night, Rebel in her bed, Q in hiding. Sometimes he divulged a great secret about the cabal that he had not shared with his other followers, but usually they made small talk or flirted. At Q's request, Rebel had sent several nude photos. Q had not reciprocated. Prophets did not send pictures of their private parts over the Internet.

In mid-November, after the fake news declared that the president had lost the election, their conversations turned serious, dark. Q wondered whether Rebel was prepared to engage in violence to bring about the Storm. Rebel assured Q that she was. And what if her act of violence resulted in her arrest? Was she prepared to face temporary imprisonment until the Storm had passed and the cabal had been punished? Was she prepared to trust the plan? Yes, she answered. She would do anything to save the children.

It was then, in late December, that Q revealed to Rebel that she was the chosen one—the one who would commit the act that would bring about the Storm. She was not surprised by the nature of Q's order; it was the only way to prevent the cabal from seizing control of the White House. Nor was she surprised she had been selected. She was uniquely positioned to carry it out. She was the only one.

Q had ordered Rebel to make no changes in her life that might raise a red flag. With the exception of the handwritten letter explaining her actions, she had maintained strict operational security. It was lying on her nightstand, the letter, beneath her compact Glock 32 .357.

In the apartment's galley kitchen, she started the Krups and skimmed a few patriot message boards while waiting for the coffee to brew. She was wearing her favorite nightshirt, a football jersey bearing the number 17—Q being the seventeenth letter of the alphabet. The patriot threads on Reddit were pretty tame, but on some of the hard-core sites there were posts about attacks on government buildings and the coming civil war. Rebel added an incendiary post of her own—anonymously, of course—and then tossed out a few thoughts on her Q Bitch account, which met with a quick response from her Q-starved followers. Finally, she switched to her real-name account and railed against the incoming administration's plan to rejoin the Paris climate accord. Within the first minute, she received more than a thousand likes, retweets, and quotes. The adulation was like a drug.

She carried a cup of coffee into her bedroom and dressed for the gym. It seemed a prosaic thing to do, given the fact she had been chosen to bring about the Great Awakening, but Q had been adamant about keeping to her usual schedule. She worked out religiously for two hours each morning, one hour of cardio followed by an hour of resistance, and then showered and changed for work in her office. Even a mild case of Covid, which she had hidden from her colleagues, hadn't disrupted her routine. A variation now would be noted by her staff. Besides, she needed to clear her head. She was spinning again, hearing voices.

Trust the plan . . .

Her phone pinged with a message. The tone told her it was Telegram, and Telegram meant that it was Q. He wanted to know whether she had a minute to talk. Breathless, she typed a response.

For you, my love, I have all the time in the world.

Are you alone?

She told him she was.

The plan has changed.

How?

He explained.

Are you sure?

Trust the plan.

With that, Q was gone. Rebel dropped her phone and the Glock 32 into the gym bag and went into the frigid morning. She headed up Kentucky Avenue to Lincoln Park, then made a left at East Capitol. The voices were whispering in her ear. Trust the plan, they were saying. Enjoy the show.

64

WASHINGTON

THE OUTGOING PRESIDENT LEFT THE White House for the final time at 8:17 a.m. the following morning, making him the only chief executive in more than a century and a half not to attend the inauguration of his successor. The Washington he left behind was an armed camp, with twenty-five thousand National Guard troops deployed around the city, the most since the Civil War. A sealed red zone stretched from Capitol Hill to the Lincoln Memorial, and from I-395 to Massachusetts Avenue. The green zone, restricted to residents and employees of local businesses, was even larger. Bridges were closed, downtown Metro stops shuttered. Miles of seven-foot non-scalable fencing, in some places reinforced with concrete barriers and strung with razor wire, gave the city the appearance of a giant prison.

As the president departed Joint Base Andrews, the president-elect arrived for mass at the Cathedral of St. Matthew the Apostle. Gabriel, in his room at the nearby Madison Hotel, heard the sirens of the massive motorcade as it moved through the empty streets. His phone rang a few minutes after nine, as he was finishing dressing. It was Morris Payne calling from Langley.

"I've been trying to reach you," he said by way of greeting.

"Sorry, Morris. I've been crushed with work."

"Is that any way to treat a friend?"

"Are you, Morris?"

"In a few short days you will realize I was the best friend you ever had."

"Actually, I think I'm on fairly good footing with the new administration."

"I'll say. There's a nasty rumor going around that you're attending the inauguration as a guest of the president."

"Where did you hear that?"

"I was given a heads-up by the Secret Service. They also told me about this so-called threat from a Russian asset called Rebel. Needless to say, I should have heard about Rebel from you."

"I didn't want anything to be lost in translation."

"Translate this," snapped Payne. "Rebel is total bullshit. Rebel is a fantasy you've created to ingratiate yourself with the new crowd and get an invite to the inauguration."

"If anyone should be attending the inauguration, it's your boss."

"It's better he left town. The country needs to move on. And if you ever repeat that, I'll denounce you from the highest mountaintop. Which is exactly where I'm headed."

"When are you leaving Langley?"

"As soon as you tell me what really happened in France on New Year's Eve."

"Someone called the Russian president from a secure phone in Washington and told him that I had placed an agent close to Arkady Akimov."

Payne said nothing.

"Who knew about my operation, Morris?"

"The people who needed to know."

"Was the president one of them?"

"If he was," said Payne before hanging up the phone, "he didn't hear it from me."

GABRIEL PULLED ON AN OVERCOAT and a scarf and headed downstairs. Masked, he walked through the frigid, sunlit morning to Capitol Hill. Agent Emily Barnes of the United States Secret Service, an athletic-looking woman in her mid-thirties with freckled cheeks, met him at the edge of the red zone.

She handed him a set of credentials. "Are you armed?"

"No. Are you?"

She patted the side of her heavy jacket. "A SIG Sauer P229."

Gabriel hung the credentials around his neck and followed the agent to a checkpoint, where he was thoroughly searched. Inside the red zone, they made their way to the East Front of the Capitol. The outgoing vice president, no longer speaking to the man he served faithfully for four years, was just arriving.

Agent Barnes led Gabriel through a doorway that gave on to the ground floor of the Capitol's North Wing. "What did you think of our Beer Hall Putsch?" she asked.

"It made me sick to my stomach."

"How about the guy with the Auschwitz hoodie?"

"I wish he had been walking down a street in Tel Aviv wearing that shirt instead of through the halls of the Capitol."

She pointed out a doorway. "That's the Old Supreme Court Chamber. The justices met there until 1860. Samuel Morse sent the first Morse-coded message from that room in 1844."

"What did it say?"

"'What hath God wrought?'"

"How prophetic."

They climbed a flight of stairs to the second level of the Capitol. The Great Rotunda, defiled only two weeks earlier, glowed with the warm light streaming through the upper windows of the dome.

Agent Barnes turned to the right. "You've been assigned a seat down on the lawn, but the president-elect asked us to give you a quick tour of the platform to put your mind at ease."

They emerged through a doorway onto the temporary structure abutting the West Front: one hundred and sixty thousand pounds of scaffolding, thirteen hundred sheets of plywood, a half million nails, twenty thousand pounds of grout and mortar, and twelve hundred gallons of gleaming white paint. Like the rotunda, it bore no traces of the damage inflicted just fourteen days earlier by the insurrectionists.

The three previous presidents and their wives had arrived and were mingling with the other dignitaries. A few members of Congress were searching for their seats, including a universally loathed and poorly groomed senator from Texas who had attempted to overturn the results of the election. Agent Barnes was describing some of the extraordinary measures the Secret Service had taken to secure the event. Gabriel was gazing at the two hundred thousand American flags fluttering in the cold breeze blowing across the empty Mall.

Shortly before eleven a.m., the president-elect's family stepped onto the platform. "We should go downstairs to our seats," said Agent Barnes.

"*Our* seats?"

"I'm afraid you're stuck with me."

"Poor you."

They entered the Capitol, descended a flight of stairs, and emerged onto the lawn that two weeks earlier had been trampled by the marauding insurrectionists. Their seats were next to the camera platform. The first female vice president in American history, the daughter of Jamaican and Indian immigrants, was administered the oath of office at 11:42 a.m.; the new president, at 11:48. Nine minutes before the constitutionally prescribed start of his term, he took to the podium to deliver his inaugural address to a nation ravaged by illness and death and torn by political divisions. As Gabriel rose to his feet, he scanned the platform for a Russian asset code-named Rebel.

"Don't worry," said the young Secret Service agent standing at his side. "Nothing is going to happen."

HE DECLARED THAT THIS WAS America's day, democracy's day, a day of history and hope. The nation, he said, had been tested by a crucible for the ages. And yet its institutions, the very institutions his predecessor had spent four years trying to destroy, had risen to the challenge. He called on Americans to end their uncivil war—a war that pitted red against blue, rural versus urban, conservative versus liberal—and assured them that their democracy would never fall to a mob like the one that had invaded the Capitol. Gabriel, awed by the majesty of the ceremony, hoped the president would be proven correct. The world's oldest democracy had survived its brush with authoritarianism, but it had been a near-death experience.

When the speech was over, a country music star sang "Amazing Grace," and the youngest inaugural poet in American history declared that the country wasn't broken, simply unfinished. Afterward, the new chief executive withdrew to the President's Room, a gilded chamber on the Senate side of the Capitol, where congressional leaders looked on as he signed an Inauguration Day proclamation and several nominations to cabinet and sub-cabinet positions.

Next they moved to the Great Rotunda for a traditional presentation of gifts, a ceremony that ordinarily takes place during the inaugural luncheon. One of the gifts, a framed photograph of the ceremony that had occurred only moments earlier, was bestowed by the House minority leader, a Californian who had repeatedly claimed that the president had not won the election. The president, intent on bridging the nation's cavernous political divide, accepted the gift graciously.

The final event before his departure took place on the steps of the East Front. There the president reviewed a parade of troops from every branch of the armed forces, a ceremony dating back to George Washington's first inauguration that symbolized the transfer of power to a new, duly elected civilian leader. Power had indeed been transferred, thought Gabriel, watching the ritual from the East Plaza, but it had not been peaceful.

At the conclusion of the ceremony, the largest motorcade Gabriel had ever seen assembled at the base of the steps, and the new president settled into the back of his limousine. By two fifteen he was headed down Independence Avenue toward Arlington Cemetery for a wreath-laying ceremony at the Tomb of the Unknown Soldier.

"I told you nothing would happen," said Agent Barnes.

"That's where you're wrong," replied Gabriel.

"What do you mean?"

"You live in an extraordinary country. Take good care of it."

"Why do you think I work for the Secret Service?" She offered Gabriel her elbow in farewell. "It was a pleasure meeting you, Director Allon. I have to say, you're not what I expected."

"Really? How so?"

She smiled. "I thought you'd be taller."

THE RAZOR WIRE SPARKLED IN the brilliant winter sunlight as Gabriel walked down the gentle slope of Constitution Avenue. He crossed the empty boulevard at New Jersey Avenue and headed north, past the grassy plateau known as Lower Senate Park. In the deep silence of the locked-down city, he could hear footfalls behind him, muted, the occasional chirp of rubber against concrete. Female, he reckoned. Perhaps fifty kilograms, slightly out of breath. The footfalls drew closer as he approached the intersection of Louisiana Avenue. He slowed, as though to take his bearings, and turned around.

Caucasian female, mid-forties, five foot one or two, solidly built, professionally attired, visibly agitated. No, thought Gabriel suddenly. She was spun up out of her mind. In her right hand was a gun, a compact Glock 32 .357. It was a lot of fire-power for so petite a woman. Fortunately, it was pointed toward the sidewalk. At least, for the moment.

Gabriel smiled and addressed the woman in a voice he reserved for those of unsound mind.

"Can I help you?"

"Are you Gabriel Allon?"

"I'm afraid you have me confused with someone else."

"You drink their blood, eat their flesh."

"Who?"

"The children."

Dear God, no. She was down the rabbit hole. A terrorist Gabriel might have been able to reason with, but not this one. Unprotected and unarmed, he had no choice but to try.

"You've been deceived," he said in the same placid tone. "There's no cabal. No one's drinking the blood of children. The Storm will never happen. It's all a lie."

"The Storm will begin after I kill you."

"The only thing that will happen is that you will destroy your life. Now place the gun gently on the sidewalk and walk away. I promise not to tell anyone."

"Pedophile," she whispered. "Bloodsucker."

Gabriel stood with the stillness of a figure in a painting. Twenty-five thousand National Guard troops, another twenty thousand police officers and security personnel, and not one had noticed the professionally attired QAnon adherent standing on New Jersey Avenue with a loaded .357 in her hand.

Three meters separated them, no more. For now, the gun was still pointed at the ground. If he waited until she started to raise it, he would have no chance to disarm her. He had to make the first move and hope she wasn't law enforcement or ex-military. If she was, his life would doubtless end at the corner of New Jersey and Louisiana Avenues in Northeast Washington.

Her lips were moving, like a suicide bomber reciting a final prayer. "Trust the plan," she was whispering. "Enjoy the show."

Too late, Gabriel rushed forward, shouting like a madman, as the woman's right arm levered into firing position. The powerful .357 round tore through him like an artillery shell. As death's darkness fell over him, he heard two more shots, the double tap of a trained professional. Then there was nothing at all, only a voice calling to him from across the green fields of the Valley of Jezreel. It was the voice of his mother, begging him not to die.

PART FIVE

ENCORE

65

WASHINGTON

TWELVE INTERMINABLE MINUTES ELAPSED BEFORE the first ambulance was able to make its way through the military checkpoints. The EMTs were confronted with two gunshot victims, one female, the other male. The female, a compact woman wearing a woolen overcoat, had been shot twice in the back and was unresponsive. The male, moderate height and build, perhaps early sixties, was bleeding heavily from a cavernous through-and-through wound a few centimeters beneath his left clavicle. He was no longer conscious. He had a pulse, but barely.

He was still alive when the ambulance reached George Washington University Hospital, but he died in the level-one trauma center at 2:47 p.m. Resuscitated, he died a second time while undergoing surgery, but once again doctors were able to restart his heart. Shortly after six that evening, he was stable enough to be moved to the critical care unit. The hospital listed his condition as grave, which was optimistic. He was alive, but barely.

The doctors were not told the name of the patient whose life they were desperately trying to save, but the phalanx of Secret Service agents and Metropolitan Police officers standing watch outside the trauma center's doors suggested he was a man of some importance. So, too, did the arrival of several officials from the Israeli Embassy, including the ambassador. He confirmed that the patient was a senior official of the Israeli government involved in security and intelligence. It was essential, he said, that his identity, even his presence in the hospital, remain a secret—and that he survive.

"Please," begged the ambassador, his eyes damp with tears, "do not let this man die. Not like this."

The comment was a reference to the identity of the woman who was allegedly responsible for the patient's grave condition: Michelle Lambert Wright, a four-term Republican congresswoman from Indiana. According to the FBI, which had assumed responsibility for the investigation, Congresswoman Wright had followed the Israeli from the East Plaza of the Capitol to the corner of New Jersey and Louisiana Avenues, where, after a brief conversation, she shot him once with her personal .357 Glock firearm before being shot twice herself. The FBI did not identify the person who killed the congresswoman, only that the individual was an agent of the Secret Service.

At the request of the Israeli government, the FBI also withheld the name of the senior Israeli official who was lying close to death in the critical care unit. But late that evening the

Washington Post identified him as Gabriel Allon, the director-general of Israel's vaunted secret intelligence service. The *Post* also revealed the contents of two troubling manifestos, discovered in the dead congresswoman's Capitol Hill apartment, that suggested she was a mentally unstable adherent of the sprawling conspiracy theory known as QAnon. The first manifesto detailed her motives for assassinating the forty-sixth president of the United States on the day of his inauguration. An updated manifesto, composed the day before the ceremony, explained why she had targeted Allon instead.

The White House press secretary revealed additional shocking details during an extraordinary briefing the following afternoon. Allon, she said, had traveled to Delaware on Monday, January 18, to warn the then president-elect about a threat to his life on Inauguration Day. The plot, according to Allon, was Russian in origin and involved a figure inside the US government who held extremist views. Subsequent forensic examination of Congresswoman Wright's phones and computers revealed that she had been in contact with someone claiming to be the shadowy Q. He had ordered the congresswoman to assassinate the new president in order to unleash the prophesized Storm and bring about the Great Awakening. But on the morning of Tuesday, January 19, he had given her a new assignment.

It was not surprising, given America's fractured politics, that the revelations only served to widen the partisan divide. A far-right Republican congressman from Florida dismissed the so-called manifestos as clever forgeries planted by operatives of the "deep state." His colleague from Ohio went further, suggesting that it was Congresswoman Wright, not Gabriel Allon, who had been targeted for assassination. When confronted with

closed-circuit video showing the congresswoman clearly shooting Allon first, the Ohioan held his shaky ground. The video,
he declared, was a deep-state fake, too.

The battle on cable news and online was even more fierce,
as rival networks and purveyors of opinion waged a holy war
over the terrible incident that had stained Inauguration Day in
blood. There was talk of violence in the streets, of civil war
and secession, even another attack on the Capitol. Those who
remained faithful to the discredited prophecies of QAnon saw
evidence that the forecast Storm was brewing, with one noted
Q influencer predicting it would begin the instant of Allon's
death. But those who had clawed their way out of the rabbit
hole and back to reality saw something more dangerous—proof
that QAnon, once dismissed as a harmless conspiracy theory,
had turned lethal. They called on the remaining community
of believers to switch off their social media accounts and seek
professional help before it was too late.

Nearly lost in the rancor was the fact that Gabriel Allon, by
inadvertently making himself the target of the Russian assassination plot, might well have saved the republic. Unconscious
and on numerous means of life support, he was oblivious to the
events swirling around him. Finally, three interminable days
after the shooting, he opened his eyes for the first time. When
asked by his doctors if he knew where he was and what had happened, he indicated that he did. He was alive, but barely.

THE CIA GAVE CHIARA AND the children the run of an old
safe house on N Street in Georgetown. Barred from the hospital by Covid restrictions, they anxiously awaited each update

on Gabriel's condition. Forty-eight hours after regaining consciousness, he showed signs of marked improvement. And when another two days passed with no further complications, the doctors expressed guarded confidence the worst was behind him. That evening Chiara traveled from Georgetown to Foggy Bottom in an embassy car, just to be nearer to him. When told of her proximity, he smiled for the first time.

They spoke briefly by video call the following morning. Chiara told Gabriel that he looked wonderful, which wasn't at all true. Drawn and gaunt, his face etched with pain, he looked positively dreadful, scarcely like himself. Nevertheless, the doctors assured her he was continuing to make good progress. The .357 round, they explained, had left a tunnel of destruction in its wake—torn blood vessels, soft tissue damage, shattered bones. His recovery, they warned, would be lengthy and difficult.

As if to prove them wrong, he rose from his bed and took a few hesitant steps along the corridor. He walked a little farther the following day, and by the end of the week he was able to make a complete circuit of the critical care unit. This earned him the privilege of a room with a window overlooking Twenty-Third Street. Chiara and the children waved to him from the sidewalk, watched over by a team of embassy security guards in khaki vests.

The new president telephoned that evening. He said he had been receiving daily updates and was pleased by Gabriel's progress. He asked whether there was anything he could do.

"Impose crushing sanctions on Russia," answered Gabriel.

"I'm announcing them tomorrow along with the seizure of several billion dollars' worth of looted assets hidden here in the United States. We'll hit them with another round of sanctions once the intelligence community determines to their satisfaction that the Kremlin was behind the attempt on your life."

"Better mine than yours, Mr. President. I only hope you can forgive me for ruining your inauguration by getting myself shot."

He allowed himself to be debriefed by a team from Langley and submitted to a video interview with the FBI. Agent Emily Barnes of the Secret Service, who was on administrative leave pending an internal review of her actions, rang him from her apartment in Arlington.

"Sorry, Director Allon. I should have put her on the ground the instant she raised that gun."

"Why were you even there?"

"She walked right past me at the Capitol. We're trained to spot people who are contemplating an act of violence. She might as well have been wearing a neon sign. When she followed you down the hill to New Jersey Avenue, I knew you were in trouble, but . . ." Her voice trailed off.

"She was a member of Congress."

The following morning, he walked five full circuits of the floor, which earned him a rousing ovation from the nursing staff. For his reward, he was poked and prodded by the doctors, who signed the papers authorizing his release. The bill for his care was astronomical. The president insisted on paying. It was, he said, the least he could do.

For the first time in three weeks, Gabriel dressed himself in proper clothing. Downstairs, a CIA security man helped him into the backseat of an armored SUV. The driver took him on a final tour of the snow-covered city—the Lincoln Memorial, the Washington Monument, the Capitol, the corner of New

Jersey and Louisiana Avenues. The sidewalk was stained with blood, his or hers, Gabriel could not tell. He stood there for a moment, hoping to hear his mother's voice, but she was lost to him once more.

Their last stop was the old redbrick safe house on N Street in Georgetown. During the drive to Dulles Airport, Chiara rested her head on Gabriel's shoulder and wept. At times like these, he thought, there was comfort in familiar routines.

66

NARKISS STREET, JERUSALEM

For a month after his return to Israel, he remained hidden away in his apartment in Narkiss Street, surrounded by a small army of security men. Most of his neighbors viewed the additional barriers and checkpoints as a small price to pay to live in close proximity to a national treasure, but a few chafed under the restrictions. There was even a small band of heretics who wondered, not without some justification, whether the shooting in Washington had really happened. After all, they pointed out, he had once misled his enemies, and his fellow countrymen, into believing he was dead. Another grand deception on his part was hardly beyond the realm of possibility.

The skeptics hastily withdrew their objections, however, on the day he made his first appearance. The occasion was a much-anticipated meeting with the prime minister at Kaplan Street. The video of his arrival shocked the country. Yes, he was still strikingly handsome, but his hair was a touch grayer, and it was evident from his deliberate movements that his body had been invaded by a large-caliber bullet.

He met with the prime minister for more than an hour. Afterward, the two men fielded questions from reporters. It was the prime minister, as usual, who did most of the talking. No, he answered bluntly, there would be no changes in leadership at King Saul Boulevard at this time. Day-to-day control of the Office would remain in the hands of deputy director Uzi Navot until Gabriel was sufficiently recovered. His doctors had set a tentative date of June 1 for his return to duty, which would leave seven months on his term. He had informed the prime minister he would not serve a second term and had suggested a possible successor. The prime minister, when asked for his reaction, described the candidate as "an interesting choice."

Unbeknownst to the Israeli public, Gabriel and the prime minister used the meeting to add their signatures to a document known as a Red Page, an authorization for the use of lethal force. It was executed a week later in downtown Tehran. A man on a motorcycle, a limpet mine, another dead Iranian nuclear scientist. Regional analysts interpreted the operation as a pointed message to Israel's enemies that the Office was functioning normally, and for once the analysts were right. The new administration in Washington, which was trying to lure the Iranians back to the nuclear negotiating table, offered only a muted expression of disapproval. Gabriel's near-death experience on Inauguration Day, declared the analysts, had paid dividends at the White House and the State Department.

Much to Chiara's dismay, Gabriel insisted on overseeing the assassination from the ops center at King Saul Boulevard. But for the most part, he made the Office come to him. Uzi Navot was a frequent visitor to Narkiss Street, as were Yossi Gavish, Eli Lavon, Rimona Stern, Yaakov Rossman, and Mikhail Abramov. Once or twice a week they gathered in the sitting room, or around one of Chiara's lavish dinners, to review current operations and plan new ones. Occasionally, they pressed Gabriel to reveal the name he had whispered into the ear of the prime minister, but he steadfastly refused. They were confident, however, that he would never entrust the Office to an outsider, which meant that one of them would have the misfortune of following in the footsteps of a legend.

But it was clear the legend was not himself. He tried to hide the pain from his troops, and from his wife and children, but sometimes the smallest movement brought a grimace to his face. His weekly visit to Hadassah Medical Center rarely passed without one of the doctors remarking that he was lucky to be alive. Had the slug entered his chest a few millimeters lower, he would have bled to death before the ambulance arrived. A few millimeters lower still, they declared, and he would have died instantly.

They prescribed for him a set of exercises to regain his strength. He read stacks of classified documents instead. And when he felt up to it, he painted. The works were filled with power and emotion, the sort of paintings for which he would have been known had he become an artist instead of an assassin. One was a portrait of a madwoman clutching a gun.

"It's much better than she deserves," said Chiara.

"It's total crap."

"You're too hard on yourself."

"It runs in the family."

It was then, standing before his easel, that he told Chiara for the first time how he had heard his mother's voice as he was dying. And how he had tried to convince the madwoman depicted in the painting, a congresswoman from America's heartland, to lay down her gun.

"Did she say anything to you?"

"She called me a bloodsucker. And it was quite obvious she believed it to be true. I almost felt sorry for her. Even if I'd had a gun . . ."

Chiara finished the thought for him. "You're not sure you would have been able to use it."

Despite the subject matter, Chiara thought the painting was of sufficient quality for hanging, but Gabriel consigned it to the storage facility where he kept his mother's paintings and works by his first wife, Leah. Near the end of April, as Israel's aggressive national vaccination campaign allowed much of the country to reopen, he was allowed to visit her for the first time in more than a year. The hospital where she resided was atop Mount Herzl, near the ruins of the old Arab village of Deir Yassin. Afflicted with a combination of acute post-traumatic stress syndrome and psychotic depression, she had no knowledge of the global pandemic, or of Gabriel's near-fatal shooting in Washington. Seated beneath an olive tree in the cool of the walled garden, they relived, word for word, a conversation they had had on a snowy night in Vienna thirty years earlier. She once again asked Gabriel to make certain Dani was strapped into his car seat properly. Now, as then, Gabriel assured her the child was safe.

Emotionally drained by the encounter, he took Chiara and the children to Focaccia on Rabbi Akiva Street, the Allon family's favorite restaurant in Jerusalem. Their photographs were soon trending on social media along with a lengthy discussion of Gabriel's order, chicken livers and mashed potatoes. *Haaretz,* Israel's most authoritative daily, felt compelled to publish several hundred words on the sighting, including quotes from two of Israel's most prominent physicians. The general consensus was that Gabriel was starting to look a bit more like himself again.

The next night they made a long-delayed pilgrimage to Tiberias to celebrate Shabbat with the Shamrons. Over dinner, Ari upbraided Gabriel for allowing himself to be shot by an American congresswoman—"The indignity of it! How could you have been so careless?"—before turning his attention to the future. Not surprisingly, he had been talking to the prime minister about Gabriel's succession plan. The prime minister was intrigued by the idea of appointing a woman but was not sure whether Rimona was ready for the job. Shamron reckoned it was a fifty-fifty proposition at best, though he was confident that, with dogged persistence, he would be able to drag her across the finish line.

"Unless . . ."

"Unless what, Ari?"

"I can convince you to stay for a second term."

Even the children laughed at the suggestion.

At the conclusion of dinner, Shamron asked Gabriel to join him on the terrace overlooking the Sea of Galilee. After settling into a chair along the balustrade, he ignited a foul-smelling Turkish cigarette with his old Zippo lighter and returned to the subject of Gabriel's brush with death in Washington.

"Another first on your part," Shamron pointed out. "You are the only chief in the history of the Office to have killed in the line of duty. And now you are the only one to have been shot."

"Do I get a citation for that sort of thing?"

"Not if I have anything to do with it." Shamron shook his head slowly. "I hope it was worth it."

"It's quite possible I saved the new president's life. He won't forget that."

"And what about the other members of his administration?"

"They're only Democrats, Ari. It isn't as if Hezbollah is going to be running the State Department."

"But can we count on them?"

"The president and his team?"

"No," said Shamron. "The Americans."

"The president has assured his traditional European allies that America is back, but they're not yet convinced. Not after what they went through the last four years. And the attack on the Capitol has made them even more skeptical."

"As well it should," replied Shamron. "Who were these creatures who vandalized that beautiful building? What do they want?"

"They say they want their country back."

"From whom?" asked Shamron, incredulous. "Have they not read their history? Do they not know what happens when a nation tears itself apart? Do they not realize how lucky they are to live in a democracy?"

"They don't believe in democracy anymore."

"They will if it vanishes."

"Not if their side is in control."

"An authoritarian regime in the United States? A ruling family? Fascism?"

"These days we call it majoritarianism."

"How polite," remarked Shamron. "But what about the minorities?"

"Their votes won't count."

"How will they manage that?"

"You know the old saying about elections, Ari. It's not about the voting, it's about the counting."

"Your friend from Moscow figured that out a long time ago." Shamron crushed out his cigarette. "I assume you're planning to retaliate?"

"The Americans are doing that for me."

"There are sanctions," said Shamron knowingly, "and then there are *sanctions*, if you understand my point."

"I've been working on and off for the Office since I was twenty-two, Ari. I know what you mean when you refer to sanctions. In fact, I'm old enough to remember when we used to refer to an assassination as negative treatment."

Shamron lifted a hand in inquiry. "Well?"

"After giving the matter careful consideration, I'm inclined to let it go."

Shamron glared at Gabriel as though he had questioned the existence of the creator. "But you *must* respond."

"Do you know how many Russians I've killed or kidnapped since the outbreak of our private little war? Even I'm not sure I can count them all. Besides, I took something more important from him than his life."

"His money?"

Gabriel nodded. "And I proved to the Russian people that he's nothing but a thief. Who knows? With a bit of luck, the next government citadel to be stormed by its own people will be the Kremlin."

"A popular uprising in Russia?"

"It's his biggest fear."

"My biggest fear," said Shamron, "is that soon after you move to Italy, I will read a story in the newspaper about your body being fished from a Venetian canal. Which is why you must delay your departure until the situation has settled."

"How long do you think that will take?"

"Ten or fifteen years." Shamron gave a mischievous smile. "Just to be on the safe side."

"Chiara and the children are leaving the day after my term expires, with or without me."

"Has it been that bad?"

"Washington was the final straw."

"But not the final act, I hope."

"I promised my wife that I would spend my last years on earth making her happy. I intend to keep that promise."

"And what about *your* happiness?" asked Shamron.

Gabriel made no reply.

"Do you still grieve for them?"

"Every minute of every day."

"Is there any room in your heart for me?"

"You're not going anywhere."

"I trained you to lie better than that, my son." Shamron was silent for a moment. "Do you remember that day in September when I came for you?"

"Like it was yesterday."

"I wish we could do it all over again."

"Life doesn't work that way, Ari."

"Yes," he said. "Isn't that a shame."

67

MASON'S YARD, ST. JAMES'S

THE FIRST REVIEW OF THE newest recording of Dvořák's beloved Cello Concerto in B Minor appeared on the website of *Gramophone* magazine. The soloist was the previously unheralded Isabel Brenner; the conductor, the legendary Daniel Barenboim. Their personal chemistry, wrote the reviewer, was evident from the cover photograph, and from the power of their performances—especially Ms. Brenner's, which was noteworthy for its haunting, luminous tone. The fill-up material was Dvořák's "Waldesruhe" and Brahms's Cello Sonata in F Major. For the chamber pieces, Isabel was accompanied by the pianist Nadine Rosenberg, perhaps best known for her long collaboration with the renowned Swiss violinist Anna Rolfe.

The concise artist's biography contained in the press materials documented Isabel's remarkable journey from obscurity to musical success—at least a portion of it. Born in the ancient city of Trier, she had studied the piano under the tutelage of her mother before taking up the cello. At the age of seventeen she was awarded a third prize at the prestigious ARD International Music Competition, thus guaranteeing admission to the conservatory of her choice. Instead, she earned degrees in applied mathematics from Berlin's Humboldt University and the London School of Economics, and embarked on a career in the financial services industry—for which firm, the biography pointedly did not say.

But a sharp-eyed business reporter from the *Guardian*, a classical music enthusiast herself, remembered that an Isabel Brenner had been linked to the notorious Russian Laundromat at RhineBank, the recent collapse of which was currently battering global financial markets. The reporter rang the high-powered lawyer representing Anil Kandar, the former RhineBank executive now on trial for money laundering and fraud, and asked whether Isabel Brenner the cellist was also Isabel Brenner the dirty German banker.

"Same girl," replied the lawyer.

The story unexpectedly produced a notable increase in sales, as did a rave five-star review in *BBC Music* magazine. But it was Isabel's sensational interview with Anderson Cooper on *60 Minutes* that propelled the album to number one in both Britain and the United States. Yes, she admitted under questioning, she had worked for RhineBank's Russian Laundromat, but only as a means of gathering information and collecting incriminating documents. She had given those documents to the investigative reporter Nina Antonova and to the legendary Israeli spymaster Gabriel Allon, who had enlisted her in an operation against

Arkady Akimov. With Allon guiding her every move, she had penetrated Arkady's inner circle and had helped to launder and conceal several billion dollars' worth of looted Russian state assets.

"Arkady trusted you?" asked Cooper.

"Implicitly."

"Why?"

"Music, I suppose."

"Were you ever in danger?"

"Several times."

"What did you do?"

"I improvised."

THE INTERVIEW WAS A GLOBAL sensation, especially in Russia, where early the following morning Arkady Akimov's smashed body was discovered in the courtyard of an apartment building on Baskov Lane in St. Petersburg, having landed there after a fall from an upper-floor window. Police declared the death a suicide, despite the fact the body showed signs of multiple blunt-force injuries.

Isabel, who was in hiding at an undisclosed location, declined to comment. Nor did she discuss the matter when she arrived in Britain in mid-July for her debut concert at London's Barbican Centre. Tickets were impossible to come by—only half the usual number were available for purchase—and security was unusually tight. Among those in attendance were the Swiss financier Martin Landesmann and his wife, Monique.

After thrice returning to the stage to acknowledge the adulation of the crowd, Isabel was whisked clandestinely across

London to a quiet backwater of St. James's known as Mason's Yard. There, in the glorious upper exhibition room of Isherwood Fine Arts, she was fêted as though she were a member of the family, which indeed she was.

"Miraculous!" declared Julian Isherwood.

"Truly," agreed Oliver Dimbleby.

Sarah pried Isabel from Oliver's grasp and introduced her to Jeremy Crabbe, who was similarly entranced. Reluctantly, he surrendered her to Simon Mendenhall, the smooth-as-silk auctioneer from Christie's, and Simon delivered her to Amelia March of *ARTNews*, who was the only reporter in attendance.

After providing Amelia with a suitable quote for her article, Isabel excused herself and approached the one man at the party who seemed to have no interest in meeting her. He was standing before a landscape by Claude, a hand pressed to his chin, his head tilted slightly to one side.

"Better than that still life in the safe house by the lake," she said.

"Much," agreed Gabriel.

She looked around the room. "Friends of yours?"

"You might say that."

"Where's Mr. Marlowe?"

"Avoiding that woman over there."

"She looks like someone I saw in a fashion magazine once."

"You did."

"Why on earth would he want to avoid *her*?"

"Because he's currently living with that one over there."

"Sarah?"

Gabriel nodded. "She's another one of my restoration projects. So is the former fashion model."

"And I thought my life was complicated." Isabel regarded him carefully. "I have to say, you look rather good for someone who's lucky to be alive."

"You should have seen me a few months ago."

"How bad is the scar?"

"I have two, actually."

"Do they still hurt?"

Gabriel smiled. "Only when I laugh."

HE WAS THE FIRST TO leave the party. Not surprisingly, no one seemed to notice he had gone. Isabel departed soon after, but the others lingered until nearly midnight, when the last of the Bollinger Special Cuvée finally ran dry. On her way out the door, Olivia Watson blew Sarah a decorous kiss with those perfect crimson lips of hers. Through a frozen smile, Sarah whispered, "Bitch."

She supervised the caterers while they packed away the empty bottles and dirty glasses. Then, after arming the gallery's security system, she went into Mason's Yard. Christopher was leaning against the hood of the Bentley, an unlit Marlboro between his lips.

His Dunhill lighter flared. "How was the party?"

"Why don't you ask Olivia?"

"She told me to ask you."

Frowning, Sarah slid into the passenger seat. "You know," she said as they sped westward along Piccadilly, "none of this would have happened if I hadn't found that Artemisia."

"Except for Viktor," Christopher pointed out.

"Yes," agreed Sarah. "Poor Viktor."

She lit one of Christopher's cigarettes and accompanied Billie Holiday as the Bentley flowed along the Brompton Road into Kensington. As they drew to a stop in Queen's Gate Terrace, she noticed a light burning in the lower level of the maisonette.

"You must have forgotten—"

"I didn't." Christopher reached inside his suit jacket and drew his Walther PPK. "I won't be but a moment."

THE DOOR WAS AJAR, THE kitchen deserted. On the granite counter, propped against an empty bottle of Corsican rosé, was an envelope. Christopher's name was written in stylish longhand on the front. Inside was a high-quality bordered correspondence card.

"What does it say?" asked Sarah from the open doorway.

"He's wondering whether you and I ought to get married."

"Truth be told, I've been wondering the same thing."

"In that case . . ."

"Yes?"

Christopher returned the note card to the envelope. "Perhaps we should."

AUTHOR'S NOTE

THE CELLIST IS A WORK of entertainment and should be read as nothing more. The names, characters, places, and incidents portrayed in the story are the product of the author's imagination or have been used fictitiously. Any resemblance to actual persons, living or dead, businesses, companies, events, or locales is entirely coincidental.

Visitors to Mason's Yard in St. James's will search in vain for Isherwood Fine Arts. They will, however, find the extraordinary Old Master gallery owned by my dear friend Patrick Matthiesen. A brilliant art historian blessed with an infallible eye, Patrick never would have allowed a misattributed work by Artemisia Gentileschi to languish in his storerooms for nearly a half century. The painting depicted in *The Cellist* does not exist. If it did, it would look a great deal like the one produced by Artemisia's father, Orazio, that hangs in the National Gallery of Art in Washington.

Like Julian Isherwood and his new managing partner, Sarah Bancroft, the inhabitants of my version of London's art world are wholly fictitious, as are their sometimes-questionable antics. Their midsummer drinking session at Wilton's Restaurant would have been entirely permissible, as the landmark London eatery briefly reopened its doors before a rise in coronavirus infection rates compelled Prime Minister Boris Johnson to shut down all non-essential businesses. Wherever possible, I tried to adhere to prevailing conditions and government-mandated restrictions. But when necessary, I granted myself the license to tell my story without the crushing weight of the pandemic. I chose Switzerland as the primary setting for *The Cellist* because life there proceeded largely as normal until November 2020. That said, a private concert and reception at the Kunsthaus Zürich, even for a cause as worthy as democracy, likely could not have taken place in mid-October.

I offer my profound apologies to the renowned Janine Jansen for the unflattering comparison to Anna Rolfe. Ms. Jansen is rightly regarded as one of her generation's finest violinists, and Anna, of course, exists only in my imagination. She was introduced in the second Gabriel Allon novel, *The English Assassin*, along with Christopher Keller. Martin Landesmann, my committed if deeply flawed Swiss financier, made his debut in *The Rembrandt Affair*. The story of Gabriel's blood-soaked duel with the Russian arms dealer Ivan Kharkov is told in *Moscow Rules* and its sequel, *The Defector*.

Devotees of F. Scott Fitzgerald undoubtedly spotted the luminous line from *The Great Gatsby* that appears in chapter 32 of *The Cellist*. For the record, I am well aware that the headquarters of Israel's secret intelligence service is no longer located on

King Saul Boulevard in Tel Aviv. There is no safe house in the historic moshav of Nahalal—at least not one that I am aware of—and Gabriel and his family do not live on Narkiss Street in West Jerusalem. Occasionally, however, they can be spotted at Focaccia on Rabbi Akiva Street, one of my favorite restaurants in Jerusalem.

It was the German powerhouse Deutsche Bank AG, not my fictitious RhineBank, that financed the construction of the extermination camp at Auschwitz and the nearby factory that manufactured Zyklon B pellets. And it was Deutsche Bank that earned millions of Nazi reichsmarks through the Aryanization of Jewish-owned businesses. Deutsche Bank also incurred massive multibillion-dollar fines for helping rogue nations such as Iran and Syria evade US economic sanctions; for manipulating the London interbank lending rate; for selling toxic mortgage-backed securities to unwitting investors; and for laundering untold billions' worth of tainted Russian assets through its so-called Russian Laundromat. In 2007 and 2008, Deutsche Bank extended an unsecured $1 billion line of credit to VTB Bank, a Kremlin-controlled lender that financed the Russian intelligence services and granted cover jobs to Russian intelligence officers operating abroad. Which meant that Germany's biggest lender, knowingly or unknowingly, was a silent partner in Vladimir Putin's war against the West and liberal democracy.

Increasingly, that war is being waged by Putin's wealthy cronies and by privately owned companies like the Wagner Group and the Internet Research Agency, the St. Petersburg troll factory that allegedly meddled in the 2016 US presidential election. The IRA was one of three Russian companies named in a sprawling indictment handed down by the Justice Department in February 2018 that detailed the scope and sophistication of the Russian interference. According to special counsel Robert S. Mueller III, the Russian cyber operatives stole the identities of American citizens, posed as political and religious activists on social media, and used divisive issues such as race and immigration to inflame an already divided electorate—all in support of their preferred candidate, the reality television star and real estate developer Donald Trump. Russian operatives even traveled to the United States to gather intelligence. They focused their efforts on key battleground states and, remarkably, covertly coordinated with members of the Trump campaign in August 2016 to organize rallies in Florida.

The Russian interference also included a hack of the Democratic National Committee that resulted in a politically devastating leak of thousands of emails that threw the Democratic convention in Philadelphia into turmoil. In his final report, released in redacted form in April 2019, Robert Mueller said that Moscow's efforts were part of a "sweeping and systematic" campaign to assist Donald Trump and weaken his Democratic rival, Hillary Clinton. Mueller was unable to establish a chargeable criminal conspiracy between the Trump campaign and the Russian government, though the report noted that key witnesses used encrypted communications, engaged in obstructive behavior, gave false or misleading testimony, or chose not to testify at all. Perhaps most damning was the special counsel's conclusion that the Trump campaign "expected it would benefit electorally from the information stolen and released through Russian efforts."

An exhaustive five-volume report released by the Republican-led Senate Intelligence Committee in August 2020 went even further, portraying senior Trump advisers as eager to obtain assistance from America's primary global adversary. The report, the culmination of a three-year investigation, detailed a complex web of contacts between the Trump campaign and Russians linked to the Kremlin and the Russian intelligence services. It said "the single most direct" connection was Paul Manafort, the veteran Republican operative with a taste for high living—his vast wardrobe of expensive clothing included a $15,000 ostrich jacket—who briefly served as the campaign's manager. Manafort, suggested the committee, was compromised by the fact he had earned tens of millions of dollars representing pro-Kremlin political candidates in Ukraine. He was also deeply indebted to the Russian oligarch Oleg Deripaska, whom the committee characterized as a "proxy" for the Kremlin and Russia's intelligence services.

But even Oleg Deripaska must have been taken aback when, in the early-morning hours of November 9, 2016, Donald Trump appeared before stunned supporters in a Manhattan hotel ballroom as the president-elect of the most powerful nation in the world. After settling into the job, Trump heaped praise on authoritarian thugs, entertained antidemocratic European populists at the White House, rolled back US efforts to promote democracy around the world, and disrupted relations with traditional allies such as the United Kingdom, Germany, France, and Canada. And once, during an Oval Office meeting with the Russian foreign minister and ambassador to Washington, Trump divulged highly classified intelligence supplied by a close ally in the Middle East—intelligence that was so sensitive it was not shared widely within the US government. That Middle Eastern ally was Israel, and the breach reportedly put at risk an operation that had given Israeli intelligence a window on the inner workings of the Islamic State in Syria.

But perhaps most unsettling was Trump's determination to withdraw the United States from NATO, a bedrock of the postwar global order. Former White House chief of staff John Kelly is reported to have said that "one of the most difficult tasks he faced" was trying to stop Trump from pulling out of the alliance. John Bolton, after resigning his post as national security adviser, wrote that he was convinced Trump would withdraw from NATO if elected to a second term.

Trump's obsession with undermining NATO, and his peculiar fealty toward Vladimir Putin, raised uncomfortable questions about his loyalty, as did his performance at a highly anticipated summit meeting with Putin in Helsinki in July 2018. With the Russian leader standing at his side, Trump challenged the conclusion of his own intelligence community that Moscow had meddled in the election. Even fellow Republicans condemned him, with the late senator John McCain of Arizona calling the remarks "the most disgraceful" by an American president in memory. That evening, a once-unfathomable sentence, composed by columnist Thomas L. Friedman, appeared in the *New York Times*: "There is overwhelming evidence that our president, for the first time in our history, is deliberately or through gross negligence or because of his own twisted personality engaged in treasonous behavior."

Friedman was not alone in his concerns over the president's conduct. According to legendary reporter Bob Woodward, Dan Coats, the former conservative Republican senator from Indiana who served as Trump's first director of national intelligence, feared the president of the United States was acting as

a Russian asset. Coats, wrote Woodward in his 2020 masterpiece *Rage*, "continued to harbor the secret belief, one that had
grown rather than lessened, although unsupported by intelligence proof, that Putin had something on Trump."

Coats was no doubt alarmed by the lengths to which Trump
went to conceal details of his face-to-face encounters with Putin. On one occasion, after a meeting in Hamburg, Trump reportedly took the extraordinary step of seizing his interpreter's
handwritten notes. According to the *Washington Post*, there is
no detailed record, anywhere within the files of the US government, of five meetings between Donald Trump and Vladimir
Putin.

The US intelligence community concluded that Putin, determined to help keep Trump in office, authorized a second
Russian intervention during the 2020 presidential campaign.
Historically unpopular, damaged by his inept handling of the
coronavirus pandemic, Trump nevertheless became the first
incumbent president since George H. W. Bush to be denied
reelection by the American people. He received 232 electoral
votes, far short of the 270 required, and lost the popular vote by
more than seven million votes, a margin of 4.4 percent. Since
1960, five elections have been closer. And yet none of the other
losing candidates—Richard Nixon, Hubert Humphrey, Gerald
Ford, Al Gore, and John Kerry—refused to concede defeat, disrupted the formal transition of power, or incited a violent insurrection. But then, no other presidential candidate in American
history ever solicited, accepted, and exploited the assistance of
a hostile foreign power. That distinction is Donald Trump's
alone.

Trump's refusal to accept the results of the election has left

America dangerously divided. It has also served to further radicalize the Republican Party. Pippa Norris of Harvard's Kennedy School of Government has concluded that Trump's GOP is now an authoritarian populist party that is "willing to undermine democratic principles in pursuit of power," much like the far-right Alternative for Germany, Austria's Freedom Party, and the Hungarian Civic Alliance led by strongman Viktor Orbán.

Recent polling would appear to support Professor Norris's conclusion. A large swath of Republican voters no longer believes in democracy. Even more alarming, a survey by the conservative American Enterprise Institute found that 39 percent of Republicans support the use of violence to achieve their political goals. Many speak openly of civil war. The party's congressional delegation now includes two members—Lauren Boebert of Colorado and Marjorie Taylor Greene of Georgia—who have expressed support for elements of the far-right anti-Semitic conspiracy theory known as QAnon. Before winning her deep-red Georgia district, Greene also expressed online support for executing FBI agents and Democratic members of Congress, including House Speaker Nancy Pelosi. Another Republican member of the 2020 freshman class, Mary Miller, quoted Adolf Hitler favorably during a fiery prepared speech delivered on the day before the Capitol insurrection. And yet the gentlelady from southeastern Illinois remains a member in good standing of the House Republican Conference.

All of which Vladimir Putin surely finds to his liking. Yes, Donald Trump ultimately disappointed him by failing to deliver an American withdrawal from NATO, but the domestic damage Trump has left in his wake will pay dividends for years to come. The Capitol siege alone was worth Russia's investment. Those white supremacists, neo-Nazis, anti-Semites, and QAnon conspiracy theorists who sacked the temple of American democracy on Donald Trump's behalf were also doing Putin's bidding. So, too, were the talk radio and cable news hosts who stoked the insurrectionists' rage with baseless fantasies of a stolen election. A politically divided and destabilized America—an America drifting toward white nationalism, authoritarianism, and isolationism—will pose no challenge to Putin at home or in the lands where he aims to extend Russia's malign influence. As far as Vladimir Putin is concerned, it was money well spent.

ACKNOWLEDGMENTS

NEEDLESS TO SAY, I DID not set out, in the late summer of 2020, to write a novel that featured an insurrection inspired by an American president and an inauguration conducted under the threat of an armed assault by US citizens. But in the days following the Capitol siege, I resolved to include the near death of American democracy in my story of Russia's relentless war on the West. I jettisoned my existing ending and rewrote much of my manuscript in a span of six weeks. Such an undertaking would not have been possible without the editorial and emotional support of my wife, CNN special correspondent Jamie Gangel, who was reporting on the very events about which I was writing. She reviewed my final substantive changes while sitting on the set of the network's Washington studios, waiting to go on the air. My debt to her is immeasurable, as is my love.

I spoke with several intelligence officers and Russia analysts while writing *The Cellist*, and I thank them now in anonymity, which is how they would prefer it. My frequent conversations with Republican members of Congress and senior administration officials during the four turbulent years of the Trump presidency provided me with a unique view of a White House, and a federal government, in disarray. My depiction of the CIA director withholding Russia-related intelligence from the President's Daily Brief is based on information given to me by an unimpeachable source.

Anthony Scaramucci, founder of the investment firm Sky-Bridge Capital, gave me a thoughtful tutorial on the brazenness of Russian money laundering that shaped my operation against Kremlin Inc. Obviously, the mistakes and dramatic license are mine, not his. Bob Woodward was a source of both information and inspiration. His matchless reporting and writing on the final, chaotic year of the Trump presidency undoubtedly changed the course of history.

Dr. Jonathan Reiner, the director of cardiac catheterization at George Washington University and a CNN medical analyst, took time out of his busy schedule to treat Sarah Bancroft for exposure to a deadly Russian nerve agent, and Gabriel Allon for a cavernous through-and-through gunshot wound near his heart. CNN political director David Chalian graciously checked my election-related copy for accuracy, and David Bull reviewed those portions of the story involving the discovery, sale, and restoration of my fictitious painting by Artemisia Gentileschi. One of the world's finest art conservators, David would have been a much better choice for the project than Gabriel, who, after all, was simultaneously running an operation and an intelligence service.

I consulted hundreds of newspaper and magazine articles,

far too many to cite here, along with dozens of books. I would be remiss if I did not mention the following: Steven Lee Myers, *The New Tsar: The Rise and Reign of Vladimir Putin*; Masha Gessen, *The Man Without a Face: The Unlikely Rise of Vladimir Putin*; Anders Åslund, *Russia's Crony Capitalism: The Path from Market Economy to Kleptocracy*; Karen Dawisha, *Putin's Kleptocracy: Who Owns Russia?*; Luke Harding, *Shadow State: Murder, Mayhem, and Russia's Remaking of the West*; Bill Browder, *Red Notice: A True Story of High Finance, Murder, and One Man's Fight for Justice*; David Enrich, *Dark Towers: Deutsche Bank, Donald Trump, and an Epic Trail of Destruction*; and Craig Unger, *House of Trump, House of Putin: The Untold Story of Donald Trump and the Russian Mafia*.

My dear friend Louis Toscano, author of *Triple Cross* and *Mary Bloom*, made countless improvements to the novel, and my eagle-eyed personal copy editor, Kathy Crosby, made certain it was free of typographical and grammatical errors. Any mistakes that slipped through their formidable defenses are mine, not theirs.

I owe a debt to Michael Gendler, my Los Angeles super-lawyer, that I cannot possibly repay. Also, to the many friends who provide much-needed laughter at critical times during the writing year, especially Jeff Zucker, Phil Griffin, Andrew Lack, Noah Oppenheim, Andy Lassner, Sally Quinn, Elsa Walsh, Peggy Noonan, Susan St. James and Dick Ebersol, Jane and Burt Bacharach, Stacey and Henry Winkler, Donna and Michael Bass, Virginia Moseley and Tom Nides, Nancy Dubuc and Michael Kizilbash, Susanna Aaron and Gary Ginsburg, Cindi and Mitchell Berger, Marie Brenner and Ernie Pomerantz, and Liz Cheney and Phil Perry.

A heartfelt thanks to the remarkable team at HarperCollins,

especially Brian Murray, Jonathan Burnham, Jennifer Barth, David Koral, Leah Wasielewski, Leslie Cohen, Doug Jones, Josh Marwell, Mark Ferguson, Robin Bilardello, Milan Bozic, Frank Albanese, Leah Carlson-Stanisic, Carolyn Bodkin, Chantal Restivo-Alessi, Julianna Wojcik, Mark Meneses, Sarah Ried, Beth Silfin, Lisa Erickson, and Amy Baker.

Finally, I am grateful for the love and support of my children, Lily and Nicholas. Their resolve and determination in the face of a world turned upside down was a source of inspiration, as was the bravery of the police officers who fought to defend our Capitol on January 6, 2021. Writing a novel seemed a rather trivial pursuit by comparison.